'A marvellous psychological drama on many levels . . . For fans of suspense, especially suspense with a feminine perspective, *Close To Me* is as good as it gets' *New York Journal of Books*

'Gripping, claustrophobic and often deeply unsettling, *Close To Me* exerts a magnetic pull from its first pages' Kate Riordan, author of *The Girl in the Photograph*

'Taut, compelling, well-paced. ADDICTIVE' Will Dean, author of *Dark Pines*

'Keeps you guessing, and then just when you think you know, you find another twist in the road. Gripping and suspenseful' Michelle Adams, author of *My Sister*

'*Close To Me* reveals itself like a buried memory, the details peeking out and keeping the reader guessing until all is discovered in the shocking conclusion . . . sure to have readers thinking about the story and how much they can trust their own recollections long after the final page' Cate Holahan, author of *The Widower's Wife* and *Lies She Told*

'An intriguing, well-told, tightly knit story that will hold you to the last page and make you put one hand on the banister whenever you're at the top of the stairs' *SHOTS Crime & Thriller Ezine*

KT-163-793

The
Hidden
Wife

AMANDA REYNOLDS

WILDFIRE

First published in 2019 by
WILDFIRE
An imprint of HEADLINE PUBLISHING GROUP

1

Cataloguing in Publication Data is available from the British Library

ISBN 978 1 4722 6155 7

Typeset in Dante MT by Palimpsest Book Production Limited,
Falkirk, Stirlingshire

Printed and bound in Great Britain by
Clays Ltd, Elcograf S.p.A.

Headline's policy is to use papers that are natural, renewable
and recyclable products and made from wood grown in sustainable forests.
The logging and manufacturing processes are expected to conform to
the environmental regulations of the country of origin.

HEADLINE PUBLISHING GROUP
An Hachette UK Company
Carmelite House
50 Victoria Embankment
London EC4Y 0DZ

www.headline.co.uk
www.hachette.co.uk

For Chris

'The goal of all art is the human face'

Paul Cézanne 1839–1906

Where do they go, the lost souls?
Are they hidden in plain sight, walking amongst us?
Or lost forever, no more than a fading memory . . .

Thirty-Three Hours Missing

Max Blake is pacing his spacious kitchen, his movements clumsy, his demeanour unpredictable. He looks like he hasn't slept. He looks like a man desperate to find his missing wife. He looks like he's lying.

Detective Sergeant Katie Ingles, Katherine to her mother, Katie to everyone else, removes her coat and runs her hands through her unwashed hair as she stifles a yawn. The baby is keeping her up at night, and although she's not the one breast-feeding and her parental leave is long over, she feels obliged to be there for her wife, making tea and watching Netflix at three a.m. Today was meant to be her day off, a chance to catch up on some much-needed rest, but despite her exhaustion she's alert to Max's every move. She catches DC Chris Green's eye and they exchange a look, in agreement about the husband, it would seem. Max had waited too long to alert them to his wife's absence and his story is inconsistent. He's hiding something. Quite possibly a body. She walks to the patio doors and looks out. There are too many places to keep secrets at Brooke House. It's huge, filled with long corridors lined with locked doors, not to mention the acres of grounds.

Twenty-four hours since the call came in, an hour since her DI rang her at home and said he wasn't upgrading the risk assessment, not yet at least, but he'd decided to bring in CID. It's a high-profile case, he can't afford to take any chances. None of them can. The team has an energy to it, conversations passed liked batons, everyone eager to get on with the investigation, although the likelihood is they won't find Julia Blake alive and well. It's already been too long. At least the dog handlers are here. She has a good feeling about bringing them in – it will save time if nothing else – but it's still a near-impossible task.

DC Chris Green is making tea and trying to keep the husband calm, but Max is agitated, demanding information and reassurance when they can offer neither. Katie's colleague could easily flatten Max Blake if he wanted to. Chris is a big guy, a gym addict, he told her on the drive over, but he appears to favour a softer approach.

'You need to sit down, Mr Blake,' Katie reiterates, dragging herself from the view as the dogs head into the wooded area beyond the long sweep of lawn.

'Do you have a husband, detective?' Max demands, walking towards her. 'Is he missing?' His face is too close, his blue eyes fixed on her. Chris steps forward and Max backs off.

'The search for your wife is ongoing,' Chris tells him, his expression splitting into one of his famous grins, a flash of perfect white teeth beneath the sparkly hazel eyes. 'OK if we call you Max?'

'I really don't care,' Max replies, pacing again.

'We're doing all we can,' Katie tells Max, and he makes a derisory sound in the back of his throat.

She resists the urge to do the same.

Max Blake, celebrity author and a bit of a wanker if first impressions are anything to go by. What husband goes to bed alone on the night of their tenth wedding anniversary? He didn't even check on his wife's whereabouts until the next morning. His account doesn't stack up; not to her. She takes a mug of tea from Chris and sips the hot brew. The rain has gathered pace, bouncing off the patio furniture and filling the wine glass left on the table. She can still hear the dogs barking, although they've disappeared from view. 'And you've no idea where Julia might be, none whatsoever?' she asks, not bothering to turn round.

Max's reflection walks towards her. 'Don't you think I'd have told you if I did?'

She asks him again to sit down and to her surprise he does, although he can't keep still, his hands tapping on the scrubbed oak table, his right leg bouncing up and down. He's wearing jeans, and a blue fitted shirt, leather brogues. Her lip curls at how put-together he is despite his puffy red eyes.

'Can you talk me through the last forty-eight hours?' she asks, taking the seat closest to the patio doors. 'As much detail as possible.'

Katie watches the dogs emerge from the trees, their noses to the grass as they're guided towards the front of the house. Their next stop should be the outbuildings: a pair of holiday lets and a converted barn located down a fork in the gravel drive. Then the garages at the side of the property. She checks her phone. Still no bloody signal.

'What are they doing?' Max asks, gesturing towards two uniformed officers pacing on the grass.

'Every possibility is being looked into, Mr Blake,' she tells him. 'For now, you are our best bet. You need to help us to find Julia.'

'I just feel so bloody useless.' Max wipes his face with his hands. 'I can't think straight.'

'Tell me about Saturday,' Katie prompts, looking up at Chris. He extracts a notepad from his jacket, then hunches over the kitchen counter, pen in hand.

'How did you and your wife spend your day?' Katie asks, exchanging a look of exasperation with Chris as Max leans his head into his hands. The author's slim wedding band glints back at her. 'It was your anniversary, I believe.'

Max lifts his head, his eyes bloodshot. 'As I've already said, more than once, Julia was on the phone whenever I saw her, arranging things for our celebration: caterers, wine, flowers.'

Mobile phone records would usually be their great hope. They haven't found her handset in the house as yet, so if Julia's used it since midnight on Saturday it will be their first break-through, but as the location of Brooke House is so remote, at least a mile from any signal and the only reliable WiFi disappearing as soon as you step away from the house, the landline records might be their best bet anyway. 'And your day, Mr Blake? Tell me what you did on Saturday before the party.'

'Apart from picking up a present for my wife in town first thing, I was in my study, writing. I have a set routine. I get up early, work until lunchtime, every day of the week, and most weeks of the year.' He glances up, as if she should react to this. 'Julia and I usually have a light lunch together, then I do a few more hours before dinner.'

Katie's tempted to confess that she's a big fan of his books. It might create a better rapport, massaging Max's not inconsiderable ego, but her DI told her to play it safe, the world will be watching and it's not her style to ingratiate herself, that's Chris's domain. 'Your wife took care of all the arrangements for the anniversary party?'

'Yes, Julia is very good at entertaining. Her forte, creative things. Photography in particular.'

Katie had noticed the black and white prints on the walls as she'd toured Brooke House, mostly arty shots of the rooms and grounds, but there was one of Julia on Max's desk that particularly caught her eye. 'Your wife is a professional photographer?'

'She was studying photography in London when we met, but she left part-way through her course. It was something she wanted to go back to in a more serious way.'

Talking about happier times is settling Max, and it's all useful background information, but the large clock on the kitchen wall is ticking vital seconds away. Katie's limited patience is tested with each lost moment. 'Your wife is twenty-eight now so she must have been what, seventeen, eighteen, when you first met?'

'I'm not aware that's a crime,' Max replies, meeting her smile with a cold stare across the table.

Not a crime to be almost twenty years older than your spouse, Katie concedes, although she does not say so to Max, but notable. 'Tell me about the rest of your Saturday.'

'Our dinner guests were due at seven, so I changed then met Julia outside.' He gestures towards the patio. 'She looked stunning, as always.'

'What was she wearing?' Katie asks.

'I'd bought her a new dress, long and floaty, low-cut. I couldn't take my eyes off her. I remember thinking that after ten years of marriage our lives couldn't be more perfect. And she was wearing the necklace, of course.'

'Necklace?' Katie glances at Chris and he flourishes his pen as if he's about to knock up a sketch. 'That's the gift you'd picked up in town?'

'Yes, it was a commission, spelling out her name. The dot above the letter I is a one-carat diamond.'

Katie makes a mental note of the design, imagining it around the missing woman's throat. It's unique, could be crucial.

'Who was invited for this special anniversary dinner?' Katie asks.

Max looks outside at the patio furniture. Katie too. She counts eight chairs, but they could have brought out more.

'There was Jonny, my publisher, and his partner, Matthew. Theo Smythe, he's in charge of the *Herald*.' Katie nods, the editor of the local newspaper well known to her. 'And Theo's wife Nicky. And Fiona and Lawrence Townsend. I've known the Smythes and Townsends since I bought this place back in 2001, Jonny even longer. I can write down their contact details for you, but I fail to see what relevance this has to—'

'Three couples besides you and your wife?' Katie asks and Max nods. 'Anyone else?'

'Two of Julia's friends arrived from London as we were finishing dinner.'

'And their names?' Katie asks.

'Ben Fortune is an old friend of my wife, from her college

6

days, and there was a woman with him. I don't recall her name.'

'Ten years of marriage and you don't know the name of one of your wife's closest friends?' Katie asks, injecting deliberate reproach into her tone.

Chris shoots her a warning look and she frowns back at him. She can be a bit direct at times, she knows that, but it needs asking.

'She wasn't a close friend as far as I know,' Max snaps back, deep lines creasing his smooth and slightly tanned face. 'I'd certainly never met her before.'

'What time did they arrive?' Katie asks.

'Must have been around eleven. They'd caught the last train from London, then a taxi from the station. I wasn't expecting them, Julia hadn't said.'

Chris looks up from his notes, listening as Katie asks, 'Why didn't your wife tell you they were coming?'

'She knew I wouldn't want Ben here, making our dinner guests feel uncomfortable, which is exactly what happened.'

'You don't like him?' Chris asks.

Max shakes his head. 'I've only met him once, maybe twice before, but no, I don't like him. He's normally off his face on something, which hardly helps.'

'Drugs?' Chris asks.

'Wouldn't be surprised. He was definitely drunk. As soon as Julia took them down to the swimming pool everyone else made their excuses and left. It was humiliating.'

Katie gets up from the table and returns to the patio doors. She can't see the pool, roughly fifty metres away down a steep slope in the grass, but she imagines loud voices would travel up from there, especially if you were seated outside on a pleasant summer's evening as Saturday night had been. The storm hadn't broken until the early hours of Sunday morning, the rain still falling over twenty-four hours later.

'Ben has remained a good friend of your wife?' she asks, turning back. 'Even though you and he didn't get on.'

There's a pause before Max tells Katie, 'It's up to my wife who she sees, don't you think?'

Chris leans across the table, placing a mug in front of Max and exchanging a knowing look with Katie as he withdraws.

'What did you do after your dinner guests had left?' she asks.

Max explains how he finished his wine on the patio and then, maybe half an hour later, he went down to the pool.

'How much had you had to drink?' Katie asks.

'A glass, two at most,' Max replies. 'To be honest I'd usually drink more but I had a headache, concentrating too much on my new book.' He smiles for the first time, and Katie is inclined to believe him.

'So you weren't drunk? she asks, pressing the point.

'No, not at all,' Max insists and again he seems genuine.

'What happened when you reached the pool?' she asks.

'I told Julia I was going to bed,' Max explains. 'But she wanted to stay up a bit longer. Her friends had only just arrived and I suppose it was reasonable to spend some time with them.'

Katie nods, distracted as the extra officers she'd requested, four of them in total, follow the same path across the lawns the dog handlers took, one of them spotting her and gesturing towards the front of the house. She checks her phone and frowns, then looks over at Chris who nods, passing her his notebook and the chewed pen before he leaves the room.

'Where's he going?' Max asks. 'Have they found something?' *Something?*

Katie closes the notebook on Chris's sketch and sits down beside Max. 'So you went to bed alone on your tenth wedding anniversary because your wife chose her friends over you? Friends you hadn't invited. One you'd never met and the other you didn't like.'

'Yes, I suppose in essence that's right, but—' Max looks at the kitchen door as it clicks shut, voices the other side. 'Can you tell me what's happening, please?' He's polite but his irritation is clear, his jaw set.

'Did you argue with your wife?' Katie asks, ignoring his question.

'We had words, but that doesn't mean—'

'And you didn't think it was strange when she didn't come to bed all night?'

Max opens his mouth to speak but then Chris rushes back in, his face full of barely contained anticipation as he skids to a halt just inside the door and beckons Katie towards him.

She grabs her coat from the back of the chair, still damp, and exchanges a few whispered words with Chris, the detective's large frame then barring Max's exit as she slips out.

She can hear Max calling to her as she walks down the long, dimly lit corridor, but by the time she's across the rug that covers the wide entrance hall he's been silenced. The front door is opened for her by a uniformed officer, the stone steps wet and slippy as she quickly descends. Then she's running, towards the fork in the drive that leads to the outbuildings.

Nine Months Later . . .

Chapter One

Don't You Trust Me?

The number of hits on the *Herald*'s carefully curated website is particularly poor this afternoon, the digits on the large screen above our desks flicking from 373 to 375, then back again. It's mesmeric, addictive if you're not careful. Held to ransom by a random target we rarely, if ever, meet. Let alone exceed.

'Five hundred is unrealistic,' Simon remarks, pausing to look up, his quick fingers temporarily suspended above his keyboard. 'Best to ignore it, Seren.'

Beneath the disappointing number, today's stories are listed in descending popularity, Simon's, about a spilt tanker of milk, the most popular by some way. Mine, a continuing saga of missed refuse collections, is much further down the 'hit parade' as our editor lamely refers to it; Theo's quip amusing him each time.

'Yeah, totally unrealistic,' I reply, closing my laptop. 'We could do with a serial killer moving into the area.'

Simon laughs, remarking that if I'd wanted a regular supply of murders and kidnappings I've chosen the wrong paper. It's another recycled gag, but I smile as I get up, stretching out my back and shoulders and circling my neck to ease out the writer's stoop I fear I'm developing. There was a time – only last summer in fact, when I joined the *Herald* as a junior reporter fresh out of university and full of idealistic nonsense – I'd have been shocked by the gallows humour of the news desk. Now I'm the one cracking the bad taste jokes.

'I'll see you tomorrow,' I tell him, picking up my heavy shoulder bag and shoving my laptop inside.

'Fingers crossed for some bad news,' he says, typing again. 'Serial killers beware, Seren's on the case!'

I rush past our editor's glass-fronted office, purposefully staring at my phone. Theo will hold me up by at least ten minutes, maybe more, and whilst his advice is always appreciated, I'm ready to call it a night. I'm within touching distance of the double doors when I hear, 'Seren! Got a minute?'

I could swear he does it on purpose, counting to ten after he spots me dashing past. I catch our receptionist's eye as I turn back and Lynda returns to her apparent absorption in last week's print edition, fanning out copies on her desk.

'Seren!' Theo booms again.

Simon hasn't looked up, but I notice Fran, our deputy editor, has spotted my about-turn, watching as I open Theo's office door. I swallow a catch in the back of my throat as the smoky air hits me. Our esteemed leader is seated behind his enormous and wildly messy desk, a stubby cigar held between his gritted teeth. 'Ah, there you are, Seren! Glad I caught you.'

'You know you're not allowed to smoke in the office.' I point a finger at him and waggle it from side to side. 'Apart from the fact it's illegal, Fran will totally lose her shit if she catches you again. She's not looking happy as it is.'

The threat of Fran's disapproval is enough to prompt Theo to remove the cigar, although he doesn't extinguish it, balancing the fat wodge of tobacco on the edge of an overflowing ashtray nestling amongst the scrunched sheaves of paper in an open drawer beside him. Smoke curls a thin line into the polluted air, a snake uncoiling from its basket as he mutters something about not giving a flying fuck what his deputy editor thinks, he's in charge around here.

'Looking for something?' I ask as I take the seat opposite him.

He's squinting at the clutter on his desk. His refusal to adopt the paperless system Fran favours is also a cause of much contention. *'I run a bloody newspaper, woman! Paper is my business.'* Trouble is, it isn't a 'paper' any more, the weekly edition our only physical output since the *Herald* became a predominantly digital publication, much to Theo's disgust. 'I had it right here . . .' he says, rummaging through the piles of files and printed documents.

I retrieve his glasses from beneath a crumpled disposable napkin and hold out the silver-rimmed frames. 'Try these.'

He frowns, snatching them out of my hand as he gestures towards the television on the wall, the sound switched off. 'You been following this?' he asks, sliding on his specs. 'Terrible business.'

The five o'clock local news is on, a short segment after the

15

national headlines and before the weather, the rolling banner across the bottom of the screen captioning a familiar photo of a girl wearing the uniform of a nearby comprehensive school. I tell him how I really need to go now but Theo shushes me, turning up the volume to listen to the distraught parents' appeal for any information about their adopted daughter, thirteen-year-old Emily Plant. I've seen the photo many times in the months since I joined the *Herald*, the details of her disappearance already well known to me. Another tragedy to absorb and compartmentalise as best as I can. If the last seven months have taught me anything it's that despite all advice to the contrary, sometimes it's best to look away. I start tapping on my phone, scrolling through social media for anything interesting to write about tomorrow. When I look up a female reporter is talking directly to camera, her red lips moving soundlessly as Theo mutes the programme again.

'Poor bastards,' he says, grimacing at me. 'The parents, I mean.' He roots around in his paperwork again as I fidget. 'Ah, here it is.' He holds up a printed sheet of A4. 'I've had an email from Max Blake.' Theo waits for some indication I know who he means, but I've never heard of the guy. 'Bestselling author,' he prompts, an upwards inflection in his voice as if he were asking me a question. 'Local man, philanthropist, writes thrillers. Ring any bells?'

'Oh, actually,' I say, holding up a pointed finger. 'I think my dad reads his stuff. He's a big deal, right?'

Theo sighs. 'God, Seren, you're so bloody young. Yes, he's a very big deal.'

'Trashy stuff, badly written?'

'I quite like his books myself.' Theo takes off his glasses and rubs at his eyes, producing a squelching sound that turns my stomach. 'The point is, his wife disappeared nine months ago. I assume you remember that? It was, as you say, a big deal.' I shrug, and Theo rolls his eyes. 'I know you're relatively new to this, Seren, but he's a big celebrity, and this story was only last May. When did you join us?'

'Two months after that.'

'And you didn't have access to the internet in deepest Wales?'

The tease is an old favourite of his, but he knows I haven't lived at home full-time for years. Not since I left for university. Although he has no concept why I've barely visited since I moved here, keeping my distance from the seaside town in South Wales where I grew up.

I skimmed over my personal circumstances at my interview, concerned that the inevitable questions about triggers and over-laps, coupled with my age and lack of experience, might affect my application, although academically I was well qualified for the position of Junior Reporter. In truth my reticence was probably more to do with my obsessive need to keep my back-story private. The only person round here who knows everything is my flatmate, Izzy, and that was forced on me.

'Seren? Are you listening?' Theo passes across an old copy of the *Herald*, dated Monday, 29th May last year. It's a thin volume, the paper printed daily back then.

I read aloud Simon's uninspired headline: 'Local Author's Wife Goes Missing'.

'Read it,' Theo instructs me. 'All of it!'

17

"'Julia Blake, twenty-eight, was reported missing from their Gloucestershire home by her husband, bestselling author Max Blake, forty-seven, yesterday morning.'" I look up. 'Wow, that's a big age gap!'

Theo directs me back to the rest of the article and I scan it quickly.

> . . . *investigation into the circumstances of Mrs Blake's disappearance from Brooke House late on Saturday night . . . police tape everywhere, and dogs . . . Detective Sergeant Katherine Ingles . . . 'At this difficult time, we ask that the family's privacy be respected . . . painstaking work.' Julia was wearing a long 'floaty' dress in bright colours . . . no coat or jacket . . .*

I finish and push the newspaper towards him. 'And they still haven't found her, the author's wife?'

'No body and no developments for months,' Theo replies. 'Early on they found evidence of foul play in an outbuilding, but I—'

'Oooh, what evidence?' I ask, leaning forward so my elbows rest on the edge of his desk.

'Julia's blood,' he says. 'But before you jump to any conclusions, there was nothing to pin it directly to Max, and that's off the record about the blood.' Theo taps the side of his nose, protective of his sources, although I know he's good mates with the DI, a fellow golfer. Personally, I don't see the point unless you can use the information, but Theo loves the fact he's 'in the know'.

'The investigation ground to a halt after a few weeks,' he tells me as he crushes the lit end of his cigar into the ashtray. 'The official line was the investigation was ongoing, but I think the police just hit a wall. No new leads, plenty of cul-de-sacs, and a million other demands on their time. Or maybe there's something I don't know.'

'But he killed her, surely?' I say. 'Her blood was found. Seems pretty damning evidence.'

'He was arrested, but never charged.' Theo sighs and points the remote at the television, switching off the silent weather report. 'OK, full disclosure; Max is sort of an acquaintance of mine. Well, to be honest we go way back.'

I nod, knowing this means nothing. Theo's been the editor of the *Herald* for over a decade and a reporter for almost twenty years before that. He keeps everyone on his radar, mentally logging details he might one day need, an inside track to possible future exclusives. It's a tragedy his talents are largely wasted in this genteel, relatively crime-free town, especially now the paper is reliant on the whims of the click-bait generation. We haven't spoken about it much but I know he's worried about his future, as well as the prospects for his beloved *Herald*.

'I met Max when his first book came out,' Theo explains. 'Must have been, gosh maybe eighteen, nineteen years ago.' His tired eyes skim the ceiling as he tries to recall the date. 'Back then he was happy with a review in the *Herald*. How times change.' He sighs. 'We've always covered his attendances at any local functions, first as a single man then later with Julia, of course. She was much younger than him, as you spotted.

19

You can imagine the comments when he first introduced her to everyone, she was barely eighteen.' He shakes his head at the thought of Mrs Max Blake.

I look at the blank television screen and then back to Theo, wondering where this is going and how long it might take. Theo loves to tell a story and normally I don't mind, but I'm starving and my feet ache. 'Sounds like you knew her pretty well.'

'No, not really. Max was more our friend. Although my wife did have a soft spot for Julia.' He stops talking and pulls a corner of his shirt free of his waistband and wipes his glasses. 'We were sometimes on the same table as the Blakes for charity dinners, and we were at their house the night Julia went missing.'

'Shit!' Now he has my attention.

'Yes, quite.' Max raises an eyebrow. 'We were invited for dinner along with two other couples to celebrate the Blakes' tenth wedding anniversary. It was a bit awkward, to be honest, especially for Jonny, Max's book editor; they still had to work together, after all.'

'Why was it so awkward?'

'Julia was goading Max, as usual, drinking too much and saying she was bored. Then two of her friends turned up from London. Max didn't seem to know they were coming. Their celebrations normally went on into the early hours, but Max made it obvious he wanted the rest of us to leave, so we did. Nicky was worried, said she had a bad feeling about it all, but what can you do?' Theo looks up as if he's just recalled I'm here.

'I wonder why Max stayed with her, she sounds a right—' I stop myself before I say any more. The woman is probably dead.

'Look them up, the Blakes, I mean,' Theo tells me. I nod, but only to keep him happy, my stomach grumbling. 'There's loads of coverage,' he says, oblivious to my waning interest. 'We ran the story until it was bled dry, which as you can imagine didn't do much for my friendship with Max.'

'No, I don't suppose it did,' I reply, glancing at the door.

'Am I keeping you, Seren?' he asks, regarding me over his glasses.

'Sorry, no. You were saying you'd lost touch?'

'Yes, but it wasn't just me. Max has retreated from all public life.'

'You think he killed her?'

'No, I don't. He completely adored her.'

'And she loved him back?' I ask, a spark of curiosity flaring as I imagine Max's tragic and troubled trophy wife.

Theo shrugs. 'I can't imagine Max was easy to live with.'

'I should get going,' I say, standing up. The mint gathering dust in the bottom of my bag is calling to me.

'He's asked to meet you, Seren,' Theo announces as I reach the door. 'First time he's agreed to speak publicly since Julia went missing.'

I spin back. '*Me?* I don't understand.'

'I know. It's unbelievable. Ah, here it is!' He passes a printed email across his desk. 'Read it for yourself.'

The message is carefully worded, a little pretentious and verbose, but undeniably articulate. I pause after the first para-

21

graph and sink into the chair again. 'How would he even know I exist?'

Theo leans over and taps the sheet of paper. 'No bloody attention span, you millennials. I blame smartphones.'

I read to the end and look up, still confused. 'He liked the article I wrote about missing persons? Is that true? That was nothing, a few paragraphs. I barely scratched the surface.'

'I've asked him much the same thing, although not in so many words, but the truth is, Seren, I don't want to overly question Max's choice. He's outright refused to be interviewed by me, or anyone since Julia vanished, but whatever his motives, he's changed his mind and feels he can talk. I'm not going to say no, unless . . .'

'Unless what?'

'Unless you tell me it's not for you. But we need this story, Seren. You understand that, don't you?'

'I'm going to interview a murderer!' I reply, sitting up and grinning manically at Theo.

'Um, hang on a minute. Let's not jump to any conclusions here. Max was devoted to Julia.' He catches my eye, and apparently my train of thought. 'And don't tell me that makes it even more likely he was involved. I know the stats, but I also know Max.'

I start listing high-profile cases where relatives have made emotional pleas for loved ones they know have come to harm, often at their own hands. Who knows why – maybe to deflect attention, or to appease detectives who suspect them of wrongdoing. It's a common phenomenon. Love, rage, jealousy; all powerful motivators.

'Yes, that is of course sadly true,' Theo concedes. 'And if you'd rather not interview him, I completely understand.'

Something in Theo's tone sets off alarm bells. I study him more closely, setting aside my excitement to work out what's going on here that I don't understand. 'Don't you trust me to do this?'

'Of course I do,' he replies, waving away my doubts with a flick of his hand. 'But if it makes you feel uncomfortable in any way, then so be it.'

'I've said I'll do it,' I reply, still puzzled by Theo's reticence. He's probably worried it's too much responsibility on my young shoulders, or maybe he's nervous in case he's misjudged his former friend. Either way, there's no way I'm refusing. 'I can't believe Max asked for me by name,' I add, keen to move on.

'No, neither can I,' Theo says. 'But it was a good piece, Seren. It truly was.'

I poured my broken heart into the article I wrote for the printed edition, my first proper opinion piece and a subject still so raw I'd wondered why I pushed for the opportunity once it was finally granted to me. The reaction to it had been good, but fleeting. I'd thought all my hard work had been for nothing, my words about the tragic and often unresolved cases of missing persons and the devastating fall-out for those left behind quickly forgotten. Tomorrow's chip paper, as they say. But now this. Theo picks up the email from Max to quote a line aloud. *'Seren's beautiful articulation of the pain of unresolved loss resonated with me.'* He takes off his glasses and sighs. 'Now, the practicalities. The house is extremely remote. I tried to persuade him out, suggested you meet him for coffee or lunch in town, but

23

he claims he's far too busy. I can go with you if you'd like, just for the first meeting?'

'No, there's clearly a difficult history between you.'

'Max and I aren't sworn enemies, Seren. He understands that I had a job to do; nothing personal.'

'I'll be fine. It's not like he's a serial killer! Not that I'd say no to that, either.' I stop talking, giddy now with anticipation. 'He really asked for me? This is amazing.'

I spot Simon walking towards Theo's office, his brow furrowed as he mouths at me, *'I thought you'd gone home?'*

Theo raises a hand to stop him and Simon turns back at the door.

'I don't want to upset anyone,' I say, watching as he walks off. Simon is senior to me, with many years of experience, and Fran, as she often reminds me, is Theo's second-in-command.

'You're going to have to toughen up, Seren,' he tells me. 'This is a cut-throat business. You think Fran or Simon would hesitate if Max asked for them?'

Theo turns his chair to the shelf behind him and studies the piles of books and magazines, extracting a thick hardback and passing it to me. The book jacket is black and red, a flame licking up from the bottom of the glossy cover. I read the blurb on the back, something about an anti-government plot and the one man who can foil it, despite insurmountable odds. Inside, the middle-aged author looks out from a posed headshot, his gaze caught by something in the middle-distance. He's trying a bit too hard in his trendy leather jacket and open-collar shirt, but there's a handsomeness to his smooth-skinned expression, and the blue eyes are startling in their colour and intensity.

'Homework,' Theo tells me, waving the book away when I try to return it. 'Read it! And everything else you can before you meet him tomorrow.'

'*Tomorrow?*'

'Yes, eleven a.m. sharp! Max suggested after five-thirty, but I said no, you were only available in the day. It's a bugger of a place to find, even in the light. Fine once you know it, but there's no house sign or any landmarks to speak of.' He scribbles the address on a Post-it note and talks me through an indecipherable map he fashions on the reverse side, sticking it on Max's book. 'And do your research on his backlist too, Seren. These literary types love to be flattered.'

I reassure him I can do this, it's my job after all, but Theo is in full flow, warning me not to be intimidated by Max Blake's celebrity. 'Remember you're there to do your job. Impress him with your professionalism, but it's a delicate matter, it will take skill and time to draw him out; long as you need. And if you have any concerns at all—'

'I'll be fine.' I tuck the book under my elbow, the note fluttering to the carpet. 'Like I said,' I tell him, bobbing down to retrieve the bright blue slip of paper, 'it's my job.'

'I mean it, Seren.' He clears his throat. 'You have to set the right tone, from the start. Don't let him—'

'Let him what?'

'No, it's fine.' He smiles again. 'I trust you.'

His words would be more encouraging if his focus wasn't directed to the news desk where Fran is chatting to Simon. Theo takes out his heavy silver lighter to balance it between the fingers and thumb of his left hand. The wrinkled skin pouches around his old-fashioned signet ring as he lights the cut end of a fresh cigar, a fizz and hiss as the tobacco crisps and curls. Theo is impossible at times, and not just the cigars. His private education informs both his views and his accent so he can appear pompous and overbearing, but he's been good to me, taking me under his wing and treating me more like a daughter than a junior. I'm not sure how I'd have coped without his kindness.

'Don't worry about those two,' Theo says. 'I'll buy Simon a pint and explain to him. He's a decent chap, bound to see sense once I put him straight. The story comes first, remember, and this is a bloody big deal for the *Herald*, not just you.'

'And Fran?'

'She's not in charge!' Theo blusters. 'I am!'

His outburst sends me to the door, but he stops me again before I leave. 'No one knows what happened to Julia that night,' he says, serious now. 'Go to Brooke House with an open mind, Seren, but take care of yourself, OK?'

round here is beautiful. Even on a drizzly day like today the tall, honey-coloured houses manage to look regal. They're mainly converted into apartments, some now repurposed as bars or shops too, but they must have originally been built as substantial family homes, filled with affluence and the scuttle of servitude. I'd assumed I wouldn't be able to afford the inflated rentals this area commands – exclusive and elegant and within walking distance of town and work, although I always drive – but here I am, living the dream. The letting agent's warning that the small, top-floor two-bed had a bath, but no shower, and was already occupied by a 'bubbly girl', should have alerted me to the compromise I was about to make, but in many ways it's been the opposite of that . . . with a few caveats.

The first time my parents met Izzy was when they brought the last of my belongings from home; the bigger items I hadn't managed in my tiny car. I'd acclimatised to Iz's eclectic fashion sense by then, barely noticed it in fact, but she was looking particularly striking that day, her exercise gear clinging to her curves, her hair, electric pink at the time, corkscrewed into tight curls, her calves bare above shiny red Doc Marten boots. Seeing her through the filter of my traditional parents only amplified the impact. I'd immediately sensed my father's discomfort as he dropped the case he was carrying and extended a hand to introduce himself. Iz, being Iz, pulled him into a bear hug followed by a double-kiss. Mum was treated to the same, but soon we were all laughing, Mum's hand flying to her mouth as she listened to Iz's account of her ineptitude at 'Boxercise' and her desperate desire to lose 'at least three stone'. Izzy was, as I recall, eating a chunky Kit-Kat at the window, the street is quiet. Too early for the bars to be filling up for the evening and too late for the shops to be open, just the odd pedestrian or car. People going about their lives unaware they're observed. I drag myself away, collecting up mugs from the coffee table, which leave faded rings behind them. The irony is Izzy spends her days clearing tables at the café on the corner, which probably explains her apathy at home.

The kitchenette is even messier, congealed fat in the grill pan and toast crumbs strewn across the counter, as if Izzy has been feeding an imaginary flock of birds in here. Dumping everything in the crowded sink, I run hot water and squeeze washing-up liquid over the dirty dishes. 'Beans or soup?' I ask the silence, peering in my almost empty food cupboard. I open a can of Cream of Tomato, a satisfying stream of bright orange liquid filling my mug. Max's book in my hand, I lean against the bubble-filled sink as the soup turns in slow circles around the microwave. There's definitely something unsettling about the intensity of Max's gaze, but it's a publicity shot. I'll reserve judgement until I meet him in person.

Propping my laptop against my knees, my feet lifted to the table in front of the sofa, I type Julia's name one-handed. The hot soup burns the tip of my tongue, my taste buds swelling in protest, but I'm soon lost in a rabbit hole of research, tabs open in a line across the top of the screen. Theo was right, there are plenty of photos of the Blakes to look at, one cropping up more than most, taken at a New Year's Eve ball just a few months before she vanished. Julia is in a long black dress, plunging neckline, blond hair in an effortless up-do. Max is beside her in a dinner suit, both of them smiling at the camera;

the perfect couple. Although, if you look closer . . . I click on the image, enlarging it. Julia's smile is forced, as if she's displeased to be there, and Max could be her father, despite his attempts at sharp dressing and the subtle highlights in his greying hair.

Next I log on to a press cuttings website and search for any news clippings of the Blakes. The media seemed to treat Julia as an appendage to her celebrity spouse before she went missing, notable only for her youth and beauty, if she's mentioned at all. One article briefly references her fundraising efforts, but the accompanying photo shows Max deploying giant scissors whilst Julia hovers uneasily in the background.

The emphasis changes after Julia disappears, an explosion of media interest in Max's missing wife. The same black-tie photo is overused but cropped down to show only Julia's plunging outfit and beautifully made-up face; a simple but impressively large single-stone diamond pendant revealed in the detail. Julia's confident if posed smile seems to highlight her vulnerability this time, although it's the same image I'd studied before.

The particulars of the night she vanished are repetitively churned, both in the *Herald* and national media, although Theo's insider information about Julia's blood being found in an outbuilding has never been made public as far as I can tell. That hasn't stopped the collective finger of blame pointing to Max, sources 'close to the couple' recounting tales of epic arguments and a deeply flawed relationship. Then again, there's always a 'friend' willing to dish the dirt when prompted by the prospect of temporary fame or cold hard cash.

I consider my tepid soup. I was starving earlier but the

thought of Julia's spattered blood has put me off my supper. I'm still typing up my notes when I hear a familiar and heavy footfall coming up the stairs.

Izzy is wearing every primary colour: a red tee-shirt, blue joggers and a yellow beanie hat. She's sweaty, loud, and impossible to ignore as she flops down on the sofa beside me. My laptop bobs dangerously on my knees, her boobs doing the same beneath her inadequate sports bra. I steady my laptop with one hand and push Iz away with the other as she tries to read what I've been writing. 'Izzy, don't! You know I hate that.'

'I need a beer.' She jumps up, the sofa lifting. 'Want one?'

I raise an eyebrow and she laughs, always quick to mock my preference for 'a nice glass of Merlot'. *'You're bloody posh for a Welsh girl!'*

'Are you still working?' she asks, heading to the kitchenette. 'Or dare I hope you've finally signed up to that dating app I sent you?'

'How was Body Pump?' I ask, looking over the back of the sofa. 'Any luck tonight?'

She screws up her nose, then bends down to reach into the fridge, her knees clicking loudly. 'Nah, that instructor is definitely straight.' Izzy twists the top off a bottle of beer and takes a foamy gulp. 'She didn't look my way once, even when I fell on my arse and dropped the F-bomb.'

I laugh, then make a sad face.

'Don't worry,' Iz tells me. 'I'll win her round.'

'I'm sure you will, but what about Dom? Is that all over?' I ask hopefully.

I totally respect Iz's fluid sexuality but I find it hard to see what it is about Dom that attracts her; beyond his obvious beauty. He's mean-spirited and he uses her, which makes him rather ugly in my opinion.

'Nah, still seeing him but we keep it casual,' she replies, descending quickly, beer sloshing down her sweatshirt.

I close my laptop and forgive her clumsiness, if not her allegiance to Dom. Her presence is always reassuring, the darkness that can appear from nowhere and threaten to engulf me pushed aside by Izzy's infectious optimism. She brushes at the damp patch on her top, pulling it away from her chest to peer at the damage, then she downs the rest of the beer in one go, her bright pink lips clamped around the neck of the cold bottle, her throat pulsating, a satisfied grin when she's done.

'Good?' I ask, smiling back.

'It's all you need, isn't it?' She raises the emptied bottle in front of us. 'A beer, friends, family.' She glances at me, realising her mistake, but she hasn't offended me. I just wish my life was as simple as hers.

Whilst Izzy jumps in the bath, a good decision, I return to my research, trawling the web for more references to the Blakes, but only finding endless links to Max's thrillers. Theo was right, Max is a big deal, his books translated into every conceivable language. I recognise some of the covers, tucked-away memories of bookstore displays I must have passed when I was shopping with Mum and Dad on a Saturday morning, or maybe when I was older and kicking around town with Evan. Not that my ex-fiancé shared my love of literature, he was more likely to read DIY manuals than fiction. 'Opposites attract,'

Mum used to say, long after the engagement had ended. She and Dad are carved from the same piece of driftwood, but not everyone is that lucky.

I sit back and chew my nail, wondering where else I can look for the Blakes, although Izzy's bath-time attempts at 'I Will Always Love You', the Whitney version, are proving distracting.

Facebook yields little information – no personal profile for Max other than a faceless author page promoting his books and advertising signings now long passed. Julia has also resisted the lure of social media, but I do find a dedicated page for the college she attended in central London to study photography. Theo gave me the college's name when I'd emailed him earlier to ask if he had any background information on Julia that might be helpful to me. 'Be careful,' he'd told me in his reply. 'Keep your enquiries discreet.'

I search through the lists of past students, but can't spot a Moresley, her maiden name. I decide to post a comment, asking if anyone remembers Julia or might have kept in touch, hoping someone will reply.

I'm still scrolling through when Izzy emerges in her giraffe onesie, a towel wrapped around her bright blue hair, Smurf-like fronds clinging to her make-up-free face.

'You should go to bed, Seren. You look tired,' she says, a cloud of talcum powder dusting my laptop screen as she leans over the back of the sofa. *Facebook?* Is that what you call work these days?'

'Yes, I do, actually. What time is it?'

'Almost eleven.'

'*Really?* I had no idea it had got so late.'

I stretch my arms above my head and haul myself up whilst Izzy hovers in the manner of one of her customers waiting for a table. Then she fashions a pillow from her damp towel and lies down in the space I've vacated, shifting on to her side as she picks up the remote and starts flicking through the channels, her blue hair fanned beneath her like radioactive seaweed.

'You should get some rest too,' I tell her, scooping up my empty mug and her discarded beer bottle. 'Are you opening up the café tomorrow?'

'Nah. I'm on twelve till four.' She sighs. 'I need to look for something new, babe. That place is doing my head in.'

I nod, but she's been saying the same for months.

'You OK?' she asks, looking up at me. 'You seem . . . on edge?'

'Thing is,' I tell her, a thumb jabbed in the top of her beer bottle, my laptop clamped under my elbow, 'I've got a big interview tomorrow, an exclusive.'

'That's so exciting!' She sits up. 'Anyone famous?'

Izzy always imbues my work with a level of excitement and glamour it doesn't warrant, but for once I can justify some of that expectation.

'Max Blake, he's an—'

'Max Blake, oh my God! Are you joking?' Izzy thuds towards her bedroom, rummaging around noisily before she emerges with tattered paperback copies of three of Max's books. 'I've got more, do you think he'd sign them for me?'

'I guess I could ask.' I take the books and Izzy jumps over the arm of the sofa to land heavily on the cushions, an ominous crack sounding somewhere beneath her. She looks up at me, her eyes wide.

'Did you break something?' I ask, placing the books, mug, bottle and laptop on to the table before crouching down to feel for any damage.

'Fuck, Seren,' Izzy says, tapping me on my back so I look up. 'He killed his wife, didn't he?'

'No one knows that, not really,' I say, getting up. 'They've never found a body.'

Izzy stares up at me, a rare moment of stillness. 'No, I guess not, but even so . . .'

'All part of the job,' I tell her, walking towards my bedroom with as much swagger as I can muster.

'Don't forget my books,' she calls after me, holding them up.

The call comes in the hour before first light, as they often do, although I don't register the time as I sit up and stare blank-eyed at the screen. The number is withheld, no response at the other end when I whisper a hello. The silence sounds familiar, unrecognisable to anyone but me, nothing more than a held breath. I wait, preserving the connection for as long as possible, listening for clues: the swell of the sea, or the roar of a road, someone calling his name. I close my eyes and try to imagine his face, fading too quickly from my memories, the sharpness of recall smudged by time. I imagine limbs dusted with sand, beads of sweat across a tanned forehead. He's older, more confident. I keep my voice low and say, 'I love you, please come home.'

There's a soft click at the other end and the call ends.

I turn away from the widening band of light that travels across the carpet then up the bed. Izzy rattles through the door at speed, her arms thrown around my shoulders. She's telling me it will all be fine. I need some rest, that's all. Then I'll feel better. Everything is at its worst in the middle of the night. She smells of sleep and beer and talc and shampoo: fusty and warm beneath her onesie, her chest squashed against mine. I pull away and wipe my eyes. 'It's him, Iz. I know it is.'

She inclines her head and stands up, pausing in the doorway before she leaves. 'You need to tell the police, Seren. These calls have been going on long enough.'

Fifty-Seven Hours Missing

Katie leaves the DI's briefing with a heavy heart. They're still holding Max, but the evidence found at the cottage is circumstantial and soon they'll have to charge him or let him go. Traces of Julia's blood found on the side of the bath had seemed like the breakthrough they'd been waiting for. The dogs had gone crazy in Lavender Cottage and the samples taken have been matched with Julia's DNA, but Max claimed, after his initial outpouring of emotion and denial of any understanding how it might have got there, it must have been from when Julia shaved her legs the night of the party.

'She sometimes gets ready in the cottage,' he'd told them. 'So as not to disturb me when I'm mulling over the day's work. The subconscious, you see, it often irons out a knotty plot. I can still be absorbed, sometimes hours after I've left my desk. My wife understands that and allows me some space.'

'It doesn't scan,' Katie told her DI in the meeting and he'd nodded. 'Why would she be using the bath in an outbuilding, a pretty crappy one at that, when she has an enormous en suite right next to their bedroom that's filled with enough products to start a salon? That cottage was empty, nothing in it except a few sticks of furniture.'

The DI had said it was possible Max was telling the truth, but there'd been a murmur of disapproval in the room. It was clearly an elaborate and flimsy lie, and the obvious attempt to clean up had only incited further suspicion.

'Nice bath, though,' DC Chris Green had observed from the back of the room. 'Max's PA said Julia was hoping to renovate both cottages as holiday lets. No expense spared, it seems. The bath cost three grand according to Julia's credit card bills.'

A collective gasp had rippled around the room at the extravagance of the purchase.

'Shame she accidentally hacked open a vein with her Gillette whilst she was in it,' Katie had observed, perhaps more harshly than she'd meant.

Katie returns to her desk to try Julia's sister again. Jacqui Moresley has already been notified that her younger sibling is missing, but according to the officer Katie spoke to at the local police station – his accent so pronounced she'd taken a moment to attune to the Scottish lilt – Julia's only surviving blood relative didn't sound that bothered about her 'wee sister'.

'Julia was always running away as a child,' Jacqui tells Katie, the small-talk, not that there was much, soon over. 'Good move getting away from that husband of hers, if you ask me. Not a nice man. Although he's loaded, I'll give him that.'

Katie grabs two espressos from the machine before collecting Chris on their way to the interview room.

'Last chance before we have to release him,' Chris says, holding the door.

Max looks like shit and smells terrible, sweat and fear clinging to him. Chris taps on the screen of the laptop to start the recording. A red light comes on above them and the camera hums to life. *Showtime!*

'Where's your wife's car?' Chris asks Max after reminding him of his rights.

'*Sorry?*' Max stares at the immaculately presented detective.

'Where's your wife's white Range Rover, registration J-U-L-1-A?' Chris asks.

'It's in the garage,' Max replies, trying to move his chair away and finding it's bolted down, his solicitor stilling him with a shake of his pudgy head.

'We've checked all the garages at Brooke House and it's not there,' Chris says, leaning in. 'Your Porsche was in one and your assistant's green Polo was parked outside another. The other two were empty apart from some cleaning equipment: mops, buckets, gloves, bleach. We've taken the used items away, but the point I'm trying to establish right now is, where is Julia's Range Rover, Max?'

'It's being repaired,' he explains. 'That's what I meant; a repair garage.'

'What's wrong with it?' Katie asks.

'I caught it on the gate. It's narrow.'

'Which repair garage?' Chris demands.

'A local chap, Mim arranged it.'

'When did you hit the gate, Max?' Katie asks. 'Brooke House gate, you mean?'

'Yes,' Max replies, addressing her. 'It happened early Saturday morning as I left for town.'

'Did your assistant 'Mim' arrange the clean-up in the cottage too?' Chris asks.

'I've told you, I don't know why there was blood, or bleach, but most likely my wife had shaved her legs in there. The cleaners would know. Or maybe Mim, she's very thorough.'

'I bet she is,' Chris says, staring at Max.

'What is it you're not telling us?' Katie asks, not expecting an answer. 'What happened in Lavender Cottage in the early hours of Sunday morning? Was there a fight after her friends left? A bigger argument than they witnessed?'

Max says nothing, his solicitor taking over, suggesting that if they're not going to charge his client they need to release him. And just like that, the case against Max Blake crumbles.

They watch as Max walks away from the large purpose-built police headquarters, Chris crushing his empty coffee cup one-handed. Max pauses to look up at the second-floor window, and although Katie knows he can't see them through the tinted glass, for a moment she imagines he's smiling at her. Then he's gone, driven away in his assistant's tatty green car, his secrets taken with him. *For today.*

Chapter Three

Beginning to Think This is a Bad Idea

My windscreen wipers scratch across the rain-drenched glass, a stray tendril of loose rubber flailing to and fro as they pivot back and forth. I'm lost, no point denying it. And tired, although it's barely eleven in the morning, my eyelids drooping as if I'm jet-lagged. I rub underneath each one, checking in the rear-view mirror that I haven't spoiled the carefully applied flicks of eyeliner. I'd wanted to arrive well prepared and looking my best, but lack of sleep and now my impending lateness have combined to cover me in a cold sweat. The repetitive screeching continues as I slow down to study Theo's Post-it note instructions, still indecipherable. He'd warned me Brooke House is impossible to find, but I'd stupidly assumed I could follow the GPS on my phone. My current position is shown as central to a large patch of green with a white spidery line zigzagging across it. I haven't passed any landmarks in the last mile, not since the farm where a field of dim-looking sheep contemplated me through the heavy rain. I screw up Theo's note and drive on, snatching a tantalising glimpse of chimney stacks and landscaped grounds off to the right, the trees parting as the hills dip, but then the road climbs and Brooke House is gone again.

'*Fuck!*' I slam on the brakes and pull into the hedgerow, allowing a speeding van to whizz by, the faded signwriting in view for a second, 'Barry Bostwick, Motor Mechanic and Body Repairs', before my car is deluged with spray from a deep puddle. 'A thank you would be nice!' I shout after the driver, although the van has already disappeared.

The GPS map freezes as the last bar of signal evaporates. *Shit!* I throw my now useless mobile on the passenger seat and concentrate on the winding lanes that seem to lead nowhere, no sign of any other properties let alone the impressive estate I spotted earlier. It was sloppy of me to rely on technology alone. I should have printed out a proper map, or at least had some idea of direction before I set out. I turn around and park by another hedge, my car fighting the brambles as I let out a groan. I'm massively late, despite allowing loads of extra time. My head is resting on the steering wheel when I hear a car roar up behind me, horn blaring. I check my mirror and raise a hand to wave them past, their lights dazzling as they flash on and off. '*Come on!*' I say under my breath, although the driver won't be able to hear me, the rain pounding down as the sleek silver bonnet edges closer.

As the sports car draws level I notice the driver impatiently circling his hand. I stretch across, winding the handle to lower the passenger-side window. Their window glides smoothly down, coming to rest at the top of a low-slung door. I can't see them that well through the squally weather, but a deep voice asks, 'Are you lost?'

'Yes,' I call back, holding up my phone. 'No GPS. I don't suppose you know where Brooke House is?'

He leans nearer the open window, ice-blue eyes meeting mine, their colour so intense it's startling, a flash of anger in them, or perhaps it's conceit as I begin to make the connection. 'Oh my God, you're Max Blake!'

'I am,' he replies, frowning. 'And you're late!'

'Yes, I'm so sorry. These lanes are a maze and there's nothing to—'

'Follow me!' he says, interrupting. Then, appraising my car with barely concealed disdain, he adds, 'I'll drive slowly.'

Despite his promise, the Porsche pulls away at speed, my little car stuttering behind as I press hard on the accelerator to catch up. Red brake lights blur up ahead and Max glances in his mirror before the car speeds off again, the personalised number plate, MAX1 disappearing round bend after bend. We pass the farm again, the sheep now bleating as the silver sports car roars past, then my car a few seconds behind. The lanes twist and turn, water spraying as we hit puddles, the ditches overflowing, until finally Max slows and makes a sharp right turn. I look for a sign but there's nothing to indicate Brooke House might lie beyond the inauspicious entrance. I follow, negotiating the narrow gate more cautiously than he did, a muddy lane beyond.

Our convoy of two makes its way along the bumpy track, the unmade road hugging a high ridge that slopes away steeply to our left, a thick hedge to the right with trees behind. The Porsche, throaty and loud, disappears over an incline. My car crests the hill slowly behind it, the double-fronted mansion I'd spotted ages ago waiting in the bowl-shaped valley below. It reminds me of a dolls' house, the windows like eyes either side of the large front door. It must be worth millions, but there's an emptiness to it as we draw near, the eyes dead, as if the life has been ripped from them.

The Porsche follows the sweep of a semicircle of gravel drive and comes to rest by a set of grand stone steps that lead up to a large front door, the sports car's low-profile tyres kicking up stones as they skid to a halt. I pull my car in behind, but then the door of Max's car flies open and he roughly waves me on. 'Round that side,' he says, pointing a key fob as I wind down my window. 'Past the kitchen,' he tells me. 'There are some garages. You can park beside them.'

The kitchen is a generous annexe that looks to be a more recent addition, a green Polo parked by the block of garages that lie just beyond it. I grab my coat and run back through the rain, glancing into the single-storey extension which has been constructed in the same brick as Brooke House. The interior looks modern and airy as I snatch glimpses of it through rectangular slits of windows that run along the side. I spot cream glossy cupboards, then a long table at one end, patio doors behind, which I guess must overlook the back garden.

Max is climbing the stone steps to the front door as I turn the corner. He's five years younger than Theo, and he's aged a lot better than my worry-worn editor. Max is a little shorter than Theo, stockier too, but he dresses well, his tailored tweed jacket stretching across his broad shoulders as he jogs up the last two steps. His hair, mainly blond and cut in a foppish style, is lifted and tugged by the inclement weather that rushes up the steps behind him. He goes inside without a backwards glance. It's a disgusting day, and he's clearly annoyed I was late, but good manners cost nothing. I pause, raising my phone to take a photo of the house. Then a voice from inside barks, 'Are you coming in, or what?'

The entrance is as large as the footprint of most new-builds, a cavernous space dominated by an enormous monochrome rug, black and white stripes running across the vast hallway until they reach the foot of an oak staircase which rises steeply to a galleried landing. I place the rooms in our apartment across the rug, convincing myself they would easily fit, although perhaps that's an exaggeration. It's hard to tell when everything is on such a grand scale. It reminds me of a London hotel I stayed in with Evan, just for the night, ostensibly to gather inspiration for a refurb of his family's seafront hotel in Wales although I think it was more of a gift from his parents. Brooke House has that same feel of modern and period features expertly combined.

'Julia had the hall completely redesigned,' Max tells me, taking off his jacket and hanging it on a stand beside the door, the jagged branches of the tree-shaped rack reaching up towards the ornate coving. 'The rug was a commission, took six months to make and cost almost as much as the kitchen extension, but it really makes the space work, don't you think?'

I nod, as if I have experience of commissioning bespoke

rugs that cost a small fortune, but it does look amazing, if a little imposing.

'We had a wall knocked down over there.' He points to a console table I hadn't noticed, hidden in a recess under the stairs, two enormous vases of lilies book-ending the mirrored top. Scowling, he remarks how he'd told Miriam he hates lilies, they're so 'funereal'. The dark-stained stamens are framed by large white petals, a sprinkling of ochre powdering them and the gleaming surface. 'No, I'm not a fan either,' I tell him, although he ignores my comment.

'Shall I take that for you?' He holds out a hand for my coat.

I remove it and he hangs it by his jacket on the sculptural rack, then he tries to take my bag. 'I'll need it, for the interview,' I tell him, clutching it to me. 'Who's Miriam?'

Max nods, as if that's an answer, then he leads me across the hall into a shadowy corridor, doors running along the left-hand side, ornate keys in their locks. It reminds me of a film Izzy made me watch last Halloween, although there is some brightness up ahead, a large window about halfway along on the right. I trot to keep up, Max walking at a march as I hold my mobile phone above my head in the hopes it might pick up some reception. I promised I'd keep in touch with Theo, but the only network is password protected and there's no mobile signal at all. Max has stopped by the window so I pause there too, tucking my redundant phone back in my bag.

'The house was originally constructed in the late nineteenth century,' Max says, staring out at the view of the gravel drive and the landscaped grounds beyond. The rain appears to be abating a little. 'Built by a vicar,' he continues. 'Sadly his wife passed away before the house was finished so he never lived here. Spent his dotage in one of the cottages down there.' He points out a fork in the drive which takes a sharp left and then slopes away, high hedges either side. 'Rather a tragic history, wouldn't you say?'

I'm not sure if Max is referring to the first lost wife, or the most recent, or perhaps both, but my thoughts have returned to Julia's blood, found in one of those outbuildings. I look away, resisting the shiver that threatens, fairly successfully, I think, but when I look at Max his expression is enquiring, pushing me for a response. I hold up my bag. 'I don't seem to have any reception here and I promised Theo I'd let him know the second I arrived.'

'Yes, of course,' Max says. 'You can use the landline in the kitchen.'

He leads the way again, pushing open the door at the end of the corridor and snapping on the spotlights that stud the smooth kitchen ceiling. We're in the newer annexe, an opulent space as I'd guessed from the foretastes I'd had from outside. It has the look of a show home, a long wooden counter stretching down the full length of the left-hand side, the narrow rectangular windows above it, and gleaming chrome appliances lining the oiled surface. I exhale – the room is reassuringly open and light, as if no wrongdoings could occur in here. There's even a hint of sunshine coming through the patio doors at the far end. I walk towards them, past the impressive kitchen table, oak, I think, in the middle of which is an over-sized candelabra which reaches almost to the light fitting above, a huge photographer's lamp. The candelabra is made of driftwood, the gnarled struts crisscrossed on a marbled plinth and dotted with tealights.

'Antlers,' Max tells me, noticing my interest. 'From the deer that used to live on the estate. Julia commissioned it from an artist friend.'

'Oh! I assumed it was driftwood. That's . . . wow!'

'Hideous, isn't it?' Max observes sardonically. 'An unfortunate lapse in my wife's usual faultless taste, but Julia liked to support her friends in their *artistic* endeavours.' There's an edge to the statement but then Max smiles and I wonder if I'd imagined it.

I reach across the table and feel the smooth surface of the nearest antler, almost velvet to the touch although it's been stripped back to reveal the pale interior.

'It's a common misconception that antlers are made of cartilage,' Max tells me. 'They are actually bone, that's why they're so hard.'

I remove my touch from the bloodless bone. 'So, what happened to the rest of the deer?' I ask, turning back to see Max is frowning. 'You said they *used* to live on the estate?'

'Oh, I see. They dwindled over the years,' he replies, walking to an enormous fridge. 'Can I offer you something to drink?'

'If I could make that call first?'

Max lifts a phone from its cradle on the counter and holds the handset out to me. 'I'll leave you to it, check on my emails.'

'Thanks. Two minutes.'

I contemplate the impressive view through the patio doors whilst I wait for Lynda to answer. The grounds stretch as far as I can see, undulating lawns and curved paths leading to a row of tall cypress trees. The *Herald*'s receptionist answers on the sixth ring, her trill greeting, 'The *Herald*, how may I help you?' modified to a curt, 'Please hold,' when she realises it's me. I've never been entirely sure what her issue is with me, but she once remarked, not long after I started, that Theo and I were 'thick as thieves', presenting the barbed comment as if it were a joke when clearly it wasn't.

The other side of the glass, mixed with my reflection, there's a patio table protected by wet covers, the eight chairs that surround it similarly shrouded, the legs poking out the bottom of their green plastic sheaths and standing in puddles. Next to the table two tall parasols are similarly swaddled for the winter, their height conjuring an image of an opulent canopy unfurled against the heat of a summer's evening, guests clinking glasses as an alfresco dinner is served.

'All sorted?' Max asks, walking back in.

I turn around, the phone still pressed to my ear.

'Oh, I thought you'd be done,' he says, checking his watch. 'Time is getting away from us this morning, isn't it?'

'Sorry,' I reply, hanging up. 'I love these glass doors, amazing view.'

'Another of Julia's brilliant ideas,' Max says, joining me. 'She was the making of this place, and me.'

He seems to return from a distant thought, reaching out to take the phone. Our hands connect, his fingers brushing against mine. I pull back, burned by the briefest of contact, my breath caught in my throat. Max smiles and then turns away although his eyes remain on me for a split-second longer than feels natural. I clear my throat, my hand covering my mouth, the fingers that touched his now pressed against my lips.

'Are you OK?' he asks, glancing back as he places the phone back in its base.

'Yes, fine,' I reply, unsure what just happened. 'You were saying your wife was full of ideas?'

'Yes. The kitchen extension was her suggestion, one of the first major projects she oversaw.' He pulls out a chair from the table, gesturing for me to sit down after he takes a seat. 'There's a swimming pool further down there.' He points beyond the patio and I half-stand to see the lip of a steep slope at the edge of the lawn. 'Trouble is . . . we're at the mercy of the British climate,' Max says. 'Hardly use the outside space, especially since . . .'

'Still, it must be lovely on a summer's day,' I babble, reaching into my bag for my phone. It's not until I look up that I realise his expression has completely changed, from soft and melancholy to stony and tight-lipped. 'I'm sorry, I meant . . . before Julia was . . .'

He points at my phone. 'Are you going to record the interview?'

'If that's OK?'

Max shrugs, getting up to open the fridge. He peers in, then bends down, sliding out a foil-topped bottle with a dark yellow label which he holds up by the neck. 'Might I tempt you to a glass of champagne, Seren?'

I glance at the clock above the table, not only to check the time but also to buy myself a moment to think. I can't keep step with Max's mood swings.

'It's almost the afternoon,' he says, a glint of amusement, even cheekiness in his eyes. 'And it's so rare I have company. I can hardly open a bottle of Veuve when I'm on my own, can I?' He smiles fully now, his head tilted to the side. 'Will you join me, Seren? Save me the humiliation of drinking alone.'

Keeping a clear head is difficult enough with butterflies dancing around my empty stomach, my journalistic brain refusing to engage, but I don't want to appear stand-offish, and Max's temper has definitely improved at the prospect of the champagne. It might oil the wheels as Theo would say. 'Yes, OK. Thank you.' I rest my bag by my feet, placing my pen and notebook in front of me on the table. 'But only half a glass,' I tell him. 'I'm driving.'

'House rules! Full glasses only,' Max says, glancing up from the foil he's peeling from the top of the bottle, his thumb ripping it back with ease. 'I'm joking, Seren. Of course, you can have half a glass if that's what you want.'

'Oh, right, I see. Thanks very much.'

'Do I detect a Welsh accent?' Max rotates the bottle and there's a muted pop as the cork is expertly released.

I jump at the sound; an involuntary move, as is the flight of my palm to my chest. I laugh to cover my embarrassment and tell him yes, I'm from South Wales.

'Ah, the home of poets and dreamers.' He reaches up to remove two crystal glasses from a high shelf, rows of them inside the cupboard. 'Your family still live there?'

'Yes, my mum and dad.'

I take the champagne flute he's holding out and he pours. We're close enough for me to catch the scent of his shirt –

washing powder and crisp cotton – the cuffs studded with expensive-looking engraved cufflinks. The froth rises against the sides of the glass, reaching the top then subsiding just in time, perfectly judged. As Max turns away I realise I've been holding my breath. Light-headed before I've taken the first sip.

'They must be very proud of you,' Max says as he pours for himself. He takes a seat at the head of the table this time, his back to the view, then stretches out his legs. I subtly withdraw my feet, afraid we might accidentally touch again.

'Yes, I suppose they must be quite proud,' I reply, wondering if that's true. My choices are alien to them and I know Mum would much prefer me to be close by.

'Are they connected to journalism in any way?' Max asks, holding up his glass to appraise the contents. 'I really don't like this as much as Pol Roger. What do you think?'

'I don't know much about champagne.'

Max smiles. 'So what do your parents do?' He downs the rest of his wine in one. A practised move, it would seem, as he shows no ill effects, or embarrassment in front of me, a stranger.

'My dad works in the steel works as an electrician, and Mum is at home these days, but she keeps busy, and . . . that's it.' I take a sip, the chilled champagne sliding across my tongue and fizzing in my throat. Each glass probably costs more than I'd pay for a whole bottle of passable red from the local shop. I pick up my phone and check again it's recording, then I place it between us on the table as Max refills his glass and gulps down half of that too. At this rate he'll be drunk before I've had a chance to properly start the interview.

'I'm not from a literary background either,' he says. 'Somewhat humble beginnings, in fact.' He raises his glass, waiting whilst I lift mine, a satisfying note as they connect. 'That's probably why I suffer with imposter syndrome.'

'Imposter syndrome?'

Max locks eyes with me, leaning across the table and whispering, 'Always wondering when I'm going to get caught out.'

I almost drop my glass, setting it back down with trembling fingers. 'How do you mean?'

'Publishing is a precarious business, Seren. You're only ever as good as your last book. I'm sure journalism is equally competitive.' He stands up, a hand to the table and a smile curving the corners of his mouth.

He seems pleased with himself, rattling the junior reporter by dangling deliberately ambiguous statements before her, then snatching them back. But surely it's a dangerous game? If he's going to tease me with twisted half-confessions then he must also expect me to draw unfavourable conclusions. At the very least it's inappropriate behaviour for a husband supposedly desperate to find his missing wife. The excessive consumption of expensive champagne and his suppressed but obvious delight as he toys with me are both in very poor taste.

'Shall we go through to the sitting room?' he asks, already striding towards the kitchen door.

Max is halfway across the rug when I catch him up, the unfamiliar and shadowy corridor taking me longer to negotiate. I pause to chuck my phone into my bag, slinging the straps over my shoulder as Max opens a large door on the other side of the hall.

The sitting room smells of woodsmoke, although the fire isn't lit. The huge hearth is to my right, built of Cotswold stone above head-height, although the formal room can take it, generous in proportion with high ceilings. Covetable powder-blue velvet sofas are placed either side of the fire, which is surrounded by built-in bookcases, the shelves running wall-to-wall and floor-to-ceiling. A taste of dust and a trace of mildew hang in the stale air, taking me back to the library I used to visit as a child. Max adopts a lord of the manor pose, his left hand resting on the pale honey-coloured lintel, his fingers almost touching a silver-framed photo.

'This is lovely,' I say, walking over to the large mullioned window on my left, the segmented view out on to the drive framed by dark navy curtains. The old glass is divided into small panes and whorled with age, tinting the hills in the distance to a dirty brown, like a sepia photograph. I think of the vicar's wife, dead before the house was completed, a cold draught shivering against my neck. I turn to Max and smile.

'I thought we could talk more comfortably in here,' he says, his footsteps echoing across the wooden floorboards as he closes the heavy door. 'I'll light the fire, warm us up.'

He returns to the hearth and bends on one knee to a basket filled with logs and kindling, pyramiding small pieces of wood first, a match struck against a vaporous firelighter before he adds a log, then another, prodding at them with a wrought-iron poker from the companion set beside the grate. The fire spits and crackles, the splits in the logs jangling my nerves. I take deep but silent breaths, looking anywhere but at the heavy poker.

AMANDA REYNOLDS

'Do sit down,' Max says, gesturing towards the sofa to the right of the fire.

He picks up his champagne flute from the lintel, taking a seat opposite me and crossing his legs, his other arm raised so his free hand rests elegantly along the top of the cushion beside him. He sips his drink, watching as I open my bag and remove my phone and the Moleskine notebook I've been saving for something special. I deliberately left my champagne behind. 'Are all of those books yours?' I ask, diverting his attention away from my preparations. 'I mean, you wrote them?'

'Not all of them.'

Max gets up to extract a thin hardback, then he moves my bag to the floor and sits beside me. We're not touching, but much closer than I'd prefer. I notice lines around his eyes, and dark circles beneath, the scent of his cologne strong enough to inhale. I edge away, my face burning. The fire is getting unbearably hot. I touch a hand to my cheek, drawing attention to my predicament as Max smiles and leans back, thumbing the book.

'This was my first success,' he says, handing it to me. 'I bought this place with the royalties.'

I turn the book over and open the back cover. The photo is of a much younger Max, clearly a novice in front of the camera. He looks uncomfortable, his smile laboured. I glance up, a trace of that same vulnerability in Max's expression now, much more appealing than the practised charm. But there's also something about the photograph that troubled me, jarred even, the younger man a total mismatch for my host today. When did

56

one replace the other? The inexperienced younger version eclipsed by a man who offers champagne at midday and deliberately disquiets me when he must sense I'm already nervous. And why wouldn't I be? Alone with him in this vast house, miles from anywhere, his wife possibly murdered by the same hand that so recently touched mine.

'It's a very old headshot,' Max says, prompting me to pass back the book as he rises. 'God, I look so young.' He sighs, taking a last look before replacing the book on the shelf.

'How did you meet your wife?' I ask, readying myself to take shorthand notes.

'My publisher was looking for a new image,' he tells me. 'I was what they call mid-list, which is code for, *"needs a bit of a revamp"*. Julia was assistant to this hot-shot photographer in London; an unpaid internship whilst she was at art college. The guy was a complete arse, charged a fortune and they've never used a single shot he took, but there was one photo we all loved.' He grabs a much thicker tome from a lower shelf, opening the back cover to show me the photo inside. It's an informal pose, a younger Max than today, but not quite as youthful as before, and this time the eyes instantly seek out mine, a surprisingly intimate exchange.

'Julia took that one,' he says, looking down at me. 'While her boss was messing about with exposures or something. She got me chatting and I relaxed. I suppose I was already falling in love with her.'

'It's a lovely photo,' I reply, holding up the closed hardback.

'Yes,' he says, taking it. 'And I don't usually like photos of myself.'

'Who does?' I ask, although I'd be more inclined to believe him if he hadn't shown me two in succession and asked for my opinion.

Max returns the book to the gap on the shelf then takes the seat facing me again. 'I'm surprised you still use shorthand,' he observes, pointing at my pad. 'I thought it would be an anachronism in this digital age?'

'It's quicker than rewinding a whole conversation on a phone just to find the line you need,' I explain, and he nods, crossing his legs and running an arm along the back of the sofa in the same relaxed pose as before. 'My phone recordings are more of a back-up.'

He nods, clearly a pro at this kind of thing. Whereas I'm struggling to keep my hands from shaking. I unfold my printed notes from the back of my pad and spread them out on the cushion beside me, hoping Max can't read them across the coffee table. My pen rolls off my lap, falling as I reach out to grab it. I wince as it lands with a clatter. 'Sorry.' I retrieve the cheap biro from where it's come to rest by his shiny brogues, his feet planted in front of him as he leans forward. The brogues have ridiculous tassels on them and his socks are garish, geometric diamonds in yellow and black, which somehow makes him less imposing. I straighten up and catch his amusement at my clumsiness, although he's feigning interest in an iPad he's picked up from the glass table.

'You get a signal on that?' I ask.

'WiFi,' Max replies, not offering me the code. 'Are you ready, Seren?' He glances at his watch. 'I do need to get back to work fairly soon.'

'Yes, sorry.' I look at my notes again and clear my throat.
'So how old was Julia when you first met?'

'She was seventeen as I'm sure you're aware. Eighteen when
we married.'

'And you were?'

'For fuck's sake, Seren. Is this an interview or a bloody
questionnaire? Ask me something you can't find on Wikipedia!'

'Sorry, I . . . I . . .' I try to read my next question, but the
words keep jumbling up in my head. And although he could
be more tolerant, he is right, my questions are redundant, a
rehash of everything from my research: art college, planning
applications for improvements at Brooke House, charity
dinners. 'OK, let's move on to Julia's disappearance. You've
been completely private since that night, despite the swell of
media interest.'

He looks up from his iPad. 'Can you blame me for hiding
away?'

I stare back, caught again by the passion of those bright blue
eyes, but more than that, there's a vague threat in his demanding
tone that unsettles me, as if I'm the one being questioned.

'I'm sure it must have been unbearable for you, but wouldn't
it have been better to use that exposure to help with the search?'
I hate myself for asking, but it's the obvious question.

'I don't trust journalists,' he says, brushing something invisible from his trouser leg. 'Particularly the ones who work for
tabloids. The things they printed at the time were grossly unfair.'

Not untrue?

'So why trust me?' I ask, perhaps unwisely.

'I'm hoping you'll be different,' he says, smiling. 'More . . .

understanding. And Julia loved the *Herald*, always read it on her laptop over breakfast and picked up a copy of the print edition if she was in town. She liked to see what was going on locally and she always cut out any pictures of us. I suppose that's why it feels appropriate to talk to you.'

'I see, but the *Herald*, we're hardly—' I stop myself from talking my way out of the door. 'Where do you think she is, Max?'

'I don't know.'

'Of course, but do you have any idea at all?'

'No, none.' He sighs and leans back into the squashy sofa, then he seems to think better of his retreat and edges forward again, massaging the back of his neck, a sheen of perspiration on his brow. 'The world's stopped making sense,' Max tells me. 'Everything I thought I understood about the universe is challenged, all my perceptions turned on their head.' He wipes his forehead with his palm. 'Nothing can prepare you for losing someone, can it? Not when there's no resolution, however hard you try to find one.' He makes direct eye contact now. 'That piece you wrote, Seren, about the pain of losing someone . . . It said so much more than was on the page. I feel I can talk to you. I feel as though . . .' His words peter out, the fire dying away too, the heat of it suddenly burned off. 'I feel as though you will understand.'

I look down, my pen suspended above the pad where it has hovered since his speech began. I start making notes again, but my shorthand squiggles are all over the page, barely legible. I feel exposed. Max has lifted the lid on my own thoughts, peering in and pulling them out, a jumbled mess on the coffee table between us, although I had purposefully avoided giving anything personal away in my article. I scan down my questions. When I look up, he's tapping the screen of iPad again. It's as if his impassioned speech had never been made.

'You said Julia was planning on taking up photography as a career when you first met?'

'Yes.' He looks up. 'She didn't abandon the course on my account, at least, not at first. She'd stay in London during the week, then come here at weekends, but her heart was always with me and Brooke House.'

'So she moved in quite quickly?'

'Yes, I suppose it was quite quick. We talked about it and she said it was tiresome commuting. We were happiest when we were together, so she made the house her project instead, and me, of course.' He laughs to himself, visibly relaxing as he casts his mind back to happier times. 'Julia had a good eye for both.'

'Quite a change in lifestyle for such a young woman,' I remark, the slight stirring of the cypress trees drawing my eye. 'What did she do with herself all day?'

'As I've already explained, she oversaw all the house renovations, and then of course there were her charitable causes.'

'Which causes did she support?'

'Mainly children's charities, kids in care, that kind of thing. She didn't have much of a childhood herself. Her parents are both dead and the sister . . . let's just say you can't choose your family, but you *can* choose not to see them. The police checked with Jacqui to ask if she'd seen Julia, of course; she lives in the wilds of Scotland, with a pig farmer, I believe. She couldn't have cared less, apparently. No wonder Julia cut all contact; only interested in us for one thing.' Max rubs his fingers and thumb together to indicate Jacqui was after the Blakes' money.

'And no children of your own. Can I ask why?'

There's a long pause whilst he looks down at the screen in his lap. 'You know what, I'm beginning to think this is a bad idea.'

'Max, I—'

'It was a misjudgement to open up my home and myself to your scrutiny and . . .' Max stands up. 'To be honest, I'm wondering, what's the point?'

'Max, if I've inadvertently—'

'I know what people think, what *you* think,' he says, walking towards the closed door.

He leaves the room, his footsteps falling fast as he retreats. I switch off the recording and chase after him, shoving my notes in my bag. 'Max, please wait.'

He's already opening the front door as I run into the hallway, an icy wind tracking across the stripy rug.

'I'm going to have to ask you to leave now, Seren,' he says, roughly grabbing my coat from the rack and handing it to me. 'I have things to do and this has taken much longer than I'd anticipated. I don't mean to be rude, I'm sure you're a lovely girl, but I'm on a deadline so I think it's best we end it here.'

'I have to ask these questions, Max. You must have realised that. But if you give me a chance—'

Max grips the door against the tug of the wind. 'If you don't mind?'

I find a business card in my overstuffed bag and hand it to him. 'I'll be in touch tomorrow, OK? See how you feel then. I want to help you tell your story, Max. I want to help you reach your wife. You said how much she loved to read the *Herald*.'

Max exhales, looking at me for a long second before reluctantly taking the card.

I step out, a slam of the wind, I assume, smashing the heavy door shut behind me. I dash across the rain-spattered gravel, the weak sun hidden behind the clouds as I turn the corner towards the garages. Fat drops have begun to fall again as I reach my car.

The tired engine begrudgingly turns over, relief flooding my system. Adrenalin pounds hard in my ears, my hands gripping the steering wheel as I edge past the kitchen. I know I should be disappointed to be leaving so soon, but after the tension of being alone in that house, with Max, I can't wait to get away. I swallow and press on a little faster, but at the fork in the drive I slow down, forcing myself to turn the car towards the outbuildings.

The hedges are high, branches brushing both sides of my car so I'm afraid I might lose the wing mirror for good, dark fronds of evergreens pressing in as my wipers try to clear the windscreen. As the hedges end, the gravel widens on to a small courtyard, a triangle of single-storey buildings surrounding it. To my left are two joined cottages that look empty and unloved, opposite them a similarly dilapidated barn. I get out and walk towards the left-hand cottage, but as I approach I feel a pressing need to look behind me, convinced I'm not alone. The courtyard is still, but shadows of the estate's troubled past are everywhere, even in the cottages' dull and empty windows, as though previous tragedies have left their mark. Max said that Julia loved Brooke House, but why? She had a full life in London, a burgeoning career, and she was so young. She gave it all up so easily. Did she ever regret that, try to break out? And yet somehow he kept her here, his perfect wife, in splendid isolation, other than when she was paraded at events, and then only there to adorn his arm and the pages of the *Herald*. I run back to my car and make a multi-point turn in the confined space, urgency increasing my self-induced panic. Maybe Julia never left, hidden in a shadowy world of Max's choosing, miles away from prying eyes, or worse, buried somewhere on the vast estate, deep beneath the earth, trapped here forever.

I drive away, foot down hard this time despite the narrow exit from the courtyard, the wing mirror swinging on the last strips of tape as I turn towards the main drive. I don't even look at Brooke House as I speed past the front entrance, my only thought to get away as fast as I can.

Chapter Four

You Think He Did It?

'For goodness' sake, Seren,' Theo says, unbuckling his seat belt. 'I told you to keep in touch! And what the fuck is this?' He holds up the detached wing mirror, then throws it back into the passenger footwell.

'I had to stop on my way back from Brooke House,' I tell him, recalling my battle with the elements and the last of the duct tape. 'Thought I was about to lose it for good.'

Apart from my unscheduled stop, the drive back was easier than the one out there. A cup of sweet tea on my return to the office had also helped to rationalise my fears. After batting away Fran's enquiries about where I'd been all morning and 'half the afternoon', I was then the last one standing, clock-watching until Theo finally rolled back in, a frown his only greeting as he closed his office door. I'd tapped and been granted entry, and a full hearing, but only if we took our conversation to the pub as he claimed it had been 'that kind of day'.

We walk together across the badly lit pot-holed car park, the rain still thrashing down.

'I did call,' I tell Theo, holding my coat above my head. 'Didn't Lynda say?'

Theo opens the pub door. 'No, she didn't. And what if Max had seen you snooping around? That could have been game over before you even start.'

'I just had a quick peek at the outbuildings,' I reply, avoiding his pained expression. We're crammed into the small lobby, another door facing us as we brush the rain from our coats.

'Yes, but—' he says, stepping back as the door to the bar opens and a wiry man emerges, cigarettes in hand. 'Shall we get a table?' Theo asks. 'I think I need a drink before this conversation.'

The pub Theo suggested is known for its selection of real ales rather than wine, actual sawdust on the floor and hand-written chalkboards above the bar listing the huge choice on tap. The air is thick with the heavy scent of stale beer mixed with the pungent smell of disinfectant coming from the nearby Gents' toilet. It feels like an odd choice of venue for our meeting, but Theo said he wanted a decent pint and maybe he's trying to avoid the wine bars by the office where we might bump into people from work. I consider this, debating whether I should ask him if he's noted Fran's disapproval of our close working relationship, Lynda's too, but I can't think how to word it without making us both feel awkward. Theo and I are good friends and colleagues, nothing more. I don't want to jeopardise that when we're doing nothing wrong. 'I know Max is a friend of yours, Theo,' I begin.

'Was,' he says, waving a note to attract the barman's attention.

'OK, but you knew him well, for many years,' I reply, barged by a passing drinker who's carrying two full glasses, the spillage only just avoiding my coat, now draped over my arm.

'Yes,' Theo concedes. 'What's your point?'

'That *potentially* your judgement is skewed by your previous friendship with Max.' I raise my hand to his look of outrage, a rebuff already on his lips. 'Hear me out a minute! The press releases and news reports all point to his involvement, and,' I lower my voice, 'the blood they found in an outbuilding sounds pretty damning.'

'I don't agree,' Theo replies, frowning. 'I mean about my judgement being skewed.'

'No, but—'

This time Theo asks *me* to hear *him* out.

'None of us can be certain, Seren. Only the two people who were there: Max and Julia. I'm sure there's plenty we're not aware of, despite my best efforts.'

'So you're admitting he might have killed her?'

He shakes his head as the barman approaches and I take the hint, trying to decide what to order, wine not listed on the chalkboard, whilst Theo is offered a sample of the 'guest ale'. Theo carries my half of cider and his pint of beer to a corner table for two, only a few drops spilt on the way.

'If we assume for a moment,' he says, wiping froth from his upper lip, 'that Max killed her, disposing of the body somewhere near the house, remote enough to remain undiscovered for all these months, it then feels counter-intuitive to suddenly involve the *Herald*. If he's hoping to deflect attention away from his guilt, why rake everything up in such a public way? No pun intended.'

I think of Max's obvious pleasure when I'd been wrong-footed. He clearly enjoys an audience, but I take Theo's point. It does feel like an unnecessary and risky move now that most of the press interest has died away.

'Maybe he has other reasons,' I suggest.

'Such as?' Theo asks.

'Such as emerging from his self-imposed asylum. He's very keen to tell me how perfect everything was before Julia vanished, but perfection is rarely the true picture. Maybe he's ready to move on?'

Theo places his glass down with a satisfied thump, half of it now drunk. 'Well, aren't you the wise old owl tonight. Any other insights?'

'There's the massive age gap,' I say, contemplating my gassy cider. 'Obviously he's very wealthy, but is that really enough?'

'No, I don't think the money is enough,' Theo replies. 'Maybe at first, but not to sustain a ten-year marriage.' He picks up his drink. 'But Max is charming, and clever. His books are like jigsaw puzzles, very intricately plotted. And he's good company, and generous to his friends and the charities he and Julia supported. And, so I'm told, extremely handsome.' Theo looks to me for a reaction and I shrug in a non-committal way. 'Yes, they argued, it was a tempestuous relationship, but they still led a pretty perfect life by most standards.' Theo swallows another inch or two of his pint. 'Julia was difficult when she was drunk, but she had her good points too. She certainly knew how to put on an elegant party. No expense was ever spared.'

'I didn't find Max charming,' I say, taking a sip of the cold cider, hoping it will cool my warming face. 'And I don't agree about his writing prowess, either. The plots might be intricate, or impenetrable depending on your viewpoint, but the characters are cartoonish, women referencing their breasts as they run after men who are doing most of the actual and figurative heavy lifting.'

Theo laughs. 'Maybe you're not his target reader, Seren? I don't think he'll be losing much sleep over it.'

'I think you're right,' I reply, relieved to move on.

I don't know why it's so hard to admit I'm drawn to Max, despite his sullenness, and the way his mood can change from warm to cold in a heartbeat. And despite my harsh appraisal, I did find some merit in his work, more than I'd expected; glimpses of humanity and subtle characterisation amongst the genre clichés, leading me to the conclusion Max may well be a victim of his own success, his formulaic sure-fire blockbusters a silken noose slung around his neck. Of course, he could just be a misogynist wife-murdering arsehole who knows how to turn up the charisma setting as required.

'Don't underestimate him,' Theo says, looking up at me from the beer mat he's been flipping one-handed, although he often misses the catch, a slight tremor in his hands which I've noticed before but never quite so pronounced.

'How do you mean?' I ask, happy to put my drink down. Cider really isn't my beverage of choice and, looking at my smeared glass, I'm concerned about the hygiene standards in here.

'Max is no fool, and more than likely he has his own agenda,'

Theo replies. 'He was always very good at using people to get what he wants.'

'For instance?'

'For instance, he came to me when he wanted a bit of publicity, early on in his career, then he decided he was far too important for the local paper. I know he was annoyed the way the *Herald* jumped on the conjecture bandwagon after Julia disappeared, but to be honest he'd pissed me off way before that.'

'But you'd stayed friends with him?'

'Yes,' Theo replies, enigmatically. 'Julia liked Nicky and as far as I was concerned . . . Look, Max was famous, I wasn't going to sever the connection, was I? Besides, I liked him. He was interesting company. I wasn't a massive fan of Julia, if I'm honest. She was bloody hard work. But Max was always a great host, and a night at Brooke House was always rather . . . lavish. Does that sound terribly shallow?'

I shake my head and I mean it. Who wouldn't be tempted by the grandeur of Brooke House? Not Theo, or Julia, it would seem. 'The night she went missing, did you notice anything different, any particular tension between them, other than after her friends arrived?'

Theo smiles, indulging me. The teacher watching their pupil learn to fly. 'Like I said, Julia was bored and drunk, she liked to rile Max, see how far she could push him. It wasn't unusual, or even the worst I've witnessed over the years.'

'But you said your wife had a bad feeling?'

Theo frowns. 'I wouldn't put too much stock in that. Try to deal with the facts, keep an open mind. You don't have to decide anything, that's not your job.' He finishes his drink and points at my barely touched cider. 'Ready for another?'

I shake my head and pretend to take a polite sip as he walks to the bar. I'm dreading telling him Max has already changed his mind, but hopefully the bad news will go down better after a second pint.

'So when do you next see him?' Theo asks when he returns. 'I should probably let Fran and Simon know what's going on; only fair.'

'The thing is . . .' I grimace at Theo and he pulls a face, thudding his beer down.

I desperately try to put a positive spin on my unceremonious ejection from Brooke House, but it's hard to couch it in any way other than a failure. I can see Theo's struggling to conceal his disappointment, which is so much worse than if he'd lost his temper with me. 'I'd already got quite a lot from Max, and a photo of the house,' I add, screwing up my face to show how sorry I am.

Theo is silent, his head bowed over his beer as he considers his reply. 'Give Max tonight to cool off – he's hot-headed, always has been – then send a grovelling email tomorrow. He hates calls, says they interrupt his flow.'

'OK, great.' I nod emphatically. 'I'll email first thing. I managed to leave him my card, so he has all my contact details if he changes his mind in the meantime.'

'Good girl, well done.' Theo is distracted, still deep in thought. 'If that doesn't work I'll try, but for now keep me out of it, it's between you two.' He looks up. 'It's possible he planned it this way all along, of course.'

'Why would he do that?'

Theo shakes his head to show he has no idea. Then he takes a cigar from his inside jacket pocket, returning it when I remind him he can't smoke in here.

'I suppose it's to do with his writing,' Theo says at last. 'He enjoys the game of it all, digging into people's psyches to work out their character. I've seen him do it time and again, so just be careful how you approach him, softly-softly and all that.'

'I should get going,' I tell him, pushing away my drink. 'Can I run you back to the office?'

Theo laughs. 'No, thanks. The journey here was traumatic enough. I'll have another beer then walk back to my car.' He stands as I do, an old-fashioned courtesy from a true gent, touching my arm as he says, 'Look, don't worry, Seren. If that's all you get from Max then it will have to do.'

It's generous of him to say so when I doubt it's how he truly feels, but I don't agree. This was my big break, it can't slip through my fingers after one aborted meeting, I shan't let it. I glance back at Theo as I leave, hoping for a smile to reassure me, but he's chatting to the barman, on the hunt for the next story. Theo orders another beer. One too many to drive on but it's not my place to tell him that.

It's only a five-minute journey home from the pub car park, but my phone pings with two alerts in that time. I reverse into the nearest space, a few doors down by the artisan bakers, grabbing my phone the second I'm done. The missed call and voicemail are both from Julia's sister in Scotland, Jacqui Moresley. I got her name from Theo, but I haven't been able to find any recent connection to Julia, which ties in with Max's comments about the sisters being estranged. I've called the mobile hairdressing company Jacqui owns more than once, the last time leaving a message offering to pay for any information she might offer in the search for her sister. The monetising of her loss had felt tacky, and I'm fairly certain Theo won't authorise a payment, however modest, but it seems to have got a response at last. I'll try her in half an hour, as she'd suggested.

I dash past the bike and up the stairs, ready to tell Izzy all about my disastrous first meeting with Max, but as soon as I step inside a wall of sound hits me. The volume is turned up so loud on the television my entrance goes unnoticed. Izzy eventually looks over the back of the sofa. 'Oh, hi sweetie, you OK? You look drenched.' Then Dom's angular profile pops up too. Izzy eyes me sympathetically and turns the sound down, explaining to Dom I've been working all day, I must be exhausted.

'I've actually been at the pub with Theo for the last hour,' I say, then spotting an exchange of looks between them. 'Hi, Dom.'

Dom has the same expression he always wears whenever I interrupt them, as though I'm the intruder. His beautiful face – chiselled jaw and sculpted cheekbones – is soured by the falseness he affects whenever he opens his mouth, his eyes widening as he says, 'Oh my God, Seren. You have to watch this. They basically shag their favourite at the end. They don't show it or anything, but it's hilarious. Iz and I are deciding who we'd choose. We both like the guy with the bun and a beard, or maybe the girl with a tatt on her face.'

Izzy, knowing I don't share her taste in television programmes, slumps back down, pointing out to Dom that I only watch the news and documentaries. 'I've told you that a million times,' she says, cuffing him affectionately on his toned arm.

He laughs and bounces down beside her, pulling Izzy's chunky calves into his lap. 'Soz, I forgot what a geek you are, Seren.'

I take off my coat and perch next to Iz on the arm of the sofa, quickly pulled into the dilemma of the girl choosing her 'perfect' date. As the credits roll, Iz and I agree she's an idiot for choosing the guy with good looks, but little in the brains or empathy department.

Dom looks up at me and flashes a smile. 'So, you think he did it?' He mimes the scene from *Psycho*, stabbing the air. 'Max Blake, I mean. Famous author and infamous wife killer!'

'Dom, no!' Izzy says trying to stop him. He mock stabs her instead but she pushes him off, calling after me, 'Seren, wait!'

I turn back, already halfway to my room. 'I told you that in confidence, Iz.'

'I'm so sorry, Seren.' She swipes at Dom again but he pulls her on top of him as she screams, 'You're a bloody nightmare, Dom . . . argh, stop it!'

I close my bedroom door and peel off my damp tights then the rest of my clothes, naked except for my bra as I slump down on the side of my bed. It's not so much that Izzy shared my secret that's upset me, it's more the feeling of exclusion when Dom's around. Iz is the only friend I've made since I moved here, apart from Theo, and the loneliness I'd felt in my last year at university aches within me once more. I grab my phone as a distraction, scanning Facebook for any mention of Julia. There's still nothing, although I spend a good ten minutes scrolling through the college's page before I try Jacqui's mobile again, although it's sooner than she'd asked me to call. I'm interrupted by a tentative knock. I end the call and pull on a tee-shirt. Then I open the door, but only enough to look out.

'I'm so sorry about Dom.' Izzy has a contrite expression on her face. 'I'm mortified he said something. He has no filter, or morals.'

'I'm more concerned you told him in the first place, Iz. I did stress that it's top secret.'

'I know, but I didn't think it would hurt to tell Dom.'

'This business is brutal, Iz. If someone else were to find out, another reporter . . . Who else knows?'

'No one, I swear.' She does an approximation of the points of a cross over her low-cut top. 'I only told Dom because I'm worried about you, Seren.'

'*Worried?* Why would you be worried?'

'Because, silly,' she says, smiling at me. 'You're my best mate.'

Her words are heartfelt, and touching, but I'm not ready to forgive her yet. 'You think I'm a joke, both of you,' I reply, grabbing my phone from the bed and rejecting the incoming call from Jacqui.

'No! Not at all. That's just Dom's terrible sense of humour, you know what he's like. I'm so proud of you, Seren. Your job, it's amazing. All I do is wipe tables and froth milk, but you interview murderers!'

I smile, so many replies coming to mind, most of them

rebuttals about my total lack of anything approaching amazingness. Then another thought occurs. 'You didn't say anything to Dom about the anonymous calls, did you?'

'No, of course not. I would never do that. I'm really sorry,' she says again. 'I'm a complete idiot.'

'No, you're not, but please don't tell anyone else. And tell Dom the same. It's important, Iz.'

'Absolutely, I will emphasise it to him right now, I promise.'

I close the door, flopping down on the bed to try Jacqui, the sound of her voicemail cutting in, again. I hang up and read a couple more chapters of Max's book, although it's still hardgoing. He can certainly spin a good tale, but the stereotyped female roles are more bothersome with each new scene, and my credulity is stretched to breaking point. I snap the book shut and switch off the light, the television still loud in the next room, Izzy and Dom's laughter louder still. I cover my head with a pillow and close my eyes, hoping the exhaustion of the day will take over, but all I can see is Dom's jabbing fist as he mimed Max stabbing Julia. As I drift towards sleep, Dom and Max morph into one, taunting me with cruel jokes and sly smiles, Max's dismissal compounded by Dom's, both of them mocking me.

It's dark, the room silent apart from the persistent tone which creeps into my dreams. My phone is lit up, casting a faint glow across the room as my eyes begin to focus. I reach out and knock the handset to the floor, a loud thwack as it lands. I'm out of bed and answering the call before my thoughts have caught up with my actions, my head swimming at the sudden-

ness of the upwards movement, darkness swaying around me.
'Hello?'

Silence.

There have been times when I've hated him and now, as I inwardly beg him to say something, set my mind at ease, I feel that same anger surge within me. I fight it with a bite to the softest part of my top lip, my teeth scraping the loose skin until the call ends. I listen for Iz next door, but the apartment is soundless, and cold. I resist the urge to throw my phone against the wall, focusing my energy on my breathing, pushing the knot of emotions back down. Then I notice a text message, sent just after midnight.

Sorry missed your calls. Call me first thing tomorrow, Seren. I've plenty to tell you about that bastard who married my baby sister! Jaq x

Sixty-Four Hours Missing

'You do not have to say anything, but it may harm your defence if you do not mention when questioned something which you later rely on in court.'

Katie recites the familiar speech, boring herself with the monologue, although Miriam Norris, Max's devoted PA, is rapt, nodding at every word. She hadn't been so compliant when she'd left Brooke House late on Sunday morning, speeding past the officer at the gate and almost taking out a reporter in her little green car, despite Katie's express instructions she was to wait in Max's study until she'd had a chance to question her further.

'Anything you do say may be given in evidence. Do you understand what this means, Miriam?' Katie asks.

'Yes, I do. Completely.'

'And your rights have been explained to you? Free and independent legal advice, details of how you can access a copy of the interview?' Katie glances up from the laptop screen to the frightened rabbit facing them, then a quick check on Chris who is seated beside her. He's as pissed off as she is they had to let Max go. This interview is as much a warning to Max that they haven't given up, as it is an interrogation of his right-hand woman.

'Yes, everyone has been very thorough,' Miriam replies. 'But as I explained to your colleague—'

'There's nothing to be worried about,' Katie says, eager to get on with it now. 'But if you want a solicitor called for you, we can still do that.'

The detective rakes her fingers through matted hair and waits for Miriam's response. In some instances, having a solicitor present is preferable, cutting through the laborious process and saving a client from themselves. But having met Max's representative, Katie doubts it would prove helpful today, in fact, quite the opposite.

'I'm here to assist in any way I can,' Miriam replies. 'No need to bother Max's brief again. You know he charges—'

'Right!' Katie says. 'I've asked to speak with you today as your employer reported his wife, Julia Blake, missing on Sunday morning.'

'I'm fully aware of that.'

'Yes, of course,' Katie replies, trying not to sound too impatient. 'What I wanted to ask you is why Mr Blake called you first.'

'Max relies on me a lot,' Miriam tells her with some pride. 'I would have been disappointed if he hadn't.'

'Can you please describe your movements over the twenty-four hours preceding Julia Blake's disappearance?'

'I was helping my sister on the farm. It's been in our family for two generations but now she lives there alone so I do what I can.'

'OK,' Chris says, smiling at Miriam reassuringly. 'That's Mile End Farm, near Brooke House?'

Katie makes a mental note to talk to Miriam's sister, asterisking it messily in her mind.

'Yes,' Miriam returns Chris's smile with her own sheepish grin. 'Julia asked for me to be gone by six on Friday night. It was their anniversary weekend, she had lots to organise.'

Katie makes a note on her pad and twists it towards Chris, the words 'Cleaning Company?' circled. He nods, then shakes his head slowly. Katie turns her attention back to Miriam. 'So you left Brooke House Friday night at what time exactly?'

'Around seven, I think. It was later than I'd planned as my daily catch-up meeting with Max ran on. There were a few issues with his edits that were preoccupying him. Julia was busy so he chatted it through with me instead.'

'And you went straight to Mile End Farm and stayed there until Max contacted you on Sunday morning, is that correct?' Katie asks.

'Yes, that is correct, Detective Ingles.'

'And the first you knew of Julia's disappearance was when Max called you there on Sunday morning?'

'Yes, around eight on Sunday morning, I think.'

'A full hour before he alerted us to the fact his wife was missing?' Katie asks.

'Yes, I suppose it was.'

'And you went over straight away, on a Sunday,' Katie leans back and folds her arms. 'Even though you had been given the weekend off?'

'I always came straight over if either of them needed me,'

Miriam explains, searching in her bag for a tissue which she dabs to her nose, sniffing. 'It wasn't a nine-to-five role.'

'Tell me about your relationship with Max Blake,' Katie says, running an odd scenario through her head where Miriam is romantically entangled with Max. It doesn't feel right, but you never know; stranger things have happened.

'He's my employer. I've been with him for many years now.'

'Describe your duties.'

'My official title is Personal Assistant, but I'm much more than that, of course.' She lists tasks she considers to be part of her role, including 'fixing', 'facilitating' and 'fire-fighting'.

'Does that also include arranging car repairs?' Chris asks, throwing in the comment just as they'd planned it. *Boom!*

Miriam looks suitably flustered, the tissue returned to her nose. 'Oh, I see, yes, I did go to the house with Barry on Saturday morning to collect Julia's car for repair, but I didn't see Max or Julia. The keys were in the ignition and it was parked by the garages. We were in and out without disturbing anyone.'

'Barry Bostwick?' Chris asks and she nods. 'What time?'

'Early morning. I'm not totally sure of the exact time. Max had caught the Range Rover on the gate and he didn't want Julia to find out. It's her car, you see. I picked up Barry, he's our trusted mechanic, and we collected Julia's car, but I didn't see anyone. Like I said, Max left the keys in it.'

'And your relationship with Mrs Blake?' Chris asks. 'Did you get on?'

'Julia is a sweet girl,' Miriam replies, blowing her nose. 'Sorry,

I seem to have picked up a summer cold. All this damp weather.'

'A sweet girl?' Chris repeats. 'In what way?'

Katie watches Chris as he probes Miriam about Julia, ready to jump in if needed. Despite appearances he has the makings of a great DS, his flashy grin belying a subtlety and intelligence it would be easy to miss. The tan must be fake, unless he's been away; it's been a mostly wet spring. The rain that returned on Sunday morning still shows no signs of stopping. It's washed away every scrap of evidence from the grounds and surrounding lanes, any tyre marks or footprints long gone. They've had no luck whatsoever on this case; even Julia's mobile phone, found tucked in a drawer of lingerie by her side of the bed, hadn't been used for weeks. The landline records have proved just as disappointing: only listing calls to the caterers, cleaners and florists on the Saturday, and nothing of note before that. Julia's laptop emails were equally dull, mainly online purchases, like the expensive bath, and charity requests and follow-ups, plus a few exchanges with what appeared to be a delivery company. They were hoping a witness might have come forward by now with a credible sighting of Julia, but all they've had are the usual crazies.

'Must have been a big change for you,' Chris continues. 'Having another woman in the house after all those years when it was just you and Max?'

Katie winces at Chris's leading question. Shame, he'd been doing so well.

'I know what you're trying to suggest,' Miriam replies, her smile slipping. 'You're wrong, Detective Green. Completely wrong.'

'What do you think I'm trying to suggest?' he asks, avoiding Katie's taps to his leg with her pen.

'Julia's been good for Brooke House, and good for Max,' Miriam tells him. 'I would never resent her being there.'

'Tell me about when you arrived at the house on Sunday morning,' Katie says, taking over.

'Max and I searched and searched,' Miriam says, looking down at the sodden tissue in her hands. 'It was horrible. So much rain.'

'Do you have any idea where Julia might be, Miriam?' Katie asks, trying to relax her face into a softer expression.

'I'd say if I did,' Miriam replies.

'That's not an answer,' Katie says. 'Do you have any idea where Julia—'

'No!' Miriam says, her voiced raised, then more quietly, 'I do not.'

'Why did you leave Brooke House at eleven twenty-seven on Sunday morning, despite the fact I had expressly told you to wait in Max's study?' Katie asks, not even trying to conceal her annoyance this time .

'I wanted to see my sister, she was worried about me. I'm sorry, I didn't think you'd mind as long as I was quick. Pauline was on pins, as you can imagine.'

'And your sister can corroborate that visit?'

'Yes, of course.'

'I'll be paying her a visit myself,' Katie says, eyeing Miriam sternly.

'Is that it?' Miriam asks as Katie gets up.

'For now,' Chris replies, standing too. 'But could you not go wandering again, please, Miriam? Go home to your sister and wait for us to get in touch, and don't talk to the press.'

'I can assure you I am nothing if not discreet, detective,' Miriam says, standing up too. 'But I'll be with Max at Brooke House if you need me for anything further. I still have a job to do and he needs me on hand.'

'Fine,' Katie says, glancing at the red recording light, still on. 'And one last thing, Miriam. Do you ever do any cleaning at Brooke House, or maybe in the cottages?'

Miriam's hair and features remain unmoving, her tightly permed curls as impenetrable as her closed expression. 'No, I don't, detective. That's not my job. We use a cleaning company, they're very good.'

'Oh, that's odd,' Chris says, looking down on Miriam who is at least a foot shorter than him. 'We found some cleaning equipment in the end garage: mop, bleach, cloths. I checked with the company you employ.' He glances at Katie and she nods. 'They told us they use a wholesale brand for their supplies, and they never leave anything at the property.'

'I don't know anything about that, detective. Am I OK to leave now?'

Chris smiles at Miriam, holding the door for her before he leads her back towards reception.

Katie gathers up her phone and notepad from the table and leaves the interview room, resisting the urge to punch the wall of the empty corridor as frustration lengthens her short stride.

Chapter Five

That's Not My Jules

'Seren?' Izzy's disembodied head appears around my bedroom door, daylight leaking into the darkened room. 'Shouldn't you be in work by now?'

I pull the duvet over my bare legs. 'What time is it?'

'Almost ten. I'm just leaving but I wanted to apologise again about what Dom said. I never thought he'd break a confidence so easily. I'm starting to wonder about him, to be honest.'

'It was you that broke a confidence, Iz!' I snap, sitting up.

She looks taken aback, swallowing hard. 'I said I was sorry.'

'No, I'm sorry.' I rub my hands over my face. 'I'm tired, that's all.'

'Disturbed night?' she asks, coming in. 'I take it you're not in work today?'

'No, it's my day off. I was hoping I'd be interviewing Max again, but it didn't go that well yesterday.'

'Oh, I'm sure it wasn't as bad as you think,' she says, the

mattress bending as she takes a seat. I pull my feet in to accommodate her.

'It was,' I tell her. 'He virtually threw me out. I think I've really blown it, Iz. My break-out story and I've mucked it up.'

'Did you at least get my books signed?' Izzy reaches out and pats my hand, trying to make me smile. 'Look, I'm sure he'll come round. And if not there'll be other stories. You're a brilliant reporter.'

'Thanks,' I reply, hoping she doesn't spot her paperbacks tucked under my bed. 'I honestly think I've blown it.'

'I'm sure you haven't,' she says, then she starts babbling on about her plans for tonight, how she and Dom couldn't find a table anywhere so they're going on a bar crawl instead, subvert the whole cynical construct, which is a rip-off anyway. 'It's Valentine's Day, Seren,' she says, noticing my confusion, then she stops twirling her hair and looks straight at me. 'You're not planning on seeing Theo tonight, are you?'

'No,' I say, reaching for my robe, a tangled mess on the floor. 'Why would you ask that?'

'I just worry how much time he spends with you, that's all. You don't think he—?'

'God, no!' I wriggle into one sleeve and then the other. 'Theo likes to infuse me with his decades of experience, that's all.'

'As long as that's all he's planning to infuse you with!' Izzy replies, making us both shudder. We laugh, although I notice she's still eyeing me with suspicion. 'Did he say anything this time?' she asks, gesturing to my phone.

'I thought you were asleep?'

'I heard something, but with Dom here I didn't think I should get up.'

I nod, picking up my mobile from the bedside table.

'Seren, you do know it's not him, don't you? He wouldn't want to frighten you like that. He'd want to let you know he's—'

'You have no idea what he'd do!'

'I know it upsets you.' She reaches out to touch my arm again.

I shrug her off. 'He's *my* brother, Iz. Not yours. You never even met him.'

She takes the hint, closing the door softly as she leaves. I shouldn't have spoken to her like that, but Izzy has no right to comment on what Bryn might do or say.

After I hear her leave for work I fall back into bed, scrolling through my recent call notifications. Number withheld, 04.52 a.m. Fifty seconds of silence. Fifty seconds of time with Bryn, but also fifty seconds of anger and frustration. Izzy's right about one thing, I should report the calls, but I can't, not yet. If it turns out not to be him, the caller traced to a far-flung country where someone is running a scam, then what do I have left?

There's also a missed call from a local landline number, just over an hour ago whilst I was still asleep, and they've left a voicemail. I sit up as soon as I hear Max's voice.

'Look, I've slept on it and I'd like to meet again today if that's OK? I'm working all day, so don't call back. You won't get an answer! If you're free I'll see you at five-thirty.'

And just like that the interview is back on. I didn't even have to send a grovelling email. I grab my laptop from my bag and open up my interview notes, my work-free day evaporating, not that I mind. I text Theo the good news. Then I call Julia's sister.

Jacqui Moresley's phone rings five times before she answers, 'Jaq's Mobile 'airdressing, can I 'elp you?' I pick up a strange mix of accents as we finally talk, a veneer of Scottishness undercut by a twang of East End, her Ts and Hs dropped. There's also a coarseness to her vocabulary I don't usually encounter outside of my days at the courthouse, the dull routine of chronicling the petty crimes heard there enlivened by the eye-watering language.

I clear my throat, another attempt to divert Jacqui back to my questions and away from her preoccupation with how much I'm going to pay for her 'valuable time'. 'What did you think of your sister's choice of husband, Jacqui?'

'I wasn't a fan,' she replies above the sound of a dog barking. 'He was as tight as a rat's arse.'

'You knew Max?'

'Only met 'im once. Didn't get an invite to the wedding or nothin', but he was in Waterstones in Edinburgh signing books a few years ago, so I made the journey, you know, to be friendly. He told me to keep away from 'im and Julia, said she din't want to see me and if I turned up at the house, 'e'd make sure I never came back.'

'He threatened you?'

'Aye, 'e did. He was all charm in front of the other punters waiting for their books to be signed, but 'e was horrible to me. Told me to fuck off under 'is breath.'

'Did you tell your sister?'

'That stuck-up cow? She hasn't spoken to me for years. I'm a reminder of her past, ain't I? Din't fit with her new image.'

'Did you ever ask Max or Julia for money, Jacqui?'

'What kind of shitty question is that?'

Jacqui is undoubtedly after whatever she can get, first from Max, and now me, unleashing a string of abuse when I explain my boss probably won't authorise a payment, but I'll try. I end the call as she's telling me exactly what she thinks of the 'gutter press'. I do feel bad, it was underhand, but after that reaction there's no way I'm asking Theo for her fifty quid. Besides, she'd very little to offer in return. She hasn't seen Julia in over a decade, and only met Max once. But she did say one thing that caught my attention.

'My sister wasn't into fancy clothes or gala dinners with a load of dried-up old fuckers. She was a dreamer, creative. Sure, she needed someone to love, a bit of security, but underneath she was a restless soul. I think she was 'is wee doll, you know, liked playing dress-up. You look at the photos of 'em together in the newspapers and online, that's not my Jules. That fucker turned 'er into someone else, or tried to. Dead behind the eyes, she was, and bored shitless if you ask me. I just hope she got away from 'im in time.'

Chapter Six

I'm Not the One Who's Scared

It's still light as I leave for my appointment with Max, although the day is almost done, twilight less than half an hour away. In the bridal shop below our apartment Laure is preening a slender brunette in front of the full-length cheval mirror, a slither of ivory silk hugging the girl's narrow hips, a long train fanned out behind her. I pause, caught by the tableau, wondering how the young woman, probably about my age, must feel as she contemplates her future. I move on, unlocking my car and placing my coat and the map I printed out on the passenger seat. The carrot cake I'd eaten for breakfast, and lunch, leftovers brought home by Iz from the café, lies heavily in my stomach, the waistband of my best trousers digging in. I swallow hard against the nausea, blaming the cake rather than my nerves as I drive away.

With the benefit of a previous outing to Brooke House, and the printed map – although it's not *much* help without road signs or many landmarks – I manage to only take one wrong turn. But I still whizz past the five-bar gate and have to slam on my brakes and throw the gears into reverse. The evening is closing in fast now, the vista on my left as I turn in stretching out towards the setting sun, but the wooded area to my right is a homogenous mass of brambles and dark crevices. My headlamps disturb an owl who swoops in front of the car, white underwings spectacularly unfurled as it skims the hedge then disappears into the valley. My heart throbs as I grip the steering wheel, pressing on along the bumpy track until I hear the stones of the gravel drive crunching beneath my tyres.

Relief that I've made it here quickly turns to a twinge of apprehension as I draw closer the house. It has taken on an eerie quality in the half-light, the top-floor windows in shadow, the heavy eyes either side of the stone steps now fully closed. I park by the garages as before, slipping my coat over my thin blouse and carefully walking back in the semi-gloom, my heeled boots crunching past the dark void that is the kitchen.

As I climb up to the front door I search for any signs of life, but the house looks empty. Max definitely said five-thirty and I'm bang on time. I look for a bell or knocker, spying an old-fashioned handle attached to a chain. A soft chime rings somewhere within, and an outside light comes on directly above the door. I blink and glance up to the dusty fitting, an insect caught in its glare, then I hear footfall approaching.

'Seren, you made it with no search party today. Come in! Come in!' Max steps back, watching as I wipe my boots on the Welcome mat, the hall cold and unlit. He takes my coat, slipping it from my shoulders in a practised move, then hangs it on a branch of the tree-shaped rack. 'We're in the kitchen, you'll join me in a drink?'

'*We?*' I ask, but Max is already headed down the corridor.

'I didn't think anyone was home,' I say, as I see a glint of light coming from the door at the other end. 'Everywhere was dark when I arrived.'

'I've just this minute emerged from my study,' Max replies, glancing back. 'The words have been flowing today,'

I catch a glimpse of blue eyes through the shadows and the scent of his now familiar cologne. 'That's good.'

'Yes, must have been your impending presence, Seren. Nothing like a deadline to focus the mind, is there?'

Light rushes towards us as Max opens the kitchen door. At the long wooden table, a stout woman – probably in her mid to late fifties – is poring over a laptop. She looks up at Max, then glances at me and her smile evaporates. Her face is plain and devoid of make-up, her hair a permed helmet of tight curls. She's one of those women who, far from holding on to her youth, has probably been middle-aged since her thirties, her plain looks coupled with a lack of interest in her appearance, conspiring to dull any attractiveness she may have once possessed.

'You haven't met Miriam, have you, Seren?' Max says. 'She's my assistant.'

'A little more than that,' she replies, clearly slighted by Max's introduction. 'I run both you and this place single-handedly.'

The comment is so blunt I wonder for a moment if it was meant as an in-joke between them, but Max has picked up his iPad from the kitchen counter and is tapping away, apparently oblivious. Miriam gets up stiffly from her chair, patting down her well-lacquered hair. Her eyes are cast down, my attempts to greet her with an outstretched hand resolutely ignored. I withdraw my palm, watching Max who is now perusing a wine cabinet built into the kitchen units. His PA asks if they are still going to have their daily catch-up, a grunt his only response. I attempt another introduction as Miriam busies herself collecting up papers from the table, but Max distracts me.

'This one OK with you?' he asks, brandishing a bottle under my nose.

It's a good red, even I know that, but I'm not here for social reasons. I thank him and say maybe a small one, noticing Miriam's frown and the almost imperceptible shake of her head as she zips up her laptop case with a flourish.

'If you're sure there's nothing you need?' she asks Max, then finally looking at me, she adds, 'I hadn't realised you were entertaining?'

Max discharges her with a curt response and she turns on her sensible boots and strides out; arms filled, cardigan buttoned. I hear her along the corridor, heavy steps receding, then a distant thud as the front door is closed.

'Oh dear,' I say. 'I don't think she liked me.'

'Don't mind Mim,' he replies, uncorking the wine. 'She's the same with everyone. Except me, of course. She loves me!' He flashes me a boyish grin. 'Take a seat, Seren.'

'She seemed to think I'd interrupted your meeting,' I say, pulling out the chair Miriam had been in a moment ago. Disconcertingly, I find it's still warm. 'I thought you said five-thirty?'

'Yes, I was running late. Like I said, good day with the book.

And I half-expected you to be late again.' He sits beside me and pours the wine. 'She can be a bit gruff, but Mim is a bloody good PA.'

The soft Merlot is rich and warming; much more palatable than last night's cider.

'To your taste?' Max asks.

He has a way of holding my gaze, locking me in, unblinking, until I'm the one to break eye contact.

'Yes, it's lovely. Thank you.' I put the wine down and check my phone. 'Is there ever any signal here?'

'No, never,' Max says, topping up his glass. 'Do you need to use the landline, let Theo know you've arrived?'

Reminded of Izzy's concerns about my close working relationship with my boss, I shake my head. Theo knows I have this meeting booked in. I set my phone to record and place it on the table, facing me.

'You were saying about Miriam?' I ask.

'Yes, she's been an absolute godsend, but don't tell her I said that.' He laughs to himself, then he takes another gulp of wine and stares at his glass, his smile gone. 'Everything would be a mess without Mim here.'

I wait for him to go on, struck by the sudden change in atmosphere, as if a patio door had been opened and the outside air allowed to rush in. He looks up at me and smiles, but it's obviously an effort and it soon fades, his mood reflective. He explains that 'Mim' used to live with her sister on the family farm before Julia disappeared, but she moved back in to help him cope without his wife. 'Mile End Farm, we passed it when you followed me here.'

'Oh, yes,' I reply, recalling the blank-eyed stares of the sheep. 'I remember.'

He drains his glass. 'I don't think Pauline was best pleased when Mim got the job as my PA, especially when she moved in here a few months later, but the role had ballooned from a few hours a week to full-time. That was, gosh, must be seventeen, maybe eighteen years ago.'

'Sorry, I don't quite follow . . . I thought you said Miriam moved in recently, after your wife went missing?'

Max glances up. 'Yes, that's right, but she lived with me for years before I met Julia. She had a small annexe in this very spot.'

'Julia knocked down Miriam's home to build a new kitchen?' I ask, blurting out the words before I've thought them through.

'The kitchen came much later,' Max replies, frowning. 'And it was all very amicable.' Another gulp of wine before he goes on. 'Mim and Julia always got on well, it was just easier that way.'

I open my mouth to ask him why his PA needed to leave her long-term home if they all got on so well, but he beats me to it.

'They both had their own ways of doing things and Mim was perceptive enough to realise it would be better for her to separate out work and home.' He raises his glass to clink against mine. 'It was really no problem.'

I check my notes, ticking off the points as I clarify them. 'So Miriam lived in Brooke House after she became your full-time PA?' Max nods. 'Then she moved out for, what . . . ten years roughly whilst Julia was here?' He agrees, saying that's about right. 'Then she came back last May after your wife . . .?'

'Yes,' Max snaps, on his feet again. 'So, I believe there's some salmon in the fridge for later.' He opens the fridge door, looks in and closes it again. 'Yes, should be enough for two. Red not's quite the right pairing though, is it? But on a chilly night like this . . .' He looks at me. 'You'll stay for dinner, I assume? Unless you have other plans on Valentine's night?'

'No, I don't, but—'

'Great, then that's settled.'

He pours himself another glass, crimson drops staining the scrubbed wooden surface of the table. I decline his offer of a top-up, which he accepts, remarking that he can't wait for the evenings to get lighter, as the dark nights can be discouraging at times. He's right, the blackness beyond the warmth of the bright kitchen is claustrophobic. I get up and look out of the patio doors, just able to make out the trees that edge the lawns. The rest of the world feels miles away, the grounds choked in gloom, not a flicker of a street lamp or another lit window in sight. I didn't warm to Miriam, or she to me by the looks of things, but it was reassuring having someone else in the house, and the more I hear of her years with Max, and Julia, the more sympathetic a figure she becomes. Max's reflection joins mine, his head appearing at my shoulder. I force myself not to react, but he's invading my personal space, his breath hot with alcohol, mine clouding the glass. I'd lied to Theo when I said I didn't find Max the least bit charming and now I find my emotions once again conflicted.

'There's talk of snow later in the week,' Max says, his words startling me. He moves away, clumsily banging his glass down as he slumps into the nearest chair.

'Do you have other staff here?' I ask, joining him at the table. 'Besides Miriam?'

'There's the cleaning contractors, of course. Mim supervises them, makes sure I'm not disturbed when I'm in my study. Same with the gardeners. Interruptions are a nightmare when I'm writing. I lock myself away, headphones on, oblivious to the goings-on in the rest of the house. When I emerge there's food in the fridge and a pristine home. Pass the bottle down, will you?'

'Sounds like a good arrangement,' I reply, reaching out to grab the half-empty bottle, wondering at what point Max will tip from garrulous to drunk. I can only hope his bad temper will be dulled, not magnified, by the effects of the alcohol. 'And thanks for sparing the time to see me again,' I say. 'I appreciate how busy you must be and I know we didn't get off to the best start.'

'I'm not sure if I am that busy,' Max replies, refilling his glass. He raises the bottle to me, then places it back down when I shake my head. 'My publisher can't seem to decide if my recent notoriety is a good or bad thing,' he says, leaning towards me. 'Anyway, can we make a start?'

'Yes, of course.' I move my chair away from Max's a little, our knees in danger of touching. 'Tell me about your wife. What was she like?'

Max talks expansively about his 'perfect' and 'incredible' wife, his extravagant hand gestures reminding me of Theo's theatricality, but there's little else to compare them. Theo is a born raconteur, generous to his audience, easily reeling them in. Whereas Max is self-absorbed, his charisma unwinding quickly as I feared it might; the temporary high of a good writing day and an expensive red already losing its potency. I worry he might terminate the interview as he did yesterday, but he continues to talk, telling me Julia was his muse, book ideas tumbling out of him over the last decade, one after another. If he ever got stuck, they'd talk through plot ideas, and somehow it would all make sense again. I recall the chapters I've read of his latest thriller, finding little to suggest any feminine contribution, but perhaps it post-dates his wife's influence. Max lectures me on character arcs and narrative expectation, then he jumps up from the table and announces, 'Come on, I'll show you where I write.' He pauses when he reaches the door, watching as I gather up my belongings. 'Leave your things,' he says, disappearing into the gloom and calling back, 'Come on, hurry up!'

I catch up with him at the far end of the corridor and we cross the hallway together. The lamps on the console table are switched on, the ambient glow casting odd shadows that stretch up the walls and change shape as we walk past the stairs. Max plunges us into another corridor, this one narrow and windowless, dimly lit by wall lights, the ceiling lower. I imagine we're in what must have originally been the servants' wing. At the end a closed door awaits, a brass key rattling in the other side of the lock as Max opens it. He switches on a light and a simple paper shade sends shadowy patterns across the yellowing ceiling.

It's a modest room, an old-fashioned mahogany desk at the centre. The chair this side of the desk, its back to me, is much grander than the one opposite it, the leather seat pouched and studded, but also worn, the ladder-back a half-moon of polished wood, and in daylight I assume it affords Max a stunning view through the double doors. He pulls the curtains, shutting out the inky night, then he switches on a task lamp, a pool of bright white falling across the scratched surface of his desk. 'This is where I write,' he says, his hands on the back of the cheap-looking plastic chair by the curtains. 'Well, actually there,' he says, pointing across the desk to the leather captain's chair. 'So I can look out at the grounds.'

'Must be lovely,' I say, taking in the small and rather shabby room. 'Have you always worked in here?'

'Yes, ever since I moved in; kind of a superstition of mine now. The one place I wouldn't let Julia redecorate.'

Lining the wall to my left is a huge bookshelf, mahogany to match the desk. I step closer to inspect the crammed shelves. The books are disorganised, spines turned on their sides, paper-backs piled one on top of another, some by Max but many not, although they are mainly thrillers.

'Review copies sent to me by publishers,' Max says, joining me. 'Feel free to take any you'd like. I never have time to read them all, let alone provide a quote, but I don't have the heart to throw them away.'

The room is cold and dusty, dimly lit, but Max's proximity brings heat to my skin, prickles of perspiration across my forehead and down my back.

'Thanks, but I don't read that much genre fiction,' I reply, hearing the implied insult as the words leave my lips. 'But my friend is a huge fan of your work,' I add quickly. 'She asked me to bring her paperbacks for you to sign, but . . . I forgot.'

Max places a finger on his latest hardback, the same one Theo gave me, tipping it towards him from a line of identical jackets. 'Author copies,' he explains. 'I'm not my biggest fan if that's what you were thinking?'

'No, I—'

He smiles and extracts a fountain pen from a pot of them on his desk, then he asks for Izzy's name and signs with a flourish, snapping the book shut, a flicker of triumph in his eyes as I jump.

'She'll be thrilled,' I reply, taking it. 'Thank you.'

He smiles again, holding eye contact until I look away.

'So, this is where the magic happens?' I take a seat in his leather chair and place the book on his desk, sliding a palm along the lacquered wood. My fingertips find the dusty crevice beneath the keyboard and come away powdery grey. I place the book on his desk and wipe my hand down the thigh of my black trousers as surreptitiously as I can and look up at Max.

He sits in the inferior visitor chair, an irritated look as he replies, 'Yes, that is where I write.'

I sit up straighter, regretting my impertinence. 'Shall we swap?' I ask, pointing back and forth between us as I rise from his chair, but he waves me back down.

'Let's carry on as we are,' he says, a half-smile replacing his frown.

I realise then I've been played, Max's instruction to leave behind my phone and notepad a deliberate one. Without my props I'm lost and Max knows it. I can't think of any of my prepared questions, my mind a blank. 'Can you tell me about the day Julia disappeared?' I ask, plucking something from the air as I turn the book over, then back again.

Max pauses, a hand to his mouth, the index finger covering his lips, pressing them together.

'I understand how hard this is for you, Max.'

'Do you?'

I refuse to be baited, covering my reaction with what I hope is a warm smile. 'Clearly you have things you want to say, or you wouldn't have suggested the interview.'

'I'm wondering now why I did,' he replies. 'You're hardly experienced, are you, Seren?'

I'm stung, but he's right. I'm new to this and no doubt making every mistake in the book, but the fact remains that he asked for me, not the other way around. I pick up the framed photograph in front of me, studying Julia's expression which is sullen, although I suppose you could interpret the pout as sultry, a Hollywood starlet pose as she stares down the lens, her chin tilted up, dark eyes framed by smoky eye make-up. Her face almost fills the shot, wisps of blond hair just visible, a white background behind her, accentuating the dark lashes, thick with mascara and perfect wings of eyeliner.

'She's certainly very—' I begin, my words drying up as I catch a flicker of something in Max's expression, so fleeting I almost convince myself it was never there, but it was, cold and hard. *Pure rage.* I stand the frame down, my hand shaking as I balance it carefully on the desk, turning it so Julia's penetrating eyes don't face me directly. 'Beautiful,' I say, finishing my thought. 'Was it taken recently?'

He leans across and picks up the frame, staring at it for so long the silence becomes uncomfortable, as if Julia were here and I'm the interloper, an echo of how I felt last night with Izzy and Dom.

'It was a gift,' he says, setting the photo down square in front of him. 'For our anniversary. She gave it to me just before the party.'

'What was her state of mind that day?' I ask, berating myself again for having no means of recording this conversation. I'll just have to remember the salient points.

Max gets up and parts the curtains with a finger. His face is reflected in the patio doors as he holds one curtain further back. 'Maybe I should rethink my rather harsh statement about your lack of experience, Seren. You're certainly tenacious.'

'I just want to get it right. I'm sure you do too.'

When he speaks, his voice is low and soft. 'I don't see there's much point indulging in conjecture about what Julia was or wasn't thinking that night. That's not really the point.'

'What is the point, Max?'

The room stills and I'm reminded how far from civilisation we are, only the two of us in this intimate space, the rest of the house empty. He turns to look at me, his frustration clear. It was idiotic of me to take his seat and then push him for answers he isn't ready to give. I need to build his trust first.

'Ten years!' I say brightly. 'That's quite an achievement. Must have been a very special celebration.'

'Yes, I suppose it was.'

'Suppose?'

He rubs at his temples with one hand stretched across his

forehead. 'We both said things . . . did things . . .' He looks at me, the space between us shrinking.

'*What things?*' I ask, my voice no more than a whisper.

He regards me with an unblinking stare then edges past the desk, so close I recoil, covering my sudden withdrawal with an even more exaggerated move as if I'd only meant to allow him through. He opens the door and walks out.

The lights in the corridor must be on a timer, but Max hasn't switched them back on, striding ahead until I can't make him out at all. I stretch my free hand out, Izzy's book in the other, feeling for any obstacles in my way, delicate vases on pedestals or priceless pictures on the walls I could dislodge. I try to remember what I saw on the way in, but I was concentrating on Max. I emerge into the comparative brightness of the hall. Max is already halfway across the rug, headed back towards the kitchen. 'Max, is everything all right?'

He stops and turns to look at me. 'Yes, of course. I'm hungry, that's all.'

We eat at the long kitchen table, my laptop and notebook open beside me as I pick at my food, surreptitiously making short-hand notes of our previous conversation. I'm hoping Max can't decipher the loops and strokes but either way he appears unin-terested. He opened a bottle of champagne as he dished up the poached salmon into white oversized dishes, insistent the fish must be accompanied by a glass of chilled 'fizz'. I set my phone to record before he finished dressing the accompanying salad, but I needn't have bothered. Max is morose and self-in-dulgent, talking mainly about his latest book and his publisher's concerns over the similarities to the one before. It's a good job Theo said he's in no rush for the copy. Max catches my eye and smiles. 'I know you said you're not a fan of thrillers, but have you read *any* of my books, Seren?'

I sip my champagne and place the elegant flute back down. I made a promise to myself to drink no more than half a glass but it is very good, if a little less chilled than it was half an hour ago. 'I've started the latest one,' I say, glancing down at Izzy's copy poking out of my bag. 'Enjoying it so far.'

'How old are you?' he asks, dabbing at the corners of his mouth with a linen napkin as he fixes me with a steady stare. If he's drunk he's good at covering it up, his movements steady. 'If that's not an impertinent question to ask a young woman these days?'

'I'm twenty-three.'

'Only five years younger than my wife. Actually . . .' He looks at me. 'Now six.'

I try not to fidget under his scrutiny but find I'm doing exactly that. I glance at the V-neck in my blouse and note the dappled pink skin on my décolletage. Maybe the champagne bubbles are to blame, they always go straight to my head. I cover the redness with my hand, but I'm only drawing more attention to myself.

'Julia sounds a remarkable woman,' I reply, clearing my throat. 'You think she left of her own accord that night?'

Max abandons the flakes of pink fish he'd been pushing around the bowl, dropping his fork and scraping his chair away from the table. 'What are you suggesting?'

'Sorry, I didn't mean . . . just that maybe someone is holding her against her will?'

'Oh, I see.' Max takes his chair and picks up his drink, regarding the flute in his hand before lifting it to his lips and sinking the contents. I force myself to wait, hoping he'll answer, but he says nothing.

I run my tongue over my teeth to check for salad leaves and take a deep gulp of air. 'Can I be honest with you, Max?'

He looks straight at me.

'People are curious about you and Julia, but they'd be even more interested if you could tell them something new. Is there anything at all you can think of? A tiny detail that would capture the public's attention, a regret or failing? Anything?'

He looks down at the empty glass in his hand, the stem gripped so tight I'm afraid it might snap. He places it on the table, running the pad of one thumb over the nail of the other, circling it, round and round, as if he was polishing a pebble.

'What are you scared of, Max?'

'*Scared?* I'm not the one who's scared.'

'Then who?'

'No one,' he says, clearing away the dishes as he comments how late it's got, he has emails to catch up on, a call to take from New York in a few minutes. I offer to stack the dishwasher whilst he's doing those things, but although he's relatively polite in his refusals, it's obvious there will be no further discussion. I'd prefer to part on good terms, so I start packing away my things, then pass Max my bowl and glass and thank him for his time, and the lovely dinner.

'I'll be in touch,' Max says, before closing the heavy front door, his words slurred.

Immediately I'm plunged into the shadow of the house, the moon hidden behind dense cloud. It's cold now, but I have my coat on and at least it's not raining. The kitchen is dark again as I pass by, the two cars parked next to the garages only distinguishable when I'm almost on top of them. I rummage in my bag for my keys, cursing the fact there are no outside lights, but then I stop, lifting my head. 'Hello? Who's there?' I call out. 'Is that you, Max?'

I listen again, my heart leaping from my chest. I definitely heard someone crunching through the gravel behind me, their footsteps almost, but not quite, synced with mine.

'Max, is that you? Miriam? It's Seren. Did you want me for something?'

Proceeding slowly, my key held out as a weapon, I walk towards the kitchen and slowly peer round the corner. The drive looks empty, the house pitch-back. *'Hello?'*

I sprint back to my car, my headlights on full beam as I drive away, shining across the grounds. But whoever it was has vanished.

Sixty-Six Hours Missing

DC Chris Green is enjoying himself, in a professional way of course. Katie Ingles is a good detective and a fair boss, but it's nice to be out on his own for once and asking all the questions. It's only a quick follow-up, shouldn't take long, not even strictly needed, but the initial interview was very brief and he likes to be thorough.

They're in Laura Gell's kitchen and her mum is making tea, another bonus. The remnants of a spag bol are on the side, but neither Laura nor her mum have offered him any. He'll have to make do with two sugars, maybe three.

'You said it was the agency who employed you to waitress at the party on Saturday, not Mrs Blake?' Chris asks, notebook in hand as he leans against the worktop.

'Yes, I do quite a bit of work for them when I'm back from uni,' Laura says, shifting from foot to foot in her pink trainers. 'At the racecourse mainly, but some private events too, weddings, stuff like that. I'm home to revise for my retakes so I contacted them to see if they had any work. I need the cash.'

Her mum looks over, pausing as she scrapes congealed

spaghetti into a food bin. 'Her re-sits,' she says. 'That's what she should be concentrating on, and now all this!'

'So the agency said they needed you at Brooke House,' Chris prompts, scribbling down the details.

'Yeah, I wasn't sure 'cos it's such a long way out of town, but they said they'd send a taxi for me at seven and I'd be picked up at midnight and dropped home. It was good money too, just to serve dinner and a few drinks. Gorgeous house.'

'Talk me through the evening,' Chris asks, noticing how much he sounds like Katie, her influence on him already greater than he'd care to admit.

Laura catches Chris's eye and jabs her head in an exaggerated move towards her mother who is now dropping teabags into a line of three mugs, her back to them. Laura mouths, 'I need to talk to you in private.'

'You know what,' Chris says loudly. 'I think that's all I need for now, don't worry about the tea, Mrs Gell.'

Laura's mum is encouraged to stay inside as it's started raining, or soon might. Mrs Gell considers the weather beyond the kitchen window, blue patches pushing the clouds aside, but she agrees to let her daughter see the detective out. Chris looks at the girl's pink trainers as she leads him to his car, parked outside the house in the quiet cul-de-sac.

'Look, there was this guy . . . one of Julia's friends,' Laura says, no preamble. 'Am I going to get into trouble?'

Chris shakes his head. 'Just tell me what you know.'

'Ben, he was called, and he was gorgeous. Blond hair, designer clothes, you could tell he had money.' Laura glances back at the house, her mum watching them from the kitchen window. 'And the woman with him, she was really pretty. Her name was Carys. I'm sorry, I don't know their last names. Ben slipped me a pill when I was serving champagne to them down by the pool. I don't know what it was, but fucking hell!' Laura looks up at Chris. 'You sure I won't get into trouble?'

'Drugs? You took it willingly?' Chris asks and Laura nods, then hangs her head. 'Ben suggested we went off together for a walk.' She grimaces at the handsome detective. 'Do I need to spell it out?'

'You had sex?'

'Yes, but please don't tell my mum any of this.' Laura looks across at the house, her mum elbow-deep in washing-up. 'It wasn't the greatest experience of my life.'

She's only nineteen, same age as his younger brother. Chris reminds himself to have that talk with him, the one about consent, although if he's the same as he was at that age, he's years off needing it, despite Chris's recent reputation as the heartbreaker of the team. 'Do you want to press charges?' he asks Laura. 'If it was non-consensual?'

'No, I knew what I was doing, but thanks. Mum insisted she sat in whilst I gave my statement and I couldn't say all that in front of her, could I? Sorry to mess you around, but I would have told you, promise.'

'Did you see Max or Julia after this encounter with Ben?'

Laura looks at her trainers. 'It was Mr Blake that found us, me and Ben, on the lawn, told us to fuck off out of his house. He was furious. The whole thing was so humiliating.'

'What time was this?'

'Quarter to twelve, maybe? I was a bit out of it, sorry.'

'That's OK, just do your best, Laura.'

'We got dressed and followed Max to the pool. Ben was furious with him, wanted to punch him or something, but when we got there Mr Blake was shouting at Mrs Blake. It was awful. Both of them screaming at each other. I felt so sorry for her. She'd been nice to me all evening, saying I was pretty and asking what I'm studying at uni. He was telling her he hated her, wished she was dead.' Laura looks at her mum again and shoos her away from the window. 'Ben wanted to stay with Julia after her husband stormed off, but she said she'd rather be on her own. That was the last time I saw her. The taxi picked us up by the gate.'

'Do you remember anything about the vehicle or the driver?'

'Sorry, it's all pretty fuzzy. Ben and Carys were arguing so I closed my eyes, went to sleep until they got out.'

'Thanks, you've been really helpful. And if you think of anything else . . .' He hands her his card.

Chris drives away from the sprawling estate, but he pulls in before he reaches Police HQ to flick through his notes. He spoke to Ben Fortune himself, bloody posh boy with a cocksure attitude. Chris hadn't liked him at all, even less so now. He'd conveniently missed out the part about supplying drugs and shagging a waitress on the lawn, much keener to reinforce how angry Max had been – deflecting the attention away from himself, perhaps? There was definitely another conversation to be had.

Carys had been tight-lipped according to the detective who'd called her. She'd answered the questions she was asked, but offered little else. She was an ex-girlfriend of Ben's, apparently, and if Chris were to take a guess, he'd say Carys's husband had no idea where his wife was on Saturday night.

Chapter Seven

The Faces That Stay With You

'Seren,' Theo says, turning from Fran to me as I stifle another yawn. 'Why don't you update us on your current stories?'

We're grouped in the middle of the office: Theo, Fran, me, Simon, and the intern. The standing meetings are Fran's idea, more efficient, she claims, although Theo deems them 'bloody ridiculous', refusing to participate for any longer than necessary, which is kind of the point. Theo's cue has set me up to share the details of the interviews with Max, but Fran's expression is not helping me to formulate the right words. Apparently, she hadn't taken the news of my exclusive that well when Theo broke it to her yesterday, although Simon had been magnanimous, which was generous of him.

'Are we keeping you up?' Fran asks.

'Sorry,' I reply, taking a deep breath. 'Late night.'

'Socialising?' she asks, pretending to smile when her eyes are not.

'I went to see Max Blake again,' I tell everyone else, ignoring Fran's heavy sigh. 'Although it was technically my day off.'

'How did it go?' Simon asks.

'It was good, thanks. Very promising so far.'

I played the recordings of Max when I got home and typed up my notes, awake until the early hours trying to work out an enticing new angle and realising I have very little to work with. There was still no sign of Izzy when I finally went to bed, so I guess the Valentine's Day bar crawl with Dom was a success. She was in her room snoring heavily when I'd left this morning, the relative ease of her career momentarily appealing.

'Great, so when do I get the copy?' Fran asks, folding her arms across her flat chest. 'I need to work out this week's layout for the print edition.'

'Um, not yet,' I reply, avoiding her pointed stare. 'But it's looking very—'

'Yes, you said that, but—'

'Take as long as you need,' Theo says, cutting across Fran. Then he leaves the meeting, marching to his office and slamming his door.

'Great!' announces Fran. 'So Seren has her story to work on, long as she needs, and I have a big gap to fill.' She takes over the meeting, dishing out stories to Simon and the intern, but she assigns me nothing, not even court duty.

'No worries,' I tell her, swallowing the hurt that bubbles up. 'I'll get on with my interview notes.'

Fran gives me a withering look as she walks away. I return to my desk to finish my half-written plan for the feature, although I've nothing new to add until Max grants me another audience. I need to come up with some 'bread and butter stories', as Theo calls them, the ones that fill up pages and will hopefully placate Fran, but all I have is the refuse collection situation which I've been rehashing for days.

'Penny for them?'

I look over the top of my screen to Simon who is watching me from the opposite desk.

'Just trying to come up with something better than a few split bin bags on the pavements,' I reply. 'I'm going to get myself a coffee, want one?'

'No, you're OK thanks.' He looks at the tumbling number displayed on the screen above him. 'At this rate soon none of us will have a job.'

'That bad?' I ask, and he shrugs, typing again.

The view from the kitchen window is uninspiring, a typical town centre vista. Planners in the seventies have a lot to answer for, ugly blocks of concrete everywhere, but my thoughts are back in the darkness of Brooke House, hearing those footsteps behind me. Two slices of stale white bread pop up from the toaster, reminding me why I came in. The instant coffee tastes bitter but I swallow it down hoping the caffeine will perk me up, tiredness creeping over me again as I take my late breakfast to the round table squeezed in the corner. I had two anonymous calls last night, one at three a.m. and another at five. Unprecedented and torturous. The feeling of being closer to Bryn is there in the silence, but Izzy's right, I have to report them. Maybe that will bring me the answers I crave, but also fear.

I'm on the last mouthful of dry toast when Lynda walks in. She's chatting to Fran, laughing loudly at something the deputy editor has said, replying, 'Oh, I can imagine. Nicky says Theo's getting even grumpier as he gets older.' Lynda turns to look at me, steel in her eyes as she adds, 'And she should know, twenty-five years of marriage must count for something, don't you think?'

'Is it that long?' Fran asks. She rips open a packet of soup, the powder clouding the air as she tips the contents into her special mug, her name picked out in pink glitter above a message declaring her to be *The Boss*.

'Yes, it is,' Lynda replies. 'They were going to that Michelin-starred place last night; he booked it months ago for Valentine's. Nice, isn't it, after all those years together?'

Fran walks off first, Lynda looking over her shoulder as she carries her lo-cal hot-choc back to reception. I run the tap and rinse out my mug as Theo wanders in and flicks the kettle back on. I'm about to ask if he noticed Fran's attitude in the meeting when Simon leans around the door; a problem with page seven of the weekly print edition he needs to run past Theo. Neither of them acknowledges me as I leave, the discussion ongoing.

The afternoon deadline approaches and I forget Fran's iciness and Lynda's snide comments, producing my quota of stories: school events, planning applications and the ongoing traffic issues in the town centre. Not exciting, but after a trawl through social media and a call to my contact at the council, at least I have enough publishable copy. The initial sheen of glamour journalism promised has been worn thin by the daily chore of producing at least four articles every day, but there's still the buzz of finding a good story, despite the fact it will often be derived from someone else's misery.

Simon, a gentle man in many ways, once talked of the faces that stay with you, the doors you don't want to knock on, but must. 'It's the worst day of their lives and there we are, asking to come in for a chat.' I'd nodded, recalling one particularly persistent reporter in the days following Bryn's disappearance. Dad, not usually prone to confrontation, had snatched the milk bottle from the vile man's hand and smashed it on the step. But unlike my family, some people *do* want to talk. Each to their own.

I'm proofreading my last piece of the day when an email from Max pops into my inbox, asking if I'm free in an hour. He'll be finished for the day by then.

'Something good?' Simon asks, picking up on my excitement.

'Could be,' I reply, smiling as I type my reply.

Theo's door is closed as I leave but I tap and go in, waiting for him to finish his call.

'OK if I take a few days to concentrate just on the interviews?' I ask, distracted by Fran who is tearing strips off the intern, the younger man nodding contritely. 'I'm off to see Max now and I'd like to really nail it down, give it my best sh—'

'Yeah,' Theo says, without looking up from his notepad. He seems preoccupied, but then he smiles, tells me to take as long as I need. 'Simon can pick up the slack, and Fran. All she does is shout these days. This story is big for us; needs to be right. I'm just pleased it's back on track, well done.'

I'm almost at my car when a Facebook notification arrives. Finally, a reply to my post on the college's page, the one Julia attended in London.

Chapter Eight

Sympathetic to the Cause

The drive to Brooke House is much more pleasant now I'm familiar with the route, although it's another foul day, the skies iron-grey at barely five in the afternoon. February is halfway through its slow trawl towards March, but the countryside refuses to shake off the remnants of winter and accept the emergence of spring, a storm blowing in from Siberia which the meteorologists have named 'The Beast from the East'. I glance at my phone when I can, but soon the signal will disappear and I'll have to wait until the drive back to find out if Ben Fortune responds again. He said he wants to meet up and asked for my mobile number, so maybe he'll try to call or text me instead. Either way I'm going to be out of contact for the next hour or two. Ben's Facebook profile didn't give much away – even the photo was arty rather than a smiling face – but I'm guessing he must have met Julia at college and remained in touch. He'd seemed concerned, but also guarded. I'll ask Theo

118

when I get a chance, see if he's heard of him, possibly even met him through Julia. Theo said some of her friends turned up from London the night she went missing. Maybe Ben was one of them.

I crest a hill and the view opens up.

I still look for the horizon, forgetting the Cotswolds get in the way and *my* sea is a hundred miles from here. Mum says the coastline is in your blood, it doesn't matter how far from it you travel, you'll always hear the gulls and taste the salt-spray carried on the wind. We took it for granted as children, the long stretch of damp sand only five minutes' walk from our house, our footprints washed away as we ran squealing from an icy wave, the air tangy with the dust from the steelworks. On a rare sunny day, if Bryn and I faced the horizon, our eyes almost closed, lashes filtering the sunlight, we could pretend we were somewhere exotic, the sea sparkling. I've avoided the bay since my brother slipped off his backpack on the jagged rocks and disappeared from our lives.

A month after that terrible day, and almost exactly two years ago now, a young man came to my parents' house and introduced himself as a good friend of Bryn. I was back at university by then and finding it impossible to concentrate, everything insignificant in comparison to what had happened on that cold January morning. Dad rang me after their visitor left, his voice barely more than a whisper as he explained how the boy had been polite, and respectful, tears running down his young face. Mum wouldn't talk about it, not a word, still won't, but Dad needed to finally acknowledge something that I think we'd all suspected for a long time. To this day, Mum's never mentioned Bryn's friend, at least not to me, and Dad asked me not to bring it up. Not because he minded, not that at all, or Mum, but because of all those lost chances. Although it's never that simple, is it, and rarely about one missed opportunity. I've thought about finding Bryn's friend but maybe his pain has abated by now. I wouldn't want to cause him more heartache.

I hope he loved my brother. I hope he told him so, often. And I hope, unlike us, he's managed to move on.

I spot the gnarled tree up ahead, and a slight rise beneath the tyres warns me the gate is coming up. I slow down, but as I turn in, I have to slam my foot immediately to the floor to execute an emergency stop, the tyres skidding a few yards before I come to a halt, just in time. A huge deer is caught in my headlights, transfixed it would seem, fear anchoring it to the spot as it stares back. It's so much larger than I'd have imagined. A massive stag, only a few metres away on the rutted track, completely still, eyes dark and unblinking, magnificent antlers curling up between velvet ears. The seconds stretch out, only the clicks of the cooling engine and the swish of the trees to tell me the suspended moment is real. Then the deer turns, a flash of spindle-thin legs disappearing into the woods. I smile to myself and drive on, a satisfying scrape of tyre tread on gravel as I approach the house, but then I'm back to where I heard the footsteps last night, the feeling of being watched returning. My smile gone.

Max opens the door, his expression welcoming. 'Good journey?'

'Yes, I saw a stag in the woods. It was magnifi—'

'It's a knack, finding this place,' he says, easing my coat from my shoulders. 'Mind you, the roads can play tricks on you, even after all these years.'

'I saw a stag,' I repeat, still struck by my encounter. 'My first time.'

'Where?' he asks, turning back.

'Just by the gate as I turned in, it ran off into the woods.'

Max nods curtly, then stares across the hallway, deep in thought. 'Haven't seen one in years.'

'Talking of strange goings-on . . .' I say, making light of what I'm about to ask. 'Last night, after I left you . . .' I follow him across the rug. 'I thought I heard footsteps, following me to my car. You didn't hear anyone outside, did you? Maybe round by the kitchen?'

'I wear headphones when I write,' he replies, glancing back. 'Didn't I tell you?'

'Yes, it's just that—'

'Mainly classical music, zones me out. I wouldn't have noticed a herd of elephants rampaging across the lawn.'

'So it wasn't you, then?' I ask, keeping up with him along the corridor. 'I called out to whoever it was, but no answer.'

Max pauses to hold the kitchen door. 'I guess it could have been Miriam. She can be a little . . .' he shakes his head, '. . . eccentric.'

He gestures towards a complicated-looking coffee machine as the door clicks shut behind us. I request an espresso, no sugar, hoping it will sharpen me for the interview, although I'm still preoccupied with last night's unsettling encounter. Miriam is the logical culprit, but why wouldn't she make herself

121

known? Her oddness is perhaps the most likely explanation. I set up my things on the table, pen, notebook, phone, then walk towards the patio doors. The grounds and distant hills are framed like a triptych, the bare limbs of the furthest trees silhouetted against the last of the daylight.

'It's so beautiful here,' Max comments.

'Yes, not sure it would suit me, though,' I reply, still contemplating the view. 'I mean, it's obviously a gorgeous location,' I say, glancing back. 'But when you're young it's perhaps a bit . . . remote.'

'What are you trying to say?' he asks, turning round, an espresso cup in his hand. 'That Julia must have felt trapped here?'

'No,' I lie, wishing my notepad wasn't lying open on the table, my thoughts on Julia in plain sight. 'I'm sure she loved it here.' I take a seat and quickly turn to a blank page.

'I didn't force her to move from London,' Max says, roughly setting my coffee down beside me before returning to make his. 'You couldn't make my wife do anything she didn't want to, quite the reverse.'

'No, I'm not—'

'If she felt it was too *remote* here, as you put it . . .' He grabs a carton of unopened milk from the fridge, twisting the top to break the seal. 'I would take her wherever she wanted.'

'Julia didn't drive?' I say, my tone expressing the outrage I feel. The thought of being stuck here with no independent means of escape is abhorrent. 'Sorry, I'm just surprised, most people do these days.'

'She didn't need to drive when she lived in central London,'

Max explains. 'And she couldn't have afforded lessons, let alone a car.'

'No, I guess not, but surely once she was here . . .?'

'Yes, of course,' he says, carefully measuring out the milk into a small stainless-steel jug. 'I paid for lessons, bought her a car as soon as she passed her test.'

'So she *did* drive?' I sip my bitter espresso again. 'I don't understand.'

'There's no great mystery, Seren. She was a nervous driver; that's all. Some people are. She was OK for a while after she passed her test, but she was out on her own one day and she hit a deer. She couldn't have stopped, it jumped over a hedge right into the path of her car.' Max looks at the jug in his hand, deep in thought. 'It affected her deeply, even though it wasn't her fault. That's why I wasn't particularly enthusiastic about your sighting today.'

'God, yes, I can imagine. Must have been horrible.' Max's reaction now makes much more sense.

He turns away, steam swooshing loudly into the metal jug; making further conversation impossible. I look across at the trees again, thinking of the lone stag, experiencing a freedom Julia briefly tasted then lost again so quickly, her independence snatched from her just as she'd reclaimed it. She was still a teenager when she came to live here and married Max, leaving behind student life in London to settle down with a man in his late thirties. She must have been lonely at times, her husband working in his study, the clouds gathering over Brooke House. That's a lot of pressure on a relationship, however charismatic and wealthy your famous husband might be. Max joins me at

123

the table, placing his cappuccino in front of him. His mood is contemplative as he turns his spoon in the froth, the antler candelabra casting shadows across his knotted features.

'Are you happy to make a start, Max?'

He looks up, the change in him dramatic. He looks panicked, his eyes wide with alarm, a tremor in his hand as he drops the spoon in his cup.

'Max, what is it?'

'I don't think I can do it.' He reaches across the table and grasps my hand. 'You have to help me, Seren. I need to be brave, it's the only way.'

Shocked, I pull away, his fingertips the last to break contact. 'The interview, you mean?'

He shakes his head, picking up the spoon again and stirring round and round.

'Max, if there's something—'

He draws in a deep breath, then he's on his feet and out the door before I have a chance to ask where he's going. I quickly gather up my belongings, following him along the gloomy corridor then across the hall. He's standing behind his desk when I walk in to his study, his back to me as he stares out of the patio doors at the darkness beyond. 'This place was so different with Julia in it. I'd give anything . . .' He turns and looks at me. 'You understand, don't you?'

'No,' I reply, Julia's dark eyes searching mine as I dump my bag down beside the silver frame. I'd like to turn her away, or better, flatten her face to the desk. 'What did you mean about being brave?'

He looks down at his clasped hands. Max is clearly struggling with something, unsure whether to share it. His outburst in the kitchen has left its mark. He's peeled back too many layers, exposed too much emotion, but for once he'd seemed genuine.

'I just meant . . .' He looks up and charming Max is back, the smile painted on as he says, 'You're a writer, Seren. You understand the importance of narrative.' He sits on the plastic seat and offers me his leather chair. 'That's all I meant, that I have to be brave to give you this interview, for us both to do our best and choose the right words.'

I nod, but it's clearly rubbish, and totally fake. I'm clumsy, almost dropping my bag as I juggle with my notebook, phone, and a pen. 'Tell me about the hours after you realised your wife was missing. How were they? What happened?'

Max sits back. He looks calmer, but it still feels like a polished act. 'The police were notified, of course. There's a system, I'm sure you're aware, which ranks missing persons according to how at-risk they're considered to be. If there's a history of absconding, or abuse, anything that might mean they're considered more vulnerable, the case gets immediate attention. Julia wasn't initially considered at risk.'

'Because there was no such history?'

'Of course there wasn't,' Max snaps, frowning at me. 'At least . . . Julia had been a runaway in her childhood, but she'd had a loving home here for over a decade, a stable marriage, devoted husband. I cooperated with the police, of course, even when . . .' He pauses.

'Even when they thought you might be implicated? I guess it's standard practice in cases like these.'

'Yes, but they implied we weren't happy, which was ridiculous.

We'd had a spat. I admitted that. Nothing to . . .' He sighs. 'It became their entire focus. Then they said they were scaling back the search, blaming budget cuts or something like that. The whole thing was a complete fiasco.'

'The police are stretched, Max. They have to make tough choices.'

'The right ones would be good.'

'And what about a private investigator?' I ask, but he shakes his head. 'Why not?' I persist. 'I mean, you can clearly afford it.' I look around the study, hardly illustrating my point, but he obviously has the necessary funds at his disposal.

'I thought about it, but I'd relied on the police to find her. Too much time had gone by.'

'I know the bigger newspapers use them . . . months, sometimes even years later. It might still be worth a try?'

Max shakes his head again. 'Julia and I were private people, few friends. Involving someone else, someone I don't know . . . it feels wrong.'

'You've involved me.'

'Yes, and I'm sure you can tell how hard a decision that has been.' He points at my notes. 'Can we move on?'

Max has something to hide. What other explanation could there be for not throwing every resource he has at the search? A good PI could dig into Julia's past much more efficiently than I can, turn up old boyfriends, places she might be hiding, people who might have seen her. Unless Max knows it's a pointless task, I can't see why he wouldn't want to try, if only to satisfy himself he's done everything he can now the police are no longer actively searching. I read the next question on my list, but I keep coming back to the same thought . . . why risk involving the media if he's killed her? Then something Simon told me on my first day at the *Herald* cuts through.

'You need to look past first thoughts, second, third, fourth even, and ask yourself, what's their motivation?'

Of course! If Max is a murderer, he must be desperate to clear his name so he can move on. I'm part of that plan. The young, easily manipulated junior reporter. Sympathetic to the cause, my article about unresolved loss testament to that. He wants me to engage his public, deflecting attention away from any implied guilt so his status as an author, not a potential wife killer, can be reinstated.

I mentally draw a line through my questions for today, smiling as I tell him perhaps we should leave it there for now. He seems surprised that I'm the one who's brought the conversation to an end. A minor victory for me, I hope, rather than a misjudged retreat. I suppress my pleasure at the reversal of power as I close my notebook and drop it in my bag.

He walks out and I follow, but I pause before the study door swings shut, my foot stuck out to halt its progress. I glance down the dimly lit corridor, hoping Max, already nearing the other end, won't notice what I'm up to. I point my phone at his desk, the camera zooming in on the framed photo of Julia.

'I have more to say, Seren,' Max informs me as I join him in the entrance hall.

'Yes?' I reply, taking my coat from the stand. Max insists on holding it at my back as I slip in one arm, then the other, his hands resting momentarily on my shoulders until I move away.

'And I'm keen to hear it, Max, but you have to open up to me. Please consider that.'

He nods. 'It's probably an odd thing to say, given the circumstances,' he says, opening the stiff front door. 'But it's been such a refreshing change to spend time with you, Seren.'

He smiles his most charming smile, and although I know it's a practised move, I feel my face reddening.

'Can I look forward to seeing you the same time tomorrow, or does Theo have a monopoly on your time?' he asks.

'No, he doesn't, not at all,' I reply, pleased that my gamble seems to have paid off.

I descend the stone steps quickly, a spring in my step, but when I glance back I catch something jarring in Max's eyes, something that hastens my already speedy exit. He clearly thinks I'm no longer paying him close attention, the door almost closed as a flash of unguarded emotion crosses his features, his charm evaporating into the chill air, the blue eyes sparkling, but cold, an icy wedge of unbridled loathing within, or perhaps it's fear. Then the door slams shut.

I run to my car, keys in hand. I lock the doors as soon as I'm inside, and double-check them before I look at my phone. Julia's face stares at me from the silver frame, the image clearer than I'd expected. She seems to be asking me for something, imploring me, in fact, and I know I can't let her down.

Chapter Nine

A Very Damaged Individual

The urban landscape of London fills the window as the crowded train approaches Paddington Station. I brush the crumbs from the lap of my dress and collect the rubbish from an improvised breakfast of a granola bar and a bottle of water. I must stick out as an unseasoned traveller as I sway towards the still-locked door, and I'm slow compared to the women in flats and trainers who speed past me on the platform then slam their Oyster cards on to the barrier whilst I fumble for my ticket.

Ben Fortune eventually got back to me late last night. I was climbing into bed, my notes typed up, the latest recordings from Brooke House catalogued. He was curt, as if *I* was bothering *him*, although it was him that called me, though he hung up as soon as our meeting was arranged. His accent reminded me of Theo's, public school with a nod to the common man.

Theo moaned that I'd presented him with a 'fait accompli'

when I'd called him from the train. As much a reference to the expensive ticket, I think, as my rash decision to spend the day tracking down some of Max and Julia's friends. But he'd warned me to take care, said Ben had looked like trouble when he'd turned up at the dinner party, thus confirming my supposition that Ben was a guest at Brooke House the night Julia vanished.

I find the coffee shop easily, a short walk from the station and the kind of soulless tourist spot that only exists in the capital. It might even be the same one where Evan and I ordered a greasy fry-up before catching a train back to Wales. The memory of that trip to London is steeped in nostalgia, but I know that's rarely a true representation of the past. I advise the waiter I'm meeting someone, and he shows me to a table by the window. Ben has called me twice now to change the arrangements, but each time the conversation has been kept to a minimum and his number withheld. I imagine a handsome man, tall with dark hair, maybe grown unfashionably long.

'Seren?'

I look up from my phone to a blond head of neatly cut hair, a little long around the collar, but every other supposition I'd made about Ben's appearance entirely wrong. Other than he's handsome, strikingly so, and roughly the same age as Julia. He's only an inch or two above me when I get up. Our greeting is awkward, Ben ignoring my proffered hand and taking a seat quickly. He's dressed in a designer shirt, the logo revealed on his chest when he unbuttons his overcoat, and he smells of expensive aftershave, the scent a reminder of Max, though the resemblance ends there.

'I don't have long,' he informs me, ordering a coffee and

handing the waiter the laminated menu without a please or thank you. 'What do you know about Julia's disappearance?' he asks, stony-faced.

'I was hoping you could answer that,' I reply, smiling.

'Why would I know anything about it?' he asks, looking out the window to the busy street. 'And why are you poking around after all these months?'

'I'm a journalist with the *Herald*, a local paper in the Cotswolds. I don't expect you will have heard of us.'

'I looked you up,' Ben replies. 'What I don't know, is why you're suddenly so interested in Julia?'

'I'm interviewing Max Blake, exclusively.'

'Doubt you'll get much out of him,' Ben replies, eyeing me warily. 'Guy's a total shit.' He checks his phone. 'Look, I know you have a job to do.'

'Not a fan of Julia's husband?' I ask, referencing his blunt summation of Max.

He laughs. 'You could say that. I've only met him a couple of times but I can't imagine he has anything nice to say about me, either. And before you ask, yes, I was at the party, and yes, I have spoken to the police. I told them what I know, couldn't let that pantomime continue unchecked.'

'*Pantomime?* How do you mean?'

The waiter arrives with our coffees and although the interruption is badly timed, it gives me the opportunity to check with Ben he's happy for me to record our conversation. He looks uncertain and I reassure him that, as I'd stated on the phone, I can guarantee his anonymity.

'I'd still prefer not to be taped,' he replies. 'Look, I've got a career to think of. I can't risk that, so you must cast-iron guarantee my name won't get into your paper. You can still give that assurance?'

'Yes, I can.' I put my phone in my bag and smile at Ben, but he remains serious, sipping his coffee then pulling a face and placing the cup back in the damp saucer.

'Not exactly the career path I'd have chosen,' he says. 'I had dreams of becoming a photographer. Now I'm in property management and Julia's . . .' He looks up, taking me in properly for the first time. 'What's your theory?' he asks, studying me as I consider my answer.

'Not sure it's my job to have one. Yours?'

He is similarly non-committal, a shrug his only reply, then he asks, 'And Max's take is . . .?'

'Early days,' I say, deflecting his question. 'I assume you met Julia at college?'

'No, it was actually before that.'

Ben describes the free-spirited teenager he first encountered in a wine bar in central London when Julia was sixteen. He was a year older and despite also being underage had managed to get served, but Julia had been told to fuck off by the barman.

'I chased after her and that was it. Pretty much inseparable. I'd dropped out of school, well, sort of, more asked to leave. I encouraged Julia to sign up to the college I was starting at in the September. It was quite a summer, and she loved the photography course. She found she had a natural aptitude for it.'

That period in his life clearly holds fond memories for Ben, his sharp features softening as he describes the student life they shared for almost a year.

132

'Then she was put forward by our tutor for a prize that led to a prestigious internship. That's when she met Max and after a few months she moved away. Left the course. Left me. I didn't see her again for years.'

'You clearly still had feelings for her?' I ask, pausing in my shorthand notes.

Ben juts his chin out, his jaw tense. 'I loved her, always have.' He checks himself, catching my eye, but instead of clamming up as I expect he says, 'I'd hoped over the years, that things might change, but I don't think she's ever felt the way I do.' He glances out the window, lost in the world of What-Ifs.

'Did she ever visit you in London?'

Ben frowns. 'I should go.'

'Just one more thing.' I take out my phone and tap in the code, selecting the photos icon and clicking on the one I took last night, then holding it up to Ben. 'This was taken in Max's study. Julia gave him that photo the day of their anniversary. I wondered if you might know who took it. Looks professional and I don't think she could have taken it herself, not from that angle.'

Ben laughs, a hollow sound this time. I wait for him to explain, setting the phone down between us.

'That's so typical of her,' he says, shaking his head at her as Julia watches us from the screen. 'Only she would be that fucking cruel.'

'I don't understand what you mean.'

'I took the photo, Seren,' he says, pointing at the glimpses of white in the background. 'That's my bedding. It was a few weeks before she disappeared.'

'Oh, I see, and you two were . . .?'

'Yes,' Ben replies, with obvious pride. He laughs again, but it's still without any joy. 'I've just remembered . . .'

'What?' I ask.

'Julia told me she'd commissioned a piece of art, years ago, probably not long after she married Max. Hideous antler candelabra thing. It was vile, and we'd both loathed the guy at college, well, I thought she did. He spent a week at Brooke House, apparently, collecting antlers and—' Ben looks straight at me. 'She laughed about it, said she hated the bloody candelabra, but she told Max she loved it so she could have it in the house as a keepsake of the fact she'd been fucking the guy in one of the outbuildings where he was staying. God, I'm as big a fool as him, aren't I?'

'Do you mean Max?'

Ben looks at me for a moment, then he stares at the endless stream of traffic and people outside. 'I thought that's why she asked me to the party, a stupid scenario in my head where she'd publicly announce her marriage was over, but then she said I should bring some people from our college days, more the merrier, it would be fun. I still went, of course, but she was the same old Julia. Nothing changes, and that just proves it!' He gestures again at my phone. 'Her husband must have looked at that photo every day, and the candelabra. It would have amused her to wind him up. *Fuck!*' Ben shakes his head. 'I even took an old girlfriend to the party, a pathetic attempt to make Julia jealous. When will I ever learn?'

Ben refuses to name his companion. 'She's not important, I promise. I wasn't even with her that much. There was a

134

waitress there; young girl.' He glances up at me. 'Not underage or anything like that. It was meaningless. *Pathetic*.' He glances out the window. 'Julia is beautiful and talented and when she looks at you . . . but she's a first-class bitch.'

'Did you argue with Julia the night of the party?'

'Hard to argue with someone who barely notices you.' He throws a note on the table for the coffees and tells me he needs to get back to work.

'Did she ever say anything to you about leaving Max?'

'Look, if you want answers ask him,' he says, standing up.

'You think he killed her?'

Ben leans towards me, placing his hands on the table. 'All I know is she'd had enough of him. He was old, boring like that bloody mausoleum where he lives. Whatever anyone says, Julia was a prisoner there. Don't contact me again, Seren.'

I watch him walk away, his black coat and blond hair soon indistinguishable from the crowds of tourists passing the window. I get up soon after and use the toilet, applying more lipstick and checking the tube map on my phone before I set off. I have one more appointment to keep before my return train.

The tall glass office block overlooks the river, the atrium grand, filled with illuminated cubby holes and display stands show-casing books by household names. I count ten of Max's titles before the lift doors open and a short man, balding with glasses, steps out. He takes me up to the fifth-floor cafeteria and tells me to take a stroll around the rooftop garden whilst he orders us a coffee, asking me twice if I'm sure I don't want a cookie, they're really very good.

Tentatively, I approach the Perspex barrier. It's a chilly but sunny morning and the views over the Thames are spectacular, a tourist boat chugging along the brown water five storeys below. The London Eye is turning a slow circle in the hazy London air and Big Ben and the Houses of Parliament stand solid in the distance, their spires reaching up to the sheltering sky.

'Amazing view, isn't it?' Jonny says, joining me. 'Max loved it too, not that he comes up to London much these days. Understandable, of course.'

I smile and follow Max's editor back through the sliding glass doors to the table he's chosen in a quiet corner. Two paper cups of coffee are already waiting and beside them a chocolate cookie on a napkin, the moon surface studied with Smarties.

'So,' he says, fiddling with the lanyard around his neck. 'Terrible business about Julia.'

'Yes, it is.' I place my coffee down and take out my notebook. 'I wanted to ask you about the night she went missing. I understand you were there?'

Jonny looks at his security pass, studying the inverted photo, then he considers me, his expression indicating polite discomfort. 'I've spoken to Max, of course. Called him this morning after you contacted me, so he knows about our meeting.'

'Oh, right.'

'Max has been with us his whole career, he's one of our star authors.'

'Yes, I can see that—'

'And obviously the fact that my partner Matt and I were guests of the Blakes that night shows you our friendship extends beyond the professional, which has presented me with some conflicts of interest over the last few months, this being one of them.'

'Perhaps I can reassure you? Max instigated the interview with the *Herald*, and he asked specifically to speak with me.'

'Yes, Max told me that.' Jonny smiles indulgently, then drops the security pass which swings down to rest on his striped shirt. 'I understand why Max wants to put his side of the story; I completely get that. And of course you would be a particularly pleasant confidante.'

I return his smile out of politeness, but the inference is troubling.

'Max has been vilified in the press,' Jonny continues. 'Unfairly so, in his opinion, and mine. Which of course brings its own challenges, publicity-wise, I mean.'

'Yes, I imagine it's been—'

'What I will say, and this is all I want to say . . . I've known Max for the best part of almost twenty years now, and I have never, ever doubted his story about that night. *Never.* They may have had their difficulties, but there is no way Max would ever deliberately harm Julia.'

'*Difficulties?*' I pick up my pen and open my notebook.

'You have to remember, Lauren—'

'It's Seren, actually.'

'Oh, I'm so sorry, what a lovely name. Welsh?' I nod. 'Yes, you have to remember that Julia was a very troubled young woman. She loved Max, and Brooke House became her passion, but she pushed that marriage as far as she could.'

'In what way?'

'I don't think it would be wise to comment,' he says. 'But let's just say that there was fault on both sides.'

'Are you suggesting affairs?'

Jonny shakes his head. 'Max, no.'

'Julia?' I ask, already knowing this to be the case from Ben. Jonny raises his eyebrows and sighs. 'And Max accepted this?'

'Tolerated, Seren. Just tolerated. He's a very proud man and everyone has their limit.'

'Do you think she may have left him for someone else?'

Jonny takes off his round glasses and wipes them with a handkerchief he pulls from his trouser pocket, then he blows his nose and folds the monogrammed square. 'I loved Julia, I mean *really* loved her. Matt did too. You couldn't help it. She was so charming and witty, spiky too, of course, but hilarious. We are both so cut up about it, but the thing is, Julia was a very damaged individual long before she met Max. Her childhood was, from what I gathered, entirely dysfunctional. She did her best to be a good wife, but she had no role model. Her mother abandoned her and she never settled in care. Julia had to fend for herself from a very young age. She was needy to an impossible degree. She craved stability, family, love, but she had no way to support or accept any of those ideals. I suspect there were dark times in her childhood, very dark. No one but Max ever believed she could be a perfect wife, Julia included. With all the love and the best will in the world, it was going to be a continual challenge.'

'You said there was fault on both sides. What did you mean by that if Max was faithful?'

'Perfection,' Jonny says, pausing. 'An impossible state to maintain.'

I press him to explain further but he says there's really nothing else he'd like to add, his polite refusal indicating our chat has come to an end.

He walks me to the lift and we chat about publishing and journalism until the doors open and he tells me it was nice to meet me and would I please ensure he's sent a copy of my article? I unclip my visitor pass from my coat and hand it to the man at reception, walking out into the bright air, the view, even from street level, breath-taking.

It seems there may well have been blame on both sides, as Jonny said, and right now I find my sympathies lie more with Max than his manipulative and unfaithful wife. Unless, of course, Max killed her.

Sixty-Seven Hours Missing

Katie ends the call with Chris, her full concentration required for the final part of the journey. The road has narrowed to little more than the width of her car, and the mobile signal was breaking up anyway. Plus the weather is atrocious, huge puddles as soon as she'd left the dual carriageway. Her DC was keen to share the new information he'd gleaned from the waitress, Laura, but Katie can't see that it helps much, other than filling in a few holes in their timeline, and even that sounds doubtful, the girl's grip on the exact details skewed by the alcohol and drugs she'd been given at the party. Ben Fortune is obviously a little shit, but they knew that already, and there doesn't seem to be much point authorising an expensive trip to London to confirm it. She'd told Chris to call Ben, apply some extra pressure in the light of Laura's confession and see what gives. What bothers Katie more is that Max failed to mention finding Ben and Laura on the lawn. It feels like a deliberate omission, although apart from saving his embarrassment she can't see why. She needs to look again at the timeline of events that night to see if that throws up any anomalies, but if it doesn't, Laura's testimony currently provides nothing of any use to her. They need more than a few specks of blood in the bathroom to charge Max, and time is money, as her DI reminds her often. He's already making noises about scaling back the search.

'It's not that he doesn't care,' Katie had told Chris. 'You know what it's like for him. He has to make tough decisions every day, and right now there are other cases that take priority.'

In truth she shares Chris's frustration. This rain doesn't help either, torrential since the early hours of Sunday morning. Some cases are like that. However hard you try, you always end up back where you started. But she's not given up hope quite yet.

The farmyard is a quagmire, mud enveloping the detective's shoes as soon as she steps out of the car. Katie retrieves her wellingtons from a plastic shopping bag stowed in the boot and trudges towards the farmhouse. There's a light on at every window, offering a hospitable glow despite the dark clouds, but as soon as Miriam's older sister opens the door, it's clear that the detective is not welcome. A stout woman, Pauline is not dissimilar in appearance to Miriam, although if anything she's even sturdier. One of those countrywomen who has never succumbed to a cold or a sob story, an apron straining across her midriff, a cardigan over the top although it's almost summer.

'I did phone ahead,' Katie reminds her.

'I don't know what else you want me to say,' Pauline replies.

A largish lamb, not new-born but not a fluffy sheep either, pushes at Pauline's knee, staring up at Katie and distracting the detective momentarily.

'I told you,' Pauline insists. 'I was worried about Mim after Max's call, so she popped over here to reassure me; that's all.'

'If I could just come in? It would be really helpful.' Katie eyes the lamb and it eyes her back.

'Your lot searched the farm Sunday afternoon,' Pauline replies. 'But if you insist . . .'

Katie walks back to her car in heavy rain, her hair quickly soaked and sticking to the shoulders of her raincoat. The farmhouse was messy but homely, the lamb following her from room to room. Pauline was with her the whole time too, arms folded whenever the detective turned around, the lamb bleating just the once as if it had something to say. Katie wasn't expecting to find Julia hiding in a wardrobe or under a bed, of course not, but maybe something to indicate she'd been sheltered there by Miriam and her equally odd sister. It was a long shot – she couldn't imagine much love lost between Julia and 'Mim' – but at least she's eliminated that line of enquiry.

Katie changes out of her boots then drives back the way she came, running yet another inventory in her mind of the facts gleaned so far. If she had to hazard a guess, she'd say Max hadn't meant to kill Julia but somehow, he had, their row taken down to the cottage after everyone had left. Perhaps Julia had wanted to stay there the night and Max had lost his temper, lashing out at his provocative wife. Maybe someone else was involved. And Miriam's mixed up in it too, Katie's certain of it. She just needs some proof. A body, perhaps, but lord knows where that might be. The search area has been widened as far she can push the budget, but still they've found nothing.

As she drives along the country lanes, Katie looks for Julia amongst the dense trees, then in the flooded ditches and thick hedges. Where has she gone and how did she leave? They need to pin that down, maybe by digging deeper into the repair on her car, or another round of the taxi companies, always a complete pain in the arse. She can no longer imagine Julia Blake is alive, but she can't let go of her either. Not yet.

Chapter Ten

Upstairs Window

I race the sunset as I drive along the lanes to Brooke House, the last pink rays catching the tops of the trees and settling amongst the bare branches, crows squawking and lifting on oil-slicked wings as the sound of my car shocks them from their rest. My train didn't get in until almost five and Max is expecting me by half-past. He's clearly a man of habit, and I don't want to keep him waiting, his moods unpredictable enough as it is. Theo had seemed pleased with the progress I'd made in London today, my texts receiving immediate and positive responses, but despite his assurances I know I don't have an unlimited amount of time to get this article finished.

I bump along the rough track as fast as I dare and park to the side of the garages, beside Miriam's green car as before. It's always so quiet here, as if the rest of the world has been obliterated. I walk fast towards the kitchen but a repetitive knock halts my progress. It sounds like it's coming from behind me. I turn back to investigate and find one of the double doors to the nearest garage is slightly ajar and being buffeted back and forth by the wind. I peer through the gap, but there's nothing inside except a few cans of paint lined up along the back wall. Then I notice a waterproof sheet thrown over something in the corner. I check behind me then pull the door open just enough to slip inside.

Using the torch on my phone, I scour the domed covering for a clue to what it may be hiding, my heart thumping hard as I try to talk myself out of the ridiculous notion that Julia's decaying body lies beneath. Tentatively, I pull back a corner. Beneath the tarp is a collection of cleaning equipment: plastic-wrapped mops, a shiny metal bucket and multiple sealed packs of rubber gloves, plus some large containers of bleach. Relieved it's not anything worse, I'm then perplexed by my discovery. Max told me the cleaning company come and go without his knowledge, organised by Miriam whilst he writes, so surely they'd bring their own supplies and take them away again? I suppose they might store some stuff here, but the tarp was dusty and covered in cobwebs. Although the general smell of bleach and the stains on the floor would indicate there were wet mops and buckets here at one time. I cover everything with the sheet and switch off my torch, closing the door properly as I leave, but the hint of astringent cleaning chemicals stays with me.

The stone steps are greasy with rain as I approach the front door. I ring the bell and wait, looking around me as the view disappears into the sinking sunset. The Cotswolds are blanketed

145

in a navy and denim-blue patchwork sky, feathery edges of clouds shifting slowly from left to right. I pull the chain again, twice in succession, listening for the bell jangling inside. I left my coat in the car, expecting the door to be open by now, Max greeting me with either a charming smile or an irritable frown. He knows I've visited Jonny, so I'm guessing the latter, but even that would be better than no answer at all. Peering through the glass panel to the right of the door, I spot a source of light, probably from the lamps on the console table near the stairs, but they're not directly in view so I can't be certain.

'Can I help you?'

I spin round, my palm to my chest. 'Oh, it's you! You made me jump.'

Max's personal assistant is standing on the other side of the drive, her robust frame set against the darkening landscape. She walks towards me and I can see she's wearing wellington boots and a practical raincoat, zipped to her throat, the hood covering her hair so only her round moon-face is visible. It makes her appear both child-like and sinister as she looks up the steps.

'I saw the car lights,' Miriam explains.

'Oh, I see. Sorry, I was looking for Max, we have a meeting arranged for half-five.' My teeth are chattering now, my arms wrapped around me in a tight hug.

'What were you doing down there?' she asks, pointing towards the garages. 'I saw your torch. Why were you snooping around?'

'I wasn't snooping! A garage door was open. I thought I should check no one had broken in, that's all.'

'Max must have forgotten to lock them before he left,' Miriam says, more to herself than to me.

'He's not here?'

'No,' she replies, pushing back her hood, her permed hair set free. 'He's in London for an urgent meeting with his publisher. I think your visit this morning may have ruffled a few feathers.'

'Oh, I see,' I reply, although I don't, not fully. Jonny said Max knew I was speaking to him, so why the rush to see him in person? Unless relations are more strained than either side is letting on. 'He could at least have let me know.'

'Well, that's my fault,' Miriam replies. 'I've been so busy I forgot to contact you.'

'What time will he be back?' I ask, not even attempting to be solicitous. She's wasted my time and petrol.

'He's staying the night, I booked him into the Groucho.'

'Is that so?'

'Yes, it is so,' Miriam replies, mimicking my tone. 'Despite your rather cavalier attitude to all this, Max has a publicist and an editor who knew very little about your exclusive interview before today and are both rather concerned about how it might affect Max's upcoming book tour.'

'He's promoting the new book, then?' I ask, and Miriam clamps her mouth closed, realising she's said more than she should have. 'I guess that's why he suddenly so keen to—'

I catch something out of the corner of my eye and stop talking, turning back to the door. Through the glass panel a new source of light has appeared from deep within, bright and then gone, accompanied by the sound of an unseen door opening and closing somewhere inside.

147

'The cleaners are in,' Miriam says as I turn back. 'Having a good go whilst Max is away.' She pulls her hood up against the gusts of wind that batter us from both sides, securing the ties in a bow beneath her double chin. 'Thought I'd take the chance whilst he's not here. They're very good, come at short notice. Max hates to be disturbed when he's writing, and his study in particular is in dire need.'

'I didn't see their van parked by the garages,' I comment.

'Contractors always use the service entrance and park behind the house,' she advises me. 'It's protocol.'

'And do they bring their own supplies?' I ask.

'Yes, of course.' She frowns, before she turns and walks away.

'I don't suppose you could spare me five minutes of your time?' I call after her. 'Save me an entirely wasted journey?'

She pauses, glancing up at the house before her gaze falls on me. 'I'm sorry, that won't be possible. Perhaps you could email Max? I'm sure he'll be happy to reply when he's back home tomorrow. Apologies again for not notifying you, Miss Spencer.'

'A few background questions, that's all,' I say running after her. 'Nothing that would get you into trouble with your employer, I promise.'

'I've been very clear, Seren,' she says, surprising me with the use of my first name. 'I don't know exactly why Max wants you here, but if you take my advice, you'll leave well alone.' And with that she strides off, headed in the direction of the cottages.

'Miriam!' I catch her up, the biting wind pushing through

my flimsy dress to the skin beneath; even my bones feel cold. 'What do I need to leave well alone?'

'I told Max, and I'll say the same to you. What's done is done! Now I'd be very grateful if you would leave.' Then she's off once more, head down as she marches off.

'Miriam, wait! What do you mean? What's done?'

She keeps walking, even when I draw level with her again. 'You should set off before the weather gets worse, Seren. It's treacherous on the lanes if they flood.'

I drop back, watching until she's swallowed up by the darkness.

Back in my car I turn the heater up to full blast, driving slowly down the side of the kitchen, my palm flat across the cold windscreen to wipe away the condensation. The drops of rain are landing faster than they're cleared; Miriam's warning of potential flooding looking ever more likely. I turn the corner slowly and approach the front of the house, but as I draw level with the stone steps, my wipers judder to a halt. I try switching them off and on again, but they're stuck fast.

Brooke House looks down on me as I climb out of my car, rows of dark windows watching. I shudder as a raindrop trickles inside the neck of my dress, the wind swirling around me as I locate the source of the wiper problem, a rope of rubber twisted back on itself. I manage to untangle it, jumping in my car to try again. The wipers scrape and stutter, but at least the blades are moving, clearing just enough water for me to be able to slowly move off. I take a last look at the house, but as I glance up to the window above the door I physically jump, stalling the car.

I trail a damp palm across the condensation fogging my view

and lean as close as I can to the windscreen until the seat belt locks. My heart is banging around my chest, but I force myself to stay calm, looking again.

A pair of eyes stare back at me.

I struggle with the seat-belt release, desperate now to get out as I squint through the driving rain, but by the time I'm free, standing on the gravel, my chin upturned to the window above the door, the eyes are gone.

I dash up the steps, pulling the bell chain and stepping back to check the window again. My hair hangs in wet ropes, my dress soaked through, and now I'm wondering if I imagined it all. But it hadn't felt like that. It had felt like I was being watched. I try the bell again, but I'm shivering uncontrollably, the weather forcing me to give up and run back to the shelter of my car.

The track is muddy, my wheels spinning and slipping, but the lanes are worse, slick with rivers of rain, Miriam's portents coming true. I concentrate on the road, the wipers pretty much ineffectual. The few landmarks that there were seem to have vanished, the way ahead a long, dark tunnel of trees and hedges that twists without warning. I'm disorientated, turning the wheel this way and that although my hands are stiff and cold. I pull in to a passing place, relieved to see my phone has picked up some signal, my fingers trembling as I call Theo's mobile.

'Slow down, Seren, you're breaking up. Are you OK?'

'No, not really,' I reply, my teeth chattering as I adjust the heater and blast myself with hot air. 'Max wasn't there – away for the night his PA said – but there was someone up there, Theo, a face at the window, looking down at me, as if—'

'OK, listen, stay put and I'll drive to find you.'

'No, no, it's fine. I'll be fine. Oh damn, I forgot to check for the cleaning company van.'

'What did you say?'

'No, nothing. Are you still at the office? I'll call in, update you.'

'Even I draw the line at six o'clock on a Friday night, Seren,' Theo replies, laughing.

It's not true. He works all hours – that's the nature of the job – but there's weariness in his levity.

'You remember where I live?' he asks.

I've only visited once, but I'm sure I can find it again. It's in a tiny village. A bit out of my way, but if I go up to the motorway junction instead of towards town, I can be there in twenty minutes. It would be good to go over today's events, get everything straight in my mind. 'If you're sure? You sound tired.'

'Yes, I'm . . . What's that god-awful noise?'

I laugh and explain it's just my wipers. I'm already feeling much better than I did when I left Brooke House, warmer too, and with that feeling of security comes doubt about what I really saw at that darkened window. Maybe it was just the cleaners, as Miriam had said, or nothing at all; a trick of the light. 'I'll see you soon, Theo.'

The GPS locates me and slowly plans my new route, the woman's voice directing me with reassuring certainty to turn right in one hundred metres. Then it's only a mile or two and I'll be on the main road. I drive on, feeling a bit foolish. I've always had an overactive imagination, and even more so since

Bryn's disappearance, more than once thinking I'd spotted him, only to chase down a startled stranger.

The route circles the wooded area that skirts the landscaped grounds behind Brooke House, the trees densely packed here, sections of the forest illuminated by my headlamps as I negotiate the twists and turns. I search between the trunks and branches for a glimpse of another deer or owl, glancing into the woods then back to the road ahead. Then the view opens up, a straight line between me and Brooke House.

I bring the car to a sharp halt, forcing myself to look again and make sure of what I'm seeing, because there's a light on at an upstairs window, the one above the front door. The one where I thought I saw someone watching me.

Five Days Missing

Katie enters the interview room and slides into the seat beside Chris, her notepad striking the table with force. She's had enough of Barry Bostwick. More than enough. The measly little man asked for a solicitor, then changed his mind, and then he threw up all over his cell. He's still steaming, an acidic smell to him that makes her want to retch. She clears her throat and questions herself again, wondering if it would be better to delay the interview until he's fully sober. But it's almost midnight and this is the third time they've tried to get a statement. Her keenness to tie up the details of the repair to Julia's car has turned into much more of a performance than she or Chris anticipated. Finally the on-call doctor has given his consent, so they're good to go. She gives Barry a thin-lipped smile and reads him his rights.

Chris tracked the mechanic to a pub in the wilds of the countryside, a mile or two on from Brooke House; a favourite haunt of his apparently. The team had been trying to contact Barry for days, but he was never in his workshop, his mobile going straight to voicemail – not a great way to run a business. Chris had asked the landlord of the Badger Inn to let him know the second Barry came in, and tonight he did. Chris had ordered an orange juice and listened as Barry held forth at the bar, telling the bored landlord and a few locals how he'd had a bit of luck lately, doing some work for someone with a load of cash to spread around. When he'd staggered outside to his van Chris had followed, suggesting it wouldn't be a good idea to drive home, but Barry had some objections.

Katie checks, for the record, that Barry feels fit and well enough to answer their questions, then she looks at Chris, the DC's black eye deepest purple, the socket swollen, the eyeball red and bloodshot.

'Not a good idea to hit a police officer,' she tells Barry. 'Not a good idea at all.'

'He hit me first,' Barry says, looking at Chris square on.

Chris's right hand curves into a fist and Katie gives him a warning look. She told him to leave their differences at the door. Barry will be charged for the assault later, and they'll have no problem making the charges stick. There were at least two witnesses drawn from the bar who can confirm Barry threw the first punch.

'Interview with Barry Bostwick, conducted by DS Katie Ingles,' she says, loud enough to break the tension and set the tone.

'Yeah, look, I'm a busy man, love. Two MOTs and a paint job waiting for me in the morning. I've had a day or two off, lots to catch up on. Shall we crack on?'

'You're not going anywhere,' Chris says, his teeth gritted.

Katie shoots her colleague another warning look and continues. 'You've owned a motor repair and body shop business for a number of years, I understand?'

'Yeah, last thirty years or so. Started when I was boy.' Barry grins. He's warming to his subject, pushing grimy nails through thinning hair. 'Clean licence, you can check. Then perhaps—'

'Your workshop is a few miles from town?'

'Yeah, cheaper out there. Although trade's not so good. It's not as convenient for punters as the places nearer town. I'm competing with the chains, they can buy in bulk. I'm a one-man band, always have been. Rely on word-of-mouth.'

'But very convenient for the Blakes?' Katie asks.

She can almost see the penny drop.

'Yeah, they've been good customers of mine over the years.' Barry stops picking his filthy nails and studies Katie. 'I look after them, you see. Put myself out.'

'Can you tell me about your relationship with Max and Julia Blake?' Katie asks, making notes.

'I take care of their cars, sweetheart. That's all.'

His condescending tone is pushing her buttons but she sets her irritation aside, for now. 'Max has a Porsche and Julia's car is a Range Rover?'

'Yeah, that's right. Nice motors.'

'I'd have thought they'd use the main dealers for luxury cars like that?'

'Yeah, they do. I just take care of the in-between stuff.'

'How do you mean?'

'The odd scratch or bump, like the one I've been seeing to on the Range Rover.'

'Tell us about it, Barry,' Chris says, leaning in.

'Yeah,' Barry swallows and Katie tries not to mind that he's intimidated by Chris, but not her.

'Mim called me Saturday morning,' Barry says, clearing his throat. 'Said Max had caught the front of the Range Rover as he pulled out the gate. He was going to pick up a necklace in town. Expensive, she said, a gift.'

It sounds rehearsed, almost verbatim what Max *and* Miriam both said. The jeweller was similarly primed, the handwritten receipt conveniently showing the correct date. The necklace was probably collected by Miriam, or even delivered by the jeweller. Max had just spent ten thousand pounds on the commission, and it wasn't the first time he'd purchased extravagant items for his wife at the exclusive establishment.

'Mim asked if I could rush it through quick before Julia noticed,' Barry continues, keen to finish his story. 'She said Julia would be annoyed that Max dented her car, and it was their anniversary, so he didn't want to upset her.' He grins at Katie, his right middle tooth discoloured.

'Are you in a relationship with Miriam Norris?' Katie asks.

Barry roars with laughter, asks if she's trying to make him puke again.

'I understand that Julia rarely drives,' Katie says, ignoring Barry's continuing amusement.

'No, not much.'

'Not much, or not at all?' Chris asks.

'Not sure,' Barry replies, fidgeting, a trickle of sweat descending his temple.

'So why would she care?' Katie asks. 'If she never drives the car, she wouldn't mind an accidental bump, would she? Or even notice?'

'Mrs Blake is very particular about things.'

156

'Describe to me the damage to the Range Rover, registration . . .' Katie flicks back in her notebook, 'J-U-L-1-A.'

'It was pretty bad. Max must have given it a good clonk, but he does throw his cars around. I had to bash out the wing and replace the lights, resprayed the front and passenger side. Gave it all a good valet too, inside and out. Good as new.'

'Yes, you were very thorough,' Chris says, folding his arms. 'Seems like more than a bash on the gate to me, sounds like it happened at speed.'

'Look, I don't ask questions. Mim wanted a quick repair and a full valet so that's what I did.'

'How much did she pay you?' Chris asks.

'Three hundred.'

'Very reasonable, Barry,' Katie observes. 'The rest was cash in hand was it?'

'All through the books, sweetheart,' he says, greasy palms raised in surrender. 'Mim picked me up late Saturday morning. I dropped it back early yesterday. Job done!'

'So you did all that work in what, three days?' Katie asks, taking notes again. 'That's good service.'

'Like I said, they're good customers.' He grins.

'And you returned the car how?' Chris asks.

'Drove it there, walked back. Mim was busy.'

'And no one saw you?' Chris says.

Barry shrugs, tells Chris he used the service entrance.

'That's a good four-mile round trip,' Chris observes. 'They must have been very good customers.'

'Oh, they are,' Barry replies, chuckling to himself.

'Did you see anyone at the house on Saturday morning when you collected the car?' Katie asks.

Barry shakes his head. 'Not a soul, love. Not a soul. Can I have my call now? I'm entitled.'

Chris storms out, waiting for Katie to catch up. 'That fucking tosser, laughing at us.'

'Yeah, well he won't be laughing when he's charged for that.' Katie points at Chris's black eye, accidentally prodding it with her fingertip.

'What do you reckon about the car?' Chris asks, rubbing his eye as Katie apologises. 'Max hit Julia with it? Or a crash? Barry's insistent he picked up the car late Saturday morning, but it could have been any time, for instance just before Max called on Sunday morning.'

Katie nods. 'Can you make sure all the guests are asked if they saw a white Range Rover at the house on Saturday evening?'

'Yeah, sure, but none of this explains the blood in the cottage,' Chris points out, inspecting his knuckles. 'And if Julia's Range Rover was locked up in one of the garages at Brooke House, none of their visitors would have seen it anyway.'

'Maybe Max moved the body in the car,' Katie suggests. 'After the argument. Can you get the Range Rover thoroughly checked again? I know Barry's done a job on it, but you never know, we might have missed something.'

They both know it's unlikely. Barry might be a tosser, but he's a thorough one and it looks like he's been paid well for his trouble.

Chapter Eleven

A Sick Joke

Theo and Nicky's bungalow is tucked behind a neatly clipped leylandii, hidden from view and centred in a large plot. Lights mark the driveway, triggered by my rattling car, high trees and hedges cut in sharp angles either side. I try to picture Theo on a step ladder wielding an electric trimmer, but it's not a natural fit. I lock my car and hold my coat over my head, dodging the puddles as I dash towards the lit porch.

I've been here once before, a few weeks after I started at the *Herald*. Theo and I were on our way to a summer drinks party, a very dull occasion hosted by the mayor, but Theo had forgotten his wallet so we called in on the way. I was curious to see where my boss lived, but not cheeky enough to invite myself in. Nicky walked out in her slippers to say hello, and she'd seemed friendly enough, but I got the impression I was being sized up, her questions a little too probing, as was her gaze.

Theo opens the door as I run towards it, the rain pounding down.

'The face you saw at the upstairs window,' he asks as soon as I'm inside. 'Any more thoughts?'

'And hello to you, too,' I reply, breathless.

The hall is snug, no room for furnishings on the rectangle of polished parquet flooring, although a set of golf clubs are leant up against the patterned wallpaper.

'Sorry, let me take your coat,' Theo says, padding around me. 'You're soaked.'

'I'm fine,' I tell him, pulling at my wet dress. 'Miriam said the cleaners were in, taking the chance whilst Max was away, but I don't know . . .'

'Mmm.' He nods. 'Sounds a plausible explanation. Max is a stickler for his peace and quiet.' He opens a cupboard beside him and takes out a plastic clothes hanger, draping my coat on it. The bungalow is quiet and disappointingly devoid of cooking smells. I was hoping I might be in time for dinner. According to Lynda, Nicky is a 'superb cook'.

'Drink?' he asks, guiding the way.

The kitchen is a square room with a tired feel, the surfaces littered with piles of post as well as books and magazines, much like Theo's desk. He opens a bottle of red and I realise that's where I must have got a taste for it; from Theo.

'Were there any contractors' vans parked round the back?' he asks, pouring the wine.

'I forgot to check, sorry.'

Theo graciously waves away my apology. 'She's a funny woman, his assistant. Always sneaking around. I sometimes wondered if she had a thing for Max. She came to functions with him a couple of times, like a puppy dog trailing behind. She looked a bit of a fright, to be honest. Hardly the image Max wanted to convey.'

He hands me my wine and I take a sip, considering Theo's point about Miriam. 'I've wondered that, if she likes him romantically, I mean, but she's quite a bit older than him.'

Theo shakes his head. 'They're roughly the same age, I think.'

'Poor Miriam,' I say, although I'm still annoyed with her. 'She said Max had to rush off to London to see his publicist. He's got a book tour coming up.'

'Interesting . . . so he's planning to hit the promotion trail again. I imagine any adverse publicity will be very carefully . . .' Theo continues to talk, his words drifting in and out of my consciousness as I take in the fact there's no sign of Nicky.

'Is your wife around?' I ask, pushing away my wine. 'I should say hello.'

'No, she's not,' he replies. 'Shall we go through to the conservatory? We can get our heads together.'

The conservatory is at the back of the bungalow facing the garden, heavy rain thrumming hard on the Perspex roof. Being here, in the place he calls home, has made me realise how little I know about Theo beyond his professional persona. I hadn't even thought of it as a persona until now. The conservatory is cold, tiled floor and no blinds. Theo puffs until the end of his cigar catches the flame from his engraved lighter then he looks across at me, lurking in the doorway. 'Sit down, Seren. You're making the place look untidy!'

It's a phrase my dad uses and I laugh, joining Theo on the

rattan sofa. I extract my notepad from my bag and turn to him, asking, 'Shall I start?'

'Yes, do! I want to hear about London first. How did the meetings go?'

'Good. I met with Ben Fortune first.'

'Nasty piece of work as far as I recall,' Theo says, puffing smoke.

'He wasn't particularly pleasant.' I cough. 'An ex-lover of Julia's, and from what he said they'd rekindled their relationship in the weeks before she went missing.' Theo gives me a knowing look and I return to my notes. 'Then I went over to Embankment, to Max's publishing house.'

'And you met Jonny. Great guy, isn't he?'

'Yes, but understandably cautious in what he was happy to share.'

'It's a tricky situation for him.' Theo draws deeply on the cigar. 'Max is a massive cash cow for them, but Jonny was also very fond of Julia.'

'Yes, that's what he said.'

'Don't get me wrong, he saw her for what she was,' Theo says, leaning forward. 'But Julia loved Jonny, and his partner, Matt. And they loved her back, warts and all. It was the creative thing, I think. Matt's in publishing too. Julia sucked up to them both.'

'And you? Did she suck up to you too?'

Theo places his cigar in an onyx ashtray on the coffee table. 'The local rag hardly qualified for Julia's arty set. Mind you, she loved it when her photo was in the *Herald*,' he says, smiling. 'An avid reader, I'll give her that.'

'Ben told me she'd had another lover years ago, so I think we can assume her affairs were a regular thing. Jonny said as much too, but he seemed convinced Max was a one-woman man.'

'Yes, I'd agree with that,' Theo replies.

'You think Max knew about the affairs?'

'He must have, or at the very least suspected. Everyone did.'

'I just don't get it. I mean, I know Max loved her, and she was much younger, and beautiful, but why put up with that level of crap?'

'Who can say what passions drive us?' Theo asks, delivering the line in a melodramatic, almost Shakespearean manner.

'Drive us to what, though?' I ask, looking up from my notes. I'd lost myself in them, but now I notice Theo's staring at me in an oddly intense way.

'What is it?' I ask, brushing at my nose. I have been known to draw on my face.

'Nothing,' he says. 'So, moving on.' He clears his throat and picks up his cigar, tapping it on the edge of the ashtray which is now balanced precariously on his knee. 'Anything else from today?'

'Nope; just the weirdness at Brooke House.' I spot the remnants of a microwave meal by Theo's socked feet, yellow grains of rice stuck to the fork, a slick of bright orange sauce in the plastic tray. 'She's away, your wife?' I ask.

'Yes, staying with our daughter in London.'

'Oh, I assumed . . .' I look around the mock-Victorian conservatory, mentally talking myself out of my rising paranoia. It's surely a coincidence that he's invited me here when

163

his wife isn't home. In fact, wasn't it me that suggested it? I can't recall the exact way it was decided. Besides, Nicky's presence is everywhere, in the tropical plants growing on the window sills, lemons and yuccas and cacti, and the carefully plumped cushions on the cane furniture. Their marriage is rock solid. Lynda said so. Theo stubs out his cigar and asks if I'm OK, I seem a bit distracted.

'Yes, sorry. I'm fine, just tired. Busy day. I should probably—'

'Look, I know this is all a bit . . . awkward,' Theo says, something in his tone setting off alarm bells in my head. 'But we're both grown-ups and with Nicky away . . .'

It happens quickly, Theo reaching out as I scream, *'What the fuck?!'* I jump up, the ashtray careering to the floor as Theo springs to his feet as well.

I dash into the hall and grapple my coat from the cupboard, one sleeve clinging on to a thick plastic shoulder of the hanger. I'm still wrestling with it when Theo emerges, his expression not stricken as I'd expected. No, he's smiling at me, as if I'm the one who's made a silly mistake.

'Methinks the lady doth protest too much,' he says, reaching out.

I recoil, the hanger and coat clattering to the wooden floor. 'You think I'm playing a game, Theo? Because I'm not!'

'Oh, come on, Seren,' he says, tilting his head. 'We both know why you're here. It's what we've wanted for ages.'

'No, it's not!' I shout, struggling with a sleeve, still attached by a thread to a jagged piece of the hanger. 'I thought you wanted to talk about Max. I thought you wanted to help me, that you admired me . . . professionally! *Professionally,* Theo!' I rip my coat free and throw the hanger on the floor.

'I do, Seren. Of course I do. But when two people—'

'You arsehole!' I tell him, opening the door to the thrashing rain.

Theo follows me out, calling my name in a cajoling manner. I stride away, but then something in his voice sounds wrong, almost like he's being strangled, and although it's the last thing I want to do, I slowly turn around, praying it's a sick joke, a desperate attempt to make me stay.

It isn't.

Theo's pulling at his tie to loosen it. His face, lit by the glare of the porch light, is ashen. He begins to fall, not pitching forward or tumbling back, but a lowering down of his creaking knees which then buckle beneath him. He thuds to the ground, his eyes rolling back into the lids.

I close mine for a split-second, willing this moment to rewind, then I'm beside him, my phone in my hand, telling him it will all be fine, he just needs to hang on until help arrives. 'Talk to me, Theo. Please talk to me.'

It's late, almost midnight, the apartment in darkness. I switch on the light and walk into the sitting room, sitting down to read a note Iz has left on the coffee table, thanking me for the signed hardback book from Max. Abandoned shoes and clothes lead to her closed bedroom door, a low moan from within. *Dom.* Then another, slightly deeper. *Izzy.* I clamp my hands over my ears but the moaning continues. I close my eyes, but all I can see is Theo, grey-faced and unmoving. Then flashing lights, talk of a faint pulse, a drop of hope. I'd held his hand, still warm, then watched helplessly as the paramedic hooked Theo up to a monitor, blue lights flashing then gone. I'd called Nicky from Theo's phone as soon as I got to the hospital, then waited, until almost three hours later she'd arrived from London, her lined skin pale as I'd explained he was unresponsive but still alive when they'd taken him away. She said nothing, her expression blank beneath the harsh strip lights, as she took his phone. Then she was gone too. I'd stared at the wipe-clean floor, another hour, maybe two, all humanity paraded before me, blood, tears, vomit and pain, but she didn't come back. The way she'd looked at me before she left, I wasn't surprised.

I open my eyes to read the new notification that's pinged on my phone. Not the text or call from Theo I've been praying for, however unlikely that would be in the circumstances, but something else to think about at least. I open Facebook and read the response to my post twice before I reply, my brain struggling to cope with anything other than Theo.

I should rest, but I need to get away and I won't sleep tonight anyway. I pack a bag and then I text Fran to tell her about Theo, fielding her immediate follow-up call before I can speak to Dad. He sounds tired, and concerned, but he doesn't ask why I'm driving through the night to get to them, telling me they'll wait up. Our family have had enough sleepless nights to take them in our stride.

The apartment is silent as I switch off the lights and close the door, everyone asleep but me.

Chapter Twelve

Welsh Rain

Swansea town centre is deathly quiet on a Sunday morning. The drive only took me twenty minutes with no traffic. 'On a Sunday, love?' Mum had asked. 'I thought you were here to see us.'

My dash to Wales in the early hours of yesterday morning is still a blur. I was exhausted by the time I was pulling up outside my parents' terraced house, barely able to coherently explain what the previous day had done to me, and Theo. Mum's hugs released the tears that had threatened since I left the hospital.

There's been no news, although I check my phone constantly, hoping someone will have heard how Theo is and remembered to pass that information on to me. Fran's concern has turned to impatience at my frequent messages. *He's in ICU being monitored, that's all I know. I'll let you know if I hear more.* I haven't received any anonymous calls over the weekend either, their absence allowing me to sleep, but I long for them to return, their familiar silence reassuring.

The café is part of the same chain as one near the *Herald* which lends it a familiar feel, but I'm a hundred miles away, my acquaintance with the décor an illusion. I order a flat white and watch as the tee-shirted barista executes his practised moves. It's not quirky or unique like the café where Izzy works, but the anonymity is good, as is the coffee.

It was Carys who suggested we meet in Swansea, so I guess she must live reasonably close by, but she's given nothing away and already postponed our meeting twice, once last night and then this morning, only to change her mind and reinstate it. My mug is empty by the time a slim brunette pushes open the door. She's dressed with attention to detail, the cuffs of her trench coat turned back, a belt cinched at her narrow waist, the heels of her trendy knee-high boots clacking on the floor as she approaches.

'Carys? So nice to meet you. Can I get you anything?'

'No,' she says, taking a seat.

Her tone is as rude as Ben's, but I'm just relieved she's turned up. I grab my notepad from my bag and ask if I can tape the conversation. She looks alarmed and shakes her head. 'That's fine,' I tell her. 'But please don't worry. Like I said in my message, you can remain completely anonymous.'

'I don't have time for this,' she says. 'My kids are with my husband and he wanted to know where I'm going. I had to lie to him.'

'Why?'

'Why do you think?'

'I'm sorry, Carys, I have no idea.'

'Because I should never have been at that party and as far as my husband is concerned, I wasn't.'

Synapses start to snap, connections being made. 'You were Ben's guest?'

'That's not the point,' she replies, picking at the edge of her immaculate nails, ovals of shiny red. 'I just need to tell you one thing, face-to-face, no record of it, and then it's off my conscience.' She glances around her, taking a deep breath, her fingers tapping the table and supporting an impressive collection of rocks. Her handbag, too precious to place on the floor, sits on the empty chair beside her. I don't like her one bit.

'I didn't know Julia that well,' she says, smoothing an arched eyebrow. 'I was more a friend of Ben's. It was after she left the course that Ben and I got together.'

An ex-girlfriend; makes sense and possibly casts a hint of blame her way, but enough to warrant further thought? It seems unlikely. I nod, returning to my shorthand.

'I was only in London for two years, a teenage rebellion against . . . well, this!' She stares out at the Welsh rain, then she looks at me, flint in her eyes. 'I know you've met Ben.'

'He told you to contact me?'

'God, no! I saw his message pop up on the college Facebook page. I'm always on there, in case . . .' She's fiddling with her wedding band, twisting it. 'It's a bit of a preoccupation of mine since Julia went missing, but if Ben knew I was here . . .'

'Has he threatened you?'

'No!' She looks at me like I'm stupid. 'Anyway, he invited me to his apartment in London before the party but neglected to tell me the full plan. I thought it was just going to be the two of us: fun, an escape. A child-free weekend in London. Have you got kids, Seren?'

'No, not yet.'

'I've got three. Five, three and eighteen months,' she counts them off on her fingers. 'I was literally losing my mind. I just wanted to be the old Carys again, but only for a night or two.'

'Ben had other plans, I assume?'

'He still has a thing for Julia,' Carys says, sneering. '*Pathetic!*'

I try not to point out the obvious, keeping my thoughts to myself.

'I knew I shouldn't have gone with him to the party, but I'd heard of Max, and Ben said the house was amazing. Anyway, it would have been awkward to go straight home; difficult to explain.'

'What was the party like?'

'Max didn't want us there, that was obvious, then Ben went off with the waitress.' Carys closes her eyes and shakes her head. 'I lied to my husband, told him I was in London with a few girlfriends from college. Then I was in Gloucestershire, middle of nowhere!'

'You said there was something specific you wanted to tell me?' Her justifications are flimsy and she's starting to annoy me now.

'After we left the party, Ben said something in the taxi . . . it's probably nothing. I should have told the police at the time. I saw it mentioned on the appeal. But I thought she'd turn up. Typical Julia, always looking for a bit of attention—'

'What should you have told the police?'

She fiddles with her engagement and wedding rings, twisting

them round, then back. 'Ben said he'd taken something; as a keepsake.'

'A keepsake?'

'He showed it to me. I said he should give it back, it was obviously worth a bomb.'

'What had he taken, Carys?'

'A necklace, beautiful thing, spelt out Julia's name. The dot of the "I" was a massive diamond, at least a carat, I'd say, maybe two. I'd noticed her wearing it as soon as we arrived. It was an anniversary present from Max. Lucky lady.'

'Why would Ben have taken that? Because it was valuable?'

Carys shakes her head. 'He was obsessed with her and it seemed to amuse him that he had it, said Julia would probably find it funny too, but I wondered if that was really true. It would have been pretty nasty of her to give it away on the same day she was given it. I asked him how he came to have it, but he wouldn't say and he clammed up when I told him I would contact the police. I called him a few times afterwards, threatened to report him, but then he claimed he'd lost it. There didn't seem much point risking my marriage for the sake of . . .' She places her hand on the table. 'Look, I've told you. Now it's up to you.' She slumps back in her seat, then she seems to recall something, leaning forward. 'I'll keep you to your promise. My name mustn't ever be mentioned. I can't risk my husband finding out where I was. That part of my life, it's over. I should never have been there. I've got kids, Seren. Think of them.'

'Seren? Is that you, love?'

'Hi, Mum.' I pull my key from the front door and kick my

171

wet shoes into the hall cupboard. The house smells of Sunday; roasting meat and wrung-out dishcloths. Mum is in the kitchen, peeling potatoes. I told her I'd be back by one, but it's a bit before that, my meeting with Carys short and to the point, although it's left me with plenty of questions, ones I'd normally run by Theo.

Mum turns from the sink, holding up her wet rubber-gloved hands to show why she can't immediately pull me into a tight hug. I've only been out for a couple of hours, but after almost two days of having me back at home she's resumed her role as the monitor of my every movement.

'You're nice and early, love. I hope you didn't speed – that section after the flyover has cameras on it now.'

'No, I was careful.'

She peels off her gloves, holding me for a second, her cheek cool against mine before she turns back to the sink, a potato in one hand and the peeler in the other. 'Did it go OK, your meeting?'

'Yeah, sort of.'

I check my phone, but there's still no message from Fran, or anyone else. I don't feel relieved, the knot of worry still there, but I guess no news is good news. I wish I could ask Theo about the necklace; he'd know if I should approach the police with Carys's information now or maybe piece together a bit more of the puzzle first.

'No news?' Mum asks, waving a hand between me and my phone. I shake my head and she screws up her mouth before she says, 'This celebrity interview of yours . . .?'

'Yes?' I open the biscuit barrel and pull out a chocolate Hobnob, biting off a chunk.

'You sure it's safe? I mean, his wife is missing and they think he might have . . .'

I roll my eyes and she smiles, but she looks unconvinced.

'Honestly, Mum, if the police thought he'd killed Julia he'd still be being investigated, wouldn't he? Anyway, he has no reason to harm me.'

Something flickers across Mum's face as if she's in pain, but she manages a weak smile, despatching me to the front room to keep Dad company whilst she gets on with lunch.

Dad is watching rugby. 'You all right, love?' he asks. 'Meeting go OK?'

I sit beside him and follow his line of vision, instantly bored by the drone of the commentator who is speaking in Welsh, most of which is incomprehensible to me. 'Yeah, not bad. Who's playing?' I ask, checking my phone again.

'Wales, of course.' He continues to stare at the television. 'We watched it together yesterday. Just watching the highlights again.'

'Oh, yeah, I forgot.' I tap my email icon and search for the one Theo forwarded me the day he told me about the exclusive with Max.

'You get that wiper fixed while you were in Swansea?' Dad asks.

I look up and smile sheepishly. 'Sorry, I forgot. I'll sort it soon, promise. And the wing mirror.'

I find Theo's correspondence, but it doesn't mention the name of the detective in charge of the investigation into Julia's disappearance. I type a quick email to my contact in the police press office, well, Theo's actually, asking her to forward it on to the relevant person. I read it back and press send, happy with the non-committal tone.

'Driving back tonight, or in the morning?' Dad asks.

'Not sure yet. See how I feel later.'

Dad points the remote at the television to pause the game, dropping his voice as he says, 'Haven't had much chance to chat since you got here, but Polly Pell called the other day.' His eyes dart to the serving hatch behind which Mum is clattering around in the kitchen. 'You remember Pol?' I nod. 'Spoke to your mum for ages, seems to help. I'm just glad your mother talks to someone.'

A clear memory of our Family Liaison Officer pops into my head, her kind voice, the way she'd fitted in. The way she'd flip into work mode so fast it would surprise us to hear another side to her. Pol was a trained professional with an important job to do, a police officer through and through, but her ready smile made you forget she wasn't a family friend.

Mum flings opens the serving hatch and pokes her head out. 'What you two whispering about?'

'We're wondering when lunch is,' Dad replies, smiling.

'If you mean have you got time for a swift half first, then the answer is yes,' Mum replies, smiling back.

Dad leaves for the pub and I climb the narrow stairs, past my old bedroom, running my hand over Bryn's name as I walk by his door. Four letters are burnt into the wooden plaque, a sandcastle beside them. I haven't been inside in a long while, but when I turn the handle I notice the bed is still made up, his books on his desk. It looks dust-free, so I guess Mum must come in every now and then to clean. The thought makes my heart hurt. I close the door and walk along the landing to use the bathroom, sitting on the cold seat and tearing off sheets of toilet paper to dab at my eyes. Then I lie on my bed and read some more of Max's book.

When I come back down Mum is battling with bubbling pans and spitting roasting tins. She refuses all offers of help, waving me out of her way as Dad arrives home from the pub. 'I'm best left to my own devices,' she says, asking us to lay the table.

Dad smells of the Red Lion, stale beer and fried food. He'll have made his half a pint last, chatting about rugby and telling his work mates that I'm home for the weekend. He grabs the place mats and cutlery from the dresser and Mum passes the piled-up plates through the hatch. I'm ravenous, taking my seat quickly and shovelling in forkfuls of roast chicken and potatoes, mashed with soft cauliflower. Mum raises an eyebrow at Dad and he says, 'You need any money for groceries, love?'

'No, I'm fine, thanks. Can you pass the salt?'

I think of Theo cracking sea salt over twice-cooked chips and swigging glasses of red on one of the many pub lunches we'd shared between appointments. His collar was too tight, his tie strangling him as he fell, his face—

'You sure you're OK, love?' Mum asks, reaching across to gently squeeze my forearm. 'You were miles away there.'

'I'm fine,' I assure her, noticing the extra worry lines since my last visit.

'So, this meeting,' Dad says. 'Who was it you were interviewing?'

'Someone who knew Julia Blake,' I reply, picking up my orange juice.

'That's the missing wife,' Mum tells him, placing her cutlery neatly on her plate. 'Of the author.'

'I've read a few of his,' Dad says, oblivious to the fact Mum and I are staring at one another, her eyes searching mine.

'I just worry, Seren,' Mum blurts out. 'I worry that it's too close to home,' she says, dabbing at the corners of her mouth with a tissue. 'I worry that—'

'I'm fine,' I tell her again, ignoring Dad's confusion. 'Honestly, it's nothing like Bryn.'

Mentioning Bryn's name is always a sure-fire way to send Mum scurrying from the room, and sure enough she gets up to clear the table, gathering the plates and stacking them in the serving hatch. She's hardly made a dent in her lunch, her clothes hanging off her. Dad smiles at me whilst her back is turned, reassuring me it's not my fault.

'Ooh, I know what I was going to tell you,' she says, reaching across to extract Dad's dirty knife from the white tablecloth. 'I bumped into Evan's mother in the Co-op yesterday. She asked after you.'

'*Really?*' I look at Mum over the edge of my juice glass. 'You didn't mention it.'

'Didn't I? I told her you were doing well in your job and had a nice apartment, but no boyfriend.'

I can imagine the exchange. The last time I saw Sandra she made her feelings about me very plain.

'Evan would love to see you if you want to pop in when you're visiting home.'

'She said that?' I ask, the answer clearly written across Mum's face. 'Well, there won't be time today,' I tell her. 'Not once we've finished lunch and had our walk.'

Mum turns away with a private smile sneaking its way

around her lips. It's lovely to see her cheerful; I just wish I didn't have to disappoint her, again.

The roast is followed by apple crumble then our traditional Sunday afternoon stroll along the front. The bracing sea air finds my inner ears and dives down into my lungs whilst the steelworks belch out their waste into the elephant-grey sky, a plume of steam extending across the bay. We used to go down on to the sand every Sunday, whatever the weather, finding shells or skimming stones, but today we stick to the wide esplanade. Mum's linked arms with Dad and I trail behind, feeling like a small child again, my boots scuffing the pavement. It was the same when Bryn was here, but at least we were a two-plus-two back then. Mum and Dad have been a tight unit since they were fifteen. I can't envisage one without the other, but then I never thought I'd be following on my own. I miss Bryn beside me, though it's not the gnawing ache it was at first, at least not as often. Time lends distance, a detachment to dull the stabbing pain, but it still hurts like hell, the desperate longing coming in waves of varying intensity. Bryn would probably tease me about my lack of a boyfriend, then wink at me because he'd have understood how difficult it was to break up with Evan. Or maybe he wouldn't – he was my baby brother, after all, but he'd be almost twenty-one now, a proper adult. I bend to adjust the zip on my boot, although it's fastened tight. Wherever Bryn is, he must still think of me with Evan, and the urge to correct that misconception propels me forward as I run after my parents.

Mum looks round as though she knows what I've been thinking, an annoying knack of hers. Then I spot the mischief-making in her eyes as she gestures without subtlety at someone walking straight towards us, their gait familiar, long legs taking in the distance between us too fast for me to compose myself. I lift my face to the cold air, allowing it to cool my warming skin, then I spread my fingers to hide my eyes, smiling between the gaps as Evan grins back. He bends to kiss Mum on a rosy cheek and shakes Dad's hand. Then Mum pulls Dad away from his one-sided conversation about the game, leaving us alone.

'Well, this is a surprise,' Evan says, still smiling.

'Yes, such an amazing coincidence. It's as though my mother had somehow arranged it with you?'

I feel the easiness we have with one another returning, the grey flecks in his eyes coming alive as they always did whenever he spotted me walking into his family's hotel. I saw it in Max's eyes too, when he talked about Julia, a spark lit at the thought of the other person. It's heady, that kind of adoration, hard to resist.

'Come on, Spencer!' he says, grabbing my hand. 'I'll treat you to a coffee. Bit of fruit cake too if you're lucky.'

My cake is stale and remains untouched, my coffee too milky. I don't want them, other than as a distraction, something to pull apart and stir round. The café is quiet: another couple seated but behind us, and a young mother ordering a hot chocolate at the counter. Along the esplanade, wind-swept walkers fight the elements, and below that roiling waves batter their way up the beach. Evan's grown a beard, sandy like his hair, his freckles currently lying dormant until a hint of sun sprinkles them across his nose and cheeks again. His hazel eyes are now framed by glasses, which suit him. 'I like them,' I say, pointing at the dark frames. He thanks me, smiling. I smile back, but then I recall Theo's dead-eyed stare, the fear in his expression before it had slackened. I imagine him hooked up to wires and machines . . . or worse.

'Are you cold?' Evan leans forward. 'It's not that warm in here.'

I shake my head, tell him I'm fine. I seem to be tripping out that phrase a lot lately. Evan's kindness has always been my undoing, his love almost too imperative to resist. *'You'll only hurt him again,'* Bryn whispers and I know he's right, surprised to hear my brother's voice after all this time. I look out at the bay, the waves as fierce as ever, dread seeping through me.

'Your mother is very determined,' Evan says, his expression more serious. 'Must be where you get it from.'

'Well, you know Mum,' I reply. 'She doesn't do subtle.'

Our familiarity is comforting, but fraught with the possibility of misunderstandings and further hurt. Evan used to be my universe and everything in it, but then I changed. Little by little detaching myself from our love, long before Bryn disappeared, and long before I admitted it was happening. When Evan proposed, an inevitability to it after the years we'd been together, I accepted without much thought for my own feelings. It was expected, and although I knew the love I had, still have for Evan, wasn't the right kind of love anymore, I kidded myself that by sliding a tiny chip of a diamond on to my third finger I would feel the way he did. Because I wanted to more than anything. I wanted it to be enough that he was my cheerleader and greatest champion. I wanted it because it was ungrateful and undeserving to expect more. I wanted it because the alternative was terrifying and selfish and downright stupid. Why wouldn't I want him? There was no good reason at all. It used to make my stomach clench when I looked at the ring, a reminder that one day I would break my best friend's heart, and mine. A simple piece of jewellery but so significant, like Julia's necklace.

It was the day a body washed up on the beach when I finally found the courage to tell Evan how I felt.

The rumour swelled like the high tide that bore tragedy on to the smooth, early morning sand, reaching us as we took in bottles of warming milk and spoke to anxious neighbours, keen to share what they'd heard. Pol arrived first, her hair wet from the shower, and only to confirm that it was a male, and as yet unidentified. She waited with us, making cups of tea, as alert as we were, four tightly coiled springs; five once Evan joined our vigil. For nine long hours we thought it was our misfortune, not someone else's. When it was over, after they'd come to tell us they were certain it wasn't Bryn, I took off my beautiful engagement ring and handed it back to a sobbing Evan, thinking nothing could be as painful as what we'd just experienced. He thought I'd change my mind, given time. They all did.

The window next to us is steaming up. I wipe it with my palm, reminded of the view of Brooke House as I'd cleared my fogged windscreen. The image of those enquiring eyes is still vivid, but it was dark and rainy, and that place is so atmospheric I could easily have been mistaken. I haven't heard from

Max over the weekend, but right now all I want is news of Theo. Outside the café, people are hunched over as they walk by, much like Miriam as she'd marched away from me into the night. Her warnings of bad weather have turned to certainty. I need to get home, before the forecasted snow arrives. The face looks down on me from Brooke House, staring back at my reflection, then melting away as the glass mists. The café smells of wet coats and warm bodies and coffee and soup. A child screams in their pushchair as the mother squeezes by. The Blakes didn't have children, but Julia was still young, maybe one day they would have. The buggy tips towards Evan and he catches a handle, holds it for the harried mother.

'How's the hotel business?' I ask.

'Yeah, you know what it's like out of season.' Evan fiddles with the packets of sugar and condiments slotted into a holder by the plastic menus. He selects one, amber crystals dusting the table as he twists the packet. 'We've turned the space above the kitchen into a self-contained apartment. My own place, at last.'

'That's nice.' I dab a finger into the sprinkled brown sugar, touching it to my tongue. 'I share with another girl. It's more expensive than round here, but really nice.'

'Are you seeing anyone?' Evan drops the scrunched packet into his empty cup. 'Sorry, I shouldn't have asked. None of my business.'

I consider my reply, but there's no reason to be anything other than honest. 'No, I'm not. You?'

He shakes his head and I'm filled with selfish relief, then he says, 'Actually, there is someone, but it's nothing really.'

A stab of jealously impales me. My instinct is to retaliate, invent a romance, or seize my chance, still there for the taking. 'Anyone I know?' I reply, my voice shaky.

'It's not like that, she's not . . .' He smiles at me. 'She's not you.'

'Don't,' I say and he looks away. 'I'm sorry, Evan, but it's not going to change anything. You know that.'

I tell him about my interview with a famous novelist, although he hadn't asked, explaining what a great chance it is; how it could mean promotion. 'Might even be able to have my own place like you one day.'

He looks up from his cup, his features flattened. 'But you've no plans to come home?'

I shake my head. 'I know you love it here, Evan, but I don't, not any more.'

He asks about Bryn and I tell him there's nothing to report, which I imagine he already knew, but it's kind of him to ask.

'I'm sorry, Seren. For him, and for us.'

'It wasn't because of that.'

'Wasn't it?'

'No, it really wasn't.'

There's a pause and I think we've circumnavigated all the landmines when he says, 'OK, I'm just going to say how I feel, because—'

Mum bangs on the glass and we both look up. Their walk will have taken them down the promenade towards the funfair, not that either of them are interested in the rides. Now they're back and Mum is smiling at us hopefully, interrupting at the very moment she had engineered towards. We must look very

182

much like a couple, deep in conversation across the table then springing apart. Mum's always loved Evan; even when we were teenagers and she worried we were too young to fall in love, unaware the boy she idolised was also the boy I lost my virginity to at barely sixteen. Maybe she wouldn't have minded too much if she'd known how gentle he was, how sweet. So different from the intensity Max exhibits when he talks about Julia, all-consuming and exclusive. I look away from my mother's expectant smile, pushing Max's strength of passion from my mind too and thinking instead of Julia's expression in the photo, knowing now that it was Ben she was looking at, the man she'd just—

Mum bangs on the glass again, mouthing something as Dad leads her away.

Evan and I follow the linked shadows of my parents, although they seem intent on leaving us behind. The promenade is busier now that the rain is finally desisting, the seafront filling up as the sun tries to break through.

'I heard there was a sighting,' Evan says, his words scattered by the gusts coming in off the waves. 'Few months ago, further down the coast.'

'It was nothing,' I tell him, holding my hair away from my face. 'More false hope.'

Evan shakes his head. 'I guessed it must be, but when I first heard . . .'

I'm tired now, and for the first time I can see why Mum prefers not to talk about Bryn. The bay is filled with people who knew him, who want to say how sorry they are, who mean well but open wounds that are barely healing. In the shops and hotels there are curious eyes that pity or look away, embarrassed perhaps, or at a loss how to deal with our pain. It's gone on too long, they've run out of things to say.

Evan waves goodbye at the end of the esplanade and Mum waves back, smiling at him then turning a scowl on me. Dad's already walking ahead, hand held out for Mum. I ignore her backwards glances as she catches Dad up, her mouth set in a tight line that pulls at her cheeks, still rosy from the sea air but sucked in by the cold.

'Well, I don't know,' she tells me as we turn into our road. 'If that boy's not what you want then I just don't know. He still idolises you, do you know that, Seren Spencer?'

'Leave it now,' Dad says and we both stare at him, but he's marching ahead, as surprised by his intervention, it would seem, as we are.

The Welsh rain beats incessantly against my windscreen, the sound exhausting as I cross the border back to England, the bridge swaying in the wind. Dad warned me they might close it tonight, the 'Beast from the East' on its way, but I thought I'd risk it, save ten minutes. I check my phone for the millionth time, my frustration growing at the lack of news. I was with Theo when it happened, I helped him, called for help. I have a right to know how he is.

The service station is heaving, the petrol overpriced. But I was driving on fresh air. I insert my credit card into the reader at the till and tap in my pin number. Then I grab my card and step away, sheltering behind a display of crisps and chocolate to leave a message on Theo's voicemail.

'Theo, if you get this, can you let me know you're OK? I'm so worried about you. Being there, when it happened. God, it was awful. Anyway, sending love . . . to you both, I mean.'

I hang up and stare at my phone.

I'm on a downwards stretch of the motorway, skirting the edge of Bristol and doing almost eighty, the screech of my wipers competing with the clatter of the rain, when my phone rings. I leave at the next exit and pull in as soon as I can, parking at the side of a country road that leads to somewhere I've never visited, nor am likely to. There's a tremor in my hand as I press my thumb to my phone and the notification appears; a missed call from Fran.

Chapter Thirteen

Someone to Blame

I know Theo won't be in his office, but I can't help but look for him there, a tiny glimmer of hope that clings on until the last moment. Behind the glass door Fran is already in Theo's chair, and Lynda has abandoned her post at reception and is seated opposite her. Standing beside Lynda is Simon, his hands resting on our receptionist's angular shoulders which shake violently. She is crying. Not the kind of crying you might expect at a place of work, contained and respectful. No, Lynda's producing big, ugly sobs. It's all wrong. So wrong I don't know where to start. Except I do. I should be sitting where Lynda is and Theo should be in his chair, chomping on a cigar. But Theo is dead.

Simon looks round and meets my reddened eyes with his, then Fran gets up.

'I can't believe he's gone,' I say, stepping back as she opens the door. 'How are you doing?'

'Can we have a quiet word?' Fran asks, headed for the kitchen. 'You too, Simon.'

Simon and I fall in behind her, passing the intern who is manning the phones. I raise a hand to reassure the younger man, let him know I understand this is a lot for him to cope with, and not just the phones. Then Fran glances back and her expression makes me feel like I've done something wrong. Not the wave, something else. Fran ushers us through the kitchen door and a swirl of fear rushes from my stomach into the back of my throat, forming into a half-splutter, half-cough.

Simon closes the door and Fran tells me to take a seat at the kitchen table. Then she points her phone at me and says, 'I called you, Seren. Twice, in fact.'

'Sorry, I must have—' I rummage in my bag. 'Is there any more information about why he died?'

Fran turns a chair towards her and sits astride it, facing me, but it's Simon who replies, his back to the door as he says, 'A stroke, apparently, maybe more than one. It seems pretty clear-cut.'

There's another loud sob from Theo's office. I crane my neck to see better, remarking how Lynda's making a spectacle of herself. 'We're all devastated, not just her.' Simon half-smiles, but then he glances at Fran and again I notice something off-kilter in their silent exchange, an acknowledgement of a grenade yet to be thrown, but which they both know is coming. I flick through the possibilities in my mind, a Rolodex spinning, like the old-fashioned one Theo has on his desk, all his contacts listed, years and years of connections. There's one idea that springs to mind, a stomach-flipping thought, but they surely can't think . . .? Fran's elbows rest on the back of the turned chair as she contemplates her phone. She clears her throat and at that point mine tightens.

'There's no easy way to say this, Seren.' She looks straight at me. 'Theo's wife has made an accusation.'

'*What?*' Blindsided, I shake my head.

'She claims you and Theo were having an affair, which she believes is why you were at their house on Friday night. In fact, she's alleging you were the reason he collapsed in the first place.'

The room tilts and Fran's face slides with it. She's still talking but her words are cotton wool, the room drifting away. I grasp the table and it saves me, but my chair topples. Simon rushes forward, righting the chair as I stumble to my feet. Fran is in front of me, hands on my shoulders, telling me to sit down, guiding me to do just that, then asking if I'm going to pass out, irritated by my display, it would seem. Simon sits beside me.

'I wasn't,' I say, but the rest won't come out.

'You weren't there?' Simon asks.

'I *was* there, but . . .'

His hopeful expression fades.

Fran is talking now, filling the air with malignant speculation. According to Theo's wife, she tells me, we'd been drinking wine, lots of it, and Theo had been smoking again, although he promised he'd given up. I listen, so I can correct this injustice, my defence forming like silent word bubbles which evaporate as my mind skitters. *I* was the unwitting victim of *his* advances. I helped *him*. Called the ambulance. Stayed at the hospital until Nicky arrived. This is so unfair! 'It's not true,' I manage to say. Then louder. 'It's just not true!'

Fran and Simon glance at one another.

'I'm sorry, Seren,' Fran says, not looking sorry at all. 'But we've heard the message you left on Theo's phone. You clearly cared for him, and he you, the amount of time you two spent together . . . everyone had noticed.'

'Yes, but—' I pull my bag on to my knee and search for my phone again, as if I can replay the message to prove my innocence, but it was foolish to call Theo, my words open to misinterpretation.

'Nicky was upset,' Simon tells me. 'And pretty angry. We persuaded her to leave,' he says, crouching down in front of my chair.

'She's been here?'

He nods. 'That's why Fran called your mobile, to suggest you shouldn't come in.'

I retrieve my phone and look at the screen; two missed calls whilst I was driving here. 'It's all a misunderstanding. It was Theo who—'

'We're going to arrange some counselling,' Fran says, interrupting me. 'If you feel you want to take advantage of that . . . Or you, Simon. You knew him the longest.'

Her words wash over me, leaving no trace. 'Theo was fine,' I tell them. 'I called in to discuss my meetings with Max. Then out of nowhere he . . . he—'

Fran looks down at me, but she's shaking her head, dismissing me. 'He wasn't fine, Seren. He'd had a scare before. He was supposed to watch his diet, stop smoking, cut out alcohol, but of course he didn't.'

Why hadn't anyone told me? Why hadn't *he* told me? I think of the pints of beer and endless glasses of wine, as well as the cigars. 'It was him, not me,' I tell them. 'He tried to kiss me. I backed away. I had no idea it was going to happen.'

'Seren,' Simon says, crouching by my chair again. 'We all want to help you, but right now you need to listen to Fran.'

Fran tells him it looks like the intern needs some help with the calls coming in about Theo. 'And leave the door ajar, will you?

'There's a lot of emotion out there,' she tells me, watching Simon as he takes the phone from the boy's outstretched hand. 'Theo was such an integral part of this place, of the whole community.'

I look at Fran and this time I notice the swollen eyes, her grey pallor, the sodden tissue in her fist. She's upset, genuinely so. But there's something else, a steely determination I've witnessed before, mainly when she stood her ground against Theo.

'Feelings are running high,' she says, pacing the small kitchen. 'I suggest you take a few days off, give people a chance to come to terms with what's happened. Do you understand what I'm saying, Seren? People are angry and confused. They are looking for someone to blame. Do you want that to be you?'

I get up slowly, rocking on my feet. *'People? Who?'*

'No one,' she says, fiddling with her jacket. 'Well, Lynda is saying some terrible things, but that's her, isn't it? Theo was well loved, Seren. I know he meant a lot to you too.' She places a hand awkwardly on my arm, patting it. 'I'm truly sorry for your loss, but I'm not asking you, Seren. I'm telling you. I must think of the *Herald* and of course Theo's family. They come first. Take a few days' paid leave, OK?'

'You're asking me to leave right now?'

'I'm not taking sides, but I think it's best all round, don't you?'

'It was him who made a pass at me, Fran. You have to believe that. Nothing was going on as far as I was concerned.'

'I still think it's best,' she says, folding her arms. 'In fact, I must insist.'

'Then you are taking sides!'

I walk unsteadily to the door, then across the office, one foot forward, then the other. An out-of-body experience. The air around me is silent, only the rustle of my coat and the soft fall of my boots on the carpet to accompany my progress. No one approaches me, no one speaks. I don't look up, but I see them all: Lynda, Simon, the intern. Fran catches up with me then walks ahead and opens the door. She asks if there's anyone she can call, a family member, friend? I shake my head, clutching the banister like an invalid as she calls after me that she'll be in touch soon. I push hard on the door to the street and the cold air hits my face. Then I break into a run, my cheeks already wet with tears.

I manage to drive around the corner before I have to stop, thumping the heels of my hands against the steering wheel as I scream, 'No, Theo! This is not my fault! No!'

Chapter Fourteen

The Wrong Choice of Confidant

The bridal shop is shuttered, closed on Mondays unless someone makes an appointment. I climb the stairs slowly and turn the key with a shaking hand. I'm not sure if it's a relief or not to find the apartment is empty. I feel dazed, but my skin is raw as I peel away my coat.

I run hot water into the messy tub – ignoring Izzy's abandoned razors which float to the top as the bath fills – then there's a blissful moment as I allow the scalding water to swallow me up, obliterating everything for a second or two. I break the surface, breathless, and realise my phone is ringing. I grab my mobile from the side of the sink, staring at Theo's name lighting up the screen. '*Hello?*'

'This is Nicky.' There's a long pause before she adds, 'Theo's wife.'

'Nicky, I'm so sorry about Theo.'

She sounds calm, unnaturally so. 'Has Fran told you I came to find you?'

'Yes, she—'

'Why were you at my house, Seren?' Her words are ice thrown into my gut, turning my stomach over. 'I asked you a question!'

'To talk to Theo about my day. About work, I mean. He was my boss, my mentor, I relied on him, but only professionally. Nothing more, I promise.' I can't tell her Theo made a pass at me, it would be cruel. 'I'm so sorry for your—'

'Whore!' she screams into my ear. 'You fucking wh—'

I almost drop the phone into the bath, throwing it instead to the safety of the towelling mat. I stare at it, her voice, hard and full of venom, bounces off the tiled floor. 'Seren! Answer me, you bitch! Answer me!'

I lean over the side and pick it up with a wet hand. Then I try to explain, but she continues to shout, even louder if anything. I can't hang up, it doesn't feel respectful, but when she does I switch off my phone, something I never do.

Eventually I manage to sleep, dreaming of Theo as he tells me he believes in me, he trusts me, he knows I can get the exclusive. Then Nicky is there, and we're both pointing at Theo as he falls to the ground. I gasp and sit up. The bedroom is shadowy. It's late-afternoon. My heart thumps as I switch on my phone, notifications popping up: two missed calls from Theo's number, and an email from Max asking me to call him any time after four.

Max answers on the second ring. I imagine him in his study, talking to me whilst admiring the view from Brooke House. 'I heard about Theo,' he says, which surprises me at first, although I guess it shouldn't. It's probably been announced

193

by the *Herald*. 'Terrible loss,' Max observes. 'Thought I should check on you.'

'I didn't know him as well as you did,' I reply. 'He was just my boss.'

There's a long pause before Max says, 'I wish I'd made more effort over the past few months. You never know when it will be the last time, do you?'

'No, you don't.'

'Nicky must be devastated. I always admired their relationship and they were both very kind to Julia, accepting her when not everyone did. He must have been a great mentor, as well. Seren, are you still there?'

I walk through to the kitchen and sink down on the cold floor, my bare thighs sticking to the tacky vinyl, my baggy tee-shirt all I have to protect me.

'Seren?'

'Theo made a pass at me. I was at his house when he collapsed and Nicky's put two and two together and come up with five. She's blaming me for his death, Max, which is—' I stop, wondering why I'm telling him of all people. But I had to talk to someone. 'Max, are you still there?'

'Did you reciprocate his advances?'

'No, of course not!' I sniff, wiping my nose on my tee-shirt, my nakedness exposed as I lift the hem to my face. 'You knew her, Max; would she want to know what Theo did?'

'I doubt it, would you in her position?'

'I don't know, maybe. You?'

There's another long pause then Max says, 'We need to get the interview done today or I can't see that I'll have time for you.' His tone is dismissive. 'Can you be here at five-thirty?'

'If you can promise to be there this time?' I ask, recovering my composure enough to retaliate. I shouldn't have said anything about Nicky's accusation, it was stupid of me, but I thought he might understand. Clearly Max was the wrong choice of confidant.

'Miriam was supposed to cancel our meeting. I don't know what's wrong with her lately.'

'It's OK, she has a lot to deal with, but it was a wasted trip.'

'Unlike your jaunt to London,' Max replies. 'Jonny said you were *lovely*.'

'I have to do my research, Max.'

'And I have a book to promote!'

'So I hear.' I take a deep breath. 'I don't suppose you'd consider coming to me today for a change?'

'No!' Max replies, then he hangs up.

I force myself to get up, turning on the kitchen tap and grabbing a glass from beside the sink. I drink one glass then another, splashing the freezing water on my face. Then I look around the empty room, wishing Izzy was here. I could do with someone on my side for a change. First Fran, now Max, and Nicky, of course. I consider messaging Iz, but I never want her to feel obligated to me. Sometimes she stays with Dom, disappears for days. I drink more, gulping down the cold water so fast I feel nauseous and have to lean over the sink, retching and coughing. Then I drink again, unable to slake my thirst.

Beyond the long sash window in the sitting room, a few flakes of soft snow float in the air, making their two-storey

195

descent to land on the pavement by my car. Mesmerised, I walk over and try to follow one unique flake's trajectory, but it's soon impossible to tell one from another. The fall is quickening and injecting a sense of urgency into the afternoon. The only thing I have left is the interview. I can't risk losing that, least of all because of something as random as the weather. I grab a pair of jeans and a jumper from my wardrobe and pull them on, searching under my bed for some long-forgotten snow boots. I give up almost immediately and pull on the heeled suede ones I always wear. The quicker I get to Brooke House the sooner I can be back here again, safe and warm, hopefully with Izzy for company and an exclusive even Fran can't help but be excited about.

Nine Months Missing

It's been many months since Katie read the name Julia Blake, although she's thought of her often, in amongst all the other lost souls who populate her subconscious. She scans the forwarded email again, from a journalist at the *Herald*. Katie moves on to the next item in her inbox, but now Julia has been ushered to the forefront of the detective's mind, she refuses to leave. Katie stares into space, her green tea growing cold beside her laptop. They'd been so close to discovering the truth, tantalising glimpses of what really happened that night, but after weeks of blind alleys and still no concrete proof, the DI had said enough was enough and the case was marked with the generic label, 'Missing Until Found'.

The cafeteria is busy as always, but it's a good place to think, and that's what she needs right now. The murder inquiry she's working on is brutal and unsettling. And now Julia is back, looking out at her from a silver frame. Katie's thoughts always return to that photo when she's reminded of Julia. That and the traces of blood spatters on the side of the roll top bath. But people go missing every day – there were at least three that same week, maybe more – so why has Julia remained so present? And now Seren Spencer, 'Junior reporter', has shunted Julia Blake to the front of the queue again. Katie finds DS Chris Green's name on her contacts list, glancing around her as she calls his mobile. She's in a quiet corner, shouldn't be overheard.

'Hey, how you are doing, Katie?'

Chris's friendly tone reminds her what a great guy he is, even if he did make sergeant in half the time it took her. 'Yeah, good, thanks. Tired, you know. Congratulations on the promotion.'

'Thanks. How's the family?' Chris asks.

Katie cuts to the chase; she's never been one for small talk. 'Listen, Chris, that misper we worked on back in May . . .'

'Which one?'

'Julia Blake, Max Blake's wife.'

'Oh right, I thought you meant Emily Plant. I'm back on that case again.'

'Yeah, I saw the new appeal. No, it's Julia I'm interested in. I've had a journalist get in touch via the press office, claims she's interviewing Max Blake, wants to meet up.'

'You think she's got something?' Chris asks, sounding genuinely interested.

'No, just digging, I imagine. I'll drop her a line, see what she wants. Good luck with the new appeal, looks great.'

'Thanks. It's the parents I feel sorry for, poor sods. Emily told them she was going to a friend's house to revise. Only thirteen and she was served in every bloody bar she went to. We've released some new CCTV footage. See if that jogs any memories. If anything comes up on the Blake case, can you let me know?'

'Sure. Take care, Chris.'

Katie types a reply to the reporter then she forces herself to push Julia from her thoughts, other faces crowding in, demanding her time.

Chapter Fifteen

Marriages are More Important Than a Moment of Madness

By the time I arrive at Brooke House the snow is much heavier, churning in the clear country air as dusk falls, although the roads were fine. Should still be OK as long as I'm away from here in the next hour or two. I park my car by the garages and take the chance to check behind them for a contractor's van, but it's been three days since Miriam claimed the cleaners were in the house, my overdue hunt for their van now largely irrelevant. There's a service entrance leading to the perimeter of the estate, just visible as I hold up the torch on my phone, but no vans or any other vehicles parked back there as far as I can see.

'You're early!' Max barks as he answers the door, a concerned look when he spots the snow. 'I suppose we should get on with it, looks like it's starting to settle.'

I glance behind me as I step inside, hoping he's wrong about the weather, but a more pressing concern is Max's obvious bad mood. He walks off without taking my coat, flicking on lights in the corridor as I quickly hang it up on a twiggy hook then rush after him. He's pushing open the kitchen door by the time I'm in the corridor, and he allows it to swing closed behind him without a backwards glance. I grab the door handle and follow him in, tempted to challenge his rudeness, not to mention lack of empathy, he hasn't even mentioned Theo, but something tells me to try a more concil- iatory approach. I don't have to like him. I just have to do my job. 'Look, Max—'

'You want one?' he asks, pointing at the coffee machine.

'Yes, thank you, that would be nice.'

We carry our coffees back across the hallway, barely a handful of words exchanged in the kitchen, our invisible footprints criss-crossing the rug as Max leads me towards the sitting room. I take a seat on the sofa closest to the door whilst Max, without offering an explanation, looks for something which appears to be high on a shelf to the left of the unlit fire. He uses a foot- stool to stand on, reaching up.

'You're right,' I say, watching the snow falling outside the mullioned window. 'I should try to leave fairly soon, just in case it settles.'

Max doesn't reply, but he appears to have found what he was looking for, stepping down to pass it to me.

'What's this?' I ask, setting down my coffee on the table. I take the heavy leather-bound album and open it across my lap.

Max says nothing, climbing on the footstool again. His behav- iour tonight is odd, almost manic. 'Max! Take care!' I say, glancing up from the pages I'd begun flicking through as he almost loses his footing.

Ignoring Max's worrying conduct as best I can, I go back to the album. It's filled with clippings from the *Herald*, each story featuring at least one mention of the Blakes, often with an accompanying image. I look up at Max periodically, but he seems totally preoccupied by his mission, mumbling to himself that he's sure there were more, although the seat beside me is already covered with a precarious pile of photo albums. I look through the next one and the next, amazed at the number of articles on Max and sometimes Julia, from magazines and other newspapers as well as the *Herald*, all stowed away in chronological order. There are also personal photos, as well as her professional portfolio, a large black album filled with eight-by-ten prints, showcasing beautiful shots of the house, grounds and her husband. I return it to Max as soon I'm finished, handling it over carefully as it's clearly a treasured possession. The next album, red velvet this time, is crammed with snaps of Brooke House, in various states of disrepair and then transformed room by room, before-and-afters illustrating how Julia sculpted the estate to her exacting vision. A large patio is captioned 'The Terrace' in a childish hand, which I guess is hers, and on the next page is a photo of a rectangle of clear azure water sparkling beneath a bright blue sky, a single lounger beside it. 'The Pool'.

As I'd suspected, Max has undergone a makeover too with new clothes and a better haircut, the grey replaced by ash blond, and finally the dazzling blue contacts; the contrast in eye colour from earlier photos too great to be a trick of the light. Julia's transformation of her older husband is remarkable, but also calculating. Don't you fall in love with a person because of how they are, not what you hope to make them, or is that immature of me? Other than Evan, I'm hardly experienced, but it feels manipulative and controlling. In Julia's defence, it would appear she applied the same rigorous programme to her own evolution. In the earlier photos, I imagine not long after she met Max, she is naturally pretty, but also scruffy in jeans and shapeless tops, her mousy hair shaggy and unkempt, her expression touchingly innocent at times as she stands arm in arm with her much-older boyfriend, Max. A typical student, she looks happy, if a bit challenging, the V-sign flicked in one, her tongue sticking out at him in another. Later portraits show how she blossomed into a breath-taking beauty, her poise constant, even if her look is hard to pin down; at times bordering on androgynous, then overtly feminine. It's difficult to warm to her, the dark eyes often averted, the smile a little false, but it's also impossible not to admire her style, or ignore the fragility which she tries so hard to disguise. There are no snaps of any extended family, and not even one picture of the gatherings with Theo, Nicky, and Max's other friends.

'I'm guessing it was Julia who collated all of these?' I ask as Max steps off the footstool and joins me, his mission finally complete. 'Must have taken ages.'

Max smiles. 'She kept a record of everything we did together.'

I nod, recalling how he'd told me before that she was an avid reader of the *Herald*, scanning the website and print editions for any mention of them. I take another album from the Jenga pile, this one filled with portraits of Julia taken over the years.

'Who took these?' I ask, looking up for Max's reaction.

'Some of the early portraits were taken by the other students on her course,' he says. If he means Ben, he shows no tell-tale signs of jealousy. 'Some she took herself – that one, for instance.' He leans across and points at a head and shoulders shot of his wife. 'Some were official photos from events we'd attended. She always liked to get a copy.'

Theo said Julia could easily have been a model and I can see why. She was a blank canvas on which she painted a new version of herself over and over, as if the previous one had been erased, hidden behind a relentless search for the perfect aesthetic, each reincarnation chronicled for posterity. The only constants are those dark eyes.

I ask if there are any of their wedding, imagining a lavish affair, maybe in the grounds of Brooke House, tissue paper leaves sandwiched between arty shots, but Max shakes his head.

'The wedding was a low-key affair; a spontaneous thing.' He jumps up to retrieve the frame from the lintel above the fire; the only record of their special day, he explains with a heavy sigh. 'We were married in a registry office,' he says. 'In front of two strangers Julia pulled from the street.' Max smiles at the recollection, but he is clearly displeased with the photo, explaining that one of the ad-hoc witnesses took it, frowning as he passes it to me. 'It's not even in focus.'

The photo is certainly poor, the edge of Julia's profile cut off as she turns away. Confetti flies around them, their faces slightly blurred. Julia is wearing a tulle skirt, a fine-knit jumper tucked in the satin waistband. It's an unusual bridal look but one she manages to pull off. Max is in a suit, charcoal grey, sharp edges and crisp white shirt, no tie. He looks handsome and incredibly happy, the kind of delirium that removes any self-consciousness, but when I look past the confetti I notice something incongruous in Julia's enigmatic expression, the contrast to Max's unbridled joy jarring, even in profile. I look again, trying to work out what she's feeling on what should have been the happiest day of her life. Maybe I'm wrong, reading into her expression something that was never there. She's smiling and looks happy enough, but—

Max takes the frame and gazes longingly at his wife. 'God, she was beautiful, Seren.'

He's lost in a private moment, but it's not that which troubles me as much as the use of the word 'was'. A slip of the tongue, no doubt, a reference to how she looked on their wedding day. Perfectly plausible, except I would never tempt fate by referring to Bryn in the past tense.

Max returns the frame to its place above the fire and sits beside me again, leaning over to point out a clipping from an event they attended and inadvertently knocking the delicately balanced pile of albums. They fall like dominoes, a photo slipping from between the pages and floating to the floor. I pick it up, looking at the much younger version of Julia, her expression defiant although she must only be in her early teens. I pass it to Max, expecting another eulogy about his wife's beauty, but his face falls. 'Breaks my heart,' he says. 'That poor little girl.'

'What do you mean?' I ask, but Max ignores me, tucking the photo back in the album, his eyes anywhere but on mine and, if I'm not mistaken, filled with tears.

★

'So you and Theo?' Max asks once he's returned all the albums to the high shelf. 'What's the truth of it, Seren?' He sits next to me again.

'I told you,' I reply, edging away now that the barrier built of the past is gone. 'There was never anything between us as far as I was concerned, and to be honest I'm tired of being accused of something I didn't do!'

Max holds up a hand to silence me, then he gets up and walks to the window. He delivers his lecture to his reflection, his featured hideously distorted in the whorled glass as he explains, as if I didn't know, that Nicky loved Theo for over two and a half decades. She saw him through previous health scares and the birth of their kids, not to mention two grand-children. 'Marriages are more important than a moment of madness. They have to be.'

'I understand all that, Max, and I'm sure that in your position I'd feel the same, but the point is—'

He spins back to face me. '*In my position?* What does that mean?'

'Nothing,' I say, standing up. 'Maybe we should reconvene when you're less—'

'No!' Max tells me, his voice raised. 'You should explain to me exactly what that comment meant.' His jaw tightens, his hands curled into tight fists. 'Tell me, Seren! What is it you *think* you know about my marriage?'

'I'm sorry, I should go.'

I leave the sitting room, walking fast across the hallway towards the front door, then rip my coat from the hook and grapple with the door handle which refuses to budge. Behind me I can hear Max's leather soles hitting the soft rug, each step increasing my urgency. I push down hard again, pressing my full weight against the cold metal handle which bites into my palm. The door finally frees and I propel myself out into the icy air, only just managing to save myself from careering down the flight of icy steps. I catch my breath and look up, taking in the scene laid out before me. A blueish light has descended, reflected back from a thick settling of snow, and everything, including the slippery steps, is covered in a blanket of pure white.

'You can't possibly leave now,' Max says, standing beside me. 'You'll never make it out.'

Chapter Sixteen

Indispensable

The outbuildings in the deserted courtyard look particularly unloved in the dark, the snow only partially covering their neglect. Max opens the cobwebbed door, a faded sign choked with ivy advising me my home for the night is called 'Lavender Cottage'.

'Mim is next door if you need anything,' he says, pointing at the mirror image cottage to our right, the curtains drawn across the front window, a light on inside.

'Thanks,' I call after him, his shoulders hunched against the blizzard.

I consider tapping on Miriam's door, but Honeysuckle Cottage looks almost as uninviting as its neighbour, and Miriam's proximity is hardly a comforting thought. I close the door and turn the key. Inside it feels dank, the air moist with damp spores, the smell taking me back to my student accommodation. I locate a switch and a bare bulb fizzes to life, the only source of light in the small sitting-room-cum-kitchen. A grubby-looking chintz sofa, worn and too big for the space, faces me. A battered pine table and two matching dining chairs between the sofa and a kitchenette. The kitchen cabinet doors strain against sagging brass hinges, a hob and tiny fridge squeezed in the gaps between. I look in the bedroom, smoothing the faded floral duvet, clammy to my touch, and I open the wardrobe and chest of drawers; all empty. The cottage has the feel of a holiday let – tea bags and sugar stored in the mildewed cupboard above the hob – although it doesn't look like anyone has stayed here in a long time; every surface dusty. *Lavender Cottage.* I repeat the name in my head, trying to recall in which of the outbuildings they found traces of Julia's blood, but I don't think Theo said. I tell myself it wasn't this one, it's far too unloved for Queen Bee Julia to have spent time here, but when I open the bathroom door my heart sinks. At the centre of the otherwise unremarkable bathroom sits a beautiful roll top bath, the edges curved and polished, deep sides enveloping any bather in luxury. *Julia's choice.* It must have been. It's the only item of furniture that reflects her lavish taste.

A knock at the door makes me jump and I almost slip on the tiled floor as I rush to answer.

It's Miriam, and despite my previous misgivings about Max's somewhat scary PA, I find I'm relieved to see her. Although it doesn't appear my feelings are reciprocated.

'Absolutely no way you can drive back?' she asks, her colour-less lips pressed tight as she waits for my response, motes of snow in her halo of curls.

'No, unfortunately not. The drifts by the garages are like

209

this,' I hold my hand up to waist height. 'And Max said the track would be—'

'Yes, he told me,' she snaps, shoving two scratchy towels into my hands. 'You shouldn't have come in the first place. Snow has been forecast for days.'

'You're probably right, but I was hoping I'd be finished before—'

'I wondered what he was up to,' Miriam says. 'Talking to a journalist after all these months. It makes a bit more sense now.'

'*Sorry?*' The implication is clear, but Miriam refuses to be explicit, simply shaking her head. I take a deep breath, swallowing my anger and thanking her for the towels. 'Would you like to come in?' I step aside with forced solicitousness. 'We could have that chat now.'

I put the towels down and fill the kettle, searching for mugs as Miriam takes off her boots then pokes her nose into the bedroom. Then she goes into the bathroom, the door left ajar but not enough to tell what's keeping her other than perhaps a similar admiration to mine of that incredible bath. She eventually emerges, still looking around. Then she fiddles with the controls on the radiators in the sitting room and bedroom, turning the knobs this way and that and commenting how temperamental they both are. I busy myself making the tea, an old tactic of Theo's that's surprisingly effective when you're in someone else's home asking them difficult questions. It also helps having something to do, Miriam's proximity in the unfamiliar cottage intimidating, especially as the snow has marooned me here.

'Sorry, there's no milk,' I say, looking again in the fridge in case a pint has magically appeared. 'Unless you have some?'

'I'll do without,' she replies, running her hand along the table then wiping the dust on her cardigan.

'Is your cottage exactly the same?' I ask, pointing at the shared wall, the floral wallpaper peeling in a particularly damp corner by the ceiling. It feels like an inadequate division, the prospect of sleeping here even more disconcerting with only a thin layer of plaster and paper between me and Miriam.

'A few more home comforts in mine,' she replies. 'As you would expect.'

'You haven't been in here for a while?' I ask as she inspects the kitchen, opening cupboard doors around me.

'No,' she says, adding no explanation as she takes a seat at the table.

'Must be good to be living back on the estate, though,' I observe. 'On hand to oversee everything for Max.' I place a mug of black tea and the sugar bowl in front of her, then sit down with mine, the mug warming my hands. 'Not in the best of circumstances, of course.'

The silence stretches out. She scrapes her teaspoon across the bottom of the mug, the sound setting my teeth on edge. I look around for inspiration, something neutral to kick-start the conversation and spot the barn through the cottage's small front window. 'Is that used as guest accommodation too?' She glances up, following my gaze, then a beat before she shakes her head.

'And what about this place? Many people stay here?' I look

around, the obvious neglect making it seem unlikely. 'Seems a bit . . . unfinished.'

'I wouldn't know,' she replies, sipping.

'Oh, but you would, wouldn't you? Living right next door and working here all these years.'

'I'm not around all the time.' Miriam places her mug down, then looks straight at me. 'Is there something going on between you and Max?'

I slosh my tea on to the table and Miriam dabs at it with a tissue from her sleeve. 'I'm here to finish the interview, that's all,' I tell her, taking a calming breath. 'It's unfortunate I have to stay, but . . .' I point out the snow, still falling. 'Believe me, I don't want to be stuck here, but whilst I am, I'm going to do my very best to get on with my job. Nothing else is going on, OK?'

Miriam shrugs. 'Nothing to do with me. I'm just the hired help.'

I attempt a conciliatory smile, although it's far from how I feel. 'I'm sure you're a lot more than that, Miriam. Clearly you and Max go way back.'

'I should go,' she says, getting up. 'He'll be expecting me for our daily catch-up.' She rests one hand on the door handle, using the other to pull on a boot. 'He pushed it back to six-thirty because you were coming, but it seems you're done.'

'Yes, of course.' I get up too. 'You're obviously completely indispensable. At least, that's the impression I get.' I'm waffling now, and it sounds insincere.

'I do my job, that's all. I always have and I always will. First for Max, then for them both. It's a privilege and a pleasure.'

'Of course, I can see that, but I can't help thinking it must have been difficult for you when Julia took over? I mean, you lost your home for a start . . .'

She sighs, but it appears my process of attrition, 'the broken record technique', as Theo called it, is beginning to wear her down.

'To clarify,' she says, swapping hands to pull on the second boot, 'I still ran the house, took care of Max, professionally speaking, and saw to anything Julia required of me. I was, and still am, as you say . . . completely indispensable.'

'Of course, but those functions you used to go to with Max, you must have missed that side of—'

She turns the handle and opens the door, cold air filling the already cold cottage. I follow her out, calling after her, 'Miriam, before you go. Can I have the Wi-Fi code?'

I wait, shivering by my open door, Miriam's slammed shut. With no phone signal, I feel entirely cut off, Wi-Fi my only hope of keeping in touch with the outside world. Miriam finally emerges, handing me a scrap of paper with a long series of numbers and letters scribbled on it.

'Thank you, and for talking to me, Miriam. You know, I'd never tell Max anything you'd like to say to me in confidence.'

'You're a journalist, Seren, and I'm not a complete idiot, so I'll thank you not to treat me as such.'

I don't get a chance to reply as she turns in the direction of Brooke House and strides off, her bearing heavy in her walking boots, her anorak zipped up against the blizzard. It's only as I glance away that I have the feeling she's watching me instead, but when I look back she's already disappeared.

Chapter Seventeen

Immoral But Probably Not Illegal

No one came to see me after Miriam left. No friendly offers to join Max for dinner, no food parcels left on the snowy doorstep. I eventually gave up and climbed into bed fully clothed in my jeans and jumper, socks too, but sleep didn't come easily, or last long, and the snow kept falling, despite my pleas for it to stop; every settled flake lessening my chances of an early escape. I pulled the damp-smelling duvet around me and lay there with open eyes, shivering in the freezing overnight temperatures for what felt like forever. With no night-time calls to keep my insomnia company – the WiFi has proved at best intermittent – all I could do was listen to my wild imaginings. Lavender Cottage filled with ghosts during the early hours: Julia, Theo and Bryn all visited my sleepless bed during those lonely hours.

The bathroom was the worst, the skylight rattling in the wind. On my second trip – the cold shrinking my bladder – I became convinced the sounds outside were more than the hoot of an owl or the cracking of a twig heavy with snow. There was someone out there.

I crept to the sitting room window, pulling back the thin curtain with a trembling hand. The empty courtyard was thick with cushions of dazzling snow, sparkling beneath the crisp night sky, but there were no footprints as far as I could make out, although the flakes were coming down fast enough to quickly cover any nocturnal movements. I then pressed my ear to the wall between the cottages, but although I'd heard Miriam return around nine, I couldn't discern any further signs of life through our adjoining wall. I assume it must be of more substantial construction than I'd first thought.

Returning to the bathroom, I'd opened the tiny skylight to the stars and stood on the balls of my bare feet, the tiled floor stone-cold and greasy, although it looks clean. Behind the cottages a line of trees was shimmering Narnia-like and as I rose up on my tiptoes I could just make out a light in the dense wooded area behind, arcs of brightness sweeping this way and that amongst the tightly packed trunks. *Torchlight*. I'd continued to watch until the light grew more and more distant, eventually no longer there. Then I climbed back under the duvet and waited for morning to come.

The sky is white and soft now through the bedroom window, the quality of light different, dimmer somehow, although dawn is finally here. The peaks of the far hills could be ski slopes, the winter scene like a Christmas card. My car must be completely consumed by it now, the rust disappearing beneath the drifts that were already well-established last night. I'd insisted Max and I walk round to the garages to check, but he was of course right when he'd told me there was no way out. I hear Miriam's front door slam, her boots leaving ankle-deep prints as she strides off. I tap on the window to attract her attention, but she doesn't look back. No one seems bothered I'm here.

I fill the kettle and plug my laptop in beside the kitchen table, an email from someone called DS Katie Ingles landing in my inbox as it picks up a bit of WiFi. The detective is keen to meet up to discuss my interest in Julia Blake, suggesting the day after tomorrow at ten and asking for my mobile number in case anything comes up and she has to cancel last minute. I reply immediately, hoping it will send, but it shouldn't be an issue driving the ten miles to Police HQ by then; the snow should have cleared long before that. I'll have starved to death otherwise. I laugh at my dramatics, but the thought of being stuck here for another night, even two, isn't funny at all.

I wash at the bathroom sink, splashing cold water on my face as there's no sign of any hot. I'm still wearing the jeans and jumper I slept in, but there's nothing I can do about that. I debate following Miriam up to Brooke House in search of breakfast, but Max had been so unpleasant last night the idea of seeing him quickly overrides my hunger. I distract myself by checking the email has sent, which it has. Whilst there's a burst of WiFi I settle myself at the table and check the local and national news on my laptop. There's coverage of the renewed appeal for the missing teenager, Emily Plant, snippets again of the report I watched with Theo as well as some new

CCTV images I don't recall seeing before, but mainly it's predictions of 'Travel Chaos' due to the snow.

Dispirited by the forecast, I type in the URL for a missing persons website I know well, the site once a regular landing place of mine. I check twice, but Julia isn't listed, which seems odd. It was one of the first things the police did after Bryn went missing. I know relatives can request details are removed, but why would Max do that? Unless he knows where Julia is?

The Welsh listings page still has some familiar faces but also new ones I don't recognise. Some are older, some with foreign names I can't pronounce. Many are unbearably young, with optimistic smiles and tousled hair, their whole lives ahead of them. The saddest cases, the ones I know all too well, go back years, young faces digitally enhanced to an approximation of the adult they would be now. Too many missing people. Where do they all go? Even if they're dead there must be traces left behind, a trail to follow. I scan the faces slowly, looking for my baby brother. Then he's there, staring back at me.

Bryn Spencer

Age at disappearance: 18

Missing From: Aberavon Beach, Port Talbot, South Wales

There's a link to download a poster; another pointless exercise. Dad and I must have attached hundreds to lampposts and fences, as well as a whole day spent stringing them from the railing lining the esplanade and handing them to shopkeepers along the seafront. Evan took stacks too, pressing one into every tourist's hand as they checked in to his parents' hotel. It can't have been good for trade, but my fiancé was insistent, relieved to have something practical to do. For all I know he's still handing them out, along with free tickets to the amusement park and money off at the local ice-cream parlour. I guess it's important to keep trying but there are days, perhaps creeping into the majority now, when I try to pretend it never happened. Is it selfish to want it all to go away and just be normal again? Or even to entertain the possibility he's never coming back? Terrified of tempting fate, I press my fingers on the wooden table. *Touch wood*.

I conclude by re-reading the generic advice for missing persons and their families, although nothing has changed since I last looked. There was a time when it offered me some comfort, a portal Bryn might use to make contact, even if he wasn't ready to come home, but it's become impotent, none of the carefully worded but non-committal guidance bringing us any closer to finding him. The detective in charge of Bryn's case informed us that anyone can go missing, that's their choice. It had felt like a conspiracy, yet another barrier to the resolution I hunted for in every conceivable and inconceivable place. The silent calls have stopped and I'm back to looking for answers where I know they don't exist. Pol warned us it wasn't a linear journey, but that doesn't make it any easier.

I try to empty my mind of the guilt, getting up to press my phone to the window. Not a trickle of reception finds its way in and the WiFi fades away too, which suddenly feels quite desperate. There's been no contact from Fran since I left the office. Correction, was *told* to leave the office. She promised she'd be in touch soon, but maybe she's tried and hasn't managed to reach me. I could have missed loads of calls, including ones from Bryn. He might have wanted to talk this time. I slam my hand against the glass, not hard, but enough to rattle the rotten frame.

I decide to email Fran, my fingers fast across the keys of my laptop as I ask when she thinks I might be able to return to work; I'm keen to get back, maybe remotely at first. I debate the merits of telling her I'm at Brooke House with Max, in case that might sway her decision, but she's hardly been supportive of my exclusive feature and it would mean telling her I'm stuck here for the foreseeable. I press send and watch until it leaves my outbox. Her reply is almost immediate.

Seren,

As I'm sure you are aware, the Herald *is going through a period of huge change as we move into digital-only publication. You were taken on by Theo Smythe for an initial probationary period of six months, which ended a month ago. After careful thought I can see no way we can provide you with a permanent position, especially during these challenging times for the paper.*

I will of course be happy to supply you with a reference for any potential employers and would like to take this opportunity to thank you for your hard work in the time you have been with us. I wish you the best of luck in your future career.

Best wishes,

Fran Simmons (Acting Editor – The Herald*)*

I read it again, disbelief turning to anger. Theo kept putting off my review, saying it was awkward, he'd ask Fran to do it, but he hadn't. He's made it easy for her to get rid of me. I'm only on a month's notice and the *Herald* is always looking for ways to cut costs. If I challenge her Fran can convincingly argue they can't afford to make me permanent. It's immoral, but probably not illegal, and even if it could be deemed constructive dismissal, I don't want to drag my name through arbitration, the details of mine and Theo's close working relationship placed under the microscope. Especially after Nicky's accusation.

So that's it, I'm unemployed. Fran hadn't even mentioned the exclusive with Max, always a bone of contention between us. Professional jealousy has obviously eclipsed her desire for a great story, which is total crap. Whichever way you look at it.

I sit back, staring at the grubby window whilst the snow continues to fall. I'm trapped here, with only Max and Miriam for company, the realisation of that turning my desperation to panic.

Chapter Eighteen

His Muse

By late afternoon hunger and boredom have finally driven me out of the cottage, my paranoia subservient to basic physiological and social needs it would seem. The snow is relentless, but fortunately a pair of wellington boots were tucked under the porch outside my front door. By Miriam, I assume, and the only kindness shown me apart from the scratchy towels since I was offered a bed for the night. The boots are huge, flapping around my calves, my toes scrunched to hold them on. I wrap my coat around me, the turquoise wool soft and warm. It was expensive, even in the January sales, but Mum had insisted on treating me. 'You need something grown-up, love. Now you're a career woman.' I trudge towards Brooke House, the cottages growing smaller at my back, their tiny symmetrical front windows winking yellow light on to the icy path, although Miriam wasn't at home. I'd checked; knocking on her door several times.

The ground is covered in powdery snow, untouched by footprints other than the satisfying trail I leave behind and despite everything, it is very beautiful, the evergreen hedges sagging with plump pouches of wet snow. But as I approach the house my spirits dive. The windows are dark and there's no sign of anyone inside. Then a light is switched on at the window above the door, the curtains drawn quickly across it.

I ring the bell and peer in, assuming whoever was up there will soon make their way down, but the entrance hall remains impenetrable. I knock, then ring the bell again, pulling the chain a couple more times before I give up and descend the icy steps with care. Then I head round the side of the house, in the direction of the garages.

As I'd suspected, the roof and windows of my car are covered with packed snow, glistening crystals beneath the darkening landscape. I swipe at the windscreen with an open palm, but the crust is hard ice, my hand snagging against the rough surface. I suck the grazed skin on the heel of my hand and stare at my only means of escape.

Where is everyone?

It's more sheltered behind the house, the patio slushier so the flagstones peek through in places, the outdoor furniture covers collecting enough snow to produce mini alpine resorts. When I reach the edge of the terrace I turn around to survey the rear of the house. The kitchen extension juts out, blocking most of my view, but I can't see any lights and without knowing the layout, I'm afraid to venture any further.

I'm about to give up and return to my temporary lodgings when I hear a voice in the distance. Taking a few paces onto what I discover is grass, I make my way across the lawn, the ground falling away as it approaches the edge of a steep slope. There's a swimming pool about thirty metres away, ripples forming as the wind that swirls the snow also disturbs the surface of the water, although it looks frozen in places. I shiver and wrap my coat tighter, ready to turn back, when I hear the voice again, the words indistinct but loud. Then I notice a figure seated on the side of the pool, their feet dangling in the water. As I watch, certain now that it's Max, he stands and then he steps off the side, disappearing with a soft splash.

'Max!' I run down the snowy hill, ignoring the flapping boots which slip and buckle. 'Max!'

I fall at the bottom, getting up to cross a flatter expanse. The snow is thicker here and it slows me down, the boots dragging beneath me. I kick them off, one then the other, running in socks through ice-cold slush until my socks also part company with my numbed feet. 'Max!'

I stop at the side of the pool, my chest filled with frozen air, painful as I try to inflate my lungs enough to scream his name. It comes out as a rasp. '*Ma-ax!*' There's no sign of him.

The water had looked clear from a distance, but up close it's impenetrable, the depths brackish. I throw my coat off and dive in, instantly paralysed by the cold as I sink down. I've swum in freezing temperatures before, in my experience the sea is *always* chilly, but this is so much worse, a thousand daggers stabbing my limbs, only my jeans and a jumper to protect me. Then all those early mornings for lifeguard training flood back and I remember we were taught to float first, allowing your body to acclimatise so you don't succumb to the panic and

223

drown, open-mouthed. I push away an image of Bryn thrashing in the sea – he was never as strong a swimmer as me – and wait until the fear and pain ease enough for me to kick out.

There's no method in my search, only frantic dives, my head breaking the surface then back under, my skin then bones attacked by bitter spikes as I search in vain. He must be here. There has to be time. But the water is black, the pool filled with leaves and dirt. I grow more and more desperate, and tired, swallowing and spitting out the stagnant mess.

Then I see him, his tweed jacket a swollen dome at the far end of the pool, his face concealed amongst the debris. Seconds stretch out as I carve through the thick soup to reach him. His head bobs, his body a dead weight and holding him down. I manage to drag him to the edge, but there's no way I can get him out. I can't even turn him over, every movement immediately undone by the pull of the water. I hold him up by his collar but it's exhausting, the cold clamping itself to me as I tread down hard, one bare foot then the other; not that I can feel them. I have no idea if Max is unconscious or even dead, his face turned away, no sound coming from him at all. I'm struggling to get my own breath too, dragged under again and again, my ears filling with liquid so I barely hear the call. But I do see the splash. *That's all I need. Another person to save.*

Miriam is flailing around at the other end, too far for me to reach her without letting go of Max.

'Try not to fight it,' I shout. 'It gets better if you stay calm.'

She nods, retching as she edges closer, her strokes wild, but she's strong, and determined to reach us.

'Can you hold him while I climb out?' I ask once she's within touching distance.

She grasps his collar with both hands and I reach up to the metal steps, but when I look back Miriam and Max are gone. I hesitate, but decide to climb out anyway. I'm no use to them if I go under too. I kneel at the edge and reach out, managing to grasp Miriam's cardigan, then her outstretched hand as it reaches towards me. 'That's good, can you maybe push him up a bit too? Miriam!'

She sinks, but again she proves tougher than I'd thought, forcing Max upwards. Only it's not enough. We try once, twice, and again, but each time his dead weight drags her under. 'One last time,' she splutters, and somehow she manages to get his shoulders clear enough for me to heave him out.

I fall heavily to the slabs, the weight of him sending me backwards. Miriam is out now too, helping me to turn Max on to his side in the wet snow. I run to where I'd cast off my coat, dashing back to throw it over Max's lifeless body. Miriam is on her knees, talking to him, rubbing his face and hands. 'Max, come on. Wake up for me. It's Mim. Please, Max, wake up.'

Max coughs, lifts his head, then vomits water over himself, my coat, and her knees.

'Thank God,' she says, looking up at me. 'Thank God.'

Between us we manage to get Max on to his feet, one of us supporting him under each armpit, his limp hands hanging on to us as best he can. He's drunk, the alcohol fumes on his breath overpowering, despite the stink of chlorine and regurgitated stagnant water. I still can't feel my feet although they're back inside the retrieved wellies, sloshing around. My coat is draped around Max's shoulders so I shiver violently, despite the effort of dragging a grown man up a steep snow-covered incline. 'What were you thinking?' I ask him more than once, no response coming back.

At the house, Miriam props Max between me and the kitchen wall as she tries the handles of each patio door, the far one giving. We drop him on to a chair as soon as we're inside, but he immediately slides off, slithering to the floor beneath the kitchen table.

'Come on, Max,' Miriam says, helping him into the chair again then sitting beside him. She's trying to talk sense into her boss, but he's glassy-eyed, his head lolling, eyes rolling back as he leans to the side. I look away, reminded of Theo.

'We need to call an ambulance,' I tell her, my teeth chattering as I pick up the phone from the counter. 'He could have hypothermia. We all could.'

'No!' Miriam replies, her eyes wide. 'Max wouldn't want that.'

'No,' he says. The first coherent word he's uttered since we saved his life. 'I fucking wouldn't.'

'Make us all a hot drink, Seren,' Miriam suggests as she lets go of Max and gets up, taking the phone from my hand to drop it in the pocket of her wet cardigan.

I look down at my bare feet. A puddle of greenish water has dripped from my clothes on to the pristine white floor. 'I need to get myself cleaned up first.'

Miriam directs me to the 'guest bathroom' and I leave her coaxing Max from his chair. 'Come on, Max. We need to get you changed and into bed.'

I feel around for light switches as I make my way along the corridor and up the dark and unfamiliar stairs, only finding one when I reach the landing. The lights up here are bright, illuminating lots of closed doors on either side. The bathroom is the first one on my right, as Miriam had said. It's a large room, wallpapered in a stylish print of black and purple feathers. I lock the door and take a folded towel from the rail next to a large walk-in shower. Once my hair is wrapped up, I run my quivering hands under the hot tap, although I'm not sure that's the right thing to do, recalling Mum's warnings about chilblains after we'd been in the sea. My hands are bright red by the time I take them out, but at least they've stopped shaking. My sodden jeans are hard to pull down, which is a problem as I'm suddenly desperate to pee. I wriggle the wet denim down to my ankles, then kick them off. I'm still shivering on the toilet when I hear Max and Miriam coming up the stairs.

'Dear God, Max. What were you thinking? I thought we were past this.'

'The pool seemed the right place for it,' he says, his words slurred together. Then, louder, 'I didn't ask to be fucking saved!'

She whispers something in reply.

'What's the point, Mim?' Max asks her. 'She's never coming back.'

I dry my hands on a fresh towel and open the door to poke my head out, my teeth chattering as I look around, but there's no one there. *'Hello? Miriam?'*

She appears from behind the next door along, the one facing the stairs. 'Yes?'

'Is it OK if I use the shower?'

227

'Yes, go ahead.' She glances into the room behind her then says, 'Help yourself to whatever you want. There's plenty of clean towels in there.'

'Thanks,' I reply. 'You need any help?'

'No, we're fine,' she says. 'Just that coffee for Max when you're done?'

I can hear Max ranting again, everything he says now incomprehensible or covered by Miriam's loud shushing as she closes the door. I turn the lock and look around for what I might need. There are two fluffy robes on hooks by the door and some nice products on the shelf built into the shower. I step under the powerful beads of hot water, lathering my hair and body then rinsing until the heat has seeped into every crevice and vein. When I open the bathroom door – the robe wrapped around me, my wet clothes rolled up inside the towel I dried my hair with – all is quiet on the landing.

The kitchen feels strange without Max or Miriam in it, the only signs of them a trail of footprints across the tiles. I drop my wet clothes in the sink and attempt to work out the complicated coffee machine, soon abandoning that idea to make sweet tea instead as I tease out my damp hair with my fingers.

It's tricky carrying three filled mugs up the stairs and I have to place them on the floor before I tap on Max's closed door. 'Miriam? I've brought hot drinks.'

'Coming!' she calls out.

She looks flustered when she opens the door, taking two of

the mugs from me and suggesting I take mine back to the kitchen, she'll be down soon. Then Max calls out my name and Miriam is forced to invite me in.

Max is lying in a large four-poster bed, a blood-red wall behind him. He cuts an insignificant figure, a sweat top visible above the white duvet as he pulls himself up, his hair combed back. There's a trace of a smile on his face, which strikes me as odd. Then I realise he's still drunk.

'Stop staring at me, Seren. I won't fucking bite, woman!'

Miriam tells him off for his use of 'foul language', his temper targeting her this time as she hands him a mug. 'Get the fuck out and leave us alone!'

'Don't speak to her like that,' I tell him. 'She doesn't deserve it.'

'It's fine,' Miriam tells me. 'He doesn't mean it.'

'I fucking do. Get out!'

Miriam leaves, another set of wet footprints left behind, then a slam of the door. He winces at the sound, then frowns.

'She saved your life, Max. You should be a bit more grateful.'

He surveys me across the enormous room, one eye closed, the other beady. 'Sit down, Seren. For fuck's sake!'

'Do you want me to help?' I ask, noticing he's spilled tea on himself and the pristine bedding. I take his mug and set it down on the bedside cabinet as Max brushes dramatically but ineffectually at the stains.

Facing the bed is the large window I stood beneath only an hour ago, the drapes still closed. Someone was in this room, switching a light on and drawing the curtains. Not Max. He was by the pool. Which means it must have been Miriam. She certainly appeared quickly when Max needed help, but why was she was ignoring me? She must have seen or heard me at the door. It's directly below.

Max gestures for me to come over, patting the bed.

'What's going on, Max?' I ask, taking the armchair by the window, careful to arrange the robe to cover my bare legs and feet. I'm still wearing my wet underwear after showering in it, but I feel exposed. 'Did you mean to jump in, or did you fall?'

He looks away. 'Does it matter?'

'I'd say so,' I reply, adjusting the robe again after I've tucked my cold feet underneath me. 'I mean, if you jumped in, and Miriam and I hadn't been there, well, you probably wouldn't be sitting up in bed drinking tea right now. Of course, if you fell, that's an entirely different—'

'OK!' he shouts at me. 'I know what you meant. And the answer's no, I didn't plan it.'

'Is this about Julia?' I ask, more gently. 'I heard you say she's not coming back.'

He closes his eyes, and although I don't think he's asleep, he doesn't speak again. I wait a while, pulling back the curtain to look at the bright moon whilst I finish my tea. Then I whisper that I'll see him in the morning, tip toeing out and quietly closing the door.

Miriam is in the kitchen cutting sandwiches. Her wet clothes are gone, replaced with a similar robe to mine, and her tight curls are washed, revealing pink patches of scalp that make me feel awful for her, although she seems not to care.

'Snap!' she says, smiling at me as if we were at a spa. 'Shall I take that?'

I pass her my mug, resisting an unexpected urge to hug her. I'm not sure what I'm most grateful for; that she was there to help me save Max, or because she's spreading fresh bread with real butter, the meatiness of thick-cut ham making my mouth water.

'I've popped your wet things on a quick wash,' she says, pointing to a door behind us.

I hadn't noticed it before, the sound of a washing machine within.

'The dryer's on the blink, so I'll have to give them to you damp, I'm afraid,' Miriam tells me. 'At least they'll be clean. Are you hungry? I know I am.'

She watches me devour the doorstops of thick granary, the salted butter creamy on the soft but chewy bread, the meat slicked with hot mustard. 'Another?' she asks, pushing the plate across the table towards me and picking at one herself. 'I can make more.'

I shake my head. 'I'll never fit back in my jeans if I do! But thanks.'

'I'm afraid your beautiful coat is rather the worse for wear,' she says, getting up.

'Oh, I forgot about that. Where is it now?' I ask, looking around

'I've popped it in the pantry sink,' she says, pointing to the door in the corner behind which the washing machine has now worked itself up to spin cycle. 'Was it terribly expensive?'

I nod, trying not to cry. 'A gift from my parents.'

'Oh no!' she replies, looking genuinely stricken. 'I'll put the kettle on again.'

Miriam answered an ad, she says, pouring us both fresh tea.

'In the *Herald*,' she explains, smiling at the coincidence. 'Max was writing longhand back then and needed someone to transcribe his manuscripts.' She mimes someone typing with one finger of each hand and laughs as she leans across the table and whispers to me that she didn't think his first writing efforts were that good. 'Don't tell him I said that,' she adds, looking alarmed. 'His typing's improved immeasurably too.'

It's good to see this side of Miriam, our shared trauma bonding us, it would seem, although I still think it's odd she ignored me at the front door.

'Miriam?'

'Yes?' she says, sipping her tea.

'I walked up to the house earlier, rang the bell several times. I think you were upstairs.'

'I don't think so,' she says, putting down her mug as she looks away.

I take the last sandwich from the plate, loosening the waist tie of the robe. There doesn't seem much point pressing her further; she's obviously lying.

'So you and Max go way back?' I say, returning to our previous conversation.

'Oh yes. And before you ask, I can assure you it has always been a purely professional relationship.'

I splutter, picking up my tea and swallowing fast to clear

my clogged throat. I cough again, smiling to reassure her I'm recovered. 'Sorry, went down the wrong way. I'm fine.'

'Are you sure?'

I nod, coughing again. 'I believe you, of course. But I'm still having difficulty accepting that it wasn't a problem for you when Julia came to live here?'

'Not in the least,' she replies.

'I'm sorry, Miriam, but how can you say that? You lost your home!'

She glances around the kitchen, as if she's taking in this information for the first time.

'The thing you have to understand, Seren, is Max's writing supports this way of life. Brooke House, Max, Julia . . . all of us are dependent on his success. I think it's important to always be mindful of that. The words started to flow again once Julia was here.'

'She was his muse,' I say, taking another swig of tea.

'I wouldn't call her that.' Miriam bristles, or maybe it's a shiver. 'Every writer has their peaks and troughs. It's an art, not a science. Creativity requires passion, and confidence, a certain ego. Julia was a breath of fresh air, transforming him and this place. Although . . .' she pauses. 'Maybe he'd have found his way back without her. We'll never know, will we?'

'You don't think she's coming back either? I heard what Max said.'

Miriam checks I've finished then takes my plate, pushing the discarded crusts into the sink.

'Do you think he was trying to end it all tonight?' I ask,

determined to get some answers whilst Miriam is still reasonably amenable.

'Don't be silly!' she says, swivelling the handle to run the cold tap, the grind of the waste disposal unit obliterating my attempt to discuss the events at the pool further.

I push my bare feet into damp wellies whilst Miriam runs to the pantry. She returns with my washed clothes crammed into a plastic carrier bag and a bedraggled lump of turquoise which she drapes over my arm. I rarely cry, not at the big things anyway, but for some reason this chokes me up. Miriam apologises for the state of my coat and explains she's tried to sponge the worst off, but it was a hopeless task. The stench is horrific, a mix of dirty pool water and vomit.

'It's OK, you did your best,' I say, sniffing.

'Yes, but,' she replies, looking thoughtful, 'Max will pay for a replacement, I can assure you of that.'

I must look like a mad woman in my oversized bath robe and wellington boots, the supermarket carrier bag twisting on my wrist as I walk back to the cottages alone, my coat held at arm's length, although the smell is unavoidable. Thankfully, Miriam had the presence of mind to suggest I check my coat pockets before I set out. I found my phone tucked deep inside one and mercifully undamaged, but the key to Lavender Cottage was missing from the other, presumably lying buried somewhere in the snow. I hold a spare in my hand, the silver glinting in the moonlight as I pull the hood of the robe over my still slightly damp hair.

By the time I reach the courtyard the boots have rubbed blisters on both my bare heels. I kick them off outside and close the door, relieved to be back in the cottage after this evening's dramatic events. It's only as I climb under the duvet — still wearing the robe, my wet underwear now draped on the radiator — that I recall Miriam's words, and why the phrase she used unsettled me. *The words started to flow again once Julia was here.*

She was referencing Max's writer's block, telling me how meeting Julia had rekindled his dwindling career. What's troubling me is that Max said something similar, how his words were flowing again since my arrival. I turn on to my side and push away the unwanted comparison, burying myself beneath the covers. I'm dry, well-fed now too, but the chill runs bone-deep. Brooke House has too many secrets, and the longer I'm here, the more entangled in them I become.

Chapter Nineteen

Some Kind of Saint

I climb out of bed and draw back the curtains to an eerie hush. The whiteness is dazzling, the courtyard and barn opposite covered in a fresh fall of silent snow. It must have been coming down all night.

I slept better last night, no calls to disturb me, and I was exhausted after dragging Max from the freezing water. The surfeit of sandwiches had filled me up too, making me drowsy . . . but this morning I'm empty, a pool of fear in the pit of my stomach. No one knows I'm here, my only means of communication via patchy WiFi, and no method of escape. Even when the snow clears and I'm able to leave, what do I have to go back to? No job, and possibly no home if I can't pay my half of the rent. Iz can't sub me, she's always broke. I consider emailing the detective to tell her where I am, as a precaution, maybe ask her to send help, but what exactly am I asking to be rescued from? The snow? There's no specific threat at Brooke House, just a general sense of unease.

The reek of gently warming damp wool mixed with vomit drags me from the bedroom, the stench permeating every corner of the cottage. My coat is on the radiator in the sitting room, the only warm one in the cottage and the damage is, as I'd feared, irreparable. My jeans and jumper are over the side of the bath, and on inspection still far too damp to wear and likely to stay that way for some time. At least my undies have dried out, well almost.

I fill the kettle, rummaging in my bag whilst I wait for the water to bubble. I suppose I have Theo to thank for the few essentials I have with me, his advice to always carry chargers, as well as a notepad and pen, drummed into me from day one. 'You never know when you'll be glad of them,' he'd warned, the memory now bitter-sweet. I added to his inventory a few items of my own: tampons, mascara, lipstick, a packet of paracetamol and a mini toothbrush and toothpaste, as well as a pack of plasters. I clamp one over each of my blistered heels and brush my teeth.

Feeling better, I take my black tea to the kitchen table and open my laptop. Mum's sent a long message with all their news. A busy start to the week, she says, but nothing to report. She's always careful to begin her updates with that rider, as if she'd tell me anything about the search for Bryn, good or bad, via an email. She asks if I've lost my phone, saying she tried to call me last night but couldn't get through. I reply quickly so she doesn't worry, telling her I forgot to charge it, and asking if they have any snow in Wales. She sends me a picture of the garden, not a flake in sight, although it's raining there. I look at the grey slabs that sit behind Mum and Dad's terraced house, a square of grass behind them, our old playhouse next to the wobbly fence. It might as well be the other side of the world.

The other emails are junk and the finality of that is disappointing. Fran must have already removed me from the work correspondence round-robins. To confirm that, I try to log on to the server and find my account has been suspended, my password invalid. She's erased me from the *Herald*'s staff without a moment's hesitation, along with all my correspondence with Max and Theo, and, I realise, DS Ingles. It's another slap in the face, an injustice too far. I should have refused to leave the office, stood my ground from the start, but I was in shock. All I have left is the exclusive with Max, and if the *Herald* want to cast me aside so easily then I owe them nothing. I open a blank document and start to type, the familiar feeling of anticipation energising me as my fingers begin tapping away.

It must be an hour, maybe more, before three firm raps on the door interrupt my concentration. 'Hold on a sec!' I save the document and close my laptop, cinching the robe before I answer the door.

Miriam is huddled against the cold, a padded coat adding to her substance, the fur-lined hood framing her ruddy features. I invite her in and she stamps the worst of the snow off her boots and onto the mat, stepping inside in her socks. Noticing my attention on her feet she regards mine, bare beneath the hem of the robe. 'My goodness, Seren. You'll freeze.' She looks around, pulling a face, her nose wrinkled. 'What's that awful smell?'

I look down at my coat, the offending article now thrown in a heap on the floor.

'Oh dear.' She smiles at me in sympathy and holds out an overfilled plastic bag. 'I've brought you a jumper and jeans, but I didn't think about coat or socks. Hold on!'

I wait at the open door whilst Miriam disappears into Honeysuckle Cottage. She returns bearing a pair of identical woollen socks to the ones she's wearing. They're probably the only things she's provided me with that will fit, although I don't suppose it matters if the jumper is huge. It looks lovely, not her style at all.

'Thanks.' I take the balled socks, the wool prickly in my palm. 'I'll return them when I leave.'

'Don't worry,' Miriam replies. 'I've got loads of pairs. I'm a keen walker.'

'Around the estate?' I ask, recalling the torchlight I'd seen the night before last.

'Yes, that's right. Anyway, can't stop, but I'll try to find a coat whilst I'm up at the house, and something for you to eat.' She opens the door. 'And don't forget to try on those clothes,' she calls back. 'Should be about the right size.'

I'm a bit insulted if I'm honest. Miriam must be at least three sizes bigger than me. I close the door and pull the clothes from the bag, throwing the door open again the second I realise my mistake.

'Miriam, wait!'

She's nowhere in sight, the blue-white path of snow already empty, my words echoing back.

The jeans aren't a bad fit. A bit snug, but there's enough stretch in the high-quality denim to make them wearable, and very slimming. I twist round in front of the wardrobe mirror. I'm impressed by the brand; not one I could afford myself. The soft pink jumper is a boxy shape and drapes beautifully. I check the fabric label to find, unsurprisingly, that it's pure cashmere. I admire myself again, turning to the side and affecting a pout like the one Julia has in the photo on Max's desk. To complete the look, I pile up my hair with an elastic band I find in my bag.

After the distraction of my makeover I return to work on the article, but I'm side-tracked by every rustle or creak from outside. At least my feet are warm now, although it's unpleasant to think I'm wearing Miriam's walking socks. I resist the urge to tear them off, the chunky wool in such contrast to Julia's stylish jeans and jumper.

Finished with the feature for now, I read Theo's obituary on the *Herald*'s homepage. Then the eighty-seven comments underneath which are universally complimentary. It's clear the *Herald*'s long-serving editor was well known and well liked, and although I hate to admit it, Fran has done a nice job with the obit. She's used a flattering photo too, one I recognise from Theo's LinkedIn profile, but it's Nicky's name that stands out for me. *His grieving widow.* I close my laptop, taken by a sudden need to get out of here, cabin fever setting in.

I poke my head out into the icy air, but there's no sign of Miriam returning with the promised coat. I'll just have to brave the cold without it for now. The wellington boots are a snugger fit in Miriam's thick socks, my blistered heels chafing despite the plasters.

'Did you hear me coming?' Miriam asks, striding towards me as I close my door.

I spin round. 'Where did you come from?' I ask, glancing behind her to the empty path that leads up to Brooke House, not a footprint to be seen.

She doesn't reply, staring at me as if she's never seen me before.

'*Miriam?*'

'Yes, sorry, it's just you look so . . . different. Anyway, more jeans and another jumper in there in case you need them.' She hands over a stuffed cotton tote bag, a pretty cable-knit sweater sticking out the top. 'And something for breakfast,' she says, passing me a plastic bag containing the loaf from last night and some wrapped butter. 'And finally this!' She holds out her left arm, over which is a very long, very expensive-looking camel coat.

'Miriam, this is really kind of you, but are you sure it's OK with Max? I assume these are Julia's clothes?'

'He probably won't even notice,' she says, persuading me to turn around as she holds up the coat to my back and slips it on my shoulders. 'There, turn around! Yes, that will do. You look lovely in it, Seren,' she says, with a nod and smile. 'Really lovely . . .' she trails off, bending over to brush snow from the tops of her boots.

'I'm still not comfortable about this,' I say, looking down at the hem, now dragging on the slushy courtyard. 'Besides, the snow has pretty much stopped now. I should be able to go home later.'

Miriam sighs and straightens up. 'I have no reason to persuade you to stay, but believe me, there's no way on earth you'll get your car out today. The drifts are worse than ever. It's impossible, Seren.'

'Maybe if we dug my tyres out? I don't mind doing it if you can point me in the direction of a shovel.'

Miriam regards me with disbelief. 'Even if we dug a path all the way up the drive, the track will be impassable. Unless—' She stops talking. 'No, probably best not.' She catches my eye. 'I'm sure it will all be melted soon and we can get back to the way we were.' She pats the arm of Julia's coat. 'I'm so glad it fits you. And the other things. Sorry there's not more, but most of what's left is occasion wear, not really what you need.'

I want to ask her where Julia's other clothes have gone, but a more pressing thought takes precedence. 'Unless what, Miriam?'

'No, nothing. Like I said. A day . . . two at most.'

'Miriam, if there's a chance I can get out of here before that, you better tell me now, or I'll . . . I'll march up to the house and bang on every door and window until—'

'OK!' Miriam says, her palm raised to silence me. 'There is a way, but Max really won't like it. I assume that's why he hasn't offered, at least I hope that's why. Oh gosh, I don't think I should say, but maybe it would be better if—'

'Miriam! Just tell me!'

Max is seated at his desk, hunched over his keyboard, his back to us, headphones on. He removes them slowly and turns his chair to address Miriam, ignoring me.

'This is what I pay you for, isn't it? To ensure I'm never interrupted.'

He looks terrible, his skin waxy and pale, and his voice is

croaky, which I guess is to be expected after last night's unscheduled swim.

'I'm so sorry, Max. I tried to stop her, but—'

'Yes, she did,' I say. 'But you've pushed me too far this time, Max.'

'Can one of you please tell me exactly what this is all about?' he asks, standing up. 'I am trying to write a book!'

'I'm so sorry, Max,' Miriam says, stepping forward. 'She came in through the patio door. We need to keep it locked in future, don't you think?'

Tired of them talking about me as if I wasn't here I shout as loud as I can, 'You have a fucking four-by-four, Max!'

He winces, a hand to his forehead.

'A great big Range Rover?' I prompt. 'That could easily get through a ton of snow?'

'Yes, I understand what you mean,' he says, slumping back down. 'Can you leave us alone, Mim?'

She instantly backs out, and with such deference I almost laugh, except she shouldn't be bowing and scraping to him and I'm fuming. Max instructs me to sit down and when I refuse he looks at me oddly, as if he's just noticed something. He gets up and grabs the sleeve of Julia's coat. 'Are you wearing my wife's clothes?'

'Yes, I believe they're hers.' I shake him off. 'I didn't have anything dry after last night's . . . incident.'

'So you thought you'd steal Julia's?'

'No, I did not! Miriam brought them to me. And don't blame her! If you hadn't vomited over my coat and I hadn't had to jump in a stinking pool fully clothed, then—'

'OK, I get it,' he holds his hands up. 'It was a shock, that's all. I haven't seen her things in such a long time and you and she are so . . .'

We stare at one another.

'I'd like to go home now, please,' I tell him, folding my arms.

'Can we please sit down,' he says. 'My head is pounding.'

I consider this for a moment, but he does look awful. Julia's dark eyes regard me with contempt when I take the visitor chair, which strikes me as odd as the photo is usually turned to face Max's side of the desk.

'My wife used to wear her hair up like that,' Max says, taking a packet of paracetamol from his desk drawer and throwing back a couple with a swig from his water glass. 'And that jumper was one of my favourites. The shade really suited her.'

I pull the cuffs of the pink jumper into my palms and dip my chin into the high neck, wishing I could turn away Julia's accusatory stare. 'Are you going to explain why you didn't offer me a lift home?' I ask. 'It's tantamount to kidnapping.'

'That's ludicrous!' he says, leaning an elbow on the arm of his chair, and it slides off. He doesn't seem as angry as when I barged my way in, just hungover. 'You're right about one thing, though,' he says. 'I haven't been entirely honest with you and that's bothering me.'

'Go on.'

'OK,' Max says, clearing his throat several times. 'I know about . . . I know about your missing brother, Seren. I know about Bryn.'

This was not what I was expecting to hear, not at all. Maybe it crossed my mind when I first found out about the interview, or when Max had talked about me understanding his loss, but not now. I'd anticipated explanations, confessions, declarations. Not this.

'*How?* I don't understand. How long?'

'I'm sorry, I should have been honest with you from the start, but Theo felt your situation might impact—'

'*Theo?*' I stumble to my feet.

'Seren, please. Sit down. Let me explain. It's not as bad as it sounds.'

'It sounds like you and Theo cooked up an elaborate lie to get me here. Using my personal tragedy to your own advantage. But please do tell me if I've got that wrong.'

'Theo cared for you, Seren,' Max says, standing unsteadily to face me across the desk.

'Don't tell me what Theo felt! He tried to seduce me, Max! He was grooming me!'

'Now you're being ridiculous.' Max shakes his head then grimaces, sitting back down. 'Theo was happily married.'

'*Now I'm being ridiculous?*' I thump the desk with my palm and he looks up. 'You were pretty quick to damn me. Besides, no one who's happily married . . .'

'Go on!'

I push past him to make my escape, but Max spins his chair to face me, his hand shooting out to catch hold of my wrist. I scream and he immediately lets go, but he's scared me. I run to the door and grab the handle.

'Seren, I'm sorry. Please wait. I need to explain.' Max is behind me. 'I thought if I told you we could . . .'

'We could what, Max?' I turn around and he backs away, bumping into his chair.

'I'd like you to stay and write the article,' he says, leaning against his desk. 'I know I've messed you around, been difficult, but I'm being honest with you now.'

'*Honest?* You don't know how to be honest. I can't believe I fell for all your lies, and Theo's.'

'Oh, for goodness' sake, Seren, drop the dramatics.'

'*Dramatics?*'

'Yes, dramatics!' he says, frowning back. 'You know Theo was always well researched, it can't be a shock to you he knew your brother is missing. He'd worried enough about you writing the original piece, but he said you were insistent.'

It hadn't occurred to me Theo knew about Bryn and was looking out for me. It's a shame that concern was then outweighed by his desire for an exclusive, and his desire for me. 'How noble of him to think of my feelings,' I tell Max. 'I bet he didn't protest much when you suggested the exclusive though, did he?'

'It wasn't like that,' Max replies, still perched on the edge of his desk, a hand steadying him as he falters. He looks really pale. 'I had to persuade him by pointing out you'd already written about the pain of losing someone. He eventually agreed he'd pitch it to you, but even if you agreed, he insisted I mustn't mention Bryn unless you brought it up first.'

'Theo warned me you can spin a good story when you need to,' I reply, no idea who to trust any more. 'It's all an act, though, isn't it? Charming Max with his easy manner and effortless style.'

Max looks caught between a smile and a scowl. 'Can we agree we've both got more than we bargained for?' He rubs the back of his neck above his open collar and I notice a sweat mark in the pit of his shirtsleeve. 'Circumstance has certainly thrown us together, and I for one—'

'But that's not true, is it?' I say, stepping forward. 'You could have driven me home in your wife's great big fuck-off Range Rover any time you liked, but you'd rather keep me here.'

'No, that's not—'

'You think I'm your puppet. That I'll write a sympathetic story, turn your fortunes around.'

'Now hang on a minute . . .' Max says, standing up.

'Quite a neat arrangement for you!' I say, on a roll now. 'Suspected wife killer to bereft husband in one article, and a substitute Julia into the bargain.'

I stop talking, but not soon enough. Max's expression is thunderous as he moves closer, the scent of his sweat hitting me, his palms clenched. 'That's grossly unfair and totally wide of the mark. You have no idea what—' He takes a deep breath then backs away, picking Julia's photo up from his desk. 'I love my wife with all my heart.'

I can't abide it any longer. The farce of it. The lies, the ridiculous pretence that she's some kind of saint. 'You know who took that?' I demand, standing beside him so we are both staring down at Julia's photo.

Max says nothing but his fingertips are white as he grips the edge of the frame.

'Ben Fortune.' I spit the name out. 'They'd fucked before

247

he took it, but you knew that, didn't you? She was a bitch, Max! A Grade A, first-class fucking bitch!'

There's a beat, then Max swings his arm back and the photo flies from his hand, narrowly missing me and hitting the wall beside me. We both stare at the mess on the floor, Julia's face covered in broken shards of glass.

'Max, I—'

I don't wait for his reply, rushing out the door, then along the unlit corridor, almost tripping on the edge of the rug as I reach the hallway. The front door resists, but I know it will give, then I'm down the frozen steps and across the drive, surrounded by snow, blinding whiteness stretching in every direction.

Nine Months Missing

DS Chris Green has held up the photo so many times and to so many people he now does it with little expectation. No one can remember seeing his misper and he's due to visit the family later today to update them. The latest appeal hasn't produced the results he'd hoped for, just a few false leads heading them back to the terrible conclusion Emily Plant is unlikely to be found. It's been heartbreaking for everyone involved.

As he leaves the taxi rank, he flicks through the other photos on his phone and eventually finds the one of Julia looking up at him from a silver frame, provocative as ever. *He would have . . . given the chance*. He smiles at the weirdness of that thought and goes back in.

The man behind the desk pulls an admiring expression at Julia's photo, then he shakes his head and returns to his call.

Chris leaves, empty-handed again, but there's something niggling away at him. It's to do with taxis and the fact Julia Blake vanished into thin air, but he can't quite put his finger on it.

If Barry the mechanic is to be believed, her car was at his garage from the morning before she disappeared, and Max and

Miriam's cars were both accounted for; parked in and by the garages at Brooke House respectively and not a mark on either of them, he'd checked himself. Julia didn't strike him as the kind to leave on foot, and she was wearing a thin dress and high heels, plus it was a remote location, no footpaths or bus routes. Or CCTV, unfortunately. She must have had help. Or she never left.

He and Katie had mapped out everything on a white board late one evening. Their shared frustration keeping them until the early hours as they'd obsessed about the timeline and when the various party guests came and went. Chris had interviewed them all: the pleasant gay guys in London, both in publishing, Jonny and . . . can't remember. Then there was the married couple in a fuck-off Georgian house in town. She was sour-faced, Fiona something, and her husband was a complete wanker. Lawrence Townsend; that was it. And lastly Theo and Nicky Smythe, holding hands in their old-fashioned bungalow. Theo had puffed on a cigar after his wife left for work, offering Chris a very decent port as they chatted in the conservatory. Chris had been saddened to hear of Theo's death; he'd been good company, interested in police work and in a small way responsible for Chris's early promotion. 'Seems to me you're more than capable,' Theo had told him, slapping Chris on the back as he'd seen him out. 'Go for it! Why not? We only get one life, need to live it to the full.'

No, it wasn't Max's dinner guests that troubled Chris. They'd all driven their own cars home, some of them probably over the limit, but nevertheless away from Brooke House by just after eleven.

Ben, an ex-boyfriend of Julia's, left in a taxi with Laura, the waitress, and Ben's ex-girlfriend, Carys, around midnight, or just after. But none of them could recall the car or driver in enough detail to be of any help, let alone supply a licence plate.

So what the fuck was it they'd missed? A dropped stitch, as Katie put it. That was the understatement of the year.

Chris turns around and goes back into the taxi rank for a third time, pushing past the queue again.

'A booking was made,' he tells the guy on the phone who is clearly not happy to see the detective returned. 'I've got the name of the catering company,' Chris says, checking his phone.

Chris watches as the details he provides are typed into the booking system, the calls still coming in as the hassled owner multi-tasks.

'I'm sure I spoke to your lot at the time,' he tells Chris, scratching his bald pate with one hand as he moves the mouse up and down with the other.

'Yeah, just want to make sure it's been followed up.'

They'd tried to trace the taxi driver for weeks. Hours and hours of CCTV watched, calls made, doors knocked. Chris can't recall the exact circumstances, just that they'd drawn a blank. Katie would remember it all, no doubt, but whilst he's here . . . may as well check it out.

'Oh, yeah,' the owner tells him. 'That was it. Bloody Cal Diamond. Knew I shouldn't have taken him on. Few too many no-shows on his shifts.'

'So he definitely went out to Brooke House at midnight?' Chris confirms.

'Yeah, claimed they'd already left. He buggered off couple

251

of days after that. Went travelling, spending my profits, I think. Mind you, one of the other drivers said they'd seen him in town last week; tan and dreadlocks, apparently. I told them, if you see him again tell him he owes me! All those bloody no-shows, he must think I was born yesterday.'

Chris scribbles down Cal's details again and dashes off a quick message to Katie. It's probably nothing, but he has a feeling he might have just worked his way back to the dropped stitch.

Chapter Twenty

Reason Enough to Kill

The snow is disorientating, the landscape homogenised. I barely notice where I'm going, stumbling across the uneven ground, unsure if I'm on the gravel drive or if I've reached the start of the bumpy track. Ahead of me are the woods, then miles of icy lanes. There's nowhere to run, but I do, the smashed photo frame crashing to the wall again and again in time with my feet, the things I said about Max's wife swirling in the mess of my thoughts. How could I have been so foolish? I'm stuck here, completely at his mercy.

'Seren? Wait! I'm sorry I lost my temper.'

I stop, turning back to confront Max. 'Are you going to take me home?'

He stops too, his words staccato between gasps. 'I promise I was working myself up to it . . .' He is still catching his breath, his hands to his knees, his back bent. He looks like he's about to throw up. 'It's a reminder of her . . . the car . . . you can understand that, can't you?'

'No, not really,' I reply, although I do, in a way. I still drive the car I shared with Bryn, but maybe if I had a choice I wouldn't, especially as every time I look at the broken wing mirror a pang of guilt punches my gut. 'It's just a car, Max. Or is there more to it than that?'

'I'm probably still over the limit,' he says, half-joking.

I heave a sigh.

Max takes a deep breath, looking back at the large and empty house. 'I've tried to move on, I really have. This reclusive life I live, it's not necessarily by choice. The offers that have come in since . . . they're insulting, or in poor taste. The truth is, you're right. I have enjoyed having you around. Is that so terrible?'

'You don't show it,' I reply, looking away.

'I know,' he says. 'And I'm sorry if I've been distant. I've felt conflicted. Disloyal to Julia, although of course I've no need to.'

'I'd like to leave now,' I tell him. 'Are you going to take me, or do I need to make a fuss?' I maintain my indignant attitude although we both know I have few, if any, other options.

'No, no fuss required,' Max replies. 'I was already planning on offering to take you, believe it or not. Don't look at me like that, it's true! I have a dinner, in town. A charity event. I was just reconciling myself to the fact I'll have to take the Range Rover as the snow hasn't melted.'

'*Dinner?*' I chase after him as he walks towards the house. 'I want to go home *now*, Max.'

He stops at the top of the stone steps and turns around. 'I have a routine, and it's already been severely disrupted. The book, well, deadlines have been missed, which has been tolerated by my publisher, up to a point . . .' He checks his watch. 'Around six OK with you?'

'I don't have much choice, do I?'

'Not really,' he says. I'm stomping back down the steps when he speaks again. 'I don't suppose you'd like to be my plus-one tonight?'

Wrong-footed in every sense I look up. 'Are you joking?'

Max frowns. 'No. I just thought—'

'You honestly think I'd want to join you for dinner?'

'If you let me finish!' He unclenches his fists. 'I just thought maybe it could be part of your story, background stuff. A speech, book signing. I assume you can use that? A journalist friend of mine has agreed to review the new book in exchange for a quick interview, so—'

'You're speaking to another journalist?'

'Only about the new book. I explained you have the exclusive. He's interested to meet you. Jamie Porten, you may have—'

'*Jamie Porten? The* Jamie Porten?'

'You've heard of him?'

I take a step up, then check myself, my enthusiasm getting the better of me.

'I'll drop you home straight afterwards, of course,' Max says. 'Where do you live?'

I tell Max the name of my road, reluctant to give him the full address. We agree it wouldn't be too far out of his way – the event is at a hotel the other side of town – but I'm not taking in the details, too busy processing what's been dangled before me, a carrot I fear may prove irresistible. Max doesn't know I've lost my job, but even if I hadn't, Jamie Porten would be an immensely important contact. My thoughts skip ahead to a splashy byline, a double-page spread in a national daily, the holy grail. Or maybe a glossy feature in a Sunday supplement with a brooding shot of Max in front of Brooke House. My outrage at Max's deception is already paling by comparison.

'Can I assume you're coming with me?' he asks.

'I'll need to think about it.'

Max shrugs as if it makes no difference to him, but he's clearly disappointed. He thought he'd won me round, but I can't let him manipulate me. If it feels right I can accept later, although I'm seriously tempted. It would only delay my return home by a few hours, and it's not like I'll be alone with Max other than in the car.

'Let me know by five-thirty,' he says, losing patience. 'I'll be finishing then to get changed.' He's about to close the door when he picks up on the fact I haven't moved. 'Was there something else, Seren? I do need to get back to my writing.'

'Yes, of course, it's just . . .' I've wanted to ask this question for a while, as much for myself as for the benefit of the article, and now it seems I may not get another chance. 'Do you . . .' I clear my throat and climb the remaining steps to face him. 'I was wondering if you remember the last thing you said to your wife?'

Max doesn't shift his focus from me, but there's sadness in his eyes, and maybe I'm reading too much into his expression, but is there some remorse there too?

'I do, unfortunately,' he replies. 'Do you recall the last thing you said to your brother?'

I'd like to tell him it's none of his business what I said, or failed to say, but I don't, settling on the compromise of silence.

'I shouldn't have asked,' Max says. 'But in fairness, you asked me first.'

'And you haven't answered.'

'No, I haven't.'

I take a deep breath, understanding the onus is on me to end this stalemate.

'If you must know, I told him he was a bloody useless brother,' I say, quickly adding, 'I didn't mean it!' Maybe I'm trying to convince myself, or possibly it's Bryn I'm hoping to reach, but it's Max I tell. 'It was stupid, over nothing. We shared a car, the one round there.' I point in the general direction of the garages. 'Bryn was new to driving, caught the wing mirror reversing into a parking space.' I inwardly shrink at the recollection of Bryn coming to me as an ally, afraid of what Dad might say, and how I'd let him down, allowing him to leave for the beach that day without retracting my unkind and untrue words. 'God, I wish I could take it back, say the right thing, tell him how much I—'

'I told Julia I hated her,' Max says. 'How's that for a parting shot?'

'*Why?*' I ask, my voice disappearing.

He shakes his head slowly. 'I don't blame her, Seren. I blame myself. She didn't know what she needed. She thought she did, but she was mistaken.'

'Mistaken about what?'

He's about to tell me something vital, I can feel it. Then I witness the mental retreat, the rearrangement of his features into a false mask of nonchalance as he checks his watch again, remarks how the morning's almost over, he should get back to work, too much time lost already. I can hear Theo in my head, urging me to be more assertive, dig it out of Max, whatever it is, but Theo's not here.

The front door closes and I walk away, the cold air snatching at my breath and stealing my thoughts, Julia's coat trailing on the ground, the hem snagging on the crust of ice, a million diamonds beneath my rubber soles as my blisters bite into my heels.

I follow the snowy path back down to the cottages, the high hedges guiding me along the track, Max's words replaying in my head. He hated his wife and told her so, but perhaps he didn't mean it any more than I meant what I said to Bryn. Love and hate, so often twinned emotions. But reason enough to kill? I shiver and break into a run, hobbling after a few paces.

As I reach the courtyard I stop, doubling back to a gap in the hedge. I stifle a gasp as wet snow tips from the branches down the collar of Julia's coat.

Miriam turns a key in the lock of the barn door. She pushes the handle down twice, then, satisfied it's secure, she crosses the courtyard towards Honeysuckle Cottage, slamming the door behind her. Nothing particularly surprising in that, except she looked even more shifty than usual, checking around her repeatedly.

I don't move, as though I were the one caught out, waiting

until it feels right before I follow the footprints to her door. I raise my hand to tap gently. Then I change my mind.

I keep watch from the relative warmth of Lavender Cottage, the radiators bizarrely now almost too hot to touch. The barn appears to be an empty and dilapidated building in need of renovation, so what was Miriam doing over there and why did she feel the need to lock it so carefully? I can't risk investigating whilst she's next door – she's bound to poke her head out in that ninja-like way she has of pouncing when I least expect it – but as soon as she goes out, I'll take my chance. If nothing else it will kill some time before I leave this evening, and where's the harm in a bit of snooping around?

Chapter Twenty-One

An Anomaly

I eat a lunch of bread and butter whilst Googling Jamie Porten on my laptop, my excitement for this evening's meeting building. I keep imagining the career opportunities a connection to a top journalist could provide, my expectations growing ever more unrealistic, despite my repeated attempts to rein them in. But forging a relationship with Jamie *is* important. He can open doors for me, ones that if I approached them now would be unceremoniously slammed in my face. I need to get my pitch right, tailor it to Jamie's style; and calm down a bit!

I'm disappointed to find I'm denied access to the clippings archive as I'm no longer a member of staff at the *Herald*, but it's not difficult to find Jamie's past triumphs, his big-name interviews and undercover exposés given many column inches. His no-nonsense approach was also cited on my journalism course as an example of cutting-edge if sometimes questionable reporting, so I'm familiar with most of the higher profile articles that come up. At only thirty-one, he's already made a massive name for himself. He looks smug in his official headshot, a self-satisfied grin on his handsome face; but looks, like reputations, can be deceiving. There was talk he was a whisper away from being called to the Leveson Inquiry, his methods as a new name in journalism considered controversial, although it was never proved he'd actually participated in phone hacking. He could certainly throw a lot more resources at Max's story than I have at my disposal – a private investigator, paid-for searches – but I have one thing he doesn't: the exclusive.

I stretch my humped back and circle my neck, getting up to check the courtyard again.

The snow has stopped falling, although it looks temporary, the sky still white. It's been a good ten minutes since Miriam left Honeysuckle Cottage, her door rattling mine as it was slammed shut, and there's no sign of her coming back. I pull on Julia's coat and wriggle my blistered feet into the loaned wellies, peering out at Miriam's footprints.

I begin my investigations by tapping on Miriam's door. Satisfied she's not home, I step to my right, standing in a pile of slush to peek in through her small front window. As she'd told me, Honeysuckle is a mirror image of Lavender, the interior identical and just as sparsely furnished. A small sofa faces me, covered in a hand-crocheted throw Iz would love, each square a different and clashing colour. A pang of homesickness strikes. I hope Izzy isn't worried where I am, but it's only been a couple of days since I saw her, and we hardly keep tabs on one another. I press my nose to the glass and study the interior of Miriam's humble home more carefully, noticing a few amateurish watercolours dotted around the sitting room walls, depictions of Brooke House through the seasons, but other than that the room is devoid of the 'home comforts' she'd described. I glance behind me, mindful that Miriam could appear at any moment. Then I turn my attention to the barn.

There are four windows running across the length of the low, brick-built building and a door to their right, facing me. I climb into the overgrown flower bed beneath the nearest window, my boots stomping on prickly weeds, the ground still covered with snow although it is starting to melt. Leaning closer, I rub a corner of the grimy glass with the cuff of Julia's coat. The dirt transfers to the pale beige with alarming efficiency, but it's pointless – the curtains inside are drawn tight across. Snagging the long coat on a bramble, I step along the border, but at the next window I find the same impenetrable folds of fabric, and the next. The barn has the feel of somewhere deliberately hiding secrets, which makes me even more determined to find out what's inside.

'Seren?'

I lose my footing, fingers grasping for the furthest snow-topped sill, just out of reach. 'Miriam, you shouldn't sneak up on me like that!' I regain my composure as she crosses the courtyard towards me.

'What are you doing?' she asks, placing her hands on her hips.

'Just killing time until I leave.' I take a step back into a twiggy bush then clamber out of the flower bed, clapping my frozen palms together.

'You should be inside on a day like this, keeping warm.' She pulls a thorny weed from the tangle beside us. 'I'll take a trowel to all this in the spring,' she says, throwing down the bramble.

'I was bored, thought I'd explore a bit,' I reply, watching for her reaction.

'I hear Max is taking you home?'

'Yes, after he's finished work.' I decide not to share the fact we also have a dinner date.

She nods and walks towards her door.

'What's in the barn, Miriam?'

She pauses in her step, glancing back. 'I told you, didn't I?'

'No, you said no one stays in there, but not what's inside.' I wait, but Miriam doesn't respond. 'I saw you coming out earlier, making sure it was locked up.' Still nothing. 'That's OK,' I say. 'I'll ask Max.'

Miriam is staring at the large bunch of keys in her hand, weighing up her next move.

'I'd hate to disturb him again, though,' I tell her. 'Especially whilst he's writing.'

Miriam looks up from the keys and takes a deep breath. Then she walks to the barn door and unlocks it.

I can't make out anything at first, then as my eyes adjust I see Miriam is a few paces ahead. The air tastes of dust, but there's a cleanliness to the echoing space, a newness to it. Miriam flicks a switch and bright light fills the dark void. Blinded by the intense glare, I shield my eyes, although they're already squeezed tight shut. When I blink them open, I'm amazed to see an entirely different interior than I'd expected. The walls, floor and ceiling are all painted white, with multiple spotlights overhead; the source of my temporary blindness. The curtains I'd seen from outside aren't visible in here, slatted blinds covering them up in a slap-dash fashion as if they were an after thought, and at the far end of the long, narrow room, a wide full-height screen, also white, is suspended from the ceiling, the base rolled out towards us like a carpet. Tall lamps stand around like triffids and discarded camera equipment is lying on the floor. But the most striking thing is that every wall is covered in photos, dozens of them, stuck randomly and at odd angles. And every single one is of Julia: smiling, pouting, posing, her hair up, then down, light, then dark, cut short, then long, her face tipped up to meet the lens.

'Not what you'd expected?' Miriam asks, as her eyes rove over the images, her hand lifted as if she might touch Julia's beautiful faces. She shivers. It's so draughty in here still, even with the curtains drawn.

I'm too freaked out by it all to move. 'Max had the barn converted just so Julia could come down here and take endless selfies?' I take a few tentative steps towards the white backdrop, careful not to tread on a particularly impressive-looking lens that appears to have been cast into the middle of the room.

'Please don't wander down there.' Miriam frowns at me. 'You might damage something.'

'Quite sad, really,' I observe, doubling back to stand beside Miriam. 'Must have cost Max a bomb. The equipment alone . . .'

Miriam contemplates her answer, then says, 'I had an aunt, used to visit us at the farm occasionally when I was a child.' She's pointing with the bunched keys to a spot somewhere beyond the white walls of the barn. 'Mum always warned me and Pauline – that's my sister,' she glances at me and I nod, 'not to pester Auntie Jen for anything, or even suggest we liked something, because she'd straight away buy it for us.' Miriam sighs. 'She took me into town once, just the two of us, maybe it was my birthday, I forget. Anyway, I saw this stupid doll. The hair grew when you turned a dial in her back, hideous thing. I was never a girly girl but I decided I wanted it.'

'So you asked your aunt?'

Miriam nods, a half-smile to forgive her younger self. 'I cut the hair short the second I got it home. Chopped it all off, no idea why. After that I hated it.' She looks at me again. 'I just had to have it, you see. Not because I really wanted it or thought it would make me happy, but because I knew I could.'

'So if Julia didn't want the flash car and the swimming pool and all this . . .' I sweep my hand around the studio, '. . . what did she want?'

'She wanted the one thing Max couldn't give her. He tried, but . . .' Miriam looks down at the keys, then asks if I've seen enough, marching to the door and switching off the lights before I've had time to answer.

'*Miriam?*' I follow, tripping over something heavy and probably breakable. 'Miriam, wait!'

I emerge to the intense brightness of the snow. 'A child? Is that what Julia wanted?'

Miriam ignores me, turning the key and testing the handle as I'd seen her do earlier. 'There, all secure again,' she says. 'I'll see you before you leave, I expect.' She walks towards Honeysuckle Cottage, but I stay where I am.

She looks back, then stops. 'Was there something else?'

265

'The patio door was left open and the front door to Brooke House is stiff but rarely locked. We're miles from anywhere, just you, me and Max.'

'Yes, what's your point, Seren?'

'Who are you locking out of the barn, Miriam?'

She stares at me, a long pause before she says, 'Like you said, there's some very valuable equipment in there.' Then she goes inside her cottage, slamming the door.

I trudge across the courtyard, kicking off my wet boots on the doormat. The studio was disconcerting, Miriam's insights into Max's indulgence of his wife and Julia's continuing dissatisfaction, both tantalising and frustrating in equal measure. It seemed Miriam was alluding to Julia's desire to have a baby, but maybe it wasn't that at all. And why check the barn door so assiduously when security doesn't seem to be a massive concern elsewhere? Surely Brooke House holds more valuable treasures than a few pieces of camera equipment?

Black tea in hand, I stare out of the cottage window, imagining Julia playing at being a photographer, papering the barn walls with her beautiful face, but always alone. She was clearly looking for something, or someone, to fill her solitary days. I'm looking for something too, anything I might have missed, the barn still not giving up all its secrets.

I take a sip of tea and it comes to me, an anomaly I'd noted whilst I was in Julia's studio, the bright lights and walls of photos distracting me from the real clue. I look over at the barn and count again, although I'm certain I'm right. The curtains were drawn, blinds covering them too – which is fair enough, I'm sure controlling the light is important when you're a serious photographer – but what puzzles me is that there are . . . *one-two-three-four* windows outside. I close my eyes and imagine myself back in that white box. Yep, still *one-two-three* sets of blinds. I stare at the fourth window, furthest from the front door, the one I'd been about to look through when Miriam caught me snooping around. And she called me back before I reached the white backdrop, also at that end of the barn. What's hidden back there, and why is she so determined to conceal it?

Chapter Twenty-Two

Less Reckless Now It's Official

Max steps aside from the front door to allow me in, a pair of headphones in his hand. 'Great timing, I'd just finished for the day,' he says, glancing at the snowy scene behind me. 'I hope this means you've decided to join me at the dinner tonight?'

I shrug, wiping my boots. Max's good mood is off-putting, the feeling I've been coerced into something returning.

'Let's talk in my study,' he says, setting a fast pace as he crosses the rug. 'Come on, come on!'

I follow, saying little. I guess I should be relieved our argument has been set aside, but Max's ability to compartmentalise his feelings is bewildering.

The first thing I notice as I enter the study is that the broken glass has been swept up, no trace of it on the floor, and there's no sign of the smashed frame either, or the photo it contained.

'So, how's your afternoon been?' Max asks, closing the document he was working on as he sits down at his desk.

'It was . . . interesting,' I reply, taking the plastic visitor chair.

'Oh?' he asks.

'Miriam showed me your wife's studio.'

Max manages to mask his surprise, but I caught a reaction in his eyes, I'm sure of it. He picks up a paper clip from a pot on his desk, tapping it rhythmically on the dusty surface.

'My assistant has been helpful to you today, hasn't she?' Max grinds the paper clip into the desk and I notice a few scratches in the wood where he must have done the same before. 'Anything else I should know about?'

'She's very loyal to you, Max.'

'Yes, but you know how women can be,' he replies, meeting my gaze but providing no further explanation of the abstruse and sexist comment. 'So what have you decided about tonight?'

'I'd like to join you,' I say. 'But to be clear, this is for work only.'

He frowns as if the suggestion it might be anything else is ridiculous, but I can tell he's pleased I'm coming. A bit too pleased if anything.

'It's black-tie,' he says.

'You mean formal?'

'Don't worry, I can take you home on the way. I assume you live closer to town?'

'Yes, I do, but—' I mentally flick through the options in my limited wardrobe. 'I don't have anything formal, I'm afraid.'

'Not one long dress?' he asks, as if that were incomprehensible.

'Not much call for it at the *Herald*,' I reply, thinking there's even less now I'm sacked. 'Never mind, I guess I'll have to give it a miss. Too late to go shopping.'

'Unless . . .' he says.

We're halfway down the corridor, arrangements now made, when Max stops by the window, his face in shadow.

'To warn you, Seren . . . there may be people there tonight who knew Theo. He was a popular guy, but I very much doubt Nicky will be going on her own, not so soon after . . . Anyway, I'll be around to make sure you're OK.'

'That's fine, I can take care of myself.'

'Yes, good. Best not to hide. I'm a fine one to talk – this is the first time I've been to one of these events since . . . I'm sure it will be OK, just wanted to mention.'

He walks on, the lamps in the hallway lighting our way to the front door.

'Oh, I just remembered,' I tell him, as if I have. 'I've got an appointment first thing tomorrow morning so I'd rather not be too late tonight, if that's OK?'

'Something important?'

'Dentist,' I lie.

'Is that in town?' Max asks.

'Oh, I see what you mean, yes, walking distance from mine, luckily.'

I don't even have a dentist, but the transport issue is problematic. I'll have to get a taxi over to police HQ for my meeting with DS Ingles, then back here to pick up my car once the snow has gone. I can't even claim my expenses, but there's no alternative.

'Great,' Max replies. 'I'll drop you home after the dinner, shouldn't be too late, then you can collect your car once the roads have cleared.' He opens the front door and looks out at the wintry view. It's definitely a bit slushier, but still far from the thaw I've been hoping for. 'Can you be ready by seven?' Max asks. 'There's no need to leave quite so early now.'

'Yes, true. Any idea where I might find Miriam to sort out the . . .'

Max shakes his head. 'She's a law unto herself. I'll point her your way after our meeting.'

I head down the steps.

'And I'll drive the car down to pick you up,' he calls after me. 'Can't expect you to walk up to the house in evening wear.'

'Thanks,' I say, turning back. 'And you'll let Jamie know I'm coming?'

'Yes, I'll do that now and copy you in.'

'Oh, that reminds me,' I say, walking back up the steps. 'I'm using my personal email address, problems with the work server.'

He frowns, says he won't be able to remember it, but I persist, repeating the address until he has it.

There's no sign of Miriam as I enter the courtyard and a knock on her door confirms she's not at home. I guess she's already up at the house, preparing for her 'daily catch-up' with Max. I unlock Lavender Cottage and take off Julia's coat, although it's freezing in here again, the radiator barely tepid. My plan is to finish my article on Max whilst I wait for Miriam to come back so she can help me choose one of Julia's 'gowns' as Max called

271

them, but instead I spend a while staring out the window and daydreaming about meeting Jamie Porten. If I can get some kind of 'in' from him, the feature on Max could still be my big break, and if the detective has anything to offer in exchange for my precious nuggets from Ben and Carys, I can add that in too. If Jamie can't help, I'll just have to try to sell the story freelance. *Never easy.* Then I'll start looking for a new job.

I open my laptop and the promised email arrives from Max, sent to Jamie and copying me in. My decision to tag along feels less reckless now it's official, although I do need Miriam to come back soon. I really don't fancy another trek up to the house to find her, and I'm not missing out on the chance to meet Jamie Porten just because I don't have the right dress to wear. I send the detective a quick email to confirm our appointment and my 'new' email address – hoping I've remembered her email correctly – then I wait, feeling both nervous and excited.

Nine Months Missing

Katie's in the car when her phone rings. A mobile number, and not one she recognises. Then she recalls the taxi driver she tried earlier this afternoon. He'd proved elusive during the initial investigation into Julia Blake's disappearance, but Chris, the thorough detective he is, has tracked him down. She's almost home, but she pulls into a lay-by in case she needs to make notes, glancing at the time. This should only take a couple of minutes.

'Hello, is that DS . . . *Ing-gels*? I'm Cal Diamond, you left me a couple of voicemails.'

She tries to relax him by assuring him it's routine, then she recaps Chris's conversation with the owner of the taxi company.

'Oh yeah, I remember that job,' Cal says. 'It was a pain. I got completely lost. Middle of nowhere. No GPS. I missed the fare. It happens sometimes, if you're late. Get there and they've already called for someone else.'

'How did you know?' Katie asks, hunting in her bag for a pen.

'*Sorry?*'

'How did you know your fare had been picked up by another

driver?' She pulls out a nappy and a hairbrush, feeling around in the jumble of tissues and wipes until she finds the biro and notepad she needs. 'Did you see anyone, speak to someone who told you the fare had been picked up already?'

'No, but the place looked deserted. I just assumed—'

'A long journey just to turn around and leave empty-handed. What time was this?'

'Dunno, maybe half-twelve. I was booked for midnight, but like I said, I got lost.'

'And you didn't think to tell the police you'd been at Brooke House the night Julia Blake disappeared?'

'*Shit!* It was that night? I'm so sorry. I've been out the country, travelling. That's why I was working as a taxi driver, so I could build up some savings, but it's a crap job. I was glad to jack it in. I haven't been checking my phone – trying to get away from technology, you know, go fully native.'

'OK, Cal. Let's go back to that night.' Spots of rain splutter on to her windscreen as the traffic whizzes by. The snow has turned to slush on the well-used road, but it could still be concealing black ice. They should slow down. 'You said when you arrived at Brooke House it was deserted, but think back, Cal. Did you see or hear anyone at all? Any signs of activity, lights on, movement?'

There's a pause. 'No, I don't think so. I just drove in and out. Suppose I could have missed something, but like I say, the fare had gone.'

'You're certain you didn't see Julia or Max Blake, maybe in the grounds or by the pool? Or perhaps heard voices, an argument, cars moving around? A white Range Rover parked up?'

Another pause. 'Nope, sorry.'

'OK, thanks. I'll be in touch again soon, arrange for you to come in and make a formal statement.'

'That's not it?'

'No, Cal, this is a serious matter. Like I said, I'll be in touch.'

Katie ends the call but she doesn't make a move, her phone still in her hand. There's something not right. Cal was over-talkative, and clearly nervous. He's young, could just be that, but she has a feeling he knows more than he's sharing. She'll bring him in soon. Better to talk face-to-face, it might jog his memory. In fact—

Katie tries his number but it goes straight to voicemail. She leaves a message, then she makes a note to request Julia Blake's file. She wants to refresh her memory before she meets with the journalist in the morning. The energy she'd felt as she stood in Max Blake's kitchen has returned. She's inching closer to the truth now; she can smell it. This case is far from over.

Chapter Twenty-Three

How Do I Look?

It's dark, not just outside, but in the cottage too, the only light coming from my laptop. I finish typing and straighten up, my neck stiff. The article is almost there, and it's good, even if I do say so myself. I circle my shoulders and glance at the window, jumping up from my chair as I notice a pale face is staring back.

'Miriam! Don't do that! You scared me half to death!'

She stamps her boots on the mat and comes in. 'I love watching writers at work, such concentration,' she says, staring at my laptop. 'All those amazing ideas whizzing from your brain to your fingertips.'

I dash past her, snapping the lid shut. 'I'm hardly in Max's league.'

'No, he's one of a kind,' she says, her adoration girlish, then her expression tightens as she gets down to the real reason she's here. 'Max says I need to find you a suitable gown for your dinner date tonight.'

'It's not a date, but—' I glance at my watch, not only to

check it's still doable, but also to avoid Miriam's obvious disapproval. 'Wow, we don't have much time.'

'It's put me in a very difficult position,' she says.

'*Miriam?*'

We tiptoe across the courtyard in our wellies and coats, the scene almost comical as Miriam glances about her. It's taken me several precious minutes of cajoling and pleading to persuade her to divulge her concerns, and then to accept my solemn promise I will say nothing to Max about 'her little secret'. I'm not sure why she's so worried. As far as I can tell, all she's done is move a few of Julia's clothes into the barn, but I guess it is a sensitive matter. Mum won't let anyone touch Bryn's things, the merest hint we might pack a few things away ending in a row. Miriam reminds me again that should the subject arise I'm to say the dress was retrieved from Julia's walk-in wardrobe up at Brooke House. 'Yes, I have promised,' I say, adding a smile. I need to keep her on-side.

She takes out her jailer's keys and selects the correct one, unlocking the barn door and snapping on the light. We both squint, then Miriam walks towards the far end of the long white room, past countless pairs of Julia's enquiring eyes. I follow, surprised there's space behind the white backdrop for the two of us as I hadn't noticed much of a gap, but I hadn't walked this far down. Taking out the keys again, Miriam passes them through her fingers, one by one. It's hard for her to see with me blocking the light so I step out, waiting until I hear the lock turn before I join her again. She pulls a cord just inside the door and a single bare bulb casts its weak light across a good-sized cupboard, a musty scent permeating the trapped air. The window is covered with the pulled curtains I'd glimpsed from outside, but no blind, and flimsy free-standing clothes rails line three of the walls, bowing under the weight of their cargo.

'Oh, I hadn't realised there'd be so many,' I say, walking towards the tightly packed hangers.

There must be tens, maybe even a hundred outfits stored in this damp space, the air fetid with mildew, hardly ideal for delicate silks and lace, the fabrics gossamer soft and supple to my touch. I turn back to Miriam, looking for further explanation, but instead of the shiftiness I'd expected, she's looks reflective, even sad.

'They're so pretty,' she says, running a piece of soft silk across her open palm, the fabric catching on her rough skin. 'But no use dwelling on the past, I guess.'

'Won't Max notice you've moved them?' I ask. 'Julia's wardrobe must be looking a lot emptier.'

'He doesn't go through her things, upsets him too much. Anyway, most of these have been here for ages.' She looks at me. 'We had a sort out; Julia and I.'

'Oh, I see. And she didn't want these? They're incredible,' I say, and they are, the cut and fabric clearly high-end, but as I look closer, I realise they're not to my taste either, better suited to a much older woman than me; or Julia, for that matter.

I start pushing hangers along a rail, looking for something nondescript. I've no desire to draw attention to myself in one of Julia's distinctive outfits. The exotic printed fabrics in bright primary colours remind me of Izzy and her fearless fashion sense. She'd love them, although they wouldn't fit her, and I'm concerned they might be a bit snug on me too. 'Something in black,' I say, glancing at Miriam. 'Maybe with a bit of stretch?'

'Yes, I agree, although the simpler stuff—' She glances across at me. 'That's packed away.'

I recall her previous comment about most of what's left being occasion wear. Julia's everyday stuff must be squirrelled away somewhere else, probably in packing boxes up at the main house. Which I guess is where Miriam retrieved the clothes that she leant me. 'How about this one?' I pull a dress from the rack and hold it up.

It's a black full-length shift with a scooped neck, but not too low at the bust like some of the others. The only identifying feature is a row of tiny pearl buttons which fasten down the back. It's not an ideal choice, but after another rushed search we conclude it's the best we can find. She turns away as I take off Julia's jumper to try the dress for size.

'It's a bit tight over jeans,' I say, smoothing down the fabric. 'But should be better with just underwear.'

She nods, helping me with the buttons, then she points at the hem. 'The only problem is, it's far too long.' She digs under the rails and pulls out a pair of red-soled spiky heels. I kick off a wellington boot and pull off the thick sock beneath, but the shoes are far too big. 'Do you have anything suitable with you?' she asks.

I shake my head, lifting myself up to my full height, but even balanced on my toes the fabric still puddles around me. 'Only my suede boots. They've got a bit of heel . . .'

Miriam kneels down and creases a line in the hem as I go up on my toes again. 'Leave it with me for ten minutes,' she says, getting up. 'I'm good with a needle and thread, years of crochet work. Can you manage the buttons yourself?'

She averts her eyes as I change back, telling me about the different outfits and where Julia wore them. 'She'd have looked good in a bin bag,' Miriam observes, smiling as I hand her the dress. 'That's what Max always used to tell her, but of course these were all his choice.'

'Max chose them?' I ask, pulling on a sock then boot. 'Why would he do that? Julia had impeccable taste, didn't she?'

'He liked to treat her, and of course it was important to project the right image, for his work.' She looks at the hem, turning it over, then back. 'That'll take me ten minutes at most.'

I stare at the racks of clothes again, seeing them now as tokens in the Blakes' power games. Julia wasn't the only one moulding her spouse to their desired image. Max liked to dress up his perfect wife, parading her in front of his friends to make her look older, more . . . appropriate. 'His wee doll,' as Jacqui said.

'Shall we go?' Miriam asks.

'I'll just pop these back,' I say, crawling under the rail to return the shoes to their box. It's dark, and dusty, my hand finding the corner of something cold and metallic pushed behind the rails. Curious, I get up, holding back the clothes to try the top drawer of the filing cabinet.

'Leave that!' Miriam says, poking her head through to see what I'm doing. 'It'll be locked.'

The drawer glides open. 'No, it's not,' I tell her, peering in.

There's a jumble of make-up inside and a packet of cigarettes, as well as cleansing wipes, a hairbrush, and half a bottle of vodka. Miriam is beside me now, considering my find.

'For the photo sessions,' she explains, as if Julia had been running fashion shoots from the converted barn. 'Ready now?'

I close the drawer, but instead of following Miriam out I pull open the second drawer, this one much deeper. Inside are stacks of photos, one on top of another, and like the prints on the studio walls, they all depict Julia in front of the same white backdrop, although I assume they must be rejects as the shots are badly framed, the images blurred in some cases. Then I notice some slightly different prints beneath, of varying size and quality. The edge of a girl's face catches my eye, and below that another, slightly older version of the same girl, early to late teens at a guess judging by the pierced nose and heavy eyeliner. I lift them both out, looking more carefully at the features. They could be Julia, or maybe her sister, Jacqui?

'Eh! Watch out!' The drawer has been slammed shut, my hand retracted just in time.

'Time to go,' Miriam states matter-of-factly, pulling the light cord as she walks out.

Miriam is waiting on the other side of the screen for me, her expression firm. 'I thought you were in a rush?' she asks.

'Why are those other photos hidden away?' I reply, looking round at the myriad images of Julia lining the walls. 'Did Julia hide them in that drawer? She was down here a lot, wasn't she?'

Miriam steps closer and roughly pulls the cobweb from my face, plucking a hair or two with it.

'Ouch! Take care!'

'Sorry,' she says, although she doesn't look it. 'I'll drop the dress round in a few minutes.'

She locks the barn door behind us, then marches across to Honeysuckle Cottage, the sound of her door slamming reverberating around the empty courtyard.

Miriam delivers the dress to my door with two minutes to spare. The alteration is poor, the stitches uneven, but it will have to do. She must notice my disappointment as she babbles on about how patching crochet squares together is quite different from hemming silk.

'It's fine, thank you,' I tell her, taking the dress into the bedroom.

I remove the towelling robe and edge the dress over my piled-up hair, while Miriam paces on the other side of the door. I think I've done quite a good job getting ready with very limited resources, a bracingly cold bath and a rush make-up job, plus the improvised up-do, all in under half an hour. The major snag is my lack of suitable footwear, but I've no alternative. I apply my final two plasters to cover my blisters and pull on the clunky boots. At least the long fabric mostly covers them

'How do I look?' I ask, doing a little twirl as I emerge.

Miriam steps back and admires me, then something seems to shift and she leaves.

A couple of minutes later I hear the sound of a car outside.

Max is turning a huge white Range Rover in the small court-yard, back and forth until he's facing the way he came, an impatient beep of the horn as I shove my jeans and jumper, finally dry, into my overflowing bag.

'We're late,' Max says, frowning as I clamber into the cream leather seat.

He swings the car out the courtyard and takes a sharp left, up the drive and out through the gate, barely glancing at me.

I'd worried about his reaction when he saw me, but the difficult driving conditions are demanding his full attention, the bumpy track treacherous. He's crunching the gears and cursing under his breath, but his hangover seems to have has lifted, the reek of sweated-out alcohol replaced by the pleas-antly musky scent of his cologne.

'The snow's melted a bit more here,' I say, encouraging him as he negotiates the dark country lanes.

'There's still a lot of ice and surface water. Even with four-wheel drive it can be . . .'

My phone buzzes loudly in my bag. I take it out, glancing at Max and apologising for the interuption. Two messages are from Izzy. She's heard about Theo and she's worried. I reassure her I'm fine, just out on a work thing. I'll be home later this evening. Dad has texted asking about the wiper – have I got it sorted yet? I'd forgotten about that. And lastly there's a missed call. No voicemail. Number withheld. Three a.m. this morning. My phone hadn't even rung.

'Lots to catch up on?' Max asks, eyes glued to the road.

'Yes,' I reply, tapping in my reply to Dad. 'I've been out of touch for far too long.'

I'm annoyed about the missed call, but taking it out on Max is hardly fair. I'm about to say something concilliatory about how lovely Julia's car is, when the tyres skid on a patch of unseen ice, throwing us around the bend on the wrong side of the narrow road.

Max regains control quickly, but it's clearly rattled him.

Neither of us speak until we're pulling into the venue. I'd imagined a glamorous evening, fine dining and champagne, but it's a grim-looking hotel out by the motorway.

'Looks nice,' I tell Max.

He offers a look of disbelief, his arched expression illuminated as he glances over his shoulder to reverse into a tight space. He stops the car and checks his phone.

'I don't mind as long as Jamie Porten shows up,' I say.

'Already on his way,' Max says, holding up a picture on his phone.

It's of a train table on which a can of G&T has been opened and poured, the caption beneath, 'Be there soon!'

Chapter Twenty-Four

Was it the Chicken?

Max reaches out to guide me across the badly lit car park. I tell him I'm fine, then I trip, saving myself by grabbing the side of a van beside me. Max insists I accept his help, our hands linked as we approach the dreary concrete building. It's odd to have the cool crevices of his palm flattened against mine for a moment or two, but Max feels more benign beyond the confines of Brooke House, and he soon jogs ahead. I notice the flattering cut of his navy dinner suit, then his slim wedding band as he holds the door for me. There's a handwritten sign taped to the wall that directs us towards 'Reception', a crudely drawn arrow pointing us back towards the car park.

'It's for charity,' Max says. 'Best to hold on to that thought.'

We follow a worn strip of carpet through two more doors before we reach the front desk, not a soul in sight.

'This is a good start,' Max says, drumming his nails on the counter. 'The host was supposed to meet me here.'

The woman who emerges from the back office is crammed into an unfortunate uniform of unforgiving burgundy polyester, her greeting lacklustre. Max gives his full name, clearly expecting a look of recognition as the guest celebrity, but the receptionist stares back, asking robotically if we've reserved a room.

'God, no,' Max replies, laughing nervously. 'We're here for the charity dinner.'

I lean across Max to attract her attention. 'Could I leave my coat somewhere? And can you tell me where the nearest bathroom is, please?'

'I'd leave that here too,' Max suggests, pointing at my shoulder bag, stuffed with my clothes, laptop, and all my other belongings.

She gives me a cloakroom ticket, which Max tucks in his wallet as I have nowhere to put it, then the receptionist points me down a flight of stairs towards the 'Ladies Powder Room'. My exit is halted by a florid-faced man who arrives with a pint of beer in his hand.

'Max, you wanker!' He grasps Max's hand and tells him he'll take us to the 'VIP area'. Our host's stomach is hard and round, as if a full-term pregnancy is straining beneath his velvet cummerbund. 'Paddock Suite when you're ready, young lady,' he says as I excuse myself, his smile lingering.

I stare back until his tongue returns to his mouth, a quick lick of his lips before he leads Max away, slapping him hard on the back.

The bathroom is miles away. I check my make-up then struggle with the long dress, hooking most of the fabric over one arm

286

as I sit down on the cracked toilet seat. When I emerge, a mature woman in a figure-hugging scarlet dress is reapplying her lipstick. I notice pronounced ridges in the satin fabric, her ribs defined as she leans towards the mirror. She appraises my face, reflected beside hers, then her eyes swoop down my dress. The door closes behind her sling-backs as I'm drying my hands. She hadn't smiled once.

The Paddock Suite is a large conference room currently filled with dinner suits and long dresses. Across a headache-inducing carpet, Max is seated at a table piled high with copies of his books. There's a long but orderly queue for signings, photos taken by an official photographer who already looks bored. 'Yes, smile. Now! Thanks. *Next!*'

I accept a glass of 'bubbly' from a tray, the young waiter's smile slipping as he moves on. The wine is flat and warm, definitely not champagne, but I drink it anyway, tracing the edge of the room slowly. Max raises a hand when he spots me, mouthing, *'You OK?'*

I nod and move on, settling by a table where I find our names handwritten on folded cards and placed side by side next to pink triangulated napkins.

Mrs Red Dress has sidled up and now has my name card pincered between red talons. She raises it to her eye level, squinting. '*Seren?* That's unusual. Are you a friend of Max's?'

I hesitate. My usual response, *'I'm a reporter with the* Herald' is no longer applicable. And even if it were still the case, I assume Max would rather I didn't share that information. 'Yes, that's right,' I tell her.

'Oh, I see.' She drops the card carelessly on the table and holds up her empty glass.

The waiter brings another and removes the proffered one on a tray. She doesn't even acknowledge him. He catches my eye and pulls a face behind the older woman's back.

'So how did you two meet?' Mrs Red Dress asks as I take a large gulp to finish my wine, accepting another as the waiter smiles at me.

'Thanks. Um . . .' I glance across at Max who has his arm around the ample shoulders of a middle-aged woman, a book held up between them. 'It was through work,' I say.

'Oh, I thought you said—'

'Seren is a writer too,' a smooth and confident voice behind me replies. 'Aren't you, my darling?'

I turn to look up at a face I recognise, although we've never met. He's haltingly handsome, his sardonic smile conspiratorial, as if we were old friends, or lovers. I feel myself blushing. Must be the wine.

'Yes, I am,' I reply, lifting my chin to address Mrs Red Dress. Her hand rests on the chair that should be mine, her neck, I notice, is sinewy. 'I'm a writer.' I exchange another sly smile with Jamie. He's taller than I'd expected.

Mr Porten, 'Call me Jamie, darling', excuses us, the promise of a decent drink and getting away from 'that frightful woman' whispered hotly in my ear as we retreat to the bar at the back of the room, both of us giggling. I take a moment to gather myself as Jamie orders a very expensive bottle of champagne. He rejects the first one as it's not chilled sufficiently, his excessive politeness to the bartender bordering on rude, but he leaves a generous cash tip. His dinner suit is dark navy like Max's, not black like every other man in the room, but Jamie has gone further, wearing an open collar, no tie. Mulberry cufflinks glint their iconic trees at me as he hands over a credit card, 'for the rest of the evening'. Everything about him radiates confidence, arrogance even. With Theo I'd been intimidated at first by his privileged background, but with Jamie it feels more like an exclusive club I'm desperate to join.

'Who the fuck was she to question you?' Jamie asks, pouring me a glass of the vintage champagne as he looks over at Mrs Red Dress, her back to us as she walks off. 'And where the fuck are we, dar-ling?' The last word is deliberately elongated, making me laugh as he straightens up and brushes his jacket sleeve which had been resting on the sticky bar.

'I have no idea,' I reply, sipping my drink. 'But *thank God* you're here.' I glance up, surprised by my daring familiarity, but I can't seem to reel myself in. I have the feeling of being let out of my cage; more than ready for a bit of fun. 'This is so good!' I say, holding up my glass. 'In a different class to the warm fizz I was drinking before.'

Jamie raises his champagne flute to mine then throws back the contents. 'Keep up!' he instructs me, watching whilst I down mine in two attempts. 'Good girl! I can see you and I are going to get along famously.'

'You arrived at just the right moment,' I tell him. 'Thanks for rescuing me.'

'My pleasure,' Jamie says, smiling widely and offering a mock salute as Max looks over. 'I see he's doing his thing. Been a while.'

'Yes, the first event he's attended since Julia went missing.'

Jamie refreshes my drink with a flourish, asking all about my background in journalism. His affectations are distracting, but I can see why he always gets the story. His ability to build an instant rapport, and the fact he's so easy on the eye, is a potent combination. He's already gleaned more than I'd planned to give away about my journalistic experience, or lack of it. I'll have to watch what I say, and how much I drink.

'How's the interview going?' he asks, suddenly more serious. 'You know I can definitely help you, if you're interested? I like to mentor newbies when I can. We've all been there and let's face it, it's a fucking nightmare trying to break out of regional journalism unless you know someone with a bit of clout.'

I nod emphatically, placing my glass on the bar as I launch into my pitch. 'Max has opened up a lot to me, some interesting details about his life with Julia, and the argument before she disappeared. I really think this story could be huge if—'

'*Argument?*' Jamie tilts his head. 'Do tell all!'

'Not much to say,' I reply, heeding my own advice to be circumspect in what I share at this stage.

'Come on, Seren. You'll have to give me a bit more than that if we're going to elevate this story beyond the local rag. Something juicy, something new!'

'OK . . .' I glance over at Max but he's busy signing books. 'He told Julia he hated her, last thing he said to her before she vanished.'

Jamie appears impressed, asks if there's more.

'I'm still drafting my copy,' I reply, sipping my drink. 'But maybe we can keep in touch via email, see if we can find a better home for my exclusive?' I stop short of telling him I no longer work for the *Herald*, hoping it's enough to declare my intent to shop the story around.

Jamie smiles. 'Fair enough. I can see you've got your head screwed on.'

I gush a thank you, although he hasn't specified what he's offering to do, and I'm afraid to ask. I've also managed to slosh champagne down myself.

'So, tell me, dar-ling,' he says, gallant enough to pretend he hasn't noticed my clumsiness as I brush at my chest with my free hand. 'Has he actually admitted doing away with her yet? Ah Max!' Jamie greets Max with a bear hug whilst I choke on a mouthful of champagne, spluttering as Jamie says, 'How the fuck are you, old man?'

'Less of the *old man*, you cheeky sod.' Max clasps Jamie's hand. 'Let's find somewhere to talk and I need a drink. You two look like you've started without me! You OK, Seren?' Max throws me a reproving look, distracted then by a hovering fan, a mature gentleman brandishing a pen and an expectant smile. 'Time for a break from this bloody circus,' Max whispers through gritted teeth.

We find a table and Max and Jamie catch up with one another's news, book stuff mainly, whilst I try to recover from a bout of unexpected hiccoughing, downing more champagne to quell the urge, silent convulsions coming thick and fast. Max orders a second bottle and I ask the summoned waiter for a glass of water, aware I need to slow down if I'm going to keep a grip on the evening. Max glances at me again, then he asks Jamie what we've been discussing.

'Just talking about you,' Jamie says, winking at me. Then he turns his charm on Max who is in his element as he describes the premise of his 'work in progress'.

I've heard about Jamie's near-total recall, the use of tapes or shorthand apparently a hindrance to his 'interviewees' candour'. I'd thought it was an urban myth, possibly of his own creation, but it seems not. His technique is enthralling, the way he teases and cajoles Max for information about his 'troublesome' latest book, drawing him out, although he's careful not to encroach on my territory, tactfully avoiding the subject of Julia. Max tells him I've been doing a great job with the interviews and he can't wait to read my article, which makes me feel like a child whose parent is trying to convince a potential employer what an amazing candidate I am. Jamie winks at me again, which helps, as does the resumed supply of bubbles. He orders a third bottle, tipping the last drops of the second one into my glass as Max drones on and on.

'Ah, there you are!' The host has found us, throwing up his pudgy hands to Max. 'Dinner is served!'

Dinner is dire, the bland food only enlivened by a passable bottle of red Jamie has sent over. I raise my glass to him across the table and he lifts a piece of limp broccoli to shake it in the air, making me giggle, although I do seem to be finding everything funny; the recent gravy incident in particular. It was hardly the poor waitress's fault, you couldn't swing a small cat between the tables, but it was very unfortunate.

Mrs Red Dress is being sponged down, much to her voluble disgust, her continuing scowls only encouraging Jamie – seated next to her – to be more and more outrageous. He demands the waitress be immediately 'horse-whipped' and I have to hold my paper napkin over my face to cover my hysteria. Max whispers that I might like to slow up on the Merlot and maybe eat a little something. I open my mouth to tell him what he can do with his advice, but he's dragged back to a conversation with Mrs Red Dress's dullard husband who seems to think he's an authority on every subject, talking loudly when he has nothing interesting to say. 'Wan-ker,' Jamie mouths to me and I burst out laughing, barely able to stop. Maybe Max is right? I push my glass away and purse my lips like a naughty schoolgirl. Then Jamie widens his eyes in mock-horror, setting me off again. God, it's great to have a friend for the evening.

'I'll call you soon,' Jamie promises as he plants a kiss on each side of my hot face, apologising that he has to leave before dessert with a 'Sorry, not sorry'. He shakes Max's hand and makes him swear he will *never* invite him to one of these 'bloody awful things' again, the words aimed like missiles across the table, zap, zap, zap as he out-scowls Mrs Red Dress. 'If it wasn't for Seren I might never forgive you.' He kisses me again, on the forehead this time, a hand to mine as he asks, 'A quick word, Seren?' I nod enthusiastically and Jamie leads me to the bar for a round of tequila shots and a chat about 'next steps'.

Max's long stares eventually drive us outside where Jamie lights up a cigarette and exhales a column of smoke into the night sky whilst we wait for his taxi.

'He's married,' Max tells me when I return, my untouched dry chicken still waiting for me beside a deflated pavlova.

'I wasn't—'

'Max!' The host claps him on the shoulder, ending our conversation. 'Time for a few words if you don't mind?'

The audience are rowdy, the round tables littered with emptied bottles as Max makes his way to the far end of the room. I test a couple on our table and find a cheap-looking Pinot that's still half-full, sloshing some into my empty glass. I'll need something to get me through the rest of the evening, now Jamie has gone.

'It's funny,' Max begins. He's stepped onto the small stage, an effusive introduction over, the mic handed to him by the host who trips back down the steps on surprisingly light feet.

High-pitched feedback cuts in, the host apologising to Max as adjustments to levels are made. Max continues, apparently unfazed.

'Seeing old and new faces here tonight,' he says, his voice carrying above the clatter of plates being cleared. 'I wonder why I left it this long to join all my dear friends and readers again.'

There's a raucous round of applause, books held aloft. It appears to be carefully choreographed, but maybe that's uncharitable, although Max's smile does look a bit . . . fake. I swig my wine, screwing up my face as I swallow.

Max's voice booms out again. 'I'm sure many of you know that my darling wife, Julia, has been missing for many months now.' He walks a few paces, then back. 'Being here without her . . .' he pauses, and I notice a few furtive glances in my direction. 'It's not easy. But when I heard what tonight's cause is, well, I had to get involved.'

Max points at a woman standing to the side of the room, her face concealed behind the notes she's reading. I hadn't noticed her before, but everything's got a bit fuzzier since the tequila.

'I'd like to introduce someone to you who does sterling work for tonight's charity,' Max says. 'As well as being a dedicated police officer. Polly Pell, everybody!'

I snap my head up from my wine. *It can't be.*

There's a round of applause and the woman lifts her sparkly dress to carefully negotiate the steps, then she takes the microphone from Max and smiles nervously, thanking him as he backs away. I've never seen Pol in heels, or a dress of any kind. Her usual uniform was black trousers and a white shirt. It can't be our Pol, the family liaison officer who held hands, made tea, said how sorry she was when she left us for the last time. I close my left eye and try to concentrate. This is surreal. Am I drunk enough to conjure people from my past? I push my wine away and ask for the carafe of water. Mrs Red Dress pours for me and slides the glass over.

'Thank you, Max.' Pol speaks into the mic, the Welsh lilt unmistakable, although her face is sliding in and out of focus. 'The charity we are all here for tonight . . .' There's a ripple of applause. 'Thank you. This charity helps in the search for

295

missing persons, but more than that it provides ongoing support to friends and family.'

I slide down in my chair, afraid she might notice me, but I'm right at the back of the room, the VIP table located closest to the bar, and she's reading from her notes again, only glancing up to smile at those nearest the stage. I've almost convinced myself it's fine, no need to panic, when she says, 'I first came into contact with the charity through my role as a Family Liaison Officer with South Wales Police, some very difficult case highlighting to me—'

I get up too quickly, knocking the table. The water glass topples to its side, landing in the already soggy mess of my uneaten meringue. Faces swivel as I grab the back of my chair to steady myself. 'Sorry, I need to, sorry, excuse me.'

Pol is still talking, her amplified voice nervous. I can't make out the words, but I know she'd never mention me, or Bryn. Still, I have to get out of here. I weave between the tables, my progress slow, all eyes on me, or so it feels, tripping, stumbling, apologising. Then a hand is round my waist, a swish of damp red fabric beside me as Mrs Red Dress walks me out of the room with a firm word and a firmer grasp, Pol's speech growing fainter.

'I'm OK,' I insist, shaking her off as we reach the corridor, the air a bit cooler out here, although . . .

'You don't look it,' she says. 'Come on, let's pick up the pace.'

I splash cold water on my face as she lights a cigarette, wafting her hand above the smouldering tip and looking up at the ceiling as she exhales. 'Can't see a detector,' she says, leaning against the tiled wall by the dryer. 'But there's bound to be one. Always is these days.'

She hasn't reprimanded me but I can feel the judgement there, her languid form a red stain against the white porcelain, a skinny arm raising the cigarette to her feathery lips. I lean over the sink, my hands grasping the sides, holding on. The room spins, Mrs Red Dress's reflection rendered in jagged movements, like bad CGI. The acid in my throat threatens, although I'd thought that was the last of it.

'You feel better now?' she asks, spritzing a mini perfume in the air.

'Yes, thank you. Must have been the chicken.'

'Really?' She drags on her cigarette and drops the emptied perfume sample in the bin. 'In fairness,' she says, looking at me with mock-pity. 'It could have been the chicken. I left mine.'

So did I.

'I'm fine,' I tell her, a pathetic version of my face staring back as I wipe my mouth with a damp paper towel. 'Much better now. And sorry about that.' I look round at the cubicle and thank God I made it in time; well, sort of.

'I'm a nurse,' she replies, surprising me. 'I'm used to it.'

'Oh, I . . .'

'You assumed I'm a lady who lunches, nothing better to do than drive my husband home when he's had too much to drink.'

'No, I . . . I didn't think anything . . .'

She laughs. 'I'm just messing with you, Seren. Can you

imagine me in a uniform, and wearing clogs? Oh my God!'
She laughs again, a crack of phlegm in her throat as she lifts
a spiked stiletto from the floor to illustrate her point. 'As
if!'

I look around for my bag to repair my make-up then
remember it's in the cloakroom, the ticket in Max's wallet. I
wipe under my eyes with a damp finger instead.

'Yes, we knew Julia well,' she says, continuing a conversation
I don't recall us starting. She takes another deep drag then
passes me a slim compact and a folding brush from her tiny
bag.

I take them, but don't want to share such intimate items.
I'm surprised she does. 'I'm OK, but thanks,' I say, passing them
back.

'*Really?*' she says in the same incredulous tone as before. 'I
didn't think you had a problem borrowing other people's
things.' She points her cigarette at the hem of Julia's dress, then
she drops the compact back in her clutch bag, running the
brush through her long hair. 'I know a good seamstress if you
need anything else *adjusted*.'

'I don't know what you mean.' I turn from the mirror, ripping
off a few sheets of toilet roll from the cubicle and wetting it
to dab under my eyes, the smeared eyeliner refusing to budge,
my lipstick a stain around my mouth.

'Oh, come on,' she says. 'I'd know that neckline anywhere,
and the tiny buttons down the back. Julia wore it to a Gatsby-
themed New Year's Eve ball the year before last. It's couture.
One of a kind. Well, it is now!' She laughs, exhaling smoke
then fanning her hand through it. 'You look like her *and* you're

wearing her dress. It hardly takes a leap of understanding to work out what's going on with you and Max.' She pulls stray hairs from the bristles and drops them in the sink, folding the brush and returning it to her bag, the whole operation achieved with the cigarette still clamped between two long red nails.

'No, you're wrong, Max and I are—'

'*Friends*. Yes, you said. Or was it work colleagues?' She takes a final drag then runs the end of the cigarette under a dribble of water. 'Don't get me wrong. I'm not saying any of us liked Julia that much – the way she treated Max was vile – but to replace her this quickly, and so . . .' She pulls a face as she looks at me. '*Completely*.'

'Thank you for looking after me, but I need to find Max.' I grab the door handle, but she stops me with another question.

'What *is* your relationship with Julia's husband?'

I close my eyes and the room spins even faster, my head touching the door as I look down at my boots, the floor moving beneath them. 'I can't tell you, it would be unprofessional.'

She snorts. 'Say what you like about Jules, but at least there was an honesty to her gold-digging. And she would *never* have worn those boots, Max wouldn't have allowed it! Unless your profession is a little older than I'd imagined?'

My hand slides from the door handle as I spin round, almost losing balance. 'I'm a journalist, if you must know! I'm inter-vening, I mean *interviewing* Max, Mr Blake, to write a piece about his wife's disappearance. Satisfied now, you stupid old cow?'

Her eyes are bloodshot, her walk more of a stagger than a

glide as she pushes past me and heads up the stairs, her lip curling as she looks back. 'Max won't appreciate you showing him up so I suggest you get a grip, girl.'

Pol is standing at reception as I stagger past. I avert my eyes and rush on, hoping she hasn't noticed me. But why would she? I'm as out of context as she is. I feel terrible hiding from someone who's only ever shown me kindness, but I can't face her, not in this state.

'Where have you been?' Max snaps, jumping up as I near the table.

Mrs Red Dress shoots me a meaningful look as I fall into my chair.

'Sorry, I . . .' I look down for my bag, the carpet patterns swirling dangerously. Then I remember again where it is. 'Can we go now? I'd like to go.'

He frowns. 'Maybe in half an hour or so.'

I hold up a warning hand as he offers me more wine. 'I'm not feeling well, Max.'

He turns to look at me properly. 'God, you do look awful. Was it the chicken? I should have warned you.'

A wave of nausea swims up from my roiling stomach. I bend forward to catch my breath, my head lolling on to the front of Julia's dress then down to my knees.

'Seren, get up!' Max hisses, lifting the edge of the tablecloth to peer down at me. 'What are you doing?'

I catch Mrs Red Dress's eye as Max helps me up, her right hand raised, opening and closing in a sardonic wave. Max places a palm in the curve of my back, asking if I'll be all right to walk to the car. 'I'll come back for your coat and bag, we just need to get you—'

'I'll be fine,' I tell him, swinging my arm around his waist. 'Let's get the fuck out of here, dar-ling!'

Nine Months Missing

DS Chris Green selects DS Ingles' contact on his phone, tapping his hands on the desk as he waits for her to pick up.

'Chris, what you got?'

Typical Katie, straight to the point. He explains the break-through they've finally had on the Emily Plant case, the CCTV images they released sparking a flurry of calls with potential sightings, one of which was of particular interest to him, and, he thinks, to Katie as well. 'You remember Laura, the waitress who was at the Blakes' the night Julia went missing?'

'Hired by the catering company, shared a taxi with Julia's friends.'

Katie's encyclopaedic recall is always impressive. 'Yes, that's right. I've spoken to her and she thinks she's remembered something else. You know we never traced the driver who made the pick-up out at Brook House that night?'

'You've found him?'

'No, not exactly, but Laura thinks the taxi that eventually collected them also dropped someone off, and more than that, she thinks it was Emily Plant.'

'Emily was at Brooke House?'

'Yeah. We've never had any reason to link the two mispers, they went missing from locations miles apart, but it was on the same night.'

There's a pause before Katie says, 'Why would Emily be going to Brooke House?'

'No idea,' Chris replies. 'The CCTV of her taken in town ends at 23:27 and she's partially obscured because she's in a group – that's why we hadn't used it before, the quality just wasn't good enough, but this was a last-ditch attempt, throw anything at it we could. She looks quite different from the school photo. She's wearing a long dress, a maxi, is that the right word?'

'What about her friends?' Katie prompts.

'They've always said the same. That she left them after that CCTV capture, they assumed to walk home, but she was in quite a state. Served in every bloody bar she went to, but she was heavily made-up. Looked a lot older. Laura said she froze when she saw the latest appeal.'

'Is she certain it was Emily in the taxi?' Katie asks.

'She sounded pretty convinced. Laura was out of it on drink and drugs, but when she saw Emily's face—'

'Not a particularly credible witness.'

'No, but they'd walked up to the gate to wait for the taxi as it was late, so she had a good view as the car pulled in.'

'Cal said he was late, that's why he missed the fare. Did Laura confirm a time?'

'She's sketchy on that too; but after midnight.'

'So let me get this straight,' Katie says. 'Either the driver I spoke to, Cal Diamond, the one who claims he missed his fare, did make the pick-up at Brooke House and is lying for some reason, or there's another driver not coming forward. Either way, whoever collected Emily in town then took her to Brooke House?'

'Yeah, if Laura's sighting is correct, and we've now got a connection between Emily Plant and Julia Blake on the night they both went missing.'

'You free now?' Katie asks Chris, already looking up Cal's number. He better answer or she'll be banging on his door herself this time, however late it is.

Chapter Twenty-Five

An Inauspicious Exit

I peel my head from the pillow, eyelids glued together. My mouth tastes disgusting, tongue fat and furry, throat scraped dry, lips like Velcro. My freezing feet rest limply on the duvet which is pinned beneath me. As though someone had dropped me from a height; which has a ring of truth to it now I think about it. Except I can't think, cognitive function obliterated by the decimation of brain cells deep within my skull: zap, zap, zap! It must have been Izzy who put me to bed, maybe with Dom's help. I cringe at the thought as I slowly rest my head back on the pillow. The fabric of Julia's dress is puffed out around my waist and shoulders, the smoothness of it comforting, but my legs are bare gooseflesh, the slippery black silk ridden up to my hips. I dare to crack open one eye, the room already light although the thin curtains are still drawn, the floral duvet—

Shit! I'm back in Honeysuckle Cottage.

Ignoring the pounding rhythm in my temples, I scan the room for clues, but apart from my discarded belongings – boots, underwear, Julia's coat – there's nothing. I try to rewind my confused recollections. I know I left the hotel with Max after I'd thrown up. That was in the Ladies' bathroom in front of Mrs Red Dress. *Oh God.* Then Max had poured me into Julia's car and warned me not to vomit on the leather upholstery whilst he went back to get my coat and bag from the cloak-room. I groan, trying to recall what happened next, but after that . . . nothing.

I panic, sitting up too quickly. Max was angry. Oh God, was I sick on the way back here? No, I was all right, I'm sure of it. A vision of the wine bar at the end of my road returns. Max is beside me, asking me something, shouting it in fact. I look down at my half-naked body, my stomach clenching. I have a vague recollection of ripping off my tights and knickers in the pitch black as I'd rushed to the bathroom to pee and I don't feel like I've had sex. No, I'd know if . . . I dig my feet into the bedding and lift my hips to pull down the twisted dress. I can't recall anything happening between Max and me, but the missing pieces of last night are deeply troubling. Why would he bring me back here after we were right outside my apartment?

I turn slowly on to my side, curling into a foetal position to dangle a limp arm to the floor, my fingers feeling around. They find a glass of water which almost topples. I lift it to my lips and down it in one dribbled set of gulps as I hang over the side of the bed. Ignoring the queasy feeling the cold liquid induces, as well as a memory of my head in my lap under the tablecloth,

I grab my phone, squinting at the screen. A missed call at 04.17 a.m. Number withheld. I scream in frustration, then hold my head.

This is bad; very bad.

Casting aside my phone, which has barely any charge anyway, I walk tentatively into the sitting room in search of my bag. It's hooked on a chair by the table, my laptop still inside. Thankfully it picks up a weak signal, downloading just one email as I take a seat. It's the one I'd hoped to find. Perking up a little, I lean closer to read the title, in caps, 'NO HARD FEELINGS, DARLING'. I smile, wincing at the thought of my less than professional conduct in front of Jamie, but he left before the real carnage began, and judging by the light-hearted tone he's seen the funny side.

Then I start to read.

'Seren!' Max's bellowing voice is followed by three hefty thumps on the front door, each one making me jump. 'Seren! Wake up! Open the door!' He thumps again. 'SEREN!!!'

'I'm awake, Max! Wait! I'm—'

Max volleys through the door as soon as I unlock it, his iPad held up to me like a weapon. Jamie's sensationalist headline and the unflattering photo of Max, the one taken a few days after Julia's disappearance, thrust in my face. 'Have you seen this?' he demands.

'Yes, I just—'

'You stupid, stupid, girl!'

'I'm so sorry, Max. I was drunk. I had no idea—'

'No idea, that's about the size of it.' He stops talking and lets the iPad fall to his side, his focus shifting to me. 'Or is this what you and Jamie were planning last night? I saw you, chatting and laughing like old friends. Then he left early.'

'No, Max, honestly. I don't remember telling him half of this stuff.' I catch his expression. 'Look, I'm sorry, I really am, but he's screwed me over as much as he has you.'

It's an unwise comment, Max's fury building as he demands to know how I find our two situations comparable. 'I've been branded a suicidal wife killer whilst you got blind drunk and spilled your guts to a tabloid journalist. Not to mention over the pavement *and* my best shoes and by the look of it—' He points at the bedraggled hem of the dress.

A memory returns in vivid technicolour. We were outside the wine bar, as I'd recalled, but I'd been too drunk to remember which door led to my apartment. Max storms out, shouting at me, 'Take off my wife's dress and get the fuck off my property!'

'Seren?' Miriam pokes her head around the open door. It's been a good minute or two since Max stormed out but I haven't summoned up the energy to get up and close it. I slumped down in front of my laptop after he left, staring at the headline as if that would make it disappear. 'Are you OK?' she asks. I heard shouting and Max wouldn't—'

'Oh God, Miriam, what have I done?'

'I'll put the kettle on,' she says, coming in.

Miriam makes tea, very loudly, or so it seems. I stay at the table and torture myself with the full horror of Jamie's story. It's on the front page of the tabloid he currently writes for, his headline and column inches cleverly avoiding a libellous accusation, instead quoting 'a source close to the Blakes' which I guess must be me. Everything I remember telling him is there and so much more, the heart ripped out of a feature I've barely finished writing. *Shit! Shit! Shit!* Why did I drink so much? I was completely crazy, acting like a teenager. Not the sensible teen I was, but the stupid one everyone else seemed to be at uni. Jamie's shafted me, and I deserve it. What a fucking idiot. Naïve and drunk, and stupid. He even mentions Max's suicide attempt and I'd decided I would never write about that. Mr Jamie Fucking Porten has played me like the expert he is; flattery, alcohol, false promises and even a goodnight kiss. Although I think the clumsy advance was mainly mine. *Oh God.* I'd even had a cigarette with him whilst we'd waited for his taxi, and I never smoke. His parting comment comes back to me, something about how he'd 'see me right' and for a second a glimmer of hope bubbles up, then I realise all over again that I'm an absolute fucking idiot.

Miriam puts a mug of black tea by my laptop and takes the other chair.

'Why are you being so nice to me?' I ask.

'Because you're a young girl who's made a silly mistake and I'm not going to punish you when you're already doing a good enough job of that yourself.'

'But Max?' I ask, wiping my nose on the inside of my wrist. 'He was so angry.'

She extracts a tissue from the cuff of her cardigan and passes it to me. 'We've weathered worse than this. Not for a while, but it's all been said before, well, most of it. How are you feeling this morning? You look better than I thought you might after the state you arrived in last night.'

'You saw me?'

'Heard you first,' she says. 'I helped Max get you inside and then you passed out on the bed. I sat with you a while, got you some water, but you were snoring away, so I left around two.'

'It was you who put me to bed?' I close my eyes on the shame, but it's also a relief it was Miriam, not Max. 'Thank you, and sorry.'

'So . . .' she says, pointing at my laptop. 'Can you write something for the *Herald* to counter all that rubbish?'

I look at Jamie's insensitive headline, then Miriam, and although my head is thick with hangover, I realise I've underestimated her. She's looking for a way to fix things for Max, her sympathy only a preamble to this suggestion. I close the laptop to hide the awfulness of it all. 'No, I'm afraid he's already said everything, and some.'

Miriam frowns. 'You shouldn't give up so easily, Seren. You know Max a lot better than that awful man does.'

She doesn't understand. Jamie's much more high profile than I am. Anything I write will look like a copy of his, not the other way around, and besides, my article was never going to be the pity piece Max, and now Miriam, seem to assume I was writing.

'I worked hard for that exclusive, gave up everything for it,' I tell her, using the tissue again. 'It was all I had left, and I threw it away.'

'All you had left?'

'I lost my job at the *Herald*, Miriam. I'm not even a journalist anymore.'

Miriam pats me on my arm. 'Well, at least the snow's melted overnight. You can drive your car home once you feel up to it.'

'Oh God, what time is it?' I ask, remembering my appointment with DS Ingles. I'm still obligated to share everything I know with her, and maybe Miriam's right, there might be something to be salvaged from this mess, particularly if the detective passes on anything new in return for the information I have about the necklace.

'Almost half-nine,' she tells me. 'You in a hurry?'

Miriam is outside when I open the door a few minutes later. I'm dressed in my own clothes and just about functioning, the bright morning sunshine waking me up, as did the ice-cold water I splashed liberally on my make-up stained face. The courtyard is wet with slush, the gravel peeking through in places.

'You all set?' she asks, coming over.

I blink, my head like a lump of lead. 'Yes, thanks so much for everything.' I hold out Julia's coat. 'I've left everything else on the bed. I think the dress is ruined, sorry.'

'Do you have another one?' she asks, taking the coat.

I shake my head.

'Then let's call it quits,' she says, handing it back. 'Look after yourself, Seren. I hope it all works out for you, whatever you do next.'

She's clearly relieved I'm leaving, but her concern for my welfare feels genuine. It was never personal for her, and in that realisation I understand so much more about her than I have before.

'Thanks, Miriam. I thought you were quite scary at first, but you've been kind to me and I appreciate that.'

'I'm sorry I was less than welcoming,' she says. 'It was silly of me, to think that you and Max were . . . I saw you, at the door before the incident down at the swimming pool. I was upstairs, closing Max's curtains and I . . . well, I ignored you. It was childish of me and I'm sorry.'

'That's OK.' I smile and hold up the key to the cottage, dropping it into her palm. 'Hope you find the other one on one of your walks.'

'I assume you're not saying goodbye to Max before you leave?' she asks, closing her hand around the key.

'No, I don't think he'll want to see me, do you?' I slide on the sunglasses I found at the bottom of my handbag. 'Anyway, don't want to interrupt him when he's working. He's never keen on that.'

I hitch my heavy bag on to my shoulder, and set off, but I pause to look back at Miriam one last time before I turn the corner. She's already gone.

Brooke House looks empty as I approach, the eyes half-closed against the sunlight, tiny rivers of melting ice running down the stone steps. There's no point ringing the bell. Max will be at his desk, headphones piping music into his ears as he types. Anyway, even if by some miracle he were to hear me, I don't want to see him. It's an inauspicious exit, disappointment and the hangover draining me, my blistered heels sore and no plasters left to cover them. I head across the drive, then down the side of the kitchen, a final glance inside before I reach the garages.

Careful not to bang my car door against Miriam's, I put my bag and Julia's coat on the passenger seat, winding down the window to gulp in some cold air as I strap in. I can do this, I tell myself. It's just the worst hangover I've ever had, but if I concentrate . . . I turn the key in the ignition, the engine throaty at first, then it stutters to a halt. *'Come on!'* I try again, another flutter of hope, then the hoarseness of a flooded engine tells me it's useless. *Shit!* To add insult to injury, the wipers spring to life, screeching across the glass to clear the remnants of snow.

I grab my bag and sling on Julia's coat, jogging then hobbling back to the front of the house.

I bang hard on the door and pull on the bell many times but as I'd expected, Max doesn't hear. Or if he does he's decided to ignore me. I scream in frustration and run down the wet steps, stress compounding my headache. I will definitely be late now, but maybe not by too much if I can persuade Miriam to give me a lift over to the new Police Headquarters on the other side of town. I've no idea what I'll tell her. I certainly can't share the real reason I'm meeting with a detective. I'll work out an excuse on the way.

But there's no answer at Honeysuckle Cottage either. I'm overheated after running around in Julia's coat, my bag heavy on my shoulder as I regret again last night's binge drinking. Casting around for ideas, I catch sight of something in the distance, at the edge of the wood that runs round the back of the cottages. The same wood I'd peered at from the bathroom skylight, watching as arcs of torchlight retreated. The sunlight is dazzling, no need for a torch right now, but if I'm not

Nine Months Missing

DS Katie Ingles studies the stills from the CCTV recording outside the bar. The grainy images of Emily Plant – heavy make-up, long dress – are just as Chris had described them. She selects the clearest one and slides it across the table to Cal Diamond. She's been impressed with Chris's tenacity. He's certainly helped her out with her misper, never letting go of Julia Blake or Emily Plant. They've agreed she will lead the interview, but Chris's silent presence beside her is reassuring.

'Do you recognise this girl?' she asks Cal, directing him to the print with a tap of her finger.

He shakes his dreadlocks and she reminds him to speak up, for the recording. 'I don't recognise her,' he says firmly.

'We have a witness placing you at the Blakes' house on the night of Saturday May the twenty-seventh last year, with this girl in the back of your car,' Katie tells him. 'You need to tell us the truth this time, Cal. No more games.'

He's only a young lad, twenty-one. His skin tanned and inked from his travels. He's been around the world in the last nine months, seen places Katie has never been, or is likely to go. But right now, he's testing her patience.

'OK,' he says. 'I do.'

'You do recognise her?' Katie asks.

He looks directly at the frozen image. 'Her name's Emily Plant. I nearly didn't pick her up, thought she might vom in the back of my cab. She was in quite a state when I tracked her down.'

'OK, let's backtrack,' Katie says. 'Tell me what happened that night – everything, this time. No more lies, OK?'

He nods. 'I was supposed to collect Emily at half-eleven outside the wine bar, but she kept me waiting. I drove round and round the one-way system. That's why I was late for the pick-up at Brooke House.'

'It was prearranged that you'd collect Emily?' Katie asks, glancing at Chris. 'By whom?'

'Mrs Blake.'

'So you knew Julia Blake?' Katie asks.

Cal gulps down half the bottle of water Chris has pushed his way. 'Sort of. I'd driven Julia,' he glances up. 'Mrs Blake, I mean. I'd driven her home from the station a few weeks before, after she'd been to London visiting a friend. Must have been April, beginning, I think, I can check the date. We got chatting, she was that kind of fare. You can tell, if they want to talk or just stare at their phone. She said she wasn't a phone type of person, there was no signal out where she lived and she preferred more creative pursuits. She was a photographer.'

Katie nods. 'So you took her home?'

'Yeah, she asked me to drop her at the gate, but she didn't get out, not straight away. Said she wondered if we could keep in touch . . . what was the word she used? *Discreetly*. I thought she was hitting on me at first, she was a good-looking woman, but turns out that wasn't what she wanted me for.'

Katie leans forward. 'And what was it she wanted?'

Cal swallows. 'She suggested I set up an email address that looked genuine, and we had this kind of code. She'd say it was a delivery, a package she'd missed that she needed me to drop off or pick up. Her husband was pretty controlling, I think. Hardly let her out of his sight. I liked her a lot. She always paid me in cash, and she was nice, very kind. She put a word in for me with the catering company when she booked the waitress, said they should use me for the pick-up as I could be trusted with a woman late at night. She was thoughtful like that, knew I needed the money for travelling, and a pick-up and drop-off would really help me out. She always tipped generously too. She said she'd like to travel one day. I got the impression she was bored, living in the middle of nowhere.'

'So Julia Blake recommended you to the caterers, specified they were to ask for you in particular?' Katie asks, glancing again at Chris. *Why didn't anyone uncover this detail at the time?* Another dropped stitch, but people only ever answer the questions put to them. The knack is working out the right ones to ask.

'Yeah, midnight pick-up. But like I said, Emily had made me late.'

'You told your boss you missed the fare,' Chris tells Cal.

He looks at Chris across the table, then Katie. 'Sometimes I'd call in fares as a no-show and pocket the cash. Not all the time, just the odd one.'

'So you *did* make the pick-up?' Chris asks.

317

Cal sighs heavily. 'I dropped Emily off first, down by the outbuildings, just past the house . . .' Katie nods. 'That's where I always took her, and Mrs B was always good for the money when I next saw her.'

'Did you see her that night?' Katie asks.

'No. I didn't. Honestly, I didn't. I just dropped Emily then I went straight back to collect the catering company fare before I lost it. It was supposed to just be the waitress, Laura, but there were three of them waiting by the gate. The man asked me to drop him and his girlfriend at that burger van near the station that's always open late.' Chris nods. 'Then I took Laura home, out on the new estate by Asda. She said she wanted me to drop her a few streets away, so she could sober up a bit before she faced her mum. She looked pretty wasted.'

Chris sighs at the carelessness of the boy, knowing what can happen when young girls walk home on their own in that state.

'The guy paid in cash for the whole fare,' Cal tells them. 'The final drop-off included. I assumed the catering company would have paid in advance so his cash would have been easy money but turns out they hadn't. That's why I lied and said I'd missed the fare. Am I in trouble?' Cal waits for Chris to reply, which he doesn't. 'Look, you can understand why I took off, can't you? I knew it would look bad that I'd been there that night, but I'd been planning on quitting my job for ages. I just hurried up my plans.'

'So you *had* seen the appeals for Emily and Julia?' Katie asks, trying and failing to keep the anger from leaking out. Her team could have made this connection nine months ago if Cal hadn't fled the country. Of course they'd discussed the fact that Emily and Julia went missing on the same night, but so did some guy who turned up after a two-day bender. It was a coincidence, nothing at all to suggest that there was a link. 'I thought you said you liked Mrs Blake, that she was good to you?'

'Yeah, I saw the appeals, but . . .' Cal says, wiping away snot and tears. 'I didn't see Mrs Blake that night, I promise. Or Mr Blake.'

'What were the deliveries?' Chris asks, leaning in to read aloud from his notes, *'She'd say it was a delivery, a package she'd missed that she needed me to drop off or pick up.'*

'Emily,' Cal says, snivelling. 'Emily Plant was the package.'

Chapter Twenty-Six

A Dreadful Accident

'Miriam! Wait!'

We've come a long way from the house but Miriam is still walking fast, and with purpose, her sturdy legs clearly used to the terrain. I call after her, but the gap between us is widening. I hoist my bag on to my shoulder and break into a run, although my blisters are on fire and Julia's coat is flapping around me, my boots sinking into the mud. Miriam crosses a road, the same one, I think, where I stopped to call Theo before I drove to his house. That night feels like years ago, but it's been less than a week.

I look for Miriam as I approach the twisting lane, just making out her red coat disappearing into a denser wood on the other side. I force myself to follow, my lungs filling with cold air, but I manage to gain a little ground, enough to notice Miriam is carrying something; a bunch of lilies exactly like the ones in the hall that Max said he hated. The heady scent fills my nostrils as if I was close enough to smell the perfumed petals dangling at Miriam's side, but she's still way out in front, so far in fact that I give up shouting her name.

I debate turning back, feeling nauseous again. Miriam has disappeared and Brooke House is just visible behind me. I could try rousing Max, or just wait at the cottages for Miriam's return. There's now no chance I can make my appointment on time. But as I catch sight of Miriam again, lilies in hand, a queasy feeling washes over me and this time it's nothing to do with my hangover.

The canopy grows denser as Miriam pushes further in, bare-limbed trees connecting above, a few leaves clinging on from last year. I keep my distance, the sounds different in here, cracking twigs amplified in the stillness. Miriam flits between the outstretched branches and tangles of raised roots so I lose her bright red anorak more than once. Then it's there again, hood up as the wet trees drip their melted snow. The ground is clogged with water and ice, mud sucking at my inadequate footwear, but Miriam is nimble, as if she's come this way many times before. I recall her telling me how she knows every path in, out and around the estate. I try to convince myself this is just one of her long walks, but why the lilies? My chest heaves as I rush to keep up, but I'm determined to see this through. The story has shifted, and I must follow it.

Miriam has reached a clearing, a tranquil spot, or at least it would be if I wasn't terrified, my pulse thudding in my ears as I hang back. Watching as Miriam places the flowers down and begins talking to herself. 'Almost there,' she says, then, to the flowers, 'Aren't they nice?'

She pushes back her hood and picks up the bunched stalks, the petals flapping as she presses on, deeper and deeper into the forest. I follow, keeping up until suddenly, she disappears. Then I notice the steep slope she must have clambered down. I move closer, lying on the spongy moss to peer over the edge, my bag now beside me. In the dip, a little further down the bank, a fast-flowing stream passes a fallen tree, the branches kissing the water. Miriam is beside the tree, continuing her one-sided conversation with the cut flowers. 'Have you been all right? I'm sorry it's been a while. I tried, the other night, but I had to turn back. Too risky, you see.'

She wipes her eyes and covers her mouth, then without warning she looks up. I freeze, burying my face in the remnants of autumnal leaves, their gossamer spines breaking free from last year's lush growth. I inhale their earthy scent, all the seasons passed through them and composted to provide new life. It's intoxicating, but I force myself to look again. Miriam has moved on, the lilies now resting on the fallen tree as she lifts her right foot and plants it on the gnarly bark.

There's a moment of dark comedy as she's temporarily marooned, her chunky legs astride the wide trunk, wedged there. She wriggles to reposition herself and slithers down the other side, landing with a thud, then she dusts herself down and claps her hands together, grabbing the flowers before she disappears again. I balance on my haunches, my thighs soon aching from the effort of crouching silently, a hand to the sodden bank to support myself as I strain to see where she's gone this time. Miriam has dropped to her knees behind the fallen tree. I lean over as far as I dare, watching as she begins

322

clearing leaves with her bare hands. Then she reaches in her coat pocket and takes out a silver trowel, scraping and digging, small clumps of loamy earth tossed aside.

It seems to take ages, one trowelful at a time, but gradually a hole appears, then widens and deepens. But oh so slowly, maybe ten or fifteen minutes passing as I wait for the full horror to unfold. Sometimes Miriam is talking. 'Poor Julia. Poor, poor Julia. All those wasted years and then this.' But mainly it's quiet, other than the scraping and digging.

She pauses, her movements like an archaeologist dusting back the sand from an ancient artefact as she uses her hands, fingers delicate, shaping something in the trench. I half-close my eyes and immediately lose balance, only just managing to save myself from a tumble down the slippery bank, my breaths ragged.

She has found something.

Poking free of the cleared ground is a piece of fabric, black, I think, although it could be any colour or print, it's so dirty. Miriam releases a single sob from her twisted mouth as she pulls at the cloth. It won't budge, so she takes her trowel again and presses the point in, carefully excavating, then using the fabric to prise something pale and waxy from its hiding place. I exhale, forcing myself not to run, appalled but transfixed as bone by bone a skeletal hand is exhumed, rings loose on the skinless fingers. She cradles it in her palm, the lifeless hand laid across hers. It's a terrible sight, but I can't look away, the only sound the fast-flowing water and Miriam's apologies.

'I'm so sorry. You poor girl. You're so missed, so loved, do you know that? I thought I'd lost you, this tree coming down so close to where we . . . but of course you're still here, you beautiful—'

The shrill sound is piercing, cracking open the moment with such force that for a long second I'm paralysed by it. Then I'm on my feet, my bag cast aside as I pull my phone from my coat pocket. I'm running, flat-out now, stumbling over the long coat as I answer my phone. 'Please, whoever this is, you have to help me!'

'Hello, Seren? Can you hear me? We had an appointment?'

'Oh my God, Detective Ingles, please help. You have to help. There's a body, Julia Blake.'

'OK. Slow down. Say that again. That is Seren Spencer?' The detective's voice is calm, reassuring.

'Yes, I'm with Miriam, Max's PA, she led me to a body, it's Julia Blake.'

'Where are you?' she asks. 'I need your exact location. *Seren?* Are you at Brooke House?'

'No,' I slow a little so I can speak; I'm panting heavily. 'But nearby.'

'Seren, listen to me!' The detective's voice is loud now, taking control. 'You're going to have to tell me *exactly* where you are.'

'We crossed a road, then into a wood.' I look around, try to get my bearings. 'I can see the house! It's ahead of me now, a long way off, and the trees are thick, I'm about thirty, forty metres from a stream, there was a steep bank—'

My phone is knocked from my hand as Miriam barrels into me from behind. I lunge after it, screaming, '*No!*' as I fall, but there's nothing I can do, her boot already crushing the screen as she grinds it into the ground beside me.

'Who were you talking to?' She looks indignant, as if I'm the guilty party.

'A detective.'

'I don't believe you.' She grabs my wrist and pulls me up.

'Let me go!' Miriam must have fifty kilos on me, the force of her determination taking me back towards the slope. 'The police are on their way,' I tell her, although she seems not to hear and I've no idea if it's true. 'You can't hurt me, they'll know it's you!'

She drops my wrist and spins round to face me, her eyes narrowing. 'Why would I hurt you, Seren? Everything I've done has been to make the best of a terrible situation.' She reaches out and I pull away but she catches the sleeve of Julia's coat. 'Come on! We'll have to move her quickly.'

'Miriam, please,' I dig my heels in, but the steep bank is soon right beside us. 'I don't want to see the body. Can't we wait here until the police come?' I try to pull away, but she digs her fingers in deeper, edging backwards, her body angled against the gradient. 'They'll help you, Miriam. I promise.'

'We have to at least try,' she says, not listening. 'I'll need your help, of course, it's a two-person job, although now . . .' Miriam falters and I take my chance, wrenching myself free of her grasp. She stumbles, falling a metre or two, then she grasps a root and holds on.

'Miriam, listen to me,' I tell her as she scrabbles back up. 'We need to let the police deal with it now.'

'No, I can fix this,' Miriam says, falling to the ground beside me and sobbing into her hands. 'I have to. I promised.'

'Miriam, it's over. You did your best for Max, but it's over.'

*

It's been a while since Miriam last spoke, my questions unanswered. But at least she's given up trying to persuade me to help her move the body. We must be roughly half a mile from the road and obscured by dense woodland. The hi vis jacket is like a mirage when I finally spot it approaching.

'Seren Spencer?' The police officer reaches down to help me up, then he catches Miriam as she hurls herself at him, his long arms easily restraining her. He's a foot taller than Miriam and probably three decades younger, but she puts up a good fight.

'The grave is down there,' I tell him, avoiding Miriam's wild stare. 'Behind a fallen tree. It's Julia Blake. Max Blake's wife.'

'No!' Miriam screams. 'You've got it wrong. That's not true!'

'*Shit!*' the young officer says, taking out his radio as he hangs on to Miriam one-handed, half-holding her up, half-pushing her away. 'I've been diverted from Traffic,' he tells me as Miriam crumples. 'I suppose I should take a look,' he says, eyeing the edge of the slope beyond which Julia's bony hand must still protrude from its makeshift burial site.

The traumatised traffic officer leads us back to the road, Miriam by his side. Tape is already flickering between branches and trunks, the cordon extending a long way. I smile to encourage him as he glances back, his skin almost as green as his jacket. His gaudily marked car – a combination of chevrons and a chequerboard of blue and green – was obviously abandoned in a hurry: the driver's door left open, keys still in the ignition. He tells me to wait as he hands Miriam over to a tall man in plain clothes. The detective is tanned and when he smiles I notice he has very white teeth.

'Where are we going?' Miriam asks as she's led away, her voice child-like. 'Can I go home?'

'Not yet,' the detective replies, placing a hand on her head as he settles her in the back seat of his car.

Then his car blue-lights the way as we head in convoy towards the motorway, me and the traffic officer following behind.

DS Katie Ingles leads me through to a small room that looks exactly the same as the one I was in hours ago. She asks me to take a seat and offers me a bottle of water.

'Is this going to take long?' I ask. 'I've given a statement.'

She takes a seat opposite me. 'How are you doing, Seren?'

'I'm OK.' I take a swig of water, my head pounding. 'Thank you for sending someone to find me.'

She looks up from her notes. 'It was lucky that traffic officer wasn't too far away.' She smiles, a note of sympathy in her expression as she tells me it was the first time he'd seen a dead body, as if I hadn't guessed. 'Anyway, let's crack on. I'm sure you'd like to go home.'

Pen poised, she asks me to repeat everything again, just one more time, looking up when I come to the part about the bones. 'Did Miriam give you the exact details of the burial?'

'No,' I reply. The thought hadn't occurred to me before. 'I assumed it was the night Julia went missing. She definitely said it was a two-person job.'

'Miriam suggested to you that she'd placed the body there with help?'

'Yes, well, no, not exactly, but she certainly knew where the body was and had been visiting regularly to place flowers.'

327

'You've been interviewing Max Blake for an article you're writing for the *Herald*?'

'It started out like that, but I'm freelance now. I can let you have all my notes and the recordings.'

'Soon as possible, please,' she says, standing up. 'Anything at all, whether you feel it's relevant or not. We'll talk again soon.'

'OK, thanks.' I get up too. 'Will you be charging Miriam? I assume Max is—?'

'If anything else occurs, do get in touch,' she says, passing me a card with her mobile number scribbled on the back. 'That's the best number to contact me on if it's urgent, but I won't be commenting on the investigation. And keep away from Brooke House.'

'I told your colleague about the necklace,' I say, stalling.

'My colleague has been through it with me, thanks. Was there anything else, Seren?'

'Actually . . . there was one more thing.'

The detective is slim, gaunt even, and not much taller than me. Messy hair, no make-up, looks tired, her phone in her hand. She's clearly busy.

'It's nothing to do with this,' I say. 'But there's something I'd like your advice on, if you have a moment?'

'OK, let's walk and talk, Seren.'

DS Ingles and I make our way towards the lifts, then down two floors and out into the bright atrium. She listens and says she understands, although she can't make any promises. 'Someone will meet you here to arrange your journey home, although it might be a wait, I'm afraid. Thanks for all your help, Seren.' She turns back and crosses the atrium, absorbed again by her phone.

There are two sets of automatic doors by reception, one closing before the next one opens, a constant to-and-fro of activity. I take a seat and stare at them, lost in my thoughts.

'There's lots you don't understand, Seren,' Miriam told me as we'd waited in the woods for help to arrive. 'But I can promise you it was an accident. A dreadful, dreadful, accident.'

An Hour Earlier

Katie is animated, her modulation rising and falling as she begins her spiel.

'Interview with Max Blake conducted by DS Katie Ingles. You do not have to say anything, but it may harm your defence if you do not mention when questioned something you later rely on in court. Anything you do say may be used in evidence. Do you understand what this means, Max?'

'Yes, I understand all that,' he says. 'What I haven't been told is why I'm here.'

Katie looks down at her notes, taking a moment to settle her thoughts. She can't wait to get started, months of frustration and dead ends leading to this, but Max remains arrogant, puffed up by his false sense of security, as if he's above all this. They watched him arrive, she and Chris, Max almost swaggering as he'd walked in wearing that stupid leather jacket. Some people are cowed by authority, but not him.

'Is there any news on my wife?' Max asks, arms folded, every hair in place. 'Because if not—'

Chris begins, as agreed. 'Can you describe the night of your wife's disappearance?'

'*This again?* I told you what happened at the time, so unless you're going to explain why—'

'We've found a body, Max,' Katie tells him, both detectives carefully watching for his reaction.

'A body? I don't— Oh, my God! Is it . . . is it her?'

Katie catches Chris's eye. Max seems genuine, but he's had nine months to perfect his act.

'We're awaiting formal identification,' Chris tells him. 'But we know it's a woman, and the body appears to have been in the ground for some time. Your assistant, Miriam Norris, led us to a place in the woods about a mile from your property. Miriam's told us the identity, Max, but we'd like to hear from you.'

'Miriam's eccentric, she says all kinds of odd things,' Max replies, affecting nonchalance.

'What kind of things?' Katie asks.

'I need to call my lawyer,' Max announces, sitting up straight, but his shoulders start to shake, his head bowed as he shields his eyes.

Katie calls home, her expression pained after she hangs up. Whatever she does is wrong these days; promises made only to be broken. She grabs a coffee then takes the chance to speak to the reporter who was there when the body was discovered. It's already been a long day but Katie doesn't feel jaded, quite the reverse, and Chris is buzzing, meeting her in the corridor once they get word the solicitor has reported in at the custody suite. Chris is walking a foot taller as he holds his pass to the door leading to the interview room.

'Tell me about the anniversary party, Max,' Katie begins. 'What time did you say goodnight to your guests?'

Max glances at his solicitor who turns to his client and nods, resting one of his double chins on his Savile Row lapel. 'You mean *my* friends?' Max asks.

Katie gives a curt, 'Yes.'

'Around eleven,' Max says. 'Not long after Julia's guests turned up, but you already know—'

'According to your original statement,' Katie says, 'you left your wife by the pool at midnight and didn't notice she was missing until the next morning?'

'Yes, that's correct.'

'But you failed to mention that before you retired for the night, you'd found Ben Fortune and the waitress, Laura Gell, how shall I put it . . .?'

'Shagging on the lawn,' Chris says.

'Yes,' Katie replies, frowning as Max's solicitor raises an eyebrow. 'Any particular reason you held that information back?'

'No comment,' Max replies.

The solicitor points out that the omission has no bearing on Max's movements that night.

'Maybe not,' Chris tells him. 'But we have a witness statement from Laura Gell confirming the taxi that collected her from Brooke House arrived with a passenger,' he informs the now scowling solicitor. 'And the taxi driver has also confirmed, the passenger he dropped at Brooke House was named Emily Plant.'

Max snaps his head up and stares at Chris, then he exchanges a look with his solicitor and repeats, 'No comment.'

Katie intervenes, losing patience with this charade. 'Take us through your movements again that night, and I'd like to remind you, Max, that anything you do say—'

'Yes!' Max tells her loudly, looking up from the stain on the table his finger was tracing. 'I get it, but still no comment.'

'So I'm guessing,' Katie says, underlining Emily's name to go back to later, 'Ben's arrival was the last thing you wanted on your anniversary?'

'I wasn't happy, of course,' Max replies. 'I've told you that!'

'*Max,*' his solicitor warns.

'I didn't like the guy,' Max admits. 'I thought you might make assumptions that weren't correct, because despite some severe provocation over the years, I have never laid a finger on him.'

Max's solicitor blusters about leading questions, reminding his client he doesn't have to say anything at this stage.

Katie waits for him to stop talking then asks Max, 'Did you speak to Ben Fortune or Laura Gell when you found them together?'

'I told them both to fuck off home, I think.'

'And then?' Katie asks.

'Then I carried on to the pool to speak to my wife, but I couldn't get a lot of sense out of her. She was drunk, and the woman Ben had brought with him was hanging around, so it was hard to have much of a private conversation. After Ben came back to the pool, I left them to it; before I totally lost my temper.'

'And went where?' Katie asks.

'To my study. Look, if this is about Ben, then forget it. I knew everything, always have. I didn't like it, but I knew.'

'You knew about what?' Katie asks.

'I knew he occasionally slept with my wife, but I also knew she was using him. It was me she loved.'

'So you went to your study?' Katie asks. 'Not straight to bed as you'd originally told us?'

'No,' Max replies, avoiding his solicitor's warning not to say any more. 'I couldn't settle to any work though, I was too worried about Julia. So I went back to the pool, but there was no sign of her there, or anyone else. Then I spotted headlights up by the gate. I watched the taxi come down the drive and then it took the turn towards the outbuildings.'

His solicitor asks for a moment with his client, but Max tells him to shut the fuck up and let him speak.

'I thought they'd be in the barn. That's where they used to meet,' he tells Katie, sweat pouring off him. 'They thought I didn't know, but of course I did.' He rubs away a tear. 'The door to Lavender Cottage was open. She was inside, and very drunk. Abusive, in fact.'

'For the recording, please, Max,' Chris tells him. 'Who was in the cottage?'

'Emily Plant,' Max says. 'And my wife.'

His solicitor slumps back in his chair and throws Max a resigned look.

'I went in and pushed past Emily to get to Julia. I could hear she was unwell in the bathroom,' Max says. 'I opened the door and—' He wipes his mouth with the back of his hand. 'She flew at me, but she was unsteady, she'd had so much to drink that night, maybe drugs, I don't know. I wouldn't trust Ben not to have slipped something into her drink. I tried to save her but the floor was slippy and she fell backwards, away from me, hit her head hard on the side of the bath. It's solid enamel, the noise was horrible.'

Max's solicitor grabs his notepad and scribbles fast, turning a note to his client who shakes his head. Max is sobbing now.

'I didn't mean to lose my temper. I would never deliberately hurt her. Never!'

'Tell us what happened next,' Katie says.

'Emily was screaming at me that I'd killed Julia, she was hysterical.'

'And your wife?' Katie asks. She can feel Chris beside her, willing her on. 'Max?'

'There was blood everywhere. On the side of the bath, the floor. It was awful. I felt so guilty and Emily was clawing at Julia after she got up—'

'She got up?' Chris asks. 'So Julia was conscious?'

'Yes, but Emily was virtually attacking her. Then Emily started pleading with me, begging me to drive her back to her parents. I grabbed the silly girl, shook her, told her to calm down, but she was panic-stricken. She kept checking her mobile, asking me why there was never any signal. I told her to go up to the house, use the phone there, but she just shook her head, kept screaming that she was scared. Julia tried to comfort her, but she shrank away, as if—' Max rubs his hands over his face. 'That's when Julia flipped out, said she was getting her car and they were leaving together. No arguments.' Max looks at the detectives. 'I couldn't let her do that. Julia said some terrible things. Things she didn't mean. I know she didn't.'

Katie watches Max with disgust as he cries, inconsolable now. 'Do you need a break?' she asks.

He looks up and shakes his head, wiping his eyes and nose with his hands. 'No, thank you. I want to say this. I *need* to say it.' He stares at Katie. 'It was all my fault. I killed Emily.'

'*Shit!*' Chris says as they walk to the cafeteria, Max's solicitor insistent his client must take a break. 'Didn't see that one coming.'

Katie doesn't want to talk, she needs to think. Max has finally admitted what happened, after all these months, the truth tumbling out of him as he'd described how he chased after his wife's car in his Porsche, refusing to accept she was leaving with Emily. As they'd sped along the dark country lanes, Julia – an inexperienced and drunk, possibly even drugged, driver – had lost control of the Range Rover. Emily, 'the silly girl' as Max referred to her, had jumped out just before Julia's car ploughed into a tree. Max had tried to brake when he'd seen Emily lying in the road, but no one could have stopped in that split second. *No one.* He'd tried in vain to revive the dead girl, then run to check on his wife, but she'd vanished. 'You can't blame her for that,' he'd said. 'She was terrified, but none of this is her fault. Blame me, but not Julia.'

He'd called Mim and they'd concealed Emily's body then searched for Julia all night in the sudden and torrential rain, but there was no sign. She'd disappeared without trace.

'I should have let them go,' Max told them. 'It was all my fault. I'm so sorry. So, so sorry.'

Chris taps his teeth with a plastic stirrer. 'Not a mark on that Porsche, I saw it myself. It was parked in the garage by the house.'

Katie nods. 'Just like driving over a speed bump, I guess. And the roads were so wet that night, even just the journey back to the house would have almost certainly washed the tyres clean of any blood or tissue.' Chris shudders and closes his eyes. 'We had no reason to link Emily to the car, Chris. We didn't even know there'd been a hit and run. Our focus was on finding Julia.'

'I'll get the Porsche checked for any damage underneath,' he says.

Katie picks at her pasta salad as Chris takes a huge bite out of a day-old egg sandwich and chews, making her smile.

'What do you reckon was going on between Julia and Emily?' he asks, swallowing.

'It's beyond disturbing that Emily was only thirteen,' Katie replies. 'But I don't know, something still doesn't add up.'

'Yeah,' Chris says, then they both look at one another, the pieces dropping into place as a lump of egg falls onto the table between them.

Chapter Twenty-Seven

Indiscretion

We've run out of conversation, the fresh-faced traffic officer and I, both silent as he drives me home. Pride was written across his face as he'd made a performance of collecting me from reception, very apologetic about the wait as he'd held every door open, including the passenger door of the police car. It had reminded me of Theo's chivalry, but he's the antithesis of Theo, the PC's youthful lack of guile engaging, if inappropriate. So far he's told me he's never seen a dead body before – 'Thank fuck!' – and observed how it must have been 'freaky' when Miriam had lifted the hand from the shallow grave and held it in hers. I suggested maybe we could talk about something else, but we haven't; nothing else in common. And now all I can think of are Julia's pale, bony fingers in Miriam's chubby ones. I don't think that image will ever leave me.

'I'll probably get a proper bollocking for saying this,' he says, breaking into my thoughts as he changes gear. 'But there's a rumour going round that the body wasn't Max's wife.'

'*What?*' I swivel in the passenger seat to face him, the seat belt cutting into my neck, amazed at his indiscretion. 'Then who?'

'Waiting for a formal ID, but apparently Max told them it was someone called Emily Plant. A schoolgirl, who's been missing for months. Hit and run, I heard. Reckon he must have buried her in the woods, with Miriam's help.'

'*Shit!*' I recall watching the appeal in Theo's office and turning away from the distraught parents, not wanting to mix their pain with my own. I had no idea it would impact me in this way. 'I don't understand. Why was Emily involved, and where's Julia?'

He shrugs, says that's literally all he knows.

'Just here, outside the bridal shop,' I tell him, still deep in thought.

He watches me unstrap, telling me how he'd hoped to become a detective in a few years' time, but now he's not so sure. 'My cousin's opening a vape shop. You know, the cigarette things?' I nod. 'Might go in with him instead – good money, he reckons, and fewer dead bodies.'

'Hopefully,' I reply, thanking him for stopping to retrieve my bag on the way over.

The narrow country lane had been closed to all traffic, the taped-off scene bringing it all back. I'd waited in the car, my muddy bag held aloft when he'd returned. It had been found where I'd left it, he told me. At the top of the bank amongst some dead leaves, the contents unharmed. Unlike my phone.

AMANDA REYNOLDS

'Yeah, no worries,' he says, accidentally flicking the wipers on. 'DS Ingles organised it all. It's been nice meeting you, Seren. Weird, but nice.'

He offers his hand and I shake it.

'I don't suppose you fancy meeting up for a drink sometime?' he asks, affecting a casual tone. 'We could try the wine bar on the corner.'

'Aren't you a bit young for me?' I reply, immediately wishing I hadn't as he turns a deep shade of red. 'Look, give me your number,' I say, rooting in my bag for pen and paper.

The flashing lights of the retreating police car attract Laure's attention. She waves from the deserted bridal shop, but I don't stop, inserting my key and running past Izzy's bike and up the stairs. The door to our apartment flies open and Izzy looks down from the second-floor landing.

'Seren!' She pulls me into one of her bear hugs then holds me at arm's length, her face stern. 'Where have you been? You look awful. Are you hurt?'

'No, I'm fine. Sorry, my phone . . .' An image of Miriam's boot smashing into it flashes up and I lean into Izzy's warm chest.

'Seren, what is it? What's happened? Come on, let's get you inside.'

Izzy's company is the best medicine. She tucks me under a blanket and joins me on the sofa, reminding me to drink my tea whilst it's hot. I recount my day, Izzy's eyes stretching wider, her mouth hanging open. I slump back on the sofa once I'm finished, feeling completely exhausted.

340

'Oh my God, that's hideous,' Izzy says, taking a third biscuit from the packet. 'A real live body!'

'Well, not exactly live, but yes.'

'So if it's not Julia, then who was this buried woman?' Izzy asks.

'I'm not sure,' I reply, mindful of Emily's parents, possibly still ignorant of the tragic news, a speck of hope in their hearts, soon to be destroyed. I've often wondered if knowing the worst would be a release of sorts, but now I'm certain nothing can be more terrible than that knock at the door.

'What will happen now?' Izzy asks.

'I expect Max, and possibly Miriam, will be charged.'

Izzy pulls a face. 'God, it's all so . . . macabre. What was this Miriam-woman hoping to achieve by going back there, pulling a hand from the ground and holding it? You think maybe Miriam killed her, whoever it was?'

'No, I imagine she's been protecting Max. She told me it was a terrible accident.'

Izzy shudders dramatically. Her hair is now a soft shade of pink. I pick up a lock and twirl it around my finger, then she holds me while I sob.

'I don't know if you've seen the headlines today?' Iz asks when I finally pull away. 'But someone seems to have written a story about Max Blake.'

'I know,' I reply, too tired to explain my idiocy with Jamie Porten. Last night feels like a lifetime ago, my hangover replaced with sadness and overwhelming fatigue.

'Well, I'm sure your story will be different,' she says, her head tilted to the side, revealing a skull earring dangling from a fleshy lobe.

I lift myself slowly from the sofa, my legs aching from the exertion of chasing around the woods, my heels now red raw and crusted with blood.

'I'll have a nice hot bath before bed,' I tell Izzy, managing a smile. 'Soak away the day.'

'The bathroom's a tiny bit untidy,' Izzy calls after me. 'Sorry, sweetie. You know what I'm like.'

'It doesn't matter,' I tell her, because I honestly couldn't care less. I'm just so pleased to be home.

Chapter Twenty-Eight

Sandwiches and Welsh Cakes

I'm looking out to sea, *my* sea, my thoughts far from here. A brand-new coat wraps me up, sensible navy, not the soft turquoise one I loved, or the stylish camel of Julia's, but nevertheless much appreciated. As was the new phone tucked inside the pocket. 'Let us look after you for once,' Dad had said, silencing my protests. 'You're still our baby girl.'

The funeral will have started by now. Theo's long, lean frame in a polished wooden box, supported on strong, caring shoulders. Work colleagues clustered together. Nicky will be in the front pew, their son and daughter either side of her. I know I can't be there, but it still draws me. As does the desire to put the record straight about what happened the night he died, or rather didn't happen. But I can't do that to Nicky, not yet. Maybe never.

Another tear escapes and tracks down my cold cheek. I never used to cry this much, not even when Bryn went missing. I brush it aside and force myself to smile as Evan approaches, his precious cargo cradled like a greasy prize. He joins me on the sandy steps, two down from the top. We're more sheltered here, a shaft of sunlight crossing my short legs and his longer limbs. He'd arrived at my parents' unannounced, his request stated simply: 'Fancy some chips on the beach, Spencer?' I'd seized the chance to escape, a welcome distraction whilst my former editor is laid to rest. Theo was a friend when I most needed one. An ally who let me down, yes, but a great mentor too. I wish I'd had a chance to say a proper goodbye.

I haven't asked Evan how he knew I was home, but word gets around quickly in a small seaside town, any comings or goings soon passed on. He hasn't asked why I'm back so soon either, although he could always read me like a book. 'The only one I'll ever need,' he used to say.

'You OK?' He touches my coat sleeve. 'You were miles away.'

'Yeah, I'm fine.'

I've found it much easier to think since I've been back at Mum and Dad's. I can't get over how I was taken in by Max. He was lying to me, lying to everyone, blood and dirt on his hands. Even Theo believed him to be an innocent man, and he was always a shrewd judge of character, or so I'd thought.

I look out at the bay again, allowing the tang of the steelworks to take me back to the past, to a time when this was my safe place. I've felt ambivalent about it for so long, but now it comforts me, as well as grabbing me by the shoulders and shaking me out of myself, the cold wind in my face and the salt-spray stinging my eyes.

'Your parents must be happy to have you around for a while,' Evan says, pulling off a glove with his teeth.

'It's only for a couple of days,' I tell him, feeling guilty as I notice his smile slide away. 'Just getting patched up a bit.'

I've been grateful for Mum's cooking and Dad's quiet concern, the house strangely restful now all their questions have been asked and answered. Well, mostly. I spared them the grim details. They were shocked enough that people I'd spent so much time with were involved in 'unspeakable things', and concerned I'd lost my job as well as the exclusive with Max. Both of them reassured me none of this was my doing, even the incident with Theo, which I'd dreaded telling my parents about but eventually shared, Mum's searing intuition coaxing it out of me. I realised last night, with another pang of guilt, how much my parents have missed me. It seems obvious now, but for so long I've felt like a poor substitute. Pol once told me that it's natural to feel some survivor guilt, but it's not as simple as being here when Bryn is not. Walking the beach alone, I've tried to clear my head, but there's so much anger and fury and sadness. Not just for Bryn, but for everything I've lost. I allowed myself to be influenced by Max's status and money, but more than that I was taken in by his false charm and well-placed flattery. My near-total lack of judgement is the hardest to accept. I was convinced he was a desperate but blameless man.

I take the tiny wooden fork Evan is holding out. 'A few more days at most,' I tell him, chewing the edge of the prongs. 'Then I'll head home.'

'I heard you lost your job,' Evan replies. 'Sorry about that.'

'Got a few ideas,' I tell him; only a half-lie. 'It'll be fine.'

Evan opens the parcel, revealing a glistening pile of inter-woven chips which we extract one by one, like a game of pick-up sticks. We have always worked instinctively together. He bends his head to look me in the eye, the windswept bay reflected in his glasses. I smile as we lick the salt and vinegar from our fingertips, the useless wooden forks abandoned. The line of the grey horizon is broken by a solitary tanker, a bleak battleship in the distance, and behind us, dog walkers and cyclists whizz by. Only when the last crispy shards have been crunched to nothingness between our sand-gritted teeth do I turn to him and ask, 'Why don't you hate me?'

'*Hate* you?' He hugs me in a brotherly way and slam-dunks the chip paper into the nearby bin. 'How could I hate you?'

'I've messed you around, though, haven't I?'

'We just want different things; I want you and you don't want me!' He laughs, then kisses me on my tear-stained cheek.

I can feel the years of love between us, as if I had never been away. His beard is soft but also a tiny bit scratchy, his gentle touch choking me up.

'Hey, I didn't mean to upset you,' he says, bashing me play-fully with a fist on my shoulder.

'I wish I could be happy here, Evan. It would make life so much simpler.'

'Yeah, it would.' He frowns, then asks, 'Are you good at your job?'

'I think so. I've got a bit to learn, well, a lot. But yes, I have some talent for it, I think.'

'Then find somewhere new. Somewhere that appreciates how amazing you are.'

The sea air whips my hair up and across my face. Evan passes his fingers gently across my lips to remove the stray tendrils. It would be easy to lean towards him and taste the sweet saltiness of his kiss, to be protected by his strong embrace and stay here with him. Close to Mum and Dad, and Bryn. I look out at the gentle waves, nothing more than white foam on flat, sludgy sand. How can they have carried my brother away and never shown us any sign of their treachery? They should be crashing against the rocks, warning us of their power.

Evan stares towards the horizon. 'What do you think happened?' he asks.

To analyse that last day is to pull apart a skein of silks, each one leading back to more and more tangled threads until my head spins. Evan and I did nothing but theorise in those first days and weeks, exhausted by the possibilities, but his directness now is refreshing, a pragmatism that sweeps a hand through the clutter in my brain and makes everything so much clearer. I've missed his simplistic approach; the characteristic I once least admired in my fiancé now his most endearing quality. Funny how we are altered in unexpected ways, perspective the most changed of all.

'I like to think he's on another beach,' I reply, stuffing my hands in the pockets of my new coat, the smooth edges of the replacement phone a pebble in my hand.

Evan holds me, his words warm whispers in my ear. 'And where is this beach?'

'That I don't know. Australia, or maybe . . .'

I look up at the steel clouds above us and shiver. Evan hugs me warm and I nestle to his side, feeling small. Scared of the resolution I desperately seek. Maybe I shouldn't have pushed for an answer about the calls. Another hope dashed, as I knew it would be. Perhaps sometimes it *is* better not to know.

'Any more idea why he left?' Evan asks.

Left is a good word to use. It describes with economy the moment my darling brother slipped off his rucksack as though he were about to dash across the rocks, darting in and out of the crevices in a final game of hide-and-seek.

I look up at the man I will always love. The only one who understands me well enough to ask that question. 'I think we all know why he left, Evan.'

'He could have talked to me,' he says, his voice cracking.

Evan was always close to Bryn, like a big brother, sharing his love of computer games and maths problems.

'It doesn't help to think like that,' I tell him. 'What ifs are useless, same as guilt.'

'It's so hard, though, isn't it? Not knowing what happened . . .' He wipes his glasses on the cuff of his jacket. 'Much worse for you, I know.'

'I suppose it allows us some hope,' I reply, sliding away from him as I rub the dampness from my face with the backs of my hands, sand scratching my cheek.

'Are you still angry with him?' he asks.

'*Angry?*'

'I don't blame you. Not that he'd have thought about it like that, I just meant—'

'It's OK, I know what you meant,' I reassure him. 'I suppose I was angry for a while. But now I just want to know he's OK.'

348

'You can still be angry sometimes if you want to.' He smiles. 'I won't tell anyone.'

Evan walks with me to the end of my road. I catch sight of Mum watching us at the window, fiddling with the net curtains.

'I'll miss you, Seren,' he says, holding me close and talking into my windswept hair.

I hug him back, feeling safe and secure and not wanting to let go of him, or the feeling.

He releases me first, and steps back. 'I'm sorry, I know I'm letting you down, Seren, but I need to make a proper break this time. It's not because I don't want to see you, but I have to at least try to move on.'

He walks away, looking back to raise a hand before he slips from view.

Mum is in the kitchen, waiting for good news. She pounces on me, wired with anticipation. I wish I could give her something to be happy for: a wedding, grandchildren, a proper family again. All I can offer her is a hug.

'I'm sorry, Mum,' I say as we pull apart. 'We were saying goodbye.'

'But you'll see him again?'

'Is Dad home?' I ask, avoiding the disappointment in her eyes. 'I'll go find him.'

Dad is upstairs, not in front of the TV, which is surprising enough, but even more so when I realise he's in Bryn's room. It's been a time capsule for the last two years, and despite

Mum's weekly flick round, Dad is sneezing and coughing as he clears Bryn's desk; books and loose change swept into a cardboard box as I join him. We work together, quietly and slowly, pausing in deference to each memento then carefully stacking everything in labelled boxes, one on top of another. A whole life contained in just six parcels. I seal them up, the sound of ripping tape a rude interruption to our thoughts. Nothing has been discarded; even scribbled study notes in Bryn's neat hand filed away. I worry what Mum must be thinking, but Dad would never have started this without her agreement.

Dad climbs the loft ladder three times, boxes passed from me to him, two at a time, heaved upwards with a reluctant heart. His wobbly trips up and down the stepladder concern me, especially as he's balanced precariously over the steep stairs, but he won't let me take over. 'Can't have you falling, can I?' he says.

He offers a quick but fierce embrace as we stand in the now soulless bedroom, surveying the results of our labours. Devoid of anything but the bed, wardrobe and desk, it's no longer Bryn's room. Only the sign on the door remains to tell anyone who wouldn't know that this was my brother's private world. One we knew so little of, but shared every day.

Mum appears, vacuum cleaner grasped in one hand, duster in the other. Dad and I watch her determined efforts, but no one says anything of significance and none of us mark the moment with even a platitude. She sprays polish on every surface, the scent of it thick and heavy. When she's finished and Dad's closed the door, we carry on as before, but something has changed. We've done a good thing and we all know it, although it has exhausted us.

Dad leaves for the pub with Mum's blessing.

'It will do him good to see his mates,' she tells me, going back upstairs and closing their bedroom door.

I leave her a while, lying on my single bed as I finish Max's book, but I can't settle, knowing Mum's in there alone. I tap lightly, edging my way in, a cup of tea in hand, the spoon rattling in the saucer. She's slipped off her shoes, her feet in Natural Tan tights tucked up behind her. I sit down on the bed and she rolls over to face me, switching off the radio.

'You hungry, love?' she asks, her voice croaky as she thanks me for the tea. 'I'll get some food ready soon. Dad won't be long.'

'Before you do that . . .' I place a hand on her arm. 'I've had some information, a few days ago, in fact.'

The teacup shakes in her hand. She sets it down, waiting for my news.

'A detective I spoke to, because of my association with Max . . .' She nods. 'I asked her to trace the anonymous calls I've been receiving.'

She stares at me, forming silent words. If I had any doubts, they are now gone.

'I thought I'd withheld our number,' she whispers, taking a tissue from the box I'm holding out.

'You did,' I say, smiling at her. 'I was very impressed.'

She laughs, then cries again. 'I'm so sorry, love. I was worrying about you day and night. I thought if I could hear your voice, know you were OK, but I didn't want you to think

I was fussing. Then when you started to speak, like you were talking to Bryn, I didn't know what to do. I thought if I went along with it there might be some consolation for you in thinking he's still out there, so you wouldn't—'

I wrap my arms around her. 'I'm not going to, Mum. I promise. Whatever happens, whatever the news, or lack of it, I will always be around for you. *Always.*'

'You won't tell your dad?' she asks, blowing her nose. 'I couldn't bear it. I'm such a silly—'

'No, you're not. You're strong and kind and gentle. I won't tell a soul, including Dad.'

'I'll make a fresh cup of tea,' Mum says, getting up.

After chicken sandwiches and Welsh cakes, I announce my decision to go home. Within an hour I'm on the train, the left-overs wrapped in foil in my bag, Dad's twenty-pound note tucked inside my purse. I fight the urge to sleep, every bit of me exhausted, but I need to say goodbye first.

The train skirts the bay, clouds gathering, the rocks almost obliterated by high tide as the coastline disappears. I place a palm to the window and watch as the waves roll in, then I close my eyes.

Izzy's message wakes me ten minutes from home.

Great news you're coming home. I've missed you! Girls' night in, babe? I'll get some beers (ha-ha! I mean wine) BTW, my hair is blond and I've dumped dick-head Dom! Will tell all when I see you. Can't wait! xxx

Chapter Twenty-Nine

How Awful it is Not to Know

Depending on your reference point, this may or may not be the first day of spring. If Theo were here, he probably would have said it doesn't matter what the bloody meteorologists say, the first day of spring will be March the twentieth this year, the vernal equinox. My new editor, Charlotte – a woman two years older than me and who has, in that seniority, assumed she knows all and I know nothing – insists March the first is *categorically* the first day of spring, no discussion. I place my mobile on the bedside table and pull my laptop on to my knees, adjusting the pillows behind me. The magazine's website is much more colourful and enticing than the *Herald*'s, Charlotte's photo choice for the banner, a field of bright yellow daffodils, providing further confirmation that winter is now officially behind us.

I click on the other tab at the top of the screen and scroll down to Theo's smiling face, details of the funeral chronicled in great detail on the *Herald*'s website. There's still not much information about Julia Blake, but it's early days and reports are limited now that Max has been charged and restrictions imposed. I close my laptop and jump in the bath.

The taxi driver arrives twenty minutes early but is still impatient. I climb in the back and tie the laces on my trainers as I ask if he knows the way. 'It's quite tricky unless you've been there.'

We pass the well-kept park, a riot of swaying spring colour filling the borders and edging the paths, and I'm reminded of the other significance of today's date, touching my coat lapel to check my daffodil is still in place. Dad will be wearing one too, taken from the vase in the hall that Mum always fills with masses of yellow blooms to mark St David's Day; the patron saint of Wales. Dad will be halfway through his shift by now, the petals wilting in the intense heat of the steelworks, but the daff will still be proudly attached to his overalls. And perhaps, somewhere, dare I hope, Bryn will remember to mark his heritage too.

Iz left a bunch of daffs in a pint glass on the coffee table. Maybe a coincidence, but she is trying a lot harder since I've come home. She's dating her personal trainer, which means I don't see that much of her, but the new love of her life, Lou, is a definite improvement on Dom.

'You said you're a journalist?' the taxi driver asks, repeating the briefest of conversations we'd struck up as we left town.

'Kind of,' I say, holding up a copy of the 'lifestyle' magazine I now write for. 'I was at the *Herald* before,' I tell him, a catch in my throat.

'Oh yes, the old guy died recently didn't he?'

I flick through the magazine for inspiration, but Charlotte's sing-song suggestion on the phone this morning that I write something *spring-like, maybe about flowers* for my first assignment isn't sparking much. 'Hopeful,' she'd said, not sounding it herself.

It's hardly cutting-edge journalism and I miss the *Herald* terribly, but it's better than nothing and she offered me 'the gig', as she called it, on the spot. I haven't given up hope of publishing my exclusive one day, but that's a long way off. If there's a trial it could take many months, and I'll probably be called as a witness. For now, spring flowers will have to do.

Charlotte also suggested a title for my piece, 'The Ten Best Places to Spot Daffodils in the Cotswolds', and now it seems an inspired choice, the buds lining not only the paths through the park, but also the country lanes.

'Here!' I tell the driver, pointing out the narrow gate, daffodils pushing up all over the grounds of Brooke House too, their smiling faces greeting us as we approach the gravel drive. I hand over the twenty-pound note Dad gave me and take another ten from my purse when the driver says the fare is actually twenty-five. 'Keep the change,' I tell him, although I can't afford to be so generous.

'Thanks, love. Want me to wait around for you? This place is a bit remote, ain't it? And after what happened . . .'

'No, thanks. I'm collecting my car.'

He still looks concerned as he leaves me, and I feel the same. Brooke House has always had that effect on me, but today especially. I keep thinking about Emily Plant's parents standing

side by side on the steps of the church they attend, their statement so full of dignity and love for the daughter they called 'a
gift from God'. I glance up at the dead-eyed windows, then
quickly turn away, heading down the fork in the gravel drive
towards the courtyard.

Miriam's green car is parked outside the open barn door, the
boot ajar as she adds to the pile of clothes, leaning in to smooth
down the expensive gowns, the tops of her bare calves exposed
above her sensible walking boots.

'You look busy,' I say, making her jump.

'What? Oh yes, I am, actually.' There's an awkward pause
as Miriam glances around her in that odd way she has, then
she says, 'You're early.'

'Yes, a bit. Sorry, is that a problem?'

Miriam glances at her watch. 'Time for a cuppa?'

I hesitate, looking at Lavender Cottage. I'd hoped to get my
car and leave straight away.

'Are you coming?' Miriam asks, opening up Honeysuckle
Cottage. 'We can have a nice catch-up.'

'Sorry I missed you when you picked up my spare car key,' I
tell Miriam, taking a seat at her kitchen table. The computer
has gone, I assume taken away by the police. In fact, the whole
place has been stripped – the throw no longer on the sofa, the
watercolours taken down from the walls, only the few bits of
furniture left behind. 'It was very kind of you, but it could
have waited until I was back from my parents'.'

'I thought you'd need your car as soon as possible.' She

smiles at me. 'Anyway, who knows how long Barry will be *at liberty* to help.'

I smile back, but it's a poorly judged joke.

'And I enjoyed meeting Izzy,' she says, filling the kettle. 'She's certainly a colourful character.'

'Iz liked you too,' I reply, not entirely truthfully.

'I loved her hair,' Miriam says. 'Thought I might even try it myself.' She giggles, patting her curls, but she seems on edge, trying a bit too hard.

'Any news of Max?' I ask, but Miriam shakes her head, closing down that conversation.

I can't push Detective Ingles for any insider information either, she's made that perfectly clear, refusing to comment on anything to do with the death of Emily Plant or Max's involvement, or the investigation into Julia's disappearance. It seems Mrs Max Blake's whereabouts are as much of a mystery today as they ever were.

According to Simon, Brooke House was searched again thoroughly after Max's arrest, but nothing new was found. Simon claimed he only wanted to check I was OK when he called round the day after I got home, but I think the primary reason was to tell me he's handed in his resignation now Fran's officially the *Herald's* new editor. He'd stayed a while which was nice, updating me on everything he knew about the case. The police are still picking their way through Barry's, and Ben's, involvement, and bail was automatically granted for Miriam, her charge of 'Perverting the Course of Justice' much less serious than Max's of 'Causing Death by Dangerous Driving'. Max is held on remand, somewhere up north I think. I've thought about visiting at some point, but I don't think I'd be allowed, and anyway, what would I say to him? He killed a thirteen-year-old girl and hid her body in a shallow grave. The fact he was able to open champagne and invite me to dinner, enjoying my company despite what he'd done, still astonishes me. Even if it was a terrible accident, as Miriam insisted it was, the very least he could have done, Miriam too, is save Emily's parents months of useless hope and desperate appeals for information. Whatever punishment Max receives will be deserved, although I suspect living with the reality of what happened to Emily will be the worst for him by far. Part of me would like to challenge Miriam again on her involvement, but I doubt she'd answer. Besides, I shouldn't really be here. Best play it safe.

'And don't worry about Barry's bill, that's all taken care of,' Miriam says, pouring boiling water.

'I can't let you pay for my car.'

'I didn't,' Miriam replies, carrying the filled teapot to the table and setting it down beside me. 'I've paid that man more than enough already. Oh, don't look at me like that, Seren, we've all got to earn a crust.'

I've no idea how she's managed to convince herself Barry Bostwick was only trying to make a decent living. He was clearly extorting large sums of money from Max and spending it down the pub, lurid first-hand accounts from fellow drinkers plentiful in the days after Max's arrest. Barry was seen at the races, gambling heavily, and he'd rather bizarrely purchased an expensive tweed jacket for the occasion. A comical photo of him with a mature blonde on his arm, featured widely.

'Thank you,' I say, taking a mug from Miriam. 'What are your plans for the future?' I ask, adding a heaped spoon of sugar and wondering if that was an unwise question: her plans may not be her own either.

'Lots to keep me occupied here,' she says, clearly unconcerned. 'And there's always work at the farm. Busy, busy, busy. How about you, Seren?'

I tell her about the magazine, how it's not exactly what I'd hoped for, but it'll do for now, although I'll probably have to supplement my income with a few shifts at the café where Izzy works.

'Ah, that's nice,' she says, as if it is. 'And the feature on Max? Will you still write that one day?'

I shake my head. 'I don't think so.'

'Well,' Miriam says, drinking from her mug. 'If you do, just remember the good things about your time here, that's all I ask.'

She checks her watch again, then she puts on her boots and anorak. I fasten my coat and we walk up to the house together, flashes of our dash through the woods making an unwelcome return.

'Miriam?' I ask, slowing my pace.

'Yes?' she says, glancing over her shoulder.

I choose my words with care. 'Do you know what happened the night Julia disappeared?'

Emily's parents have maintained a dignified silence since their public statement, but there's been plenty of speculation, especially on social media.

'You know, Seren,' she says, stopping in her tracks. 'I appreciate that you have a job to do, but you must understand that so do I. Now, let's get you to your car, shall we? I can't wait for you to see it.'

We walk towards the garages, the journey so familiar and yet strange, as if it's the first time I've been here, and of course the grounds look different without the covering of snow. I spot her car first, then mine, but I wonder if I'm mistaken, dashing ahead then glancing back to check with Miriam, who is beaming at me.

'Oh, my goodness!' I say, cutting across her explanations of the transformation. 'It's unrecognisable!'

The beat-up old wreck I abandoned here a week ago has had a complete make-over. It's gleaming, waxed and polished, which usually only happens when Dad does it and then his efforts only highlight the patches of rust on the wheel arches, but they're all gone too. Miriam continues to smile as I walk round to the passenger side and stroke the replacement wing mirror, all signs of duct tape peeled away, and again a fresh coat of paint. I can't remember seeing my tiny car in better shape. I grin at Miriam and take the key from her outstretched hand, the interior sparklingly clean too, even an air freshener in the shape of a tree suspended from the rear-view mirror. I insert the key in the ignition and turn it, breath held. The engine purrs to life, smoothly tuned, no false starts or hesitation this time, and the wipers execute perfect strokes. I wind the window down and look out. 'Miriam, this is amazing, thank you.'

'No worries,' she says.

'Can I ask you one more thing before I leave?'

'You can ask,' Miriam replies matter-of-factly, her hand on the car door. I glance at it, wishing she'd move it away.

'I thought I saw someone at the bedroom window, that time I came here and Max was away in London. I know you said the cleaners were in, but I was wondering if it might have been Julia?'

I decided on the way over it would be my parting question. I'm convinced Miriam knows a lot more than she's letting on.

She shakes her head. 'I can only repeat what I told you before, Seren. It was the cleaners.'

I hadn't thought she'd admit to anything, even if I'm right, but I'm frustrated to leave with more questions than answers.

'Goodbye, Seren. It's been a pleasure to meet you. I wish you all the luck.'

I watch her walk away, waiting until she reaches the corner of the kitchen extension before I edge my car forward. She looks back, standing in the very spot where I'd once heard footsteps. I'm convinced it was her following me that night, strange but loyal Miriam, caught up in the Blakes' wrongdoings.

I drive slowly, turning the corner to see Miriam is waiting for me. She's on the edge of the lawn by the drive, a guard of honour, ready to wave me off. I wave back, a quick glance at the empty windows as I pass the house. When I look back, Miriam is still waving. I continue on, but when I check my mirror I notice Miriam is staring up at the house, more specifically, the window above the door, Max's room. It's hard to see why though, even when I turn to glance over my shoulder. I slow down and take a good look, following her eyeline. Then I see it. A figure caught in the glare of the sun hitting the

Blakes' bedroom window. I slam on my brakes, meeting Miriam's panicked stare as I climb out of my car.

'No!' she shouts, running towards me and blocking my way. She grabs me by my shoulders. 'Please, Seren. Just leave.'

'Get off!' I shout, managing to side-step her.

'Seren, please!' Miriam screams after me as I run at full pelt towards the house. 'Please, just wait!'

I throw myself at the door, thumping my hands against it and pulling the bell.

'Does Max know she's here?' I ask, turning to face Miriam as she runs up the steps behind me.

'Seren, you don't understand. Let's go back my cottage, I can explain.'

I stare down at her in disbelief. 'God knows, I wish I didn't, Miriam, but believe me I understand how awful it is not to know. Whatever happened between them, whatever he's done, this isn't fair on Max.'

The unmistakable sound of a key turning in the lock silences our argument. I continue to stare at Miriam, afraid to turn around, then I hear a woman speak, her voice cold, each syllable slicing through me.

'No need to worry about my husband, Seren. Max knows I'm alive.'

Chapter Thirty

Ugly Beauty

Julia Blake is several inches taller than me, even though she's barefoot. She's wearing well-cut jeans and a crisp white shirt, a gold necklace at her throat, the I of Julia dotted with a dazzling diamond. Her beautiful face is devoid of make-up except for the dark flicks of expertly applied eyeliner and the long strokes of mascara on her thick lashes. She's stunning, but she looks quite different from the woman in the photo that once graced Max's desk, her blond hair now jet-black and cut in an angular bob.

'So, we meet at last, Seren,' she says theatrically, stepping aside to allow me into Brooke House.

Miriam bustles back into the kitchen with a fresh packet of tea. 'I knew I had one somewhere,' she says, holding it up. 'Back of the pantry!'

Julia's gaze remains firmly on me. She's even pushed aside

the antler candelabra which was blocking her view, calling it 'a hideous thing'. We've been temporarily side-tracked by Miriam's insistence we must all have tea, but Julia's frostiness remains palpable as we assess one another across the table. I find her intimidating, but also fascinating.

'You know, Mim,' Julia says, looking away at last. 'Seren claims she saw a stag, up on the track. Do you think that could be true?'

I frown, finding Julia's dismissal of my account incredibly rude. I'd only mentioned it to make conversation. 'I didn't imagine it,' I tell Miriam. 'It was magnificent.'

'Max shot any he saw,' Miriam replies, and Julia arches an eyebrow in an *I-told-you-so* manner.

'Why would he do that?' I ask, appalled that a man I spent so much time alone with, and in truth often found charming, would be capable of such unnecessary cruelty.

'Because I asked him to,' Julia replies. 'Max would do anything for me.'

'Even turn a blind eye?' I ask, and she shrugs. 'But to kill innocent creatures just because—'

'*Because,*' she says, in the tone of someone answering an annoying child, 'not long after I moved here I was almost killed when a deer ran in front of my car.' She looks for my approval, as if this further explanation makes it any more palatable, although I notice a flash of something less certain in her eyes.

'That's just bad luck, Julia. You can't cull them all because one got in the way of you.'

'Just like hunting, isn't it?' she says. 'Loads of people do that. The Queen, for a start.'

I sigh, unsure where to begin. 'Where's his gun?' I ask, looking around as if it might be in the kitchen.

Miriam tells me the police took it away, along with many other things. 'It was locked in his study before that,' she assures me. 'No need to worry.'

'Mim said there are physical similarities between us,' Julia says, changing tack. 'What do you think, Seren?'

'I don't think we look alike at all,' I say, glancing across to Miriam who is opening the packet of teabags with a sharp knife.

'No, neither do I,' Julia replies, tucking a lock of hair behind her ear. 'No similarities whatsoever.'

She's become a mythical creature to me, Mrs Max Blake, but now she's here, living and breathing. Her dark eyes are cat-like, the disdain within them clear, although I'm not sure what I've done to deserve it, other than spend time with the husband she chose to abandon.

'Are you going to explain to me where you've been hiding?' I ask, a quaver in my voice that betrays my nerves. I still can't get over the fact that Max had a gun in his study. I'd pushed him to the limit in that tiny room, made him so angry he'd smashed Julia's photo against the wall.

'So you can sell the exclusive story of Julia Blake, the vanishing wife?' she asks, pointing a manicured finger across the table. 'Now wouldn't that be a happy turn of events for you?'

I take out my phone but Julia reaches across and taps the screen with an oval nail. 'I don't think so, Seren. No photos.'

'I was going to tape our conversation,' I say, but she shakes her head, grabbing my phone and switching it off before she tosses it back to me.

Miriam looks alarmed, shooting Julia a warning look that she volleys back, but nothing is said. I'm not sure what their plan is, if they have one, but clearly I wasn't supposed to be party to it, at least as far as Miriam is concerned. I tuck my phone back into my jeans pocket. 'Is it OK if I ask you a few questions?'

'You're assuming I have any desire or reason to talk to you,' Julia replies. 'Which I don't.'

'*Really?* Then why open the door to me?'

'Curiosity, I suppose. You've been spending a lot of time with Max, I hear.' She glances at Miriam who nods, a carton of milk in her hand. 'Has it been fun pretending to be the new Mrs Blake?' Julia asks.

'I haven't!' I catch her amusement and bite back the urge to retaliate further. 'Anyway, I would have thought given what's happened you'd be very keen to defend yourself?'

'Defend myself from what, exactly?' she asks, her mask of superiority slipping. 'I was caught up in something awful that night.' Julia stops talking, realising her mistake.

'So you *were* involved?' I ask.

She looks away, but doesn't try to deny it, other than to point out that it was Max's fault, something he's finally acknowledged.

'But you can't expect to walk away from this without consequence? Even if the police decide not to press charges, the fact you left your husband to shoulder the blame alone will mean that popular opinion is likely to conclude you're a heartless bitch.'

Julia's watery eyes flash with anger. She composes herself enough to say, 'And how exactly will talking to you make any difference? People can think what they like, but Max has confessed.'

'Yes, he has, but you know what people are like, they always blame the woman. Men get away with murder, but us, we're different, aren't we?' I lean back in my chair. 'Up to you, Julia, but I reckon I'm your last chance before the police find you here, and they're not going to be happy. You've been messing them around for months.'

It's a huge bluff. It's unlikely any editor will risk publishing her story whilst Max is on remand, but my deliberate goading seems to be having the desired effect, unsettling her. 'Why *did* you come back?' I ask. 'Or have you been here all the time?'

Julia laughs at the latter suggestion, saying it would be impossible to hide at Brooke House.

Miriam nods. 'The police are sending patrols every day to check on the place. They would have found her straight away.'

'I only came back today,' Julia informs me.

'A little earlier in the day than planned,' Miriam says, bringing us mugs of tea and frowning at Julia as she sits beside her.

'I have every right to be here, this is my home,' Julia tells her. 'And now Max has spoken to the police I'd imagine there can only be a few formalities for me to go through.'

'Why don't you give me some background, Julia?' I say. 'I know you had a tough start in life. I'm sure that's been a big influence on you. Context is everything, isn't it?'

'I did have a very tough start,' Julia says. '*Looked after*, they

367

call it these days; hardly an appropriate phrase for what went on at Swan House.'

'Swan House?' I ask.

'Before your time, I expect. A children's home, although I was almost a teenager when I was sent there, the last in a very long and unsuccessful series of "homes".' She indicates her disdain with air quotes.

She describes the children's home, located about fifteen miles from here. It sounds awful, a place to learn how *not* to be a child. I take a biscuit when Miriam offers me the plate. I have no interest in the crumbly digestive, but hope my apparent distraction will allow Julia to carry on as it seems she's finding the next part of her story more difficult to share. I wait, sensing that's best.

'A member of staff there . . .' she says, looking down at her hands. 'He—'

Miriam removes a tissue from her sleeve, but Julia holds up her hand to refuse it.

'There was a scandal about it a few years ago,' Julia tells me, meeting my eye. 'Closed the place down. I never came forward. Couldn't face it, and Max's image is so vital to his sales . . .'

Miriam looks at Julia, the older woman's eyes filled with sympathy, although she seems to know the story already. Julia draws in a deep breath. It's dreadful for her, and my heart aches at the thought of what she's been through, it really does, but there's another, shameful part of me that's keen to get to what happened the night she went missing. If I can just keep her talking, I have a feeling we will.

'In many ways I was an entirely innocent teenager before

that,' Julia says. 'They thought I was getting fat.' She huffs at the thought. 'I was almost six months gone by the time I saw a doctor. Far too late to do anything. I was supposed to keep the baby for a few weeks, to make sure the adoption was definitely what I wanted, but I couldn't cope, not at all. So I did what I always do when it gets too much for me.'

'You ran away,' I say, managing to make and maintain eye contact. 'Where did you go?'

'London. Thought I'd be able to get work, earn a bit of cash and have some fun. I ended up sleeping rough. I'd only given birth days before; I was still bleeding. In the end I got so sick I collapsed in a park. I was picked up by some paramedics, pure chance really, they thought I was a drunk. They took me to hospital but the damage had been done, a pelvic infection and God knows what else. I'll never be able to have another child.'

'God that's . . .' I'm tempted to reach out, though she's shown little sign of emotion, her eyes dark pools of nothingness.

'I went crazy for a while,' she tells me. 'Lots of casual encounters. Then I met Ben, but of course you know all about that.'

I must show my surprise for she laughs, clearly delighted by my reaction.

'Your Facebook message gave us quite a fright,' she says, nibbling a biscuit.

'You were with him? In London? When? The day I saw him?' It makes sense now. He'd been jumpy, constantly looking out of the café window. 'Did Max know where you were?'

'So many questions! I was already on my way back here by the time you and Benny-boy were having a crappy cup of coffee. And did Max know I was with Ben? Well, I imagine he had a very good idea.'

'The face at the window . . .' I say.

'Yes, that's right!' Julia laughs. 'Mim was supposed to have cancelled your appointment, but I must admit, it was an added bonus to see the woman who's been diverting so much of my husband's attention.'

Miriam apologises for her oversight, but she looks less than happy with Julia. I imagine she'd told her to keep a low profile until she'd got rid of me. Much like today.

'I can't believe I was that close to finding you. So you've been with Ben the whole time? Apart from the odd flit back here when Max was away?'

'Correct!' she says, as if I'm a contestant on the most bizarre game show ever invented. 'A girl needs her best-loved clothes,' she says, glancing more favourably at Miriam. 'And some much-needed cash.' She flicks her dark bob and flashes me a false smile. 'Ben has various apartments around London, rentals mainly. It's surprisingly easy to disappear.'

'If you have the funds and a helping hand,' I say, glancing at Miriam who looks away.

'I thought you'd lost that?' I say, pointing at the gold 'Julia' necklace.

'Yes,' she says, feeling for the diamond. 'Ben swiped it from by the pool, the cheeky bastard.' She laughs. 'I got it back, obviously, although he took some persuading.' She raises an eyebrow to indicate her meaning.

Miriam blushes and gulps down the remains of her tea, but Julia shows no shame.

'So if Max knew you were alive . . . Sorry, I don't understand. Are you saying you left Max for Ben and your husband knew?'

'Ben was never a serious threat to our marriage.' She considers that statement. 'He's doing well for himself, a large property portfolio and all that, but it's hardly comparable to this place.' She smiles, looking around the bright kitchen. 'As soon as I came here I fell in love with Brooke House.'

'And Max,' I prompt.

'Yes, of course, and Max.' She offers a brittle smile at the recollection. 'The décor was dire, of course, but I could see the potential.' She smiles again, pleased with her joke. 'And now I'm finally back where I belong.'

I look out at the sunshine hitting the patio, the furniture uncovered now, one chair pulled out as if Julia had been sitting there earlier, drinking in the spring air. It seems Brooke House was as much of an attraction as Max, possibly more. I suppose that would explain the risk she's taken in coming back, but can she really be so naïve to think she can restart her life here with only a 'a few formalities' to deal with before everything is back to how it was before? One look at Miriam's face and I know she's thinking the same.

'Did you tell Max about your past?' I ask.

'Everything,' Julia says, picking up her tea then putting it back down. 'Not at first, but a few years ago, when the news of what went on at the house came out. Max suggested we visit Swan House, thought it would be *cathartic* for me, put everything into context. I'm not sure what he was hoping to achieve – it was an empty building by then – but it got me thinking and God knows I needed a project. It's a happy, vibrant home for many, many children these days. You should write about it.'

I don't understand why it's so important to her. It was the place where she was abused. Then she says, 'I named it after my daughter: Rebecca House.'

'Did you ever try to trace her?'

Julia shakes her head. 'I wanted to, but I didn't think it was fair. I mean, I'd abandoned her. I decided she could find me when she was older, if she wanted to.'

'I take it she did?'

Julia's eyes fill with tears and she allows Miriam to comfort her, but only for a moment, the tissue accepted as she pulls away. 'The whole time I'd been living here, almost ten years by then, she'd been less than half an hour away. Can you believe it? Mind you, it still wasn't easy for her to find me.'

'But there must have been papers, for the adoption? Couldn't she have traced you that way, if she'd wanted to?'

'I'd been using my father's surname after I left Swan House, only thing he ever gave me, then of course I became Mrs Blake, so that hadn't helped in the search. She was looking for a Julia Moresley and I was Kirkpatrick, then Blake. She was so young, trying to do it all on her own; she didn't want to upset her adoptive parents, you see, although they'd always been honest with her, told her what they knew. She'd all but given up, then she saw my photo in an old copy of the *Herald*. Her family used to have it delivered, but she never read it. It was lining a drawer, my face staring up at her. The one when Max opened

Swan House.' I nod, recalling the photo. 'She knew she was born there and there was a striking resemblance, so she took a chance. Came here demanding answers one day, just turned up out of the blue. Feisty thing, I loved her on the spot.'

'Did Max know she'd found you?'

'Yes, and although it was a shock, he could see how happy I was.' Julia's face lights up. 'We'd meet at the house, have lunch with Max, then go down to the barn,' she says. 'I have a studio there.' I nod. 'It was our special place, just me and my daughter.'

I think of Miriam locking up the barn so carefully. The place where Julia had spent precious moments with her child.

'She loved trying on my clothes, especially the hideous ones Max had chosen.' Julia laughs at the recollection and so does Mim, enlisted, I assume, to ferry the 'hideous' outfits down there. 'We'd take photos of each other, not all that good, but it didn't matter. They're so important, aren't they? Photos, I mean. All we have of the past. She looked so like me, especially at that age.'

'Sounds very special,' I say, thinking of the photos hidden away in a drawer. I'd thought they were of Julia, or maybe her sister. It hadn't occurred to me they were Julia's daughter.

'Until Max decided she couldn't come here anymore,' Julia says with disgust.

'Why would he do that?'

'A necklace went missing,' Miriam says. 'A very valuable one.'

'We have no proof it was her,' she snaps at Miriam, then turning to me Julia says, 'It was one Max bought me years ago, a diamond pendant. That's why he gave me this instead.' Julia feels for the name at her throat. 'Even if she did take a few things, what's the big deal? It wasn't like he couldn't afford it.'

'Your daughter, Rebecca,' I say, crumbling the rest of the biscuit on the table. 'She was renamed by her adoptive parents, I assume?'

Julia lets go of the necklace. 'Not just a pretty face, are you, Seren?'

'No,' I reply. 'But then neither are you. Julia Moresley, Julia Kirkpatrick, Julia Blake. Names are important, aren't they? Because Rebecca Moresley became Emily Plant, didn't she?'

Miriam closes her eyes but Julia's rage has been ignited. 'You know, some things in life are unforgivable, and losing Em so soon after I found her is one of those. Max asked me to choose. My daughter, or this.' Julia casts her gaze around the opulent kitchen she had built to her exacting design, bulldozing Miriam's home in the process. 'Can you imagine?'

I shake my head, afraid to challenge her whilst she's so unpredictable.

'Max put me in an impossible position,' she says. 'This house and everything in it, they're all his. And he'd fight me for it, make no mistake. But she was my daughter, Seren. What was I supposed to do?'

She gets up and starts pacing the kitchen. 'Everything was getting on top of me: Em, Max, the anniversary, those awful sycophants of his he always wheeled out. No wonder I was drunk by the time Em turned up. I'd wanted them to meet her. All of them. Properly introduce her. A surprise at the end of the meal. But they'd all gone by the time she finally got here. That never happened. They'd stay until the early hours.

Outstay their welcome, usually. Then the one night I didn't want them to go—'

'I don't understand what you did want,' I say, genuinely confused. 'To force Max to accept her? You can't make someone do that by humiliating them in front of their friends.'

'Why not?' she shouts, slamming her hand on the table. 'Why couldn't I demand what was mine? This place *is* mine! I built it, my vision, my creativity. Brooke House was nothing before me. Nothing! All I wanted was my daughter here with me. Is that too much to ask? Is it? I have a right to be here!'

Miriam tells Julia to calm down but she ignores her, pouring herself a glass of wine from an opened bottle on the counter and taking large gulps before she sits down again.

'What happened when Emily arrived at the party?' I ask, already guessing the trail leads down to the cottages and the blood found there.

'We'd arranged to meet at the barn as usual, but the whole evening was falling apart. Max and I had argued, Em was drunk and Ben was being a nightmare. I'd had a lot to drink too. I didn't feel well.' For the first time she looks embarrassed, setting her wine down. 'I needed to use the bathroom so we went into Lavender Cottage first. I was still in the bathroom when Max turned up. I could hear him shouting at Em, scaring her.'

I shudder as I recall being in that same bathroom.

Julia looks up and must catch my stricken expression. 'Ah yes, you've been staying there, haven't you? Did you enjoy the bath? I find it can induce a nasty headache.'

'Are you saying Max attacked you?'

'Let's just say there was a lot of blood. *My* blood.'

'Took me ages to clear it up,' Miriam says. 'Max told me to,' she tells Julia, noticing her disbelief. 'What was I supposed to do?'

'As you can imagine, I'd had enough of him by then,' Julia tells me, touching the back of her head. 'Thought I'd go away for a few days, a week at most. Enough to give him a nasty shock and show Em the sights of London. She'd never been.' Miriam squeezes Julia's arm, reassuring her as she begins to cry.

'You let Max think you were leaving him for good?'

Julia sniffs then shrugs. 'He knew I'd be back.'

'And Emily was happy to go away with you?' I ask, suspecting not, a sick feeling building in my gut.

'Em was very drunk,' Julia says, as if that answers my question, which it kind of does. 'She had no idea what she wanted.'

'To go home to her family, I imagine. But you didn't want that, did you?''

'It wasn't like that. It was Max that scared her, not me,' Julia replies, angry again now. 'He should have let us leave. I would have come back, eventually, but he wouldn't allow it.' Julia meets my eye, looking desperate. 'Max's Porsche is so fast, Seren. Too fast. My car is heavy but it still skidded. She must have thought she was going to die. She wouldn't have jumped otherwise, would she?'

'I don't know, Julia. I wasn't there.'

'Well, I was, and I'm telling you my daughter would still be here now if it wasn't for him.' She's jabbing her finger into the table. 'This is Max's doing, not mine. He was the one who killed Em.' Miriam tries to comfort her but Julia shrugs her away. 'I loved her, Seren. I wanted her here with me, where she belonged. If he'd allowed it, she'd be alive today.'

'I'm not defending Max,' I say, trying to process what she's said. 'Clearly, he shouldn't have chased after you like that – the roads round here are so dangerous – but your daughter died, Julia, and you fled the scene.'

'I saw her go under the tyres,' she says, her eyes unfocused as she relives that moment. 'It was awful, as if you could stop it, but you couldn't, like slow motion.'

'I think you should go now, Seren,' Miriam says, standing up.

Julia gets up too, grabbing Miriam's arm. 'You said you'd be quick, but you were gone for hours. I was so scared, Mim. Left alone in that creepy farmhouse. If I hadn't managed to get hold of Cal . . .'

'*Cal?*' I ask, but they ignore me.

'Pauline shouldn't have left you on your own,' Miriam says, wrapping her arms around Julia. 'Whatever needed doing on the farm could have waited until I came back.'

Julia clings on to Miriam, child-like.

'Did Cal drive you to London, Julia?' I ask, but her face is buried in Miriam's cardigan. 'OK, whatever, but I have to report all this.' I get to my feet, feeling a bit wobbly as I do so.

'No, you don't,' Miriam says, stroking Julia's hair. 'You don't have to tell anyone anything.'

I run.

Out of the kitchen and along the corridor, across the rug and out the front door, then I fly down the stone steps and up the drive to my car, not even glancing back until my doors are locked and the engine is running. I thought they'd try to stop me, but Miriam is watching from the top of the steps and there's no sign of Julia. I put my foot to the accelerator and press down hard, the gravel kicked up as I head towards the track. A few minutes at most before a signal reaches my mobile and I can call for help.

I turn out on to the lane, narrowly missing the gate before I speed along the bumpy country road. The recent bad weather has opened up potholes and crevices that almost derail me. I slow down a little, for safety's sake but also to feel in my bag for the detective's card, her mobile number scribbled on the back. There's a passing place coming up, I'll pull in there to make the call. I push my hand into my jeans pocket, feeling the reassuring shape of my phone inside.

I'm lost in the view across the valley to Brooke House as the call connects. When DS Ingles finally answers I jump at the sound of the detective's voice. 'Seren, is that you?'

'Yes, I need to tell you something.' I continue to watch the house as I speak, the eyes lifeless, the front door closed as far as I can make out, and no sign of Miriam on the steps. 'I've found her, Detective. I've found—'

'I'm sorry, you're breaking up, Seren. Are you still there? I can't—'

I allow the phone to fall from my ear as I'm struck by a violent thought, a memory breaking through unbidden and unwanted. I try to push it away but it shouts louder, demanding my attention.

It's Valentine's Day, Max and I eating cold salmon and

drinking champagne, his guard down after several glasses of wine. He was missing his wife more than ever, despite everything she'd put him through. But unlike Julia, Max was tortured by a guilty conscience. He could have welcomed Emily into their lives, however difficult that was, allowed Julia to be a mother, even though she could never give him a child of his own, but he couldn't reconcile himself to the disruption, his perfect life suddenly chaos. Maybe if he had, Emily Plant would be alive today and he might have convinced Julia to stay; if not for him, then to be near Emily, or perhaps, less palatably, because of Brooke House.

I'm certain now that Max had guessed Julia was with Ben. He might have found her if he'd hired a private detective, or told the police what he knew from the start, but he'd hoped she'd choose to come back to him, as she always had before, and he needed her to keep his secrets. Above all, I suspect he wanted to save his pride. Everyone has their limit. But when she hadn't come back months and months later he'd turned to me, an ally he'd hoped, someone who could act as his mouthpiece; the puppet who'd listen as he spun his tale and make sure it was given pride of place in the newspaper Julia had always followed and most likely still did from her hiding place in London, searching for references to Brooke House, and Max of course, but mostly herself . . . the missing wife.

I close my eyes and try to imagine Emily finding her birth mother. It must have been exciting at first. She was bound to have been impressed with Brooke House, and tempted by the wealth on show. But Julia had revealed her true self the night of the anniversary party; a damaged individual who treated everyone badly, including her devoted husband. There had been a row, a terrible argument between the Blakes, blood spilt. Max had a temper and Julia knew how to provoke him. But he loved her, I have no doubts about that.

'What are you scared of, Max?'

'Scared? I'm not the one who's scared.'

Emily must have been terrified. She wanted to go home, but as Julia drove her away from Brooke House she lost control of the huge Range Rover. They were headed for a tree when Emily jumped from Julia's car. A dreadful accident caused by Max as he chased after them far too fast.

I saw her go under the tyres. It was awful, as if you could stop it, but you couldn't, like slow motion.

I look in my mirror, the view limited, and I'm stationary. Julia was an inexperienced and drunk driver, negotiating dark lanes, a storm breaking, the Porsche gaining ground as it sped up behind them, then lost behind hedges and bends. It would have been almost impossible to witness that moment in such detail in her rear-view mirror, unless . . . 'Shit!' I hit the steering wheel with the heel of my hand. 'Shit!' Unless it was Julia driving the Porsche, not Max. Julia the one chasing the Range Rover as Max tried to take Emily home.

It makes sense. Julia was drunk, probably a lot drunker than Max, who'd finished celebrating hours before. He'd have been my choice of a safe way out if I were Emily. And if it were Julia who chased after them, then she wouldn't have been thinking straight, pushing Max to go faster and faster. She hadn't wanted to harm Emily, just make them stop, but when she rounded the corner she saw something lying in the road, something she was about to hit.

It must have been horrific, knowing it was already too late. She would done everything she could to avoid it. Then she'd have felt the bump under the sports car's hard suspension, bones cracking under the tyres, once then twice. Like the deer she once hit, except this time it was much worse. This time, Julia had killed her own flesh and blood. Her daughter's body lying behind her in the road, and up ahead her husband, already plotting a way to save his beloved wife from what she'd just done. He'd managed to get her to the relative safety of the farm, but she'd fled whilst Max and Miriam buried Emily's body and before Max had the chance to convince her that if all else failed, he would take the blame.

'Seren? Are you there?' DS Ingles asks. 'Seren, what was it you said? I didn't hear you properly. I thought you said—'

I lift the phone to my ear again, ready to tell the detective what I know. But what do I know? I can't prove any of it. That night is lost to the past. And even if I convince the police of my theory, will it change anything?

The sun catches something shiny in the distance, moving fast. Only a speck, maybe not even there, but I swear I saw it. A dash of metallic green; incongruous against the lush hills. I watch again, hoping for a final glimpse of the small car winding along the verdant country lanes, but the sun blinds me, the beauty of the valley opening up as the spring weather dapples the scene. Brooke House is vanishing once more into the shadows.

Julia has always been the queen of reinvention. A new life,

a new lie, the past buried. She doesn't strike me as the penitent type. It would be entirely in her nature to shrug off the fatal mistakes she's made. The truth lost beneath a carefully curated new image, those yet to meet her dazzled by a false and ultimately transient beauty. An ugly beauty. Her real self hidden away.

'I've found her, Detective. I've found Julia Blake,' I say, knowing it may already be too late.

Acknowledgements

There's no easy way to write a book, even when you've done it before, so below are a few special people I would like to thank.

My agent Sarah Williams, I'd never have dared to write this without her encouragement, and the incredibly talented Sophie Hicks and Morag O'Brien at SHA.

Alex Clarke and the team at Wildfire who are a complete joy to work with and everyone at Headline: Siobhan Hooper for another dazzling cover, Jo Liddiard in marketing (a social media whizz), and Phoebe Swinburn, the most passionate publicist I could wish for. My editors: Kate Stephenson for her early belief in me and this book, Claire Baldwin for her enthusiasm and insight, and Ella Gordon who guided me to a sharper version of this story as well as providing much needed support when I had my usual last-minute wobble.

Hayley Hoskins and Kate Riordan, brilliant writers and my dearest friends, for being there every step of the way, and The Ladykillers, for lunches, camaraderie and so much laughter, and the Cotswold-based authors I have met in 2018. Thank you all for your companionship, vital in a largely solitary profession.

My mentees, Nikki Smith and Kate Galley, both such gifted writers.

All the bloggers and reviewers who shout about my books. Thanks for the thoughtful reviews and wonderful photos. Your posts brighten my days.

My local bookstores for getting behind my books and welcoming me for signings and events, and Cheltenham and Stroud Literature festivals who truly made my year.

All my friends and family, but especially Chris, Beth, Dan, George, Mum, Dad, Val, Clare, David, Hannah, Morgan, and Olivia. Also my constant writing companions, Alfie and Marley.

For journalistic advice Jon Coates from the *Express*, so generous with his time, and everyone at *Gloucestershire Echo* who welcomed me and answered my endless questions. And to Nicki Pettitt, for her insight into the care system and for being a hugely enthusiastic reader.

Final thanks go to the experts who deal with the reality of missing persons every day. Josie Allan at missingpeople.org.uk, and DS Nigel Hatton who reads, checks and advises me on every police-related matter, (any deviations, intentional or otherwise, are mine) and the other officers I met at Gloucestershire Police HQ whose dedication and humility are an inspiration.

Amanda Reynolds

If you loved

The
Hidden
Wife

**don't miss out on these
twisty domestic dramas from**

AMANDA REYNOLDS

Available from Wildfire now!

WILDFIRE

**She can't remember why she's afraid
of her husband.**

CLOSE TO ME

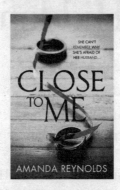

When Jo Harding falls down the stairs at home,
she wakes up in hospital with partial amnesia – she's lost
a whole year of memories.

A lot can happen in a year. Was Jo having an affair? Lying to
her family? Starting a new life?

She can't remember what she did – or what happened
the night she fell.

But she's beginning to realise she might not be as
good a wife and mother as she thought . . .

'A wonderful reading experience'
Kathryn Hughes, author of *The Letter*

'Gripping and twisty' *Take a Break*

You think you know the truth about that night.
But what if your husband is . . .

LYING TO YOU

When Jess Tidy was Mark Winter's student, she made
a shocking accusation. Mark maintained his innocence,
but the damage was done.

Karen Winter stood by her husband through everything,
determined to protect her family.

Now, ten years later, Jess is back. And the truth about
that night is finally going to come out . . .

'This dizzying novel keeps you on your toes'
Sun

'Gripping and twisty'
Laura Marshall, author of *Friend Request*